DEDICATION

Alive is dedicated to my beautiful son, Callum.
I just want to make you proud of me baby. I love you!

ACKNOWLEDGMENTS

To my son, Callum. Even though you are only two years old, you are part of the reason I am trying to make my dream come true. I love you so much little man. You are mummy's world.

To my mum, Toni. Thank you for everything that you have ever done for me, I am truly grateful. Without your love and support, I don't think I would have ever achieved what I have.

To Liam Murray. You have been the biggest help while I've been writing 'Alive'. You've been there for me through the tough times that I have faced whilst writing this book. You helped me brainstorm when I was in a writer's funk, even if some of your ideas were terrible. I will be forever grateful for you and your non-stop support.

To E J Shortall. I'm so glad that I met you on this wonderful journey. You've helped with beta reading for me on numerous occasions, given me ideas on how to make my book even better, and just been there for me when I had questions that needed answering. You are awesome!

To Jessica, Sam, Karen, Kathy, Melissa and Casey. Thank you for beta reading my book and giving me back awesome feedback. Without you lot to help and guide me, my book wouldn't be where it is now. You are all stars!

To Kendra, thank you for editing my book and doing an awesome job!

To Sprinkles On Top Studios, thank you for making me an amazing cover. I love it and am amazed every time I see it. It's going to look fantastic on my book.

PROLOGUE

"MAISIE, HURRY UP! WE'RE GOING TO BE LATE!" I hear my best friend shout from somewhere in my house. "CHLOE, SHUT THE FUCK UP AND GET IN HERE AND HELP ME!" It's not my fault we're going to be late, when Chloe knows I need her help with my dress, but she'd rather stand talking to my brother Jake. They think I'm clueless, pretending they tolerate each other for my benefit, when they obviously have a crush on each other. They should just sleep together and get it over with!

"How can I be of service, your majesty?" Oh, I just love sarcastic Chloe. I raise my eyebrows and point to the back of my dress. I'm going to look so good tonight. Matt isn't going to know what to do with himself. I bought this beautiful red dress last week. It goes down to the middle of my thighs and cuts down low on my chest, though not so low that I look trashy, but more sophisticated.

Turning back around to face Chloe, I wait for her opinion... "Matt is going to explode in his pants when he sees you in this! You look so hot, sexy lady!" That's the reaction I was aiming for. "Now tonight, Maisie, if you leave me there without a ride, I will KILL you! I don't want to end up getting a lift from Jefferson again. That boy *really* doesn't know how to take a hint! So what is it you're not allowed to do tonight? Just to make sure that I have it drilled into your head."

"I'm not allowed to leave you tonight, so you don't get pestered by Jefferson. Got it, boss."

1

"Good. Now come on. We have to leave, or otherwise, we won't find a parking space." I pick up my phone from my bed, checking to see if Matt has texted me. I haven't heard from him for a few hours. We had an argument earlier because I said I was going to arrive with Chloe to the party and not him. Oh well. Let him get on with it. Seeing that I have no message alerts, I put it in my bra, and we make our way out to my little red Honda. The radio blasts out Pink's 'Get the party started', so Chloe and me scream out the lyrics on the short ten minute journey to Matt's house party. The closer we get to Matt's, the more excited I become to see him.

Matt and I started dating when we were thirteen and have been together for just over four years now. We'd been in English together and had to partner up for assignments. We grew attached really quickly. I never could understand why he took an interest in me. He's the captain of the football team, the guy all the girls wanted because of his exceptional good looks. He's your typical blonde hair, blue eyes kind of guy. I'm just your ordinary girl who doesn't wear much makeup, and I'm not popular. Matt told me he never cared about what anyone had to say or that I wasn't popular. He loves me for me. I love him so much. He really is my soul mate.

Pulling up outside Matt's house, it's not a surprise that half of the school has turned up. Word gets around that Matt's parties are the best, so everybody who is anybody turns up. Luckily, I have a small car, so it's easy to find a parking space. Chloe meets me at the front, and holding hands, we make our way up toward the front door.

"Alright, sister, let's go get a drink and then get our freak on!" Chloe says.

The music is blasting out Robin Thicke's 'Blurred Lines' as I walk through the front yard, so I start doing a little shimmy because it's my favorite song at the moment. As soon as I get in the front door, people start pushing me around. I swear, if someone makes me fall flat on my face, I will knock them out. Now, I'm not the violent type, but these people are pissing me off! Looking around the living room, I notice that the sluts of the school are hanging around Matt's team mates, but Matt's not in sight. I take my phone out and text him to let him know that I'm downstairs so he can find me, and then proceed into the kitchen with Chloe in tow to get a drink. Looking at the table with all the alcohol on it, I see that there's a choice of warm beer or vodka. I decide to stick to the vodka. I can't stand the taste of beer! "CHLOE, YOU WANT A DRINK?" I yell to her so she can hear me over the music.

"Yeah, babe, I'll have a vodka and coke. Can you get it for me? I'm going to talk to Jimmy." She waggles her eyebrows at me as she walks off, and I just laugh. Jimmy is Matt's best friend who Chloe has been having a no strings sexual relationship with for the past 5 months.

Spotting Jamie at the breakfast bar, I make my way over to talk to him. "Jamie, do you know where Matt is? He isn't answering my messages, and I can't find him."

"Hey, Maisie! Yeah, I think he's upstairs in his room. He's pretty drunk already, so has probably gone for a lie down."

"Ok, thanks. I'll go see if he's alright. Talk to you later." I turn on my heel and walk toward the stairs. Matt doesn't allow anyone upstairs when he has a party, so it's no surprise that it's empty. I stand outside of his bedroom door and am about to turn the handle when I hear a woman laughing. Feeling confused, I put my ear to the door to hear better and wish that I didn't.

"Baby, you look so fucking hot tonight. I can't wait anymore. I have to be inside you." Vomit starts to make its way up my throat because I'm sure that was Matt, but because of the loud music it's hard to tell. My hands are starting to shake and sweat, and tears prick my eyes, but I carry on listening. I have to be sure that it's definitely him.

"Oh, Matt... baby, this feels so good. Harder, baby. Give it to me harder!"

That's all I need to hear before I open the door and see what I thought I would never see. My eyes land on my boyfriend, butt naked on top of the school's biggest slut, Megan, who has been after Matt for the last three years! I start to back slowly out of the room, trying to leave without them knowing I was here, when I hit something hard. Something crashes to the floor, grabbing Matt's attention. I freeze and watch as he turns around, looking pissed off at having been interrupted until he sees that it's me. All the color drains from his face, but he still doesn't move to get off Megan. After what feels like minutes, but was probably only seconds, he jumps off of her, stumbling in the process. I laugh humorlessly and wait for the lies to flow from his mouth. I won't let him see that he has just broken my heart and that it's lying on his bedroom floor right now!

"Maisie, baby, I'm so sorry. I didn't mean for this to happen. I've had a lot to drink..." I hold up my hand to stop him spouting off more rubbish. Of course he meant for it to fucking happen. Does he think I'm stupid and that he just fell and landed inside her? I look at Megan, seeing a huge smirk on her face. She knows she has successfully won now, but I won't give her the satisfaction of letting her see me crumple. I turn back toward a horror faced Matt, the face of the man I have loved for four years and who I thought would never hurt me.

Swallowing the huge lump in my throat, I try to stop the tears from appearing as I get ready to say goodbye to the love of my life. "Save it, Matt. I don't want to hear it. You've made it pretty clear that I'm not enough for you anymore. Now, I'm going to go downstairs, and you are not going to follow me. Do I make myself clear? You can delete my number because I never want to see or hear from you again." I turn to leave, but I have to say something to Megan before I go. "Oh, and Megan, sweetie?" She looks up at me with that fucking smirk still in place. Stupid bitch. "You're welcome to him as you have probably just given him herpes. Oh, and desperate does not look good on you." Not waiting for a reply or a last look at Matt, I turn and walk back downstairs toward the kitchen where I see Chloe and Jimmy making out. I practically run to her, wanting to leave before everyone finds out what has just happened.

When I get to Chloe, I tap her shoulder and whisper, "Chloe, we need to leave *now*! I just walked in on Matt with Megan, and I want to leave before he comes back downstairs and humiliates me."

Chloe stops what she's doing, turns to face me, and I can tell that this isn't going to be good. She is going to kill Matt.

"WHAT? WHERE ARE THOSE FUCKERS? I'M GOING TO CHOP HIS BALLS OFF!" That got everybody's attention. Well done, Chloe. There's no chance of leaving quietly now...

"Chloe, shut up and let's just go. I don't want everybody to know. Please, let's just leave," I hiss through gritted teeth.

Not bothering to see if she follows, I turn and start to make my way toward the front door, ignoring the fact that everybody is staring at me now, waiting to see if I will break apart. Well, I've got news for you people; this woman will not break in front of anybody. I will do it in the safety of my own bedroom, where I can realize that I no longer have a heart because it shattered on the floor of my ex-boyfriends bedroom not five minutes ago. Matt's voice stops me two feet from the front door.

"Maisie... please, baby, let me explain." I was so close to leaving. I take a deep breath to compose myself, and then turn to face him. He sounds all choked up, and taking a look at him, I see that he's been crying which breaks my heart, but then I remember what I saw not even five minutes ago. I wait for him to carry on. I couldn't speak even if I wanted to because of the big lump lodged in the back of my throat. God, I'm going to be sick! "It wasn't what it looked like, Maisie. I've had a lot to drink, and we had that argument earlier. I didn't know if you wanted to be with me, baby. I wouldn't have done it otherwise. You have to believe me! I love you so much! You know you're my future. Please don't let this ruin us. I couldn't live without you, baby." Lies, lies, LIES! Does he think that because he has had a lot to drink it makes up for it? "Please say something..."

"Good-bye, Matt. Don't call me or speak to me ever again." With that, I leave and don't look back. The ride home is quiet, and Chloe knows that I just need time to think without her asking me questions. I know that eventually she will want to know what happened, but I just can't talk about it at the moment.

Chloe drops me off at my house with a promise to phone me tomorrow and bring my car back, and then I make my way through the front door, careful not to wake anybody up. I can't face anybody right now. They will know something is up, and the pain is just too raw to talk about it.

As soon as I'm in my bedroom, I lock the door then fall head first onto my bed, finally letting out the big fat ugly tears that taste of heart break. Deep down, I knew that I would only be good enough for Matt for so long; I just hoped he could have proved me wrong. Thinking about it only makes me cry harder and uglier. I can feel the hollow space where my heart used to be, and the feeling of emptiness is already making me feel numb. I've never been in so much emotional pain in my life, and I'm hoping the numbness will creep through the rest of my body quickly so I don't have to feel the pain anymore. I stay like this until the sun starts to rise, and just before I fall into the slumber of sleep, I vow to myself that after today, I will never fall in love again!

CHAPTER ONE
PRESENT DAY - MAISIE

Looking around my room one last time, I make sure that I have everything I need. My room, which I have had since my childhood, is bare except for my bed and closet. Everything else is packed in my car and waiting to go to a new destination; one where there aren't any bad memories and where I can start over again.

Making my way downstairs, I drop my bag and see my mom and dad waiting for me. They have been my rock over the last three months after everything that happened with Matt, so it's going to be hard to leave them, but they know I need to do this in order to move on with my life. Stepping into my mother's embrace, I let the tears flow freely.

"Baby girl, I am so proud of you! Now you go and show what you can do and have fun. I will see you soon okay?" I nod my head and let go of her. Turning toward my dad, I see his eyes mist over, and I can't help but cry even more. I have always been a daddy's girl, and leaving is the hardest thing I've ever had to do. Giving me a hug, he squeezes me so tight, like he's afraid to let go.

"Daddy, I can't breathe. Loosen up a little, will you?" I laugh.

"No, Pumpkin, I won't. I won't ever let go. You're going to have to take me with you!" The funny thing is that he probably isn't joking. Pushing away, I pick up my bag and coat and open the front door. "Maisie, you be careful, okay? Stay away from guys and focus on your studies. If you need anything, anything at all, remember we're a phone call away, okay, sweetie?"

"Yes, Daddy. Now, I really need to leave if I don't want to get stuck in traffic. I'll call you when I arrive. Bye. Love you both," I say and then turn around.

"Love you too," they reply in unison.

Putting my bag on the passenger seat, I get into my car, which is packed with all of my belongings, and turn on the engine. As I look out of the window at my house, I think of all the fun times I've had and how much I'm going to miss living there. But then I think about moving into my dorm with Chloe, starting a new life miles away from home, and all of the drama that has happened in the past few months. I smile properly for the first time in three months and then drive off, looking at my parents one last time before I turn the corner.

****

I finally arrive at California State University and take in a huge breath at the sights that surround me. I knew this was the place I was destined to attend the minute I set eyes on it. It is beautiful. I could see myself sitting next to the fountain, reading a book under the hot California sun, and relaxing for the first time in months. I'm used to the California weather as I am a California girl born in San Francisco. I could have chosen to go to a college further away, but I love California. Plus, six hours away from my home town is long enough. If I had gone somewhere like New York, I'd have hated it. It's far too busy for me, and there aren't enough beaches. Besides, I have the company of my best friend here, and I wouldn't have it any other way.

My cell rings, startling me from my thoughts. Looking at the screen, I see Chloe's goofy face pop up. "Hey what's up?" I answer.

"Where the hell are you? I thought you said you would be thirty minutes? That was forty-five minutes ago, bitch. I'm waiting to go check out the eye candy. Maisie, don't make me wait anymore!" Chloe whines down the phone to me. Yes, she actually whined.

"I'm in the parking lot. Come down and help me with my things?" I ask.

"Okay, be down in two. Ciao." With that, the call disconnects.

I get out of the car, open the trunk, and start lifting boxes out and putting them on the floor. This is going to take about five trips. I hope we're on the bottom floor. As I am pulling the first box out of the trunk, Chloe comes bouncing over, looking all hot in shorts and a white tank top. She is beautiful with naturally wavy sun bleached blonde hair and the bluest eyes I have ever seen on a girl. Looking around, I notice quite a few of the guys are watching her. I'm not surprised, either, because she always has the guys after her. Chloe is the complete opposite of me. I have straight, dull brown hair with brown eyes and freckles. I envy her sometimes. She stops next to me and just stares at all of my stuff.

"Maisie... this is going to take forever. Please tell me you're going to unpack later?" Chloe asks, looking deflated.

"Don't worry. I'll unpack later. Now, what floor are we on? I haven't had a chance to check," I ask, dreading her answer.

"We're on the second floor, sweetie, so not too bad. Eurgh, it would have been good if your brother was here to help. We could have sat back and watched while he did all of the hard work," Chloe says. My brother attends California State University too, which is one of the reasons I selected this campus. It always helps to have a big brother here to show you around and look out for you.

"Jake will be here later." I wink at her, and she rolls her eyes at me. "Anyway, let's get my stuff to our room."

Arriving at our dorm room for the next year, I drop the boxes on the floor and take it in. The room is tiny with two single beds, two bedside tables, a desk, and a dresser. Off to the left is a door, which I'm guessing leads to the bathroom. I know that when Chloe and I have finished doing this room up, it will look cozy, so I'm happy to call this my home for the next year. I pick up the boxes and put them on the bed I assume is mine because it's completely bare. Taking in a deep breath, I turn to Chloe. "Let's go get the rest of my things then."

Fifteen minutes later, I am on the final box, while Chloe is upstairs getting ready. Picking up the box, I turn around and smash into what feels like a brick wall. I'm about to tear one into this jerk about watching where he is going when my eyes meet the most beautiful pair of brown eyes I have ever seen. My mouth is hanging open ready to start my onslaught, but my brain has completely forgotten what I'm meant to be saying. Standing in front of me is by far the best looking guy my eyes have ever set sight on. A six foot two man with muscles covered in tattoos, wearing a black t-shirt and tight, dark jeans is what I smashed into. No wonder it felt like a wall. Mr Beautiful is pure toned muscle! After scanning him from bottom to top, my eyes land on his face. He has jet black hair and the most amazing brown eyes that seem to have flecks of gold in them. To finish it off, he has a panty melting square jaw! Oh, I think I'm in love...

Coughing startles me out of my trance. I quickly shut my mouth, feeling a blush creeping onto my cheeks. To further humiliate me, Mr Beautiful then smirks, and out pops two dimples! This man cannot be real. I must have knocked myself out somehow and am now dreaming. Men this sexy do not exist. Remembering that I didn't come here to look for guys, I pull myself together and stand up straight. "Excuse me, please," I say, trying to sound confident.

"Sorry, darling," he says with a wink, then turns and walks away.

I just stand there, flabbergasted and wondering what the hell just happened. This overly good looking guy just walked into me when he could clearly see that I was here, and then one look into his eyes was all it took for me to be completely mesmerized. I acted like a fool. I'm surprised I didn't dribble all over the floor! And then he just walked off like nothing happened. Who does he think he is, calling me darling and then winking? I already know that I need to steer clear of this guy; he has player written all over him. None of that matters, though, because I didn't come here to get involved with guys. I came here to get my degree in English to achieve my dream of becoming a teacher, and no guy, especially not Mr Beautiful, will get in the way of that. Snapping out of my thoughts, I take the last of my belongings up to my room, and then get ready for Chloe's plans.

****

Chloe decided that we should check out the coffee shop, Cafe Blanc, on campus. Her theory is that all of the hot guys hang out in coffee shops. Where does she get this knowledge from? Stepping inside, I am instantly awakened by the smell of fresh coffee as it hits my nostrils. As I join the line, I look around at the booths filled with students and at the computers in the corner, knowing immediately this is where I be will hanging out between lectures. With the light mocha colored walls covered with pictures of the history of the café and worn red booth seats, it has a homely feeling about the place.

Searching around the café and looking at everyone gathered around, my eyes land on a familiar face. Mr Beautiful. He's standing with three guys, who also don't lack in the looks department, with a tall blonde girl hanging all over him. Seeing that he is engrossed in conversation, I take the time to study him further. How is it possible for him to look even more beautiful than he did earlier? Mr Beautiful puts his arms around Blondie, pulls her flush against his body, and then sticks his tongue down her throat. I feel disgusted. They are definitely not acting PG in public. Do they not have any respect for others? Some people are trying to eat or have a quiet drink in here!

"Yo, Jesse, what's up man?" Some surfer looking guy shouts at Mr beautiful. So, Jesse is his name? It suits him.

"Hey, Brandon, I've been looking for you all over, man. We have to head down to practice in thirty minutes or Coach will kick our ass!" Jesse shouts back. He pulls away from Blondie and walks over toward his friend. Hey, I'm not a stalker. I'm just going by what I've heard.

"Can I take your order please, miss? Or are you just going to stand there all day?" Swiveling my head around to face a pissed off barista, I realize that I have been staring for so long at Jesse that I forgot I was waiting to get a coffee. God dammit, why didn't Chloe say anything? I turn around to see that she is talking to a guy off to my right. Well, she doesn't hang around, does she! She could have at least told me that she was going to talk to that guy. "Well...?" the barista asks when I still haven't told her my order.

"Y-yes, sorry. Could I have a caramel latte, please?" Paying for my drink, the barista turns around to make my drink with a huff. I can't blame her really; I would have been pissed off with serving me too. The barista passes me my latte, so I turn to go stand with Chloe. Next thing I know, something bumps into me, and my latte ends up all over me. OMG, this freaking burns! Could this day get any worse? This is the second time that someone has bumped into me! Feeling pissed off because my top is starting to stick to my burning skin, and because I didn't even get to try my latte, I turn around and find Jesse with his hands held up in the air. "YOU! THIS IS THE SECOND TIME YOU'VE BUMPED INTO ME TODAY! WHAT IS YOUR DEAL?" I practically shout. I don't even care if anybody is looking. I'm so angry, I feel like I might explode at any second. Do I have this big sign on my back saying *'Please feel free to bump into me at any time, Jesse?'* What is this guy's problem? Putting my hand on my hip, I tap my foot and wait for him to reply.

"Well, aren't you a little fire cracker, darling?" Jesse says with a big smirk on his face, showing off his beautiful dimples. If he wasn't so good looking, it would be easier to be angry with him, but his dimples seem to have doused the fire inside of me, though only a little bit!

"Don't call me darling. I am not your darling! Now answer my question. Why do you keep bumping into me? You're lucky this latte is all over me, or it would be in your face right about now," I say, while shooting daggers at him.

"Okay, okay… Whatever you say, darling." He winks at me, and I feel my temper rising again.

"But for the record, this morning you bumped into me. I was just walking on the sidewalk like normal people do, minding my own business, when you turned around and smashed a big, hard, heavy box into my chest. And this time, I apologize. My friend and I were messing around, he pushed me too hard, and I fell into you. I am so sorry. Let me buy you another drink?" he asks. Staring into his hypnotizing eyes, I can't even remember what he just said. I'm sure they have powers, as I seem to be turning into a fourteen year old girl who's just discovered boys for the first time.

"O-o-kaay…" I stutter. Turning to ask the cashier for another one, my brain registers what he just said. What did he just do to me to make me forget? He isn't getting off the hook that easily. Making sure not to look into his hypnotizing eyes, I say, "No, actually, it's not okay. I can buy my own drink, thank you very much, though I wouldn't have to if you were watching where you were going! And for the record, as you put it, you could clearly see I was bent over picking something up off of the sidewalk. Now, if you didn't have your head shoved so far up your ass, you would notice this, wouldn't you? Actually, don't answer that. Of course you wouldn't. Please, just go away. You've done enough damage today already." Shaking my head, I decide that I can't even be bothered to wait for another coffee. Seeing that Chloe is still talking to some guy, I walk over to her and tell her that I'm going to go back to the dorms to unpack. She doesn't say anything, just raises her eyebrows in question, but I slowly shake my head. I know I'm off the hook for now, but later, I will have to explain everything.

JESSE

I love California. There is no place else in America that I would rather be, which is why I chose to go to college in my home town. At least this way, I will have all of my friends here with me, and I can go home every night without having to sleep in a crowded dorm room. Another plus is that I know all of the easy girls around campus. I'm not going to lie- I'm a bit of a man whore, but at least I let the girls know that I'm not looking for a relationship when we hook up. They know the score before they sleep with me, so I guess that makes them as bad as me. Oh well, that's their choice.

College starts up again on Monday, but Coach needed me today to help with the tryouts. So here I am, Friday afternoon, and it sucks ass. I could be out surfing the waves all day, but instead, I have to not only do demonstrations but watch the potential players in the scorching heat. I guess that's what I get for being captain of the football team. I'm a sophomore here at CSUF on a full football scholarship. I'm determined to be someone and do well in life to prove to my mom that I'm nothing like my pathetic excuse of a father.

Leaving my house, I hop on my baby, my Ducati. No one is allowed to ride her except me. Not even my friends go near her. They know better. I bought her cheap and done her up by myself while working over the last year because I'm a mechanic on the side of college. See, the logic behind it was that chicks dig motorbikes, especially a good looking guy with muscles and tattoos riding one. It was a win-win situation!

After starting the engine, I floor it and cruise down the road at 80mph. I love feeling the breeze run through my hair and the thrill of riding my baby fast down winding roads.

Driving past the beach, I look at the ocean. Man, it's a perfect day for surfing. I feel like turning my bike around, going home, getting my wetsuit and board, and saying *fuck football tryouts!* I know, though, that Coach will kick me off the team faster than I can say surfing. Coach Burns is a mean, old, no-nonsense bastard, but he is the best coach we could have. We didn't lose a single game last season, and we don't expect to lose this year.

I pull into the parking lot, jump off my bike, and a release a sigh. Looking around, I don't see Brandon's car. I pull out my cell phone and send him a text, asking him where the hell he is. That boy is always late. However, Brandon is like a brother to me, and he has been there for me during the hard times in my life and helped pull me through them. I don't know what I would do without him, as feminine as that sounds.

As I walk down the sidewalk toward Café Blanc to see if Brandon is there with the guys, I see a girl bending over a pile of boxes. She must be new with all the boxes she has. Yeah, she's definitely new; I would remember an ass like that from anywhere. She is wearing short shorts that show off her long, tanned legs that seem to go on forever and a yellow t-shirt. From her position, I can't see if she has boobs to match that delicious ass. Hey, I'm a red hot blooded male, so don't judge! All I know is that I have to get a look to see if she's fit. Deciding that the best course of action is to 'accidentally' bump into her, I walk closer to the edge of the sidewalk. I know this is a dick move, but I'm determined now. She is fresh meat, so she knows nothing about me or my reputation.

When I'm one step away from her, she suddenly turns and smashes straight into my chest. I'm stunned for a few seconds because whatever she has in that box is hard as shit! She looks up, and as I look into her eyes, I can tell she is going to tear into me. It will serve me right, to be honest. I am an asshole. But then something in her eyes changes, and where she was about to say something, nothing comes out and her mouth is just left hanging open. I tend to have this effect on women, and it's amazing! I notice that she is checking me out, so I take the time to also check out her goods. She's beautiful in the girl next door kind of way, with brown hair stopping in the middle of her back and the most beautiful brown eyes I've ever seen on a girl. She has a few freckles dotted across her cheeks, which make her look adorable; I could gaze at them all day. I mentally shake my head. What the fuck was that about? Carry on with your inspection. She will snap out of her daze soon, so I don't have long left! I sneak a look down at her chest and am greeted with two perfectly sized perky boobs; they would fit into my hands nicely. I could have some fun with them. She has a slim waist which leads to those beautiful long legs that I saw from a distance. She must only be about five foot four. She is tiny!

"Excuse me, please." I hear her say. I snap my eyes up to meet hers and give her my signature smirk. It works on all the girls. I've heard many girls call it a panty melting smile because it brings out my dimples, and girls are a sucker for them. That's one thing I can be grateful to my dad about. I got them from him.

Now that I've seen what I wanted to see, and I have to say I'm very pleased, I say, "Sorry darling." I give her a wink, then turn and walk off. The only thoughts in my head while I walk away are of getting dirty with Little Miss Girl Next Door.

****

Café Blanc is the local hangout between classes, and for me, it's also a great place to pick up girls. Girls love their coffee, so they are always hanging out in coffee shops. Checking the cafe, there's still no sign of Brandon. Where the hell could that dipshit be? Deciding that it might be best to call him to find out where the fuck he is, I pull out my cell to dial his number.

"Jesse, baby. Where have you been lately? I've missed you," Tiffany whines in my ear. Tiffany is my go to girl. We hook up regularly if I can't be bothered to find different pussy. She knows how I like it, which is an advantage. Sometimes, when I hook up with someone, they can be absolutely shit, and I'm left unsatisfied, so it's easier just to go see her. She's a good looking girl, which is a positive thing. At five foot seven, with long straight bleach blonde hair, wide green eyes, and a slim figure most girls would kill to have, is Tiffany Dawson.

"Tiff, I've been busy. You know I'll call you when I get a spare minute," I reply.

"Okaaaaay, I just miss you is all. Come on. Let's go over to the group." Pulling on my hand, she drags me over to our friends.

"Hey, guys. How's it hanging?" I say to no one in particular.

"Yo, Jesse, we're good man. Haven't seen much of you this break. Where you been?" Tom, one of my team mates, asks.

"Busy, my man, very busy," is the only reply they are going to get from me. I can't exactly say that I've been hooking up with a different girl nearly every night or Tiffany will get pissed off, and then who will I call? Putting my arms around Tiffany to keep her sweet, I keep up with pointless chit chat and try to act interested. I get the sensation that someone is watching me, so I look out the corner of my eye as not to make it too obvious and see the girl with the perfect ass from the sidewalk. She hasn't noticed that I've caught her staring right at me. Well, I might as well make it worth her while. Spinning Tiffany in my arms so she is facing me, I drop my head to hers and kiss her. I need to make it a little more x-rated if I'm going to give Little Miss Girl Next Door a show. Deepening the kiss, I gaze out the corner of my eye and see that she looks disgusted. Oh yeah, she is wishing it was her I'm kissing, even if her face has disgust written all over it.

"Yo, Jesse, what's up man?" Brandon shouts while walking over to us. About fucking time he showed up.

"Hey, Brandon, been looking for you all over man. We have to head down to practice in thirty minutes or Coach will kick our ass!" I make my way over to him and slap his back in greeting. Noticing that Little Miss Girl Next door is ordering her drink, I think of a quick plan to get her attention. "Hey, Brands, I need your help."

"Whatsup, brother?" he replies.

"You see that girl over there?" I whisper and point to the girl.

"The one with the brown hair? What about her?" he asks.

"I need you to do me a favor and 'accidentally' push me into her. I'll fill you in on the details later, but this is important. Okay?"

I move over so that I'm practically standing behind her, and then give Brandon the signal to push me on the count of three. One, two... He shoves me full pelt into the girl just as she picks up her drink, which ends up down the front of her shirt. Result, it's going to go see through. I just hope that wasn't a hot drink in there. Shit, it's a bit late to think of that. God, I'm such a douche! Putting my hands up in the air, in a surrender motion, I remain still and wait for her fury.

"YOU! THIS IS THE SECOND TIME YOU'VE BUMPED INTO ME TODAY! WHAT IS YOUR DEAL?" she screams at me. Jesus, this girl obviously doesn't care that everybody has stopped what they were doing and are now staring at the scene unfolding before them.

Liking her feistiness, I smirk. As I pull out my lady killer dimples, I say, "Well, aren't you a little fire cracker, darling?" A bit of the anger in her eyes dissipates. I know she's forgiving me a tiny little bit. Ladies can't resist my charm.

"Don't call me darling, I am not your darling! Now answer my question. Why do you keep bumping into me? You're lucky this latte is all over me, or it would be in your face right about now!" Okaaaay, maybe I was wrong. Wow, this girl is confusing. I never EVER have trouble when it comes to reading girls. They are like an open book to me, but this one has got me stumped!

Trying to act indifferent to the situation, I say, "Okay okay, whatever you say, darling." I wink at her for good measure. "But for the record, this morning you bumped into me. I was just walking on the sidewalk like normal people do, minding my own business, when you turned around and smashed a big, hard, heavy box into my chest. And this time, I apologize. My friend and I were messing around, he pushed me too hard, and I fell into you. I am so sorry. Let me buy you another drink?"

Little Miss Girl Next Door as I'm going to call her, because I don't have a clue what her name is, stutters, "O-o-okaay..." Staring into her eyes, I can tell she has calmed down. The fire has dimished from her beautiful eyes. She turns back to the barista, ready to order another drink. I'm completely blindsided when she whips around to face me with the thunderous look back on her face or when she opens her mouth to speak. "No, actually, it's not okay. I can buy my own drink, thank you very much, though I wouldn't have to if you were watching where you were going! And, for the record, as you put it, you could clearly see I was bent over picking something up off of the sidewalk. Now, if you didn't have your head shoved so far up your ass, you would notice this, wouldn't you? Actually, don't answer that. Of course you wouldn't. Please, just go away. You've done enough damage today already." Then she's walking away

Staring at her retreating form, I'm left wondering what the hell just happened. My plan definitely backfired. Why is this girl immune to my charms? I've only seen her twice, and I already know that I need to figure her out.

CHAPTER TWO
MAISIE

My first semester starts today. A new chapter of my life is starting today. A lot is starting today... This is a very important time for me, and to say that I'm a little scared would be a lie. I've never been so petrified in my life. I'm starting my future by myself, without the help of my friends or family. Yes, I have my best friend Chloe, but we are taking different classes, meaning I will be all on my own. That is some scary shit!

Entering the campus office, I collect my schedule from the front desk. Checking it over, it all seems to be correct, which is great. This saves me the hassle of having to get it corrected.

I feel my leg vibrate, so pull my phone out of my pocket. Chloe is calling. "Hey Chlo," I answer.

"Maisie, where are you?" Chloe sounds half asleep. She didn't get in until three this morning from a party that she attended last night with the guy she met at the coffee shop the other day. Apparently, his name is Ryan, and he's a really nice guy, but I wouldn't know. I chose to stay in and get prepared for today rather than getting drunk with a bunch of people I don't know. Parties aren't my scene anymore, for reasons I don't wish to remember.

"I've just picked up my schedule. I have to go get my books and supplies for my classes, then I'll be back," I reply.

"WHAT? Why didn't you wake me up? How big is the line? Please tell me it's not huge?" Chloe begs through the phone.

Chuckling at my best friend, I turn my head around to look at

17

the office and see that the line is now out of the door. I'm going to have to lie, or she will never come to get her schedule.

"Erm... No, it's not very big. I'd say about ten people." Yeah, more like thirty people. Oh well. "And I didn't wake you up because you came stumbling in at three this morning. I thought you could use the sleep."

"Oh, Maisie, that was such a good party. You should have come!" I just cough to remind her. "Oh, come on, Maisie. You can't stop living your life forever. This was meant to be a fresh start for both of us, remember? You can't coop yourself up in the dorm room doing homework for the next year. I won't allow it, okay?" she rants down the phone.

"Chloe, look, you know why I don't want to go to parties, so just drop it, okay?" I'm getting pissed now. She's my best friend and has been by my side through the tough times, so she should understand more than anybody. I huff, telling her, "I'll be back when I've got what little I need for classes. I'll see you soon." Then I hang up before she can reply.

****

Two hours later, I'm finally ready for my first class. As I walk into my English class, I stare around at the huge room and decide where to sit. It's not too packed yet as I made sure that I arrived early. Picking a seat near the back, I unpack my laptop, then decide to text my mom and dad to let them know that my first class is about to start.

A bag dropping next to me startles me. I look up and am surprised to see Jesse standing there staring at me with a big smile on his handsome face. I blink a few times to see if it is actually him standing there. I know that half of the seats in this room are unoccupied, so I ask, "Do you have to pick here to sit when half of the other seats are empty?"

"I like the look of this seat. Good view from up here. Plus, it's not like we're strangers. We've had the pleasure of meeting twice now. Would you prefer to have a complete stranger sitting next to you?"

"Yes, actually, I would rather a stranger sits next to me. They probably wouldn't cause damage to me, unlike you." He can't sit here. I won't be able to concentrate on my lessons at all! My pulse is accelerating by the second with him just standing there!

"Well, tough." With that, he sits down, putting his legs on the table and crossing his ankles, with his hands behind his head. I'm about to pick up my stuff to move, when the professor walks in. Great timing, NOT! Can I ask him if he could come back in two minutes time so that I can move? Okay, I guess not... Suck it up, Maisie. He's just a guy. There are plenty of them in the world. So he may be a douche, a sexy douche at that, who is sitting next to you, but that doesn't mean you have to talk to him. I focus my attention on the professor and try to ignore the beautiful man sitting next to me.

Luckily, I get through the whole lecture without having to speak to Jesse, but as I make my way out of the door, a hand lands on my shoulder to stop me.

"Save me a seat tomorrow, darling." I can feel Jesse's hot breath on my ear. Shivers run down my back, and goose bumps cover my arms. Damn you, traitorous body!

"My name's not darling. It's Maisie," I whisper.

"Well then, *Maisie*, save me a seat tomorrow. I like sitting next to you." Then he's off down the hall, and I'm stuck on the spot. My legs won't move! I can't keep letting him affect me like this. He's such a cocky jerk and thinks he is God's gift to women, by the looks of it. Well, I'm going to have to show him that I'm not all women. I will not fall for his charm, and he definitely won't be sitting next to me tomorrow.

JESSE

When I stepped into my English lecture this morning, the last person I expected to see was the girl who has been playing on my mind all weekend. I woke up this morning with a plan of keeping my distance if I ever bumped into her again. It's not in my nature to be thinking about a girl for forty-eight hours straight. I've turned into a pussy, and I don't even know her, but when I saw her sitting there looking all sexy, that plan went right out the window!

Sitting next to her for ninety minutes was torture. I kept getting whiffs of strawberry every time she moved. I just wanted to sniff her neck for hours on end, and I would have had it not seemed creepy. I was entranced by the smell of her. I noticed that when she was confused, she scrunched up her nose. It is the cutest thing I have ever seen! Oh God, now I'm calling her cute. I need to get laid pronto.

When class finished, I was going to go straight to football practice, but I couldn't help myself. I had to say something to her. I knew my speaking into her ear had affected her the minute her skin got covered in goose bumps. Maisie is what she said her name is. It suits her; a sweet and innocent name for a sweet and innocent looking girl. I know I should just turn around and forget all about her because I will just end up breaking her heart, but every time I think about letting her go, I feel like someone has kicked me in the gut. Not good, Jesse. Love is a disease, remember? Look at what happened to your mother. Do you want to end up like that? No, so forget about her. It's easier said than done, though, isn't it? She's a challenge. I never give up on challenges.

I tried harder during practice today than I ever have in my life. I battered myself, but Maisie only escaped my mind for a few hours.

Deciding on an early night, I fall asleep picturing the darkest pair of brown eyes I have ever seen.

CHAPTER THREE
MAISIE

Two weeks have passed since I started at CSUF. My life has become pretty routine. I wake up in the morning, get dressed, go to my classes, then come home and do my assignments. To say my life is tedious is putting it mildly. But I'm happy with it. I don't want dramatic. I want peace. I've not seen much of Chloe recently, either. She's made a lot of new friends, ones who actually want to do the whole college experience and party. We still hang out in our room, or go to Cafe Blanc, but it's not as often as we used to. I know I can't hold her back, so I don't mention that I wish we spent more time together.

I haven't spoken to Jesse since he sat next to me. When I next had English, I made sure to arrive just before the professor and get a different seat, so that he couldn't sit next to me. It's childish, but something about him affects me. Also, the guy just screams trouble! I don't need my broken heart to be broken even more.

It's Saturday, and I promised Jake that I would attend his party tonight. Chloe is ecstatic that she finally got me to accept. I, on the other hand, would rather be watching boring reality shows all night than hanging around a bunch of loud drunk people that I don't know. I didn't bring any clothes with me to wear to a party, so right now we are on our way to the shopping mall. The girly side of me is bursting out of the seams. I love shopping. Chloe and I used to go and spend all of our money on clothes of the latest trends.

Venturing around the mall, the first shop we stop in is Hollister.

"We need to find you something that will make you look hot to trot, baby girl. How about this?" Chloe holds up a knee length lilac dress with a round neckline. I shake my head then carry on looking through the racks.

"Look, I know you don't want to come tonight, which I understand. I really do, Mais, but this will be good for you. Forget about what happened last time. You don't know anybody here, and you need to get out there and make friends. This party is the perfect place. So, stop looking at granny clothes and find something sexy okay?" she says with a sad smile on her face. She's right. I do need to forget about what happened and move on with my life. This is what the new start was about, so I need to start living.

"Okay." I smile a true genuine smile.

"Well, that was easy." We both laugh. "Let's find you something to wear then!"

****

Twenty minutes later, we are in the changing room with armfuls of clothes. Most of the clothes I try on aren't right for me. I have one outfit left to try, and I love it. It's perfect for tonight, and I could wear it during the day as well. I'm wearing a black leather faux skirt with a black crop top covered in gold studs. Twirling in front of the mirror, I smile at my reflection. I'd forgotten what it felt like to get dressed up. I don't look trashy or too done up. This outfit is just the right amount of dressy, and I don't have too much of my flesh on display.

"I think this is the one, Chloe. I love it! I'm never taking it off!" I laugh to my smiling best friend. "I just need to find some shoes now."

"You look amazing!" Reaching up, she wipes a tear off her face.

"Why are you crying, silly girl?"

"Because I finally have my best friend back! I'm so happy right now. I thought I'd lost you forever..." Chloe looks down at her feet. I draw her in for a hug, telling her I'm sorry over and over until we are both in tears.

It's a while before we are all out of tears. "Come on. Let's buy these then go get something to eat. I'm starving."

Chloe decides to get the lilac dress. It looks beautiful with her blonde hair.

****

We sit down in a booth at one of the diners in the mall, and the waitress comes over to take our order. We both order cheese burgers and fries with a diet coke; our usual. I know I should start a conversation and ask Chloe what's been happening in her life recently. I've missed out on a lot because I've been in my own little world filled with books and homework, but I honestly don't know where to start. I decide to start with the guy she met in the coffee shop.

"So how's Ryan?"

"I wouldn't know. We haven't spoken for a few days. He turned out to be a douche. I mean, we were only hooking up and sometimes hanging out, but he never once told me he was in a long term relationship. I found out he has a girlfriend back home, so I ended it, but then he couldn't understand why. I feel sorry for his girlfriend. She doesn't have a clue." I feel proud of Chloe in this moment for ending things, not being a home wrecker.

"I feel for his girlfriend. I'm glad you ended things with him, though." I smile at my best friend. "So how are your lessons going?"

"Oh, they're really good! My art teacher, Professor Longhorn, is a genius. I've learned so much already. I'm glad I went with Art instead of business, like my parents wanted. I would have been miserable. Can you imagine me being in an office nine till five? It would drive me insane." We both laugh. The image that pops into my head is hilarious; Chloe wearing a suit and carrying files. What a joke! Chloe wouldn't last two minutes in an office. She doesn't like to be bossed around, which is why she chose art. This way, she has her own deadlines and is free to express who she is in her drawings.

"Oh God, I have a stitch!" My tummy muscles aren't used to this kind of strain anymore. I haven't laughed in months. I calm myself down as our food arrives, so we tuck into it.

"Ooooooooh, that was good. I needed a good meal. I don't know how much longer we can live on noodles, Chlo," I say, wiping my face on a napkin.

"We have to live on noodles. We're students, which makes us

poor. Most of the time, I would kill for one of Mom's home cooked meals."

"I really miss your mom's lasagne." I pull a sad face, which makes Chloe laugh at me. "Don't laugh at me, bitch! I'm really fed up with eating the same thing every day. It's making me miserable, especially now that I can taste your mom's lasagne."

"Okay. I'm sorry." She's still laughing at me, though. Her laughter finally subsides after I shoot daggers at her. "Let's stop talking about what we obviously can't have right now. It's not doing us any good. Tell me. How are your lessons going so far? Make any new friends?"

"Yeah, my classes are going surprisingly well. I'm not failing, which is a bonus." I haven't spoken to anybody since I started lessons, not if you don't count Jesse. I wouldn't call him a friend. Plus, I haven't spoken to him in two weeks. Maybe he finally decided to stop pestering me and realized I wouldn't give him what he was obviously looking for. Looking over at Chloe, I realize I've taken too long to answer the rest of her question. Oh, what have I got to lose? She won't tell anyone. It's not like anything interesting has happened. "No, I haven't made any friends, but do you remember that guy at the coffee shop who made me drop my latte all down myself?" Chloe nods. "Well, his name is Jesse, and he's in my English class. After the sidewalk and latte incident, I hoped not to bump into him again, what with the campus being huge. So when he decided to drop his bag down next to me on my first day in English, I knew that the Gods were out to get me. I had to sit next to Jesse for the whole class, unable to concentrate because I'm not blind. He is probably the best looking guy I've ever seen, and for some reason, he just affects me, Chloe. No one has affected me except Matt. Jesse looks like he could break someone's heart with the click of his fingers. I don't need that in my life. So the next day, I made sure to arrive just before the professor so that I didn't have to sit near him. I've been doing it ever since."

Chloe looks like she's trying to process everything I've just told her. I don't blame her. Thinking about all of what I just told her, it's actually pretty confusing. I made it sound like I have a crush on him. I don't even know the guy.

"Maisie? You do know that you can be friends with a guy without having to date him, right? Just because you don't want to get into a relationship with him, doesn't mean you can't talk. You'll never make any male friends if you're always questioning their motives. Not all guys have motives, sweetie." She's right, not that it matters now. I haven't spoken to Jesse for weeks. He's most probably given up trying to talk to me. I'll just keep it in mind for when the next guy talks to me.

"You're right, except I don't think Jesse wanted to be just friends." Looking at my watch, I notice it's getting late. "We need to leave if we're going to make it to Jake's party. It's six o'clock already, and I've still got to shower." We pay the bill, and then walk back to my car.

****

I'd forgotten how long it takes to get ready for a party. I haven't been to one in four months. I used to party every weekend, but after walking in on Matt and Megan, I hardly left the house, let alone partied. I didn't want to be humiliated anymore than I had been, and with Matt being popular, everybody sided with him. It didn't matter that he was the one in the wrong. People who I thought were my friends turned their backs on me. I got told that I wasn't enough for Matt, hence why he went elsewhere. In the end, it was just easier not to leave the house. That way, I didn't have to hear what people were saying about me.

Going to this party tonight is a big step for me. I just need to remind myself that nobody here knows who I am. I don't have a boyfriend, so it won't be a repeat of what happened before.

It's just after nine when Chloe and I arrive at Jake's house. Jake is a year older than me, so he shares a house with some of his best friends just off of campus. I've never met any of his friends, but it's no surprise that they are overly good looking. Jake is definitely a lady's man. Come to think of it, he's always got a different girl on his arm, though they have never been girlfriends. Chloe and I make our way over to tell Jake we're here. When I tap him on the shoulder, he stops his conversation and turns to face us.

"Hey, Maisie," he says, pulling me into a bear hug.

"Nice to see you too," I laugh, pulling out of his embrace.

"Why haven't you been to see me since you arrived?"

"Yo, Jake? Who's this pretty little thing, and why have you been keeping her hidden?" a guy who I'm guessing is Jake's friend asks.

"Evan, shut the fuck up, man. This is my little sister, Maisie, so stay away, unless you want me to chop your balls off." Jake warns, giving Evan a serious look. The other guys laugh, but say nothing. Smart guys.

"Alright. I hear you. Nice to meet you, Maisie," Evan winks at me. Evan is really good looking, in the surfer boy kind of way. He must be around five foot eleven and has longish shaggy blonde hair, but it suits him. Looking into his eyes, which are the brightest shade of green I have ever seen, I smile at him.

"Nice to meet you too, Evan. This is my best friend, Chloe." I point to Chloe, taking the focus off of me. She has been quiet since we arrived. I'll have to ask her what's wrong when we get a moment. I see Chloe look at Jake, and then turn toward Evan.

"Hello. Would you show me to the drinks please?" Chloe asks, giving Evan a flirty smile. Oh God. Jake must have pissed her off. This isn't going to end well, especially if Evan flirts back with her. Why do they do this to each other? Either date or leave each other alone. It's simple really. I give it an hour before Jake has found a girl just to make Chloe jealous, in which case, she will probably end up sleeping with Evan just to spite him. Then, in the morning, when the alcohol has worn off, she will be in depression mode for a few days until her and Jake sort it out again. It's been the same situation for the last few years. I told them both years ago that I'm not getting involved. I won't be made to choose between my brother and my best friend. So far, they haven't gotten me involved, but it will happen eventually, unless they finally decide to give it a shot or call it quits.

"Of course I can, pretty lady. Please follow me." Evan holds his arm out for Chloe to take. I focus on Jake, noticing his jaw tighten and his fists clench as he watches Chloe leave with Evan. I just shake my head at their behavior.

"Jake, please don't do anything stupid, okay? I'm going to get a drink then find somewhere to sit quietly."

Pouring myself a vodka and coke, I make my way to sit down on the sofa. Well, this party sucks already. I've only been here twenty minutes, and already I want to leave.

Avicii's 'Hey Brother' starts playing. I quietly sing along, lost in my own little world. I love this song. I think it's the country accent used in the song. Tapping my foot to the tune, I don't notice that someone has sat next to me.

"You look like you're having fun, darling." At the sound of the voice that I haven't heard for two weeks, I turn my gaze toward Jesse. Wow, he looks extremely hot tonight. He's wearing a white t-shit that hugs his muscles in all the right places and dark jeans, and my mouth goes dry at the sight of him. Every time I see Jesse, he just gets better looking. How is that possible?

Taking a sip of my drink to wet my mouth, I respond, "I'm not." I then turn to watch people dancing on the makeshift dance floor, aka the living room.

"I can tell. You have a sour face right now. Fancy some company?" Do I want his company? I guess it can't be any worse than what I've been doing. I'm going to need more alcohol for this, though. Lifting my cup to my mouth, I gulp down the rest of my drink.

"Only if you would be kind enough to get me another drink?" I hold out my cup for him to take. "Vodka and coke, please."

"How do you know I won't spike your drink?" he asks while taking my cup.

"I don't."

"You're lucky I'm not like that, Maisie. Don't just ask random people to get you a drink in the future." Before I can tell him not to tell me what to do, he walks away toward the kitchen.

Who does he think he is, telling me what to do? Sitting back on the sofa, my mind strays to how Jesse looks tonight. How does he manage to always look so good? There hasn't been one time when he hasn't looked even the tiniest bit like shit. He always looks impeccable. Where's Blondie anyway? Why is Jesse by himself? More importantly, why is he sitting with me? It's not even like I'm very nice to him. In fact, I've been nothing but just plain rude to him! I can't help but not be rude to him. It's my defense mechanism these days. If I don't let any guy near me, then I won't get my heart shattered, except it's not that simple when I find Jesse attractive. I'm insanely attracted to him, but I can't let him in. I know that if I get to know him, he will break my heart. It's inevitable. He is even better looking than Matt, and he got bored with me. Jesse would definitely get bored with me, and then he would take what's left of my already broken heart and shatter it into a million more pieces.

"Here you go. It's not spiked, scout's honor," Jesse says, doing the scout's honor sign. It makes me laugh. "So you can laugh? You should do it more often. It's a beautiful sound." Feeling a blush creep up my neck, I look down at the floor so he doesn't see that he's embarrassed me. "Hey, don't be embarrassed," he says, putting his fingers under my chin. He tilts my head up, until I have no choice but to stare into his eyes. His beautiful eyes. "You have a beautiful laugh. Don't be embarrassed of it." He smiles then releases my face.

"Thank you." There's not much else to say to that. I need more alcohol in my system if I'm going to hold a conversation with Jesse. Gulping down the contents of my drink, I get up to refill my cup. "I'll be back in a minute. I need more vodka." Smiling at him, I make my way toward the kitchen.

JESSE

I'm left staring at Maisie's retreating form, while I stand here like a dick. I had been watching her from the corner of the room for the last fifteen minutes, ever since I arrived. Now I really do sound like a creeper. I was on my way to get a drink when I saw her sitting on the sofa by herself, drink in hand, silently singing along to Avicii's 'Hey Brother'. She looked adorable, minding her own business, lost in the song.

When I saw what she was wearing, I was blown away. There is definitely life downstairs from looking at Maisie. She looked so hot in her black leather skirt, with the black crop top, allowing me a tiny peak at her perfect tanned body. Even if only a few inches of her flesh were showing, it was definitely doing things to my manhood. I thought I could keep her company. It looked like she wasn't in her comfort zone being at this party, so when I asked her if she wanted some company and her reply was "Only if you would be kind enough to get me another drink?" I couldn't refuse. She was finally saying more than one word to me without shouting. That's progress.

Most of the girls I know would lap up compliments if I gave them. Fair enough, they were meaningless compliments to get them into bed, but they still took them without being embarrassed. When I gave Maisie a compliment, which for once in my life I actually meant, she got all embarrassed. It was the cutest thing I've ever seen, apart from her laugh. Her laugh... My God, that sound. It did funny things to my insides. I can't even explain it. I've never felt it before.

I'm standing here waiting for Maisie to come back, when I know I could be hooking up with Tiffany. I know she's here somewhere, except I'm not interested in finding her. I want to spend time getting to know Maisie.

I've tried to keep my distance from her since she moved seats in English two weeks ago, but all I can think about is her, day and night. I don't even know the girl, and she's already consuming my thoughts. I know I should walk away and forget about her, and trust me I've tried, for two weeks in fact. I just can't do it. As soon as I see her, I want to be near her. I want to call her mine, even if it means going against everything I believe. I know Maisie could break me if she wanted to, but the heart wants what the heart wants. I couldn't stay away even if I tried.

"Hello? Earth to Jesse." Maisie says, waving her hand in front of my face.

"How long have you been standing there?" I must have zoned out thinking about her. Not good.

"About a minute, so not long. Did you want a drink? I didn't know what you liked, so I got you a beer. Hope that's okay?" she says. Passing me the cold beer, her fingers graze mine with the gentlest of touches. Had I not felt a shock when our skin made contact, I wouldn't have noticed. I look into Maisie's eyes to see if she felt it, but if she did, she doesn't let it show.

"Beer's fine, thank you." I open my mouth to ask her how she found out about the party, as Jake's parties are usually pretty private, just for the popular crowd, when I hear a voice that I really don't want to hear right now.

"Jesse, baby, why didn't you tell me you were already here? I've been looking for you since I arrived. Brandon said he didn't know where you had gone to," Tiffany asks in her really irritating, high pitched voice. How have I not noticed how annoying it is before now? It's not like Maisie's gentle, smooth voice, which I could listen to all day, if I ever got a moment to talk to her properly. I notice Maisie look at Tiffany and scrunch her nose up at her. Hmm. Interesting.

"Tiff, can't you see that I'm a bit busy at the moment?" I ask, giving her a pointed look that says piss off. Not taking the hint, she wraps her bare arms around mine, rubbing her chest on me in the process. For once, it actually makes me feel physically sick.

Looking down at Tiffany wearing the shortest red dress that I have ever seen, I would usually get turned on by it, but now it does nothing for me. It would seem that these days, I like girls who wear black leather skirts with crop tops that only show a tiny bit of flesh. Trying to retrieve my arm from Tiffany's vice like grip proves harder than I thought it would. Using a little more force than I usually would on a girl, I free myself, and then turn toward where Maisie was standing, but she's no longer there.

"Who was she, anyway? I've never seen her around before. You can do a lot better. You have me remember?" Tiffany slurs, trying unsuccessfully to wrap her arms back around me.

Moving out of her reach, I cross my arms, trying to remain calm. "Look, Tiff, if I want to hook up, I will call you. And for your information, Maisie is one hundred times prettier than you because she isn't desperate. Now, if you don't mind, I'm going to go apologize to her for your rudeness." Without waiting for her to respond, I turn to the kitchen to try and find Maisie.

****

I've surveyed the whole house three times for Maisie, but I can't find her anywhere. The house isn't that big, so it shouldn't be this hard. Making my way into the kitchen to get a drink, someone laughing stops me dead in my tracks. I listen for the laugh again, and as if on cue, someone laughs. I recognize the sound. It instantly makes my heart melt. I follow the sound of the laugher out into the garden, and then stop in my tracks when I see Brandon all over Maisie. It hurts that Brandon is chatting her up when he knows I'm interested in her. For God's sake, I asked him for his help in the coffee shop. He's supposed to be my best friend. He's like a brother to me.

What hurts the most, though, is that Maisie looks like she is enjoying his company. She never looks at me like that. God, I wish she did, though.

Standing there, watching them interact for a few minutes, the hurt subsides, being replaced by anger; anger at Brandon for doing this, but mostly anger at myself for obviously not being good enough for a beautiful girl like Maisie. I don't know why I ever thought I would be. I mean, I don't even really know her, and she's already decided that she doesn't want someone like me. I'm damaged. Maybe she realizes that. No, she couldn't. I hide it well. I've had years to perfect this 'I don't give a crap' attitude, but this is the reason why I don't try to get close to girls. Feelings always mess everything up, leaving someone hurt in the process, and I'm damaged enough as it is.

I can't stand to watch this anymore, especially when Brandon does his signature move of putting the stray strands of hair behind Maisie's ear, which he usually does just before he makes his move. I won't allow him to kiss her.

Striding over to them in four big strides, I push my way between them, staring him down. "What the fuck do you think you're doing, *bro*?" I hiss to Brandon.

"Well, I was talking to this very lovely lady before you interrupted, *bro*," Brandon replies, giving me a satisfied smile. His eyes can't focus on anything in particular. This isn't good. Drunk Brandon doesn't give a fuck about anybody but himself.

"Well, conversation is over. Go find someone else to hook up with. Maisie isn't a one night stand kind of girl, Brandon." Spinning on my heel, I turn to find a completely hammered Maisie. She only left me about twenty minutes ago. How much has she had to drink? She can't even stand up straight!

A sharp pain reverberates through my skull. Spinning back around to face Brandon, who looks extremely pissed off, I raise my eyebrows. There's no point arguing. This fight is going to happen whether I want it to or not. Drunken Brandon is an angry guy, not my bro who has my back at all times.

"Come on. Hit me back. You can't just come in and take her away. She isn't your property. Go and find your own girl," Brandon says, raising his voice.

"Brandon, I think you need to go drink some water. Do you want me to take you home?" He can't drive home in this state. He may not make it.

I see Brandon's fist aim straight for my face. I'm not going to try and stop it. He can get one decent punch in before I knock him to the ground, best friend or not. His fist connects with my face, good and proper. I'm going to have a beauty of a black eye tomorrow!

"That was a good shot, but now that you've had your one free shot, it's all you're going to get," I whisper to Brandon so that nobody else over hears.

"Give me what you've got, Jesse. I'm gonna fuck you up."

I won't throw this first punch. That way, I can't get done if the cops show up. I don't have to wait long before he makes his move. Blocking his right hand from colliding with my already swelling eye, I punch him straight in the stomach, making him double over in pain. Not waiting for him to get back up, I follow it with an uppercut straight to the nose.

"FUCK!" Brandon screams, cupping his nose. Lifting his head up so we are eye to eye, his nose is gushing with blood. Shit. I think I might have broken it. Oh well, that's what he gets for breaking the code.

Bending forward so that we are nose to nose, I whisper, "Call that a warning. Stay away from her, Brandon." He just nods his head. It's sad that it took getting his nose broken to realize that he's done wrong. Tomorrow, he probably won't even remember what he's done, meaning I will have to explain without getting pissed off again.

Grabbing hold of Maisie's arm, I pull her toward the front of the house.

"What the FUCK do you think you're doing, Jesse?" Maisie spits out at me. Great. Now I have to deal with another drunk.

"Stay away from Brandon, Maisie. He will drop you as soon as he gets what he wants. Do you want to be one of those girls?"

"I'll do what I like! Who the hell are you to tell me what to do? I don't even know you! Go back to Blondie, Jesse." Maisie pulls her arm from my grip and goes to walk away. I can't let her leave being angry with me. Grabbing hold of her arm, I pull her into my chest.

"LET GO OF ME, JESSE!" Maisie screams, struggling to try to get out of my hold. I hold her tighter, and then move my lips close to her ear.

"I'm telling you what to do because I care about you, and you don't look like the kind of girl who wants a one night stand," I whisper in her ear.

"Well don't, Jesse," she whispers back dejectedly. "I've dealt with worse." I know that tone well. She's been hurt at some point, though who would want to ever hurt this beautiful girl?

"Look at me, Maisie." Her eyes stay focused on the floor. I tilt her head up, so she has no choice but to look into my eyes. "Whatever's happened in your past doesn't mean you need to degrade yourself like that. You're worth so much more." God, I'm such a hypocrite. Isn't that what I do to girls like Tiffany? Do I not use them to get what I want, and then discard them like yesterday's trash? It's always been the way I've protected my heart, though I never thought about the hearts of the women I used.

Staring into Maisie's eyes, I see the fire that was in them diminish at the mention of her past. It breaks my heart that somebody has hurt her before. When I find out what happened, and who hurt her, I'm going to seriously hurt them. Maisie looks like she has an 'I don't give a fuck' attitude, but deep down, she cares. She really fucking cares. I've always been good at reading people. I'm a master at fooling people about how I feel, so I can always spot a damaged person.

"Why are you being nice to me?" Maisie whispers so quietly that I wouldn't have heard it if I hadn't been paying close attention to her.

"I've been a dick to you since we met. I'm sorry for that. I'm not going to lie, but when I first saw you on the sidewalk, I wanted to hook up with you. Then I saw you in the coffee shop that same day, so I tried to get your attention again. Badly, I know." Maisie chuckles at that. I realize that I could never get bored of hearing that sound. "Anyway, I was shocked when I saw you in English. I knew I should have stayed away from you, as I always end up hurting women, but something about you is different. You're not like the other girls I know, Maisie. You're so much better. When I realized this, I decided to leave you alone. You can do so much better than people like Brandon and me. We don't care about anybody except ourselves, and you deserve to be treated like a princess." I watch a tear roll down her cheek, before I reach up and swipe my thumb across her face to remove it.

She starts to move forward, all the while staring into my eyes, still letting the tears flow. I pull her into my chest for a cuddle and try to comfort her as best as I can. She looks like she needs one right now, and I will take anything I can get, especially if it means I get to touch her. She leans back after a few minutes and, without warning, grabs my face and plants her lips on mine, hard. I respond, kissing her back just as eager. Her lips are just as soft as I have imagined. She tastes of a mixture of coke, vodka and strawberry. I'm guessing the strawberry is from her lip gloss, but I'm addicted to the taste of her already. Maisie tries to deepen the kiss, and I almost let her, but I don't want her to kiss me when she probably won't even remember it in the morning. Breaking off the kiss is the hardest thing I've ever had to do, and I know I'm going to regret it; however, I want her to remember every second of the next time we kiss. And there will be a next time, I'm sure of it.

"Oh God, I'm so sorry. Th-that shouldn't have happened. I've got to go," Maisie stutters, looking mortified. Before I can say anything, she runs off into the crowd. I've got to find her. She's drunk far too much to be around a bunch of people she doesn't know.

Making my way into the kitchen, I see Maisie standing with Jake and the blonde girl who I saw her with at Cafe Blanc that first day. I wonder how she knows Jake. Time to find out.

"Jake, my man. Thanks for inviting me to your party. I'm going to head off soon, so thought I would see how you are." Maisie sneaks a look at me out of the corner of her eye. I try not to laugh at the fact that she looks distraught at the fact that I am here.

"Good to see you, bro. It's been a while. Have a good summer vacation? Of course you did. You're Jesse Cohen, the man all the ladies want. I'm jealous, man!" Jake laughs, while I internally shudder. I don't want Maisie thinking badly of me when I've not even had a chance to prove anything to her yet.

"It was alright. Surfed the waves all day, so what could be better?" I laugh uncomfortably. "How about you? Any girls down in San Francisco this year?" Jake is a bit of a lady's man too. He's always telling us crazy stories about the girls back home.

"I'll have to tell you about them another day, man. They're not stories for my little sister's ears." Jake puts his hands over Maisie's ears, winking at me. Thank God, they are related and he's not interested in her.

"Jake, you're such a pig! These girls are more than a piece of meat, you know? They have feelings, unlike you, you heartless bastard!" the blonde girl suddenly pipes in, giving Jake the dirtiest look I have ever seen.

"Chloe, you're just jealous because you want a piece of me," he replies, rubbing his hands down his body while giving Chloe a smirk.

"Yeah right, and end up catching STDs? I don't think so. Plus, I rather like your friend Evan. He's a real man, and he seems like a gentleman, which you certainly aren't." Now it's Chloe with the smirk on her face, and Jake looks like someone just stole his puppy. The sexual tension between those two is really thick. I find Maisie shaking her head at them, and it makes me smile. She must be used to the bickering between them then. I'm going to have to have words with Jake and get the details.

"Anyway, it's getting late, and I have practice tomorrow, so I'm going to head off. Maisie, would you like a lift home?" Please let her say yes.

"Erm... I'm getting a lift from Chloe. Thanks anyway, though." The smile that was on my face disappears.

"Maisie, I can't drive, and neither can you. We've both had too much to drink. I'll get a lift home from Evan. I'm sure he won't mind. Go ahead. Get a lift from Jesse." Chloe smiles at me, while Maisie is shooting me looks evil enough to kill a person on the spot.

"Okay. Come on then." Maisie sighs, following me out to my Ducati. It's a good thing that I decided to bring my helmet tonight.

I give Maisie the helmet, but she doesn't put it on. Instead, she just stares at it.

"I'm not getting on that thing, Jesse. I value my life too much to willingly get on a killing machine!" Maisie near enough shouts at me.

"I'll ride slowly. I promise. Now get the helmet on, please."

"No way. I'm not getting on that thing."

"Well, I guess you're walking home then." I get onto my bike and kick the stand up.

"Fine," she huffs, putting on the helmet. Getting back off the bike, I make sure the helmet is secure, and then help her on. She wraps her arms around my chest like a vice. I like the feel of her close to me, her chest pressed so tightly against my back that not a slither of space is between us. Gunning the engine, we race off down the street, her grip getting even tighter.

****

Ten minutes later, we are at Maisie's dorm room. I never had to stay in the dorms. I didn't see the point in paying extra expenses when I live just down the road. Plus, that way, I can be there for my mom when she needs me.

"Thanks for the ride. I'll see you around sometime, maybe,"

Maisie says, trying to get off my bike.

"I'm going to walk you up. It's late, and it wouldn't be very gentlemanly of me if I didn't make sure you got in okay." She's going to protest, but I'm not taking no for an answer, especially in the state that she's in. People might take advantage of her.

"Fine, but you're not coming in. You can stand at the door." Wow. I was expecting a fight on this. She amazes me all the time. She's so hot and cold, it's confusing, and I don't *ever* get confused by women.

One flight of stairs later, and we're standing outside of her door. I should leave, but I don't want to without explaining about why I ended the kiss earlier. She needs to know that I didn't reject her.

"About the kiss earlier..."

"Don't worry about it. I've forgotten about it already. I shouldn't have kissed you, and I'm sorry." This would be an easy way out. I could just say okay and be done with it. That way, I wouldn't end up hurting her in the long run. However, I can't just leave it. I feel pulled to her for reasons I'm not sure about, but I have to find out what it means, otherwise I won't be able to forgive myself. Maisie could be the girl to change me out of my man whore ways. I have to take this chance.

"No, I won't forget about it. I only ended the kiss because when I kiss you, I want you to remember every little detail about it- the way my lips feel against yours, the way my hands will feel running through your silky hair, and most importantly, how it makes you feel inside. I got a glimpse of what kissing you will feel like earlier, but I want you to have that experience too." Wow, I'm pretty impressed with myself. I've never spoken to a girl like that before. Maisie turns me into a poet!

"I don't know, Jesse. I don't think I'm ready for a relationship yet. I've recently got out of one, and I don't know if I can handle another just yet." Her face falls when she talks about her past relationship. It must be a touchy subject.

"How about we just hang out, get to know each other, and we can see what happens in the future? I'm in no rush. We'll do things at your pace?"

"Okay. I can do hanging out. I'm not promising anything will ever happen between us, though. I don't know if I will ever be ready," she whispers the last part so quietly; I don't think I was meant to hear it. Taking out my cell from my pocket, I hand it to her to enter her digits.

"Well, I'll talk to you soon then. Sweet dreams, Maisie," I say, taking my cell from her and then walking away, her door quietly closing behind me. The ride home gives me time to think. My head is telling me I should have left her alone. No good can come of this. Love is a disease. My heart is telling me not to let her go, to get to know her and let someone in for once. Even though I should listen to my head, I listen to my heart.

CHAPTER FOUR
MAISIE

Eurgh. Somebody close the blinds. It's far too early to be up after the night I had.

Ring ring.

What is that sound? Somebody make it stop before my head explodes!

Ring ring.

Eurgh. My cell phone. Who is ringing at this time in the morning? Do they know it's not acceptable to ring before ten on a Sunday?

Reaching for my cell phone on the bedside cabinet, I answer without bothering to see who it is.

"Hello." Great. I sound like a frog. I need water, now.

"Good morning, croaky," a guy laughs on the other end of the line.

"Erm... Who is this?"

"I'm offended that you don't recognize my voice, Maisie." The guy laughs again. Jesse. How did he get my number? Come on, Maisie, think! Ohhhh, I gave it to him last night. What was I thinking?

"Oh, sorry. I'm still half asleep, and I totally forgot that I gave you my number." I mentally cringe at admitting that last part.

"After how much you drank last night, I'm not surprised. Anyway, I called to see if you wanted to hang out today? I was thinking about maybe going to the zoo. I haven't been there for a few years. What do you think?" Well, if I wasn't awake before, I sure am now.

Sitting up in bed, I squint out of the window, trying to think of a reply. Damn it. I said we could start hanging out and get to know each other. That's it. I should not be allowed to be left alone talking to a hot guy when I've had too much to drink. Why did Chloe allow Jesse to take me home, when only a few hours prior, I explained my situation with Jesse to her? I'm going to have serious words with my so called best friend. Now, I have no choice but to go and spend time with him. Alone. This is going to be fun.

"Erm. Yeah, the zoo is fine. Give me thirty minutes?" I'm in dire need of a shower. I have vodka coming out of my pores! Hang on... maybe I should stay smelling like shit. That way, he might leave me alone, and I won't have to try and get to know him? Hmm, it's tempting...

"Great. I'll pick you up in thirty. See you soon, Maisie." Wait, he drives a motorbike!

"NO, WAIT..." He's already hung up. Great, now I have to ride on his killer machine again, except I'm sober this time. Pull up your big girl panties, you idiot! It's just a motorbike. You can do this.

Checking the time, I see that I only have twenty eight minutes left. I slowly get up from my bed, and my head feels like it has been trampled on by a stampede of elephants. Where did I put my Advil? I find some in my bag, take two, and then make my way to the shower.

The scorching hot water beating down on my face feels amazing. I could stand under here all day, if the water wouldn't eventually run out. Scrubbing myself clean of any remnants of alcohol coming out of my pores, I savor the feeling of being fresh. There's nothing better than washing off grime from the day before. Making sure that I've shaved all my vital parts, so that I don't look like a hairy gorilla, I jump out of the shower and towel dry off.

Surveying my dresser, I decide to wear something comfy. I pull out a white tank top with my denim jacket and black leggings. Comfy and casual. It's not like I'm trying to impress Jesse. He's just my friend, albeit an overly good looking friend who makes my heart rate increase. Don't even go there, Maisie. Shaking my head to rid myself of inappropriate thoughts of him, I apply some mascara and eye liner. I decide to let my hair air dry, so I put on my black boots and grab my bag.

Ring ring. I reach for my cell and see Jesse's number pop up.

"Hi," I say, answering the call.

"I'm downstairs. You ready?"

"Let me just lock up. I'll be down in two minutes." Hanging up the call, I go to the window and see if I can spot him. There he is, standing right below my window, leaning against his motorbike, his legs crossed at the ankles, and sunglasses over his eyes. Wearing a black leather jacket, black t-shirt that hugs his muscles in all the right places, and black jeans with black biker boots, he looks every bit a biker. I'm not going to lie; I'm dribbling just staring at him from the second floor. I can just imagine what he will look like from up close. Calm down. You're just friends, remember. Don't be drooling all over him when you're face to face.

As I make my way downstairs, my hands start to shake. I'm nervous as hell.

"Took your time, didn't you, darling?" Jesse gives me his dimpled grin while pushing off of his motorbike, walking to meet me on the path. Oh yeah, he looks even better up close. My heart rate is rapidly increasing already. It's beating so loud, I'm sure he can hear it.

"Well, I didn't want to appear eager did I?" I say, laughing nervously. Talk about playing it cool.

"You look very nice today, by the way." I look down at the ground, feeling a blush creeping up my neck and onto my face. "Come on, then. Let's get going before the traffic gets bad." After passing me the helmet, he helps me secure it properly. Climbing onto the back of the bike, I wrap my arms around his chest, holding on for dear life, and we haven't even left yet. God, I can feel every contour of his body. It feels amazing with clothes on, so I can only imagine what it would feel like to run my hands over it with him naked. Shaking my head for the second time today to rid myself of inappropriate thoughts of Jesse, I focus on my heart beat instead. I think my heart is going to pop out of my chest in a minute.

"Maisie, could you loosen up a little bit? I can't breathe when you squeeze me like an anaconda." Loosening my grip a little bit, Jesse starts up the engine, and then we breeze down the road.

****

A journey which should have taken twenty minutes, took thirty. I didn't take into account that I was going to be riding on a motorbike, in the September chill, when I got ready today. That doesn't matter though; I was only cold for a few minutes. Jesse is like a human radiator. His heat seeped into my body, warming me from the outside in. Every time the wind blew, I got a whiff of his cologne, a spicy, woodsy smell. I hadn't smelt anything like it before, but it was quickly becoming my favorite smell. I kept taking sneaky sniffs of him throughout the journey, until it was engraved into my nostrils. Hey, I'm not being creepy! I'm just memorizing the smell in case I want to buy it for myself. Who am I trying to kid?

"Maisie, you can let go now. We're here," Jesse says, smiling at me over his shoulder. God, his smile is so beautiful. After I unwrap my arms from around his torso, I jump off the motorbike and unclasp the helmet. "What's with the sad face? You'll be able to put your arms back around me in a few hours. Don't worry, darling." Jesse smirks at me. I want to knock the smirk off of his face for that comment. His ego seems to know no bounds.

"Let me tell you something, Jesse. If this whole getting to know each other thing is going to work, then you need to stop with the unnecessary comments. I don't mind being friends, but friends don't talk to each other like that. Knock it off, okay?" That came out harsher than I had intended, but I told him last night that I wasn't ready for more than friendship. He needs to respect my wishes, even if it's not what I want deep down. I need to protect myself because he would definitely steal the rest of my heart before I could say no, but also break it before I could say look after it. Trying to be more than friends is just not worth the heart ache that will be sure to follow within a few months. Jesse said so himself last night that he's a lady's man. He uses them, and then when he's bored, chucks them before they even have their clothes back on. I don't want to be another one on a long list of girls that he's done it too. I have more dignity than that, even though last night didn't exactly prove that.

Jesse holds his hands up in the air, trying to hide his smirk.

"Okay, I can do that. I said we'll go at your pace, remember. Come on then, friend. Let's go and get our tickets." I'm not going to lie; my heart hurts when he calls me friend. I just need to remember that it was my request to be friends and nothing more.

Damn the safety of my heart!

****

I'm standing next to the orangutan enclosure, waiting for Jesse to come back with some drinks. I have to admit, today has been quite fun. We've been getting along really well, considering I've been nothing but a jerk to him since I met him. We've just been talking about a lot of random things really, but this is just what I have needed; something to take my mind off of the past few months.

Staring at the orangutans, I look at their sad faces. I know they can't help but look miserable because they don't have the muscles to smile, but they really do look fed up with life. They kind of remind me of myself recently. Maybe that's why I've been standing outside their enclosure for the last fifteen minutes. I'd hate to be trapped behind a cage and have random people staring at and taking pictures of me all day long. If they had face muscles, I'm sure they would still look miserable.

"Here's your water," Jesse says, holding out a bottle of water toward me.

"Thanks." Opening the bottle, I gulp down at least half of it. I'm sure a few drops dripped down my chin from where I missed my mouth. How attractive! If they did, Jesse doesn't say anything.

"So, what do you want to go and see now? You have a choice of elephants, lions, or tigers?" Jesse asks, looking at the map of what animals we have left to see.

"That's easy. The elephants. They are my favorite animal to see at the zoo." A big smile stretches across my face at the thought of seeing elephants. I may look crazy, but I have loved them ever seen seeing the Disney film 'Dumbo' when I was little. I have a big collection of stuffed elephants at home, which I've collected over the years.

"If I'd known elephants would make you smile this big, I would have brought you here first. Maybe I should dress up as an elephant for Halloween?" A laugh bubbles up out of me at the image of Jesse in an elephant costume. I would pay good money to see the football captain dressed as an elephant!

"That I have got to see!" I try and say between laughing. Jesse just stares at me with amusement and a big smile on his face.

"It's done then. I will dress up as an elephant for your

42

amusement. You best give me some candy for the effort. Actually, I want a whole bag of candy for that."

"You can have two bags of candy if you do that. It's going to be priceless. Will you let me take a picture?" That picture has Facebook material written all over it. I can't wait for Halloween now. Calming my laughter down to just giggles because my cheeks hurt, I wipe under my eyes to clear the moisture from my tears.

"Only if you will be in the picture as well? I'll put it as your caller ID."

"Okay, but only if I can put it on Facebook. The world has to see this!"

"That's okay with me. I'm not going to be embarrassed." Jesse laughs, walking toward the elephants.

The zoo keeper has just announced that it's feeding time. I've never fed the elephants before. Picking out some fruit from the bucket, I put my hand out, waiting for the elephant to take it. When I see one walking over to me, a huge smile overtakes my face. I wish I could touch it, but unfortunately, we're not allowed. I'll go to Thailand one day, just to ride one. Watching the elephant take the food from my hand, a flash goes off to my left. I turn and find Jesse with his cell aimed at me.

"Did you just take a picture of me?" I ask, putting my hands on my hips, trying to look stern. I hate people taking pictures of me without permission, but the look on Jesse's face shocks me. He's looking at me with complete adoration on his face. It throws me for a loop.

"Yeah, sorry. I'll delete it if you want, but you just looked so happy. I couldn't risk not taking a photo. This way, you will remember the day you fed an elephant for the first time." This guy amazes me more and more throughout the day. I've realized today, that behind the man whore exterior, Jesse is a softy at heart. It's confusing me. It would be so much easier to not like him if he was a jerk. That way, I could hate him, meaning I wouldn't have to talk to him. Except he's not a jerk. Well, not to me he isn't, and that is what is confusing me. I can't exactly just stop talking to him because he's being nice, or then I would be the jerk.

Taking the cell from him, I look at the picture that he's just taken. Wow. It's an amazing photo. I actually look really happy. I haven't seen myself this happy in months. I'm standing there, smiling up at the elephant, while he takes the food, going on with his day-to-day life. "It's beautiful, Jesse." I don't know what else to say. It truly is a beautiful picture.

"It is. You look so carefree. It's a nice thing to see for a change. I'll get it printed for you, if you want?"

"Yes, please. I want to remember this forever." Passing Jesse back his cell phone, we head off toward the lions. I really don't know what to say to him right now. I'm speechless.

JESSE

I expected more of a fight over the picture. Any other girl would have looked at it, noticed that they hadn't posed, and then made me delete and retake it. Maisie always seems to be proving to me that she's not like other girls. The picture was natural because she didn't know that I was going to take it. She let her guard down, allowing herself to shine through for a few minutes. It was a beautiful sight. I'm glad I captured the moment.

I've been browsing around the gift store for the last fifteen minutes, trying to find something to buy Maisie for her to keep as memorabilia. Maisie is on the other side of the store luckily, looking through some of the books, so she is none the wiser about what I'm doing.

I'm about to give up as I can't find anything good enough for her when I spot the perfect gift. It's a little fluffy elephant with a green top on that says 'Feed me'. This elephant would hold a lot of memories for her, which she will remember every time she looks at it.

Making my way to the check out, I pay for her gift before she realizes what I'm doing.

"That will be $18.99, please, sir," the young cashier says.

"Keep the change," I reply, handing her $20. I haven't got time to waste waiting for my change. It's only $1.01 anyway. It's not going to change my life.

Turning around to see where Maisie is, I spot her looking at the elephant that I have just bought her. I need to distract her before she decides to buy it, or otherwise, my surprise will be ruined. "Hey. You ready to go?" I ask, making her jump.

"Jesus, Jesse! Do you have to creep up on me like that? I think I just peed my pants a little," Maisie says all serious, holding her hand over her heart. Let's hope it was enough to distract her.

"I'm sorry. I didn't mean to scare you. Forgive me?" I ask, pulling a sad face and fluttering my eyelashes at her. Who couldn't forgive a face like that? Maisie doubles over in laughter, pointing at my face and trying to catch her breath. God, it's a beautiful sound to hear. I truly could listen to her laugh all day. That is going to be my goal; to make her laugh as often as possible. She glows when she laughs, and it's a sight to behold.

"St-stop pulling th-that face!" she says through her laughter, now holding onto her stomach.

"Only if you forgive me, or I'm going to keep pulling this face until you do."

"Okay, okay. I forgive you. Please, just stop. You're giving me a stitch!" I flutter my eyelashes a few more times for good measure, causing more laughter. A few people are staring at us, probably wondering what Maisie's laughing at and thinking we're crazy. Oh well, let them stare. I don't care as long as she's happy.

"It's getting late, plus, I'm pretty hungry. You want to go get something to eat?" I ask.

"Yeah, I'm hungry too. What do you have in mind?" She asks, placing the elephant back onto the shelf. Mission accomplished!

"How about pizza? There's a little pizza joint just down the road that's pretty good," I ask as we make our way out to the parking lot.

"Pizza sounds good right about now. I could eat a cow. I'm that hungry." Just as she says that, her tummy does a loud rumble. A blush appears onto her cheeks at her embarrassment of me hearing it. Putting the present under the seat compartment before she notices, I then hand her my helmet and help her secure it. I sit on my bike, and then Maisie gets on behind me, wrapping her arms in her signature vice like grip. I'd complain that I couldn't breathe, except I don't want her to loosen her grip. I like the feel of her chest pressed hard against my back, feeling the heat of her body seep into mine. It does crazy things to my body; things that shouldn't be happening when you're trying to drive a motorbike. Starting the engine, I ride off, taking extra care because of the delicate package on the back of my bike.

****

We arrive at the restaurant and are shown to our seats straightaway. I don't even need to look at the menu to know what I'm going to get. I always get this pizza when I come here. Pablo's Pizza makes the best pizza in the area.

"You're not going to look at the menu?" Maisie asks, peering over the top of her menu at me. She looks so tiny sitting in this booth. It's swallowing her up.

"No, I always get the same every time I come here," I reply, shrugging.

"What are you getting?"

"The mighty meat feast. It's the best. That way, instead of having to just choose one meat, you get a big selection."

"Hmm... That does sound good. I might get that too then. Otherwise, I'll regret it if I just get a Hawaiian," she says, putting her menu down on the table.

"How about we get a large pizza and share it?" I suggest.

"Are you ready to order?" the waitress asks. I didn't even see her walk over. I must have really been focusing on Maisie.

"We'll have a large mighty meat feast please," I say, giving the waitress, whose nametag says Kelly, a polite smile. I don't miss the way she checks me out. Women of all ages check me out everywhere I go. I'm not stupid. I'm a good looking guy, and I usually use it to my advantage. However, since meeting Maisie a few weeks ago, I haven't been paying attention to other women. Trust me. It's not through lack of trying. I've tried to pay attention to women who so blatantly want me, but every time I get close to doing anything with them, Maisie's delicate face pops into my head, and I can't help but compare everybody to her. She's ruined me without even knowing about it.

"Can I get you anything to drink?" Kelly asks, sticking her chest out toward my face. That's another thing I'm used to; women willingly allowing me to check them out. Usually, I would, but like I said, that was before Maisie.

"Just a diet coke," I say, not paying attention to her. Turning my attention to Maisie, I see that her eyes are bugging out of her head. I mentally laugh. Bless her, she's so innocent. "Maisie, what do you want to drink?" I ask because I know the waitress has probably forgotten that she is sitting there.

"A diet coke too, please." The waitress snaps her head toward Maisie, giving her the once over.

ALIVE

"Okay," Kelly says to Maisie bluntly before turning her attention back to me. Great. "Your pizza won't be long." With a wink, she's gone.

"Wow, she didn't even really acknowledge that I was sitting here until you spoke to me. Are women always like that around you?" Maisie asks, looking shocked.

"I'm not going to lie. Yeah, they are," I reply honestly.

"Hmm..." is all she says.

Maybe now would be a good time to give her the present I bought. It might cheer her up a little bit. Since the waitress left a few minutes ago, Maisie has just stared at the table, fiddling with her hands. It's a little unnerving. "I got you a little something at the zoo. I hope you like it," I say, pulling the bag off of the seat next to me and handing it over to her. She doesn't attempt to get it out of the bag, just stares at it like it's going to explode at any second. "You can have a look, you know. It's not going to hurt you."

"I know that. I'm just shocked that you bought me something, is all." She pulls the toy elephant out of the bag and just stares. Great. Maybe she doesn't like it? What made you think that you know her well enough to know what she would like, Jesse? You fool!

"If you don't like it, I can take it back. I still have the receipt. It's just, when I saw it, I thought it was the perfect thing to get you. You love elephants, and it says 'Feed me', and you fed the elephants for the first time today. This will help you remember." I'm not a person who is usually uncertain about anything. However, right now, I'm pretty uncertain to whether she likes it or not.

"NO!" Maisie says loudly, hugging the elephant to her chest. I let out the breath that I didn't know I had been holding. She likes it. Relief courses through my body. "Sorry about my reaction. I just didn't expect you to buy me anything, especially something this thoughtful. It's beautiful. It truly is," she whispers the last part so quietly I almost don't hear it.

"Hey, what's wrong?" I ask, staring at the top of her head, as her head is bent down, staring at the table again. She seems to do that a lot when she's embarrassed or thinking about things, I've noticed. "Maisie, look at me please," I ask gently. I just want to make sure she's okay.

She slowly lifts her head, looking up at me through tear filled

47

eyes. Fuck! This wasn't what I was aiming for. I just wanted to buy her something that will make her remember what she did today every time she looks at the toy. Not make her fucking cry! I'm such a stupid son of a bitch. I don't know her well enough to know what she likes. For all I know, it could be triggering some painful memory right now, and it's my entire fault. "Please don't cry. I'm sorry. I don't know what I was thinking buying you that. I don't even know you well enough to know what you like. And now look. You're crying. This isn't how I expected you to react," I tell her, getting angry with myself.

"Jesse, stop. I'm crying... I don't even know why I'm crying, but this is the most thoughtful present I've ever received. Thank you." Maisie scoots over on the seat toward me. Wrapping her tiny arms around my neck, she gives me a hug. I'm so shocked that I can't move. It feels wonderful having her arms around my neck. By the time I go to hug her back, she's pulling away and moving back over to her seat. Damn it!

"You're welcome," I reply.

Our food arrives a few minutes later, by a different waitress, thank God. I watch Maisie pick up a slice of the pizza and take a bite. God, I wish I was that pizza right now. Jesus Christ, I'm jealous of a slice of pizza. I need to sort it out!

"Mmmm," Maisie moans. She actually moans! My cock stands to attention, throbbing painfully. Right now, my mind is thinking real dirty thoughts. What I would do to her to hear that sound come out of her perfect lips again. Taking a slice of pizza to take my mind off of the situation downstairs, I take a bite, focusing on what is going on outside.

"I'm so full. I think I'm going to go into a food coma!" Maisie says, rubbing her stomach. She only ate three slices, which isn't a lot, considering we didn't get anything to eat at the zoo, and it's not even five o'clock.

"I best get you home before you go into it then, eh? Don't want you falling off the back of my bike," I reply, earning a laugh.

"Yeah, it's probably best. I have a lot of assignments to do for tomorrow, and at this rate, I'm not going to get them completed." Maisie says with a sigh.

After paying the bill, we head out to my Ducati, so I can drive her home.

****

We arrive outside of the dorms, and Maisie jumps off of the bike like a pro. "You're getting good at that now," I say smiling at her.

"At what?" she asks, scrunching up her nose. It's an adorable quirk, which makes me smile even bigger.

"At getting off the bike. You're becoming a pro. I'm amazed." Maisie smiles, shaking her head at me.

"Well, what can I say? I'm a fast learner." That makes me laugh. I hope right now she doesn't know that I'm thinking of a million things I could teach her, to see if she really is a fast learner, all of them being x-rated thoughts.

"I'm sure you are. Thank you for today. I had a good time. I'd like to do something again sometime, if you're up for it?" Please let her say yes!

"I think I would like that. I'll see you tomorrow in English. Night, Jesse."

"Night, Maisie." I wait for her to go in through the doors before leaving, then pull out onto the road and drive toward home.

The whole way home, thoughts of today flash through my mind on repeat; Maisie feeding the elephant, her face when I gave her the present I bought her, and the way she moaned when she ate the pizza. I'm strung so tight, I know I'm not going to be able to sleep unless I let off some steam. Usually, I would go and find myself a girl, but things have changed for me. The gym it is then!

CHAPTER FIVE
MAISIE

I stayed up until the early hours of the morning, making sure that my Drama paper for Professor Kendall was completed. She's a lovely lady and an amazing teacher, but you don't want to get on the wrong side of her. She will kick you out of the class before you can even say 'Act'. I've already seen one student kicked out for doing exactly what I would have done, had I not stayed up all night completing the assignment.

Luckily, I had some peace and quiet last night for a few hours, as Chloe left a note letting me know that she was out with a few of her new friends and wouldn't be back till late. I was still awake when she arrived home at eleven. She wanted to know what was happening with me and Jesse and where I'd been all day, but I didn't have the time to explain last night. I was behind on my work, especially because the damn stuffed elephant kept distracting me. I couldn't get over how thoughtful Jesse had been. I didn't know he was like that. Though, I don't think anybody knows that side of him. Every time I looked over at it, sitting on the desk, I saw Jesse's beautiful face and how worried he looked when he thought I didn't like it. I loved it from the moment I saw it in the shop. I cried because he just keeps making it harder and harder to not let emotions get involved. When he gave me the present, it was sweet enough for the walls, those walls I'd spent weeks putting up, to come crumbling down. Now, I'm left constantly thinking of Jesse, wondering when I will hear from him next and what will happen in the future. The only problem? My heart isn't ready to be broken again.

Because I stayed up nearly all night, I wake up late this morning. Noticing that I only have twenty minutes to have a shower and get ready, I rush into the bathroom. Fifteen minutes later, I'm ready to leave. Writing a note to Chloe, who must have already left for her early Art class, I tell her to meet me at Cafe Blanc at eleven, and then I'm out the door, practically running to English.

****

I arrive to my class just as Professor Jones does. Phew! Scouting the room for a seat, I see one next to Jesse at the back. I quickly make my way toward the seat. I'm about to sit down, but Jesse's bag is on it. He moves it onto the floor, so I sit down, pulling out my laptop.

"I saved you a seat. Hope that's okay?" Jesse whispers in my ear. His hot breath tickles my ear, causing the hairs on the back of my neck to stand up. Goosebumps cover my skin, making me shudder.

"Yeah, it's fine. Thanks." I whisper back, trying to ignore how close he still is to me. If I turn my head, I'm sure my lips could touch his. God, how I want my lips to touch his. From what I can remember in my drunken haze, he is an extremely good kisser. Now is not the time to be thinking about that, though. Returning my attention back to the Professor, I try to concentrate on what he is teaching us. It's easier said than done, though.

****

I don't remember anything that was said during English. The whole time I was imagining what it would be like to kiss Jesse again. Now, I'm going to have to ask Professor Jones to email me the lesson plan. Great. I'm going to look like I don't pay attention. I'm usually top of the class, but I can see Jesse distracting me, making my grades drop. I can't allow that to happen.

Packing up my laptop, I put my bag over my shoulder and make my way down the stairs. Jesse must have already left. It was nice of him to say bye to me. I don't know why I expected anything different. Maybe it was because we had a nice day together yesterday, and we actually get on great together, and then he bought me the most thoughtful gift I've ever been given. I guess I was just fooling myself that he would change and actually be interested in me. Why would a guy who looks like he could be on the cover of GQ be interested in a plain, broken girl like me? This is why I'd put up a wall when it came to him. I knew he would hurt me. I just didn't think it would be this soon. I know I told him that I just wanted to be friends, but I still thought he would try harder for me. I guess he is who he said he was.

"*Psssst!*" I jump, spinning around, and throw my fist out in front of me. My fist makes contact with something hard, except I don't know what because my eyes are still closed. "*FUCK, Maisie!*" Jesse shouts out in pain. When I open my eyes, I see him looking at me, wide eyed, and covering his nose with his hands.

"Shit! I'm so sorry, Jesse," I say, disbelief in my voice. "Are you okay?" I reach my hands out and remove his from his nose. Blood is gushing down his face. *Shit!* "No, that's a stupid question. Of course you're not okay. I just punched you in the nose, possibly breaking it. Shit shit shit!" I rush out.

"Maisie, calm down. I don't think it's broken, but I do need some tissues, or I'm going to bleed all over the floor." I look around frantically for the restrooms, spotting one to my left, just down the hall. Dragging Jesse over toward the restrooms, I tell him to wait outside. I grab handfuls of toilet paper, then rush back outside and place the tissue to his nose.

We stand in silence for a few moments, which allows me time to think. What the hell was he thinking, creeping up on me like that? How was I supposed to know that it was him behind me? My sadness at punching Jesse quickly turns into anger at him for being so stupid.

"What the *hell* do you think you were doing, creeping up on me like that? Here I am feeling sorry for punching you in the nose, when in reality, you deserve it. How was I supposed to know it was you, Jesse? For all I know, it could have been a creeper!" I say, getting all flustered.

"I didn't think you would turn around and punch me. Had I known you would do that, I wouldn't have snuck up on you. Trust me. I have to say, though, you have a good right hook for a girl. Who taught you that?" he asks, his words muffled from the tissue covering his mouth.

"My dad taught me. He always said it was good to be able to defend yourself, so when I became a teenager, he taught me basic self defense and how to throw a punch. I've never had to use it until now, though." Placing my hands on my hips, I give him a stern look. He just laughs at me, which spikes my temper up even higher. "What the hell are you laughing at? You have no right to laugh at me, especially when you're the one with the bleeding nose from said girl," I state, pointing at myself.

"I'm laughing at the serious look on your face." God, I could punch him again.

"Jesse, shut the hell up. This is not funny. I just punched you in the face because you made me nearly pee my pants! How on earth is that funny?" I really don't understand what is funny. He doesn't expect me to be happy about the situation, does he? I just punched the most gorgeous man I have ever seen in the face, probably ruining it, and all he can do is laugh? *ARGHH!*

"Seriously, Maisie, calm down. It doesn't really hurt anymore. I've had worse, but I'm impressed with the strength behind your punch. It'll help me relax about your safety." Adoration shines bright in his eyes. I like the look of it, and my anger instantly vanishes. "I'm the one who should be apologizing to you. I shouldn't have crept up on you like that, but I wanted to ask you something. Would you come to watch the game on Friday? It's the first of the season, and we're playing against our rivals, The Dirtbags. It should be a good game, and I'd like you to be there to support me. Will you come?" Jesse asks, giving me the puppy dog eyes, like he did yesterday at Pablo's Pizza. It makes me laugh all over again.

"I'll have to see if Chloe will come with me so I don't have to sit by myself, but I'll let you know by tonight." I bet he looks yummy in his football uniform, all sweaty and muddy. I wouldn't mind getting down and dirty with him. What girl wouldn't?

"That's fine. I've gotta go. I've got practice, and I'm late, so Coach is probably going to kick my ass. I'll talk to you later?"

"Yeah. Text me later."

"Will do. See ya," he says, then turns down the hallway toward the changing rooms.

I watch Jesse until I can no longer see him. It sounds stalkerish, I know, but I just can't seem to stop thinking about him. He's in my thoughts all day, every day. I don't even know when my perceptions changed from wanting to keep my distance, to being friends, to eventually ending up having feelings for him. We've only hung out with each other once, and it seems I'm hooked on him. It's worrying. I suppose what will be, will be. You can't interfere with fate. I'll just have to try to keep my heart guarded around him if I can.

I don't have any classes for two hours, but I said I'd meet Chloe at eleven. Checking my watch, I see that it's eleven already. *Shit!* She hates it when I'm late. I type out a quick text, letting her know that I'm on my way, and walk toward Cafe Blanc.

I'm about to walk through the doors of the coffee shop when the blonde girl Jesse knows comes strutting out. I move out of the way to let her past, except she doesn't move. She just stands there staring at me, so I stare right back at her. Do I have something on my face or something?

I'm getting pissed off now. I don't want to spend all day having a staring contest with her, especially when I don't even know her. "Excuse me," I say, stepping to the left to get past her. She blocks my path, putting her hands on her hips and curling her lip up at me. Okay. *What the hell is this girl's problem?*

"Is your name Maisie?" she spits out. Attractive.

"What's it to you?" I ask, sarcasm seeping from my voice. What business is it of hers what my name is?

"Is your name Maisie?" she repeats. God, she's persistent, isn't she? I don't have time for this.

"Yes. Now, could you please move out of my way?" If it's possible, her lip curls up even more.

"Stay away from Jesse. I don't want to have to tell you again." Who does she think she is, telling me who I can talk to? I have never let anybody tell me what to do, and I'm definitely not going to start now.

"Listen. I can talk to whoever I want. Who do you think you are, telling me what to do? I've seen you hanging all over him. It's quite disgusting, actually. However, don't you think if he wanted you, then he would have hung around with you at the party the other night? Instead, he was with me. I don't know who you are, or what you are to Jesse, but don't you ever tell me what to do again. I don't take kindly to strangers giving me orders. Now, if you don't mind, for the third time, could you move out of my way? I have somebody waiting for me inside." It's childish of me to throw low comments about her in my rant, but this girl needs to realize she is most probably wasting her time with Jesse. I'm not going to put up with shit from Jesse's hook ups when nothing is happening between us; although, she doesn't need to know that.

"I'm warning you, Maisie. I will make your life hell if you don't stay away from him," Blondie hisses, getting up in my face.

"I get it. You want him, however he doesn't want you. I suggest you go and talk to Jesse about this because it has nothing to do with me. I'm not going to stand here arguing with you. I have better things to do with my time. If you're going to make my life hell, then give it your best shot. I've been to hell before." Not waiting for a reply, I walk around her, having to bump my shoulder into hers to get her to move.

Some people are unbelievable! Oh well. I'm not going to dwell on it anymore. I have more important things to think about other than jealous girls in Jesse's life.

Searching for Chloe, I see her sitting in a booth in the furthest corner, two lattes on the table in front of her. I sit down opposite her and take a sip of my caramel latte. Mmmm, it takes like heaven. I've been needing caffeine all day. As I meet Chloe's eyes, I see a worried expression on her face. What's up with her?

"Who were you talking to outside?" she asks, her frown deepening further.

"Oh, I don't know her name. She warned me to stay away from Jesse," I reply, shrugging my shoulders. I'm not worried about a little threat. She's probably all talk anyway.

"Who is she?" Some jealous bitch.

"She's one of Jesse's hook up girls, but from what I can tell, I think she loves him. I don't think he feels the same, though. From what he's told me, he's never had a serious relationship. Just has sex, and then ditches them, which is why I don't want to get too close to him. It's hard though, Chloe. I've not felt this way about anyone except for Matt. I told myself not to let him in, but he was so sweet yesterday. I'm in trouble, Chloe!" Resting my elbows on the table, I place my head in my hands. After saying it out loud, I realize I've done exactly what I didn't want to happen. I've fallen for him. Hard. "I can't stop thinking about him. I'm constantly checking my cell to see if he's texted. I keep staring at the elephant that he bought me. I'm not ready to get close to anyone else yet.

You know Jesse could break me more than Matt did if I let him, but I can't seem to stop letting him in. I like his company. He makes me feel alive again. I like feeling alive again, Chloe. I don't want to go back to being half a person." I inhale deeply, trying to catch my breath.

Looking up at Chloe, I see pity shining in her eyes. I hate pity. I've seen it from everybody close to me for the last four months. "Stop looking at me like that." Pity still shines in her eyes.

"I'm not going to tell you what to do. You won't listen to me anyway. Just follow your heart, Maisie. I know you don't want a repeat of what happened with Matt, but Jesse might be different. You won't know until you give it a shot. So what if he has a reputation with women? He just might not have found the one worth settling down for yet. You might be her. Don't call it quits when you haven't even given him a chance to prove himself. You'll regret it years down the line," she says, a stern tone underlining her voice. She's right, though. She's smart at giving advice. I just wish she would listen to her own advice every once in a while. It would save her and Jake a lot of trouble.

"You're right. I do need to give him a chance. Otherwise, I'll never forgive myself. Not everybody is like Matt. I just need to realize this." Chloe nods her head at me, not saying anything. She doesn't have to. She knows she's knocked some sense into me. "Oh, before I forget, Jesse invited me to watch him play football on Friday. It's the first of the season, and apparently they're playing their rivals. I don't want to go alone, but I want to watch him play. Come with me, please?" I ask, putting my hands in a prayer pose. Chloe just laughs at me.

"Babe, you don't have to ask. Of course I will come. Next time just say, 'Hey, bitch, you're coming to the game with me on Friday'." We both crack up laughing, earning a few odd looks from other customers.

"Where have you been recently? You've hardly spent any time in the dorm room since Saturday." I hadn't really thought about where Chloe was, until now. I've been too wrapped up in myself.

"Oh, nowhere, really. I've just been hanging out with Evan. He's actually an alright guy, which is odd seeing as he's friends with your brother, the king of dickheads." Hmm, I wonder what Jake thinks about this. I doubt he knows. Otherwise, I'm sure Evan would have gone missing by now. Chloe really knows how to piss

Jake off. I don't want to be around when it all blows up in their faces.

"Chloe, do you think it's wise hanging around with Evan? You know how Jake is going to react when he finds out."

"Maisie, your brother has had years to sort his act out and ask me out. Has he bothered? No. He sleeps with a different girl every weekend, flaunting them in my face. Have I ever said anything to him about it? No. Because it's not my place. If that is how he wants to act, then that's his problem, but I won't wait around forever for him. Besides, I'm allowed a little fun in my life as well. I get along well with Evan. I'm not going to chuck away what could be good for me, just to wait for your brother to pull his head out of his ass," she says, growing frustrated.

"You know Jake's not very good at commitment. I don't know where he gets it from, either, as Mom and Dad are happily married. He does have feelings for you, though, Chloe. Even if it is weird for me to admit my brother and best friend like each other, you both need to pull your heads of your asses. Each of you is as bad as the other. However, I want you to be happy. If Evan makes you happy, then that's fine with me. Just be warned, Jake won't take it well. I suggest you tell him if something is going on between the two of you, before he hears through the grapevine. Please?" I ask, trying to get my point across. I will get dragged into this, and I don't want anything to do with it. Having Chloe explain to Jake what is happening will hopefully calm some of the storm, which is likely to follow.

"Of course. I'm sorry that you're going to have to get involved, Maisie. I just want to forget about Jake. He's done nothing but bring me heartache, which is why I'm telling you to catch Jesse before he lets you go. I don't want you to have regrets," she says, all somber. Something is up there. There's no point asking, though, because I won't get any answers.

I check the time and see that I have an hour until my next class. My stomach growls right on cue, reminding me that I haven't eaten anything today. "Do you want to order some food? I missed breakfast this morning, so now I'm starving," I explain, my stomach rumbling again.

"Yeah, I could do with something too," Chloe agrees.

For the rest of my break, we talk about how our classes are going. We don't talk about Jesse or Jake again. We've already said all that needs to be said. Now, I just have to find a way to let Jesse in. I hope he's worth it.

JESSE

My nose still hurts. Damn, that girl has an awesome right hook. Who would have thought there would be such strength behind her tiny frame? Not me, that's for sure. I now know not to piss her off.

When I turned up to practice, Coach questioned about my nose. When I told him what happened, he nearly pissed himself, laughing and telling me not to underestimate the female strength. I just told him he was right.

I missed practice, as Coach made me go to get my nose checked out. There was no point in arguing with him, or he would have benched me for Friday's game, and the team needs me.

Getting checked over by the nurse took a while. She told me that my nose wasn't broken, just bruised. I could have told her that. There wasn't any point in going back to practice, so I decided to go to the gym to let off some steam.

That's where I am now, three hours later. Exercise is usually my way to release tension, except today, it doesn't seem to be working. No matter how many weights I lift, or how far I run, all I can think about is my brown eyed beauty. I think about how I'm not good enough for her, how much I want her to be mine, and how to try and break down the wall that she seems to have put up.

For the first time in my life, when it involves women, I'm confused. Maisie is the exception to everything I know. All I know is that I want her in a way I've never wanted any other woman before. I want her for more than just a way to get my kicks. I want her to be in my future, to see where life takes us. It's a scary thought for me. I'm only nineteen, and I think I may have possibly met my future a few weeks ago.

My cell vibrates in my pocket, distracting me from my thoughts. Checking the caller ID, I see Brandon's face on the screen. We haven't really talked since Saturday night. "Hello," I answer.

"Where were you at practice today, man?" Brandon asks. Nosy bastard.

"Coach sent me to see the nurse. Maisie punched me in the

nose when I crept up on her." I laugh. Brandon full on cackles. Jesus, I think he just burst my ear drum.

"Oh man, that is just too funny. I would have loved to have seen that. How does it feel being given a bit of your own medicine? It's not fun being punched in the nose, is it, fucker?" Nothing like getting straight to the point. We need to talk about this sooner or later. He needs to know to stay away from Maisie. If he doesn't, I'll just have to punch him again.

"You deserved that," is all I say.

"I know. I'm a dick when I drink. At first, I didn't recognize who she was, not until you told me. You know what I'm like when I've been drinking. I think I'm fucking invincible, man. It was a shitty thing what I did to you. I'm sorry, bro," he apologizes.

"I'm not going to fall out with you about this, Brandon, but I'm warning you to stay away from her. She isn't like the other girls you sleep around with. Maisie is special, and she deserves someone who won't fuck her over." I'm a hypocrite. I can say to other people that she deserves better, except when it comes to me. I know I'm possibly going to fuck her over worse than the other boys in this campus probably could, but I want to try to be what she needs. She is worth fighting my demons for.

"Yo, Jesse, you there, man?" Brandon says into my ear, reminding me that I'm on the phone.

"Yeah, sorry. What did you say?"

"I said you must really like this girl." Is it really that obvious? Brandon's known me since kindergarten. There's no point lying to him, either, because he'll know.

"Yeah, man. I'm hook, line and sinker. I know I'm not better than you for her, but I just can't stay away. And trust me, I've tried. I took her to the zoo yesterday, Brandon. The fucking zoo! When was the last time I went to the zoo, let alone took a girl there? Hell, I've never taken a girl anywhere, except to bed, in my life. You should have seen her. She was so carefree for the first time since I met her. Usually, she has a wall built up, not letting anybody in. For the first time yesterday, I saw the real her shine through. Her wall went down a little bit, and now I want to completely knock it down. Man, I sound like a pussy." I laugh awkwardly. I never express my feelings. I feel like a teenage girl now.

"Wow..." is all Brandon says.

"I know, right?"

"Jesse, don't let your past ruin your future. You're not your dad, and Maisie isn't your mom. Just because you have the same DNA as that shithead, doesn't mean you're like him. Your mom would tell you the same thing. You dote on that woman, so you can love, Jesse. Wow, listen to me giving advice. I should become a counselor." I snort at that. Brandon, a counselor? What a joke. Though, he does have a point this time. I can't let my past dictate my future.

"I know. Only problem is that she just wants to be friends. She says that she's just got out of a bad relationship, which I'm guessing is why her guard is up around me. She knows my reputation, which doesn't help either. I'm just going to have to give her time, show her that I'm serious about us, and hope that eventually she feels the same."

"That's all you can do, bro. You want to meet up later? Grab a beer or something?" Brandon asks, changing the subject. I think he's done all the woman talk he can for one day, and I don't blame him. I think I need to check to see if I still have my balls.

"Not tonight. I promised Mom I'd put up her new dresser for her. I've been putting it off for the last few days, so I really need to do it for her. Tomorrow?"

"Yeah, tomorrow's good. Catch you later," Brandon replies. Ending the call, I get back to doing my weights.

For the next hour, I bench press more weights than I've ever managed. I needed to feel like a man again. For a few minutes, I had thought I had grown a vagina.

It's late when I make it home. Mom's not in, so I heat up my dinner, eat it, and then head upstairs to get started on her dresser. Putting on my iPod, Imagine Dragons, Demons plays. This song is the theme tune for my life, especially now that Maisie's walked into it. Eventually, she will see the demons that I can't get rid of. I just hope that, like the song, she will show me how and not give up on me.

CHAPTER SIX
MAISIE

Chloe and I get to the field at five for the football game. It isn't supposed to start until six, but we're meeting Jake and Evan here earlier so we can find a seat. When Chloe told me that we were going with them, I asked her if it was a good idea. Apparently, it will be fine. I also asked her if she had spoken to Jake yet. Her answer? No. Tonight is going to go really well; I can feel it. Chloe and Evan better be subtle around each other, so Jake doesn't catch wind about what is going on behind his back.

Walking over toward the concession stand where we are meeting the guys, I see the blonde girl who threatened me on Monday. She hasn't seen me yet. Thank God. I'm not in the mood for another run in with her just yet.

"Maisie, isn't that the girl from the coffee shop the other day?" Trust Chloe to mention it.

"Yup, that's her alright. Try not to draw attention to us. I'm not in the mood for her to threaten me again," I say, hoping she will listen to me for once. It's never been her strong suit.

"Don't worry. We'll be stealth like!" Chloe says, walking on her tip toes, looking like a twat.

"Chloe, stop it. You're drawing more attention to us," I say laughing.

"Alright, alright," she replies, walking normally.

We're almost past Blondie when I hear Jake shout, "Maisie, over here!" Fuck sake! That will definitely draw attention.

"Uh-oh," Chloe says next to me. She knows I'm going to kill Jake now, fucking loud mouth that he is!

When I turn around, I see Jake and Evan standing with a group of guys. Jake waves us over. I don't miss the way he checks Chloe out as we make our way toward them. Subtle, Jake. Very subtle. "Don't shout my name like that again, Jake. It's embarrassing. If you had just met us where you said you were going to, then you wouldn't have had to shout like that, fucker," I say, punching him in the stomach. He doubles over, holding onto his stomach. Serves him right.

"Fuck, Maisie. Did you have to do that?" he asks, trying to catch his breath. I think I winded him. Good.

"Yes, I did. Now stand up, you pansy. You look like a tool in front of your friends." All of his friends are just standing there laughing at him. He's going to be pissed off at me for making him look like a twat. Oh well. He just drew attention to me, so I think we're even. I'm surprised Blondie hasn't walked over to me yet. I risk a glance over my shoulder at her. She's standing there with two girls, who I'm guessing are her friends, staring at me. Joy.

"I'll get you for this, squirt." Jake says, now standing up. "Come on, then. We need to get seats before they're all taken up. Plus, we always sit in the same place." Following Jake, we all head up the bleachers. We end up sitting half way up in the middle of the bleachers. I have to admit; I have a good view.

I've been dreaming about seeing Jesse in his uniform all day. I love guys who have athlete legs; all muscle- yum. Matt had strong legs, and it was my favorite part of his body. I don't want to think about him, though. I want to think about Jesse. When we talked earlier, he asked me if I wanted to do something tonight. I haven't seen him this week, except for in class, so I agreed. Since my talk with Chloe the other day, I've decided to give him a chance, his reputation and my heart be damned. It's a risk I'm willing to take. Tonight, I'm going to show him that my guard is down and I'm ready to let him in. I'm pretty nervous, to be honest. I just hope I haven't gotten my hopes up and read the signals wrong. I think he likes me too, but I've always been inexperienced when it comes to guys.

"Oh, I forgot to ask," Jake says, nudging my arm. "How'd you know Jesse?"

"Oh, he's in my English class," I say nonchalantly.

"Well, just be careful, okay? He has a worse reputation than me. I don't want you getting hurt, or I'll have to kick his ass, even if he is a friend." The less I tell him, the better. I don't need Jake getting involved in my business and having words with Jesse. It's nice that he cares about me, but it can be a little overwhelming sometimes.

"We're just friends, Jake." I tell him rather abruptly, hoping he will drop the conversation. I hope we'll be more than friends one day; however, I don't say that out loud.

"Hey, dickwad, leave her alone. Who Maisie gets involved with is none of your business. She isn't going to turn into a whore like you, so you have nothing to worry about," Chloe interrupts. This is the first time she has said anything to Jake since we met up half an hour ago. That's unusual for her. Guess that's why she had to get her dig in when she could.

"Fuck off, Chloe. I'm just looking out for Maisie, and you're just jealous because you have no one to look out for you," Jake quips back. Oh here we go again...

"Jealous? Why would I be jealous to have a brother like you?" Chloe looks at Jake with disgust in her eyes.

"I guess it's a good thing I'm not your brother then, or otherwise, it'd be incest," he answers back, a smug smile on his face. Oh no. I shake my head 'no' at Chloe. I don't need Jake finding out about her and Evan like this. I don't want to be involved. Chloe gives me the tiniest nod of her head, letting me know that she won't. Nobody else would have noticed her nod, except we've been best friends for as long as I can remember. We can talk without anybody knowing.

A creepy smile takes over Chloe's face. "If you say so, sweetie," she finishes, and then turns around and carries on her conversation with Evan, who looks completely confused. I don't blame him. I doubt he realizes he's planted himself in the middle of their cross fire. I just raise my eyebrows at Jake.

"What?" he asks confused.

"When will you two be able to have a conversation without arguing?" I don't hear his reply as the music welcoming the teams starts up. A team wearing gold and black comes out, which I'm guessing is the Titans' rivals, the Dirtbags. Next, our team comes out wearing a navy blue, orange and white uniform. Jesse is the last to run onto the field. The crowd goes crazy when they see him. Wow. He really must be a superstar here. I didn't realize. Why would I, though? I don't usually watch football.

I'm able to check Jesse out from up here without him noticing, so I take full advantage of it. He looks sexy in his uniform, way off the hotness chart. And his legs? Oh my. Best. Legs. I. Have. Ever. Seen. They are so muscled and tanned. I just want to run my tongue up his legs. They look that good. His top is quite tight, like his usual attire, showing off his beautiful tattooed biceps. It's no wonder the women love him. I'm sitting here discretely drooling, when I'm sure all of the female population here, young and old, are doing exactly the same thing. Getting a look at his face, my eyes meet with his dark orbs, which are staring right back at me. A smirk lifts one side of his mouth up. *Shit, I've been caught.* Trying to act nonchalant, I smile back at him, shrugging my shoulders. I look more confident than I feel. If he was standing in front of me, I'm sure he'd see that my face is beetroot red right now. Jesse winks, and then turns to get in position. What position he plays, I'm not sure. "Jake, what position does Jesse play?"

"He's the quarterback," he replies, eyes on the game.

"Is he any good?" I ask, watching the ref blow the whistle.

"Hell yeah. He's the best CSUF has had for the last ten years. Jesse will go down in history. He's already got scouts turning up to his games, wanting to sign him on when he leaves." Wow. I'm speechless. Jesse never told me he was that good before. He's got an amazing future ahead of him.

I watch the rest of the game, cheering when everybody else cheers. That way, I don't look like a fool. I've sat with my hands covering my eyes for most of the game since the second minute. I've decided I don't like to see Jesse being tackled in case he gets hurt.

By the end of the first half, the score is seven-nil to us. Of course, Jesse's legendary status is accurate. He scored on the twenty-ninth minute. When he scored, I think I lost a little bit of my hearing. I thought the crowd went crazy when he ran onto the field, but that was nothing compared to how they acted when he scored. I'm blown away by how much these people love him, and also how much he loves them. When he scored, he really paid attention to his fans, joining them in the celebration.

I need a drink after all that cheering. "Jake, how long do we have to wait until the second half begins?"

"Fifteen minutes. Why? Where you off to?" he asks, looking at me for the first time since the game started. He's a huge football fan. He's just not the best at playing it.

"I'm thirsty, so I'm going to get a drink. Do you want anything while I'm there?" I ask, being the generous sister that I am.

"I'll just have a water, please."

"Chloe, I'm going get a drink. Do you want one?" I shout just to be heard over the noise. She's sitting between Evan and Jake; not a smart choice, but hey. I'm not going to tell her what to do.

"No, I'm alright, thanks. Evan got me one before the game." Jake's head swivels at her revelation. Oh shit. I'm out of here before it all kicks off.

Walking down the bleachers, I see parents who have bought their children to the game. Whether they are supporting someone playing today or have just come for fun, it's great to see. Everyone seems to be smiling. I never knew that the atmosphere at a football game could be so welcoming and happy.

Passing the restrooms, I decide I'd best go. We have another forty-five minutes before I can go again. The restrooms are surprisingly empty, considering it's half time. At least I can pee in peace now.

As I'm zipping my skinny jeans up, the door to the restrooms open. "I definitely saw her come in here, Tiff." Huh? Saw who? I hope they aren't talking about me because I'm the only one in here.

"Check the cubicles." Wait a second. That voice... Oh shit. That's Blondie. Didn't they call her Tiff? Tiffany, I'm guessing, is her full name. She looks like a Tiffany.

I hear shoes crunching against the linoleum, stopping outside of my cubicle. The door rattles on its hinges. "Someone's in this one. I'm betting it's her. Want me to have a look?" What. The. Fuck. For all she knows, I could be on the toilet, and she's willing to look?

"No, Emily. She'll have to come out eventually. We'll just wait," Tiffany commands. She's the ringleader, I'm guessing by the tone of her voice. Not wanting to look scared of them, I exit the cubicle, meeting three sets of angry glares. I make my way past them to wash my hands. They just turn and stare at me through the mirror.

Taking the lead, I ask, "I take it you've come back to warn me to stay away from Jesse again, except you've brought your posse with you this time." Drying my hands on the paper towels, I turn around to face them, waiting for my answer.

"I've been thinking, Maisie. The thing is, what I don't think you realize, is that guys like Jesse don't belong with girls like you. He belongs with a girl like me, someone of the same social status. And unfortunately for you, you don't have a social status... Yet," she replies, her glare not once leaving her face.

"And your point is?" I ask, totally confused as to where she's going with this train of thought.

"My point is that if you don't stay away from Jesse, you will have a social status, but it won't be a good one. I'll make you out to be a whore. And do you know what the best thing about my plan is?" She doesn't wait for me to answer. "It's that nobody will believe you when you try to defend yourself, because they don't know you. People know me. I'm high up in the food chain compared to you. All the guys will talk to you just for a piece of ass, not because they like you. And the girls... well, they will look at you like the piece of trash that you are." Wow, she's thought about this really hard. I know I should just tell her to do her worst, but nobody wants to be perceived as the local whore. Plus, what can I do to stop her? Like she said, I'm nobody compared to her. Maybe it's best if I just give up before anything even starts with Jesse.

"Fine. I'll stay away from Jesse. But if he ever comes back to you for sex, it doesn't mean he wants you. A bit of advice- don't degrade yourself like that." With that, I make for the exit.

"He loves me. He just doesn't realize it yet," Tiffany says confidently. I just shake my head at her stupidity and make my way outside.

The concession stand is desolate now. What's the time? Shit, the game started five minutes ago, I realize as I check the time on my phone. I don't want a drink now. I don't even want to watch the rest of the game. I just want my bed. I don't expect to move from there for the next two days. Why does the world have girls like Tiffany in it? What good do they do except try to make people's lives miserable? She's right, though; I'm not good enough for him. Jesse's proved that tonight. He has his future mapped out ahead of him. Me? I'm just going to be a boring English teacher. He should be with a model or someone equally in the same league as him, not sitting at home with a girlfriend who marks essays for a living. That's all I can offer him. I don't know why I even thought about letting him in. He deserves so much better than what I can give him.

I think I'm just going to tell Jake and Chloe I'm going back to the dorms. I'm not in the mood to sit and watch the guy who I want more than life itself, knowing that I have to let him go before I've even had him.

Plopping down next to Jake, I don't feel the pain that I should have felt in my bum from the force of sitting down on the metal bleachers. Act like nothing's wrong and you're just tired. "What took you so long?" a voice says, sounding far away. "Maisie?" the same voice says again. Returning from my thoughts, I face a worried looking Jake.

"Huh?" I ask, not remembering what he asked.

"Are you okay? You were gone a long time, and by the looks of it, you didn't return with drinks." I forgot all about getting the drinks after my run in with Tiffany.

"No, I don't feel very well. I think I might have eaten something dodgy for dinner. I'm gonna go back to the dorms, alright?" I reply, feeling sick to my stomach.

"Will you be okay walking back by yourself?" My brother can be so thoughtful sometimes. I know he cares about my safety, but I'm not going to let him miss the game just because I'm having a bad night.

"Yeah, I'll be fine. I'm just going to go straight to my room. You stay here and watch the game."

"Make sure you text me when you get in, so I know you got back safe, okay?" I just nod. Taking a glance at Jesse, I see he's really into the match. He won't even know that I'm gone, which is good. I don't want him losing focus. For all he knows, I could be in the restrooms, if he looks up and sees that I'm not there. I watch for a few more seconds, and then make my way down the stairs, my heart breaking all over again, just like it did four months ago. My good friend, heartbreak, has made himself comfy on my shoulder again, reminding me that I'll never feel alive again.

****

Walking into my dorm room, I slam the door shut, fall to the ground, and hug my knees. The tears are pouring down my cheeks like a waterfall now, fast and thick. The funny thing is that I don't even really know Jesse. It's not like with Matt. I was with him for years. I thought he was my forever. I've known Jesse for a number of weeks. I didn't want anything to do with him, but somehow, the tears and pain are just as painful as they were after what Matt did. I should have listened to my mind, not my fucking damn heart. All my heart does is cause me pain. Laughter bubbles up manically out of my mouth. If anyone were to hear, they would think someone escaped from a mental asylum. I sound pretty crazy. Maybe I am going crazy from all the bad luck I've had in the last few months. Maybe it's taken its toll on me, and I've finally cracked. I wouldn't be surprised.

I wish I had never met my beautiful Jesse. That way, I wouldn't have known what it feels like to feel alive again.

JESSE

I noticed the way Maisie came back after half time, looking like the world had just shat on her. Before half time, she seemed so happy. I even saw her cheering a few times. When we came back out after the first quarter, she wasn't sitting with her friends anymore. I just thought she had gotten stuck in the line for the toilet. I looked up ten minutes into the game, and there she was, sitting with her brother. I breathed a sigh of relief, but that relief only lasted a few seconds when I got a good look at her face. Her eyes, which shined with happiness and affection not a half hour before, were now dull and lifeless. Her skin, which looked vibrant, now looked pale. And her posture, which was confident, was now closed off. She was closing in on herself. I know that look well, except I've had years to learn how to disguise it. Maisie, it seems, is new to the game.

When she left the grounds, it took all of my will power not to run after her to see what was wrong. I was willing to possibly ruin my career for a girl who doesn't even want me, just so I could take away that pained expression on her face.

For the rest of the game, I couldn't focus. My mind was constantly straying to Maisie. What happened to make that dramatic change of mood? Who the fuck upset her? I missed so many opportunities to score, just because I wasn't paying attention. I had Coach screaming down my ear to '*Get your head back in the fucking game*' and '*What the fuck is your problem, Cohen?*' for the rest of the match. No matter how hard I tried, every time I finally focused, her beautiful distraught face popped into my mind. We ended up drawing one all in the end. No doubt the team will blame me, and

I'll probably be benched the next game. Fuck it. I don't care. I need to get the fuck out of here and over to check on Maisie.

Skipping the shower, I rush to get back into my clothes. I just have to leave without Coach catching me. I don't need him to give me a lecture right now. Stuffing my kit into my bag, I swing it on my shoulder, ready to leave.

"Where the fuck do you think you're going, Cohen? In my office. *Now.*" Not arguing, I follow Coach into his office. "Sit down." Doing as I'm told, I sit down and wait for him to tear into me. "What the hell do you think you were doing out there? You let your team down tonight, Jesse. We could have won this match, had you pulled your head out of your ass. Want to explain what has you so tied up in knots that you can't focus on what's important?" he asks, crossing his arms and waiting for my answer. Like I'm going to tell him what's got me in knots. He won't give a shit. I'll just get told football is more important than a girl and not to chuck my future away over this. He's right. Football is more important than girls, but Maisie isn't just any girl. She has a hold over me after a few short weeks that nobody else has ever managed to do. I'm not about to chuck what could possibly be the best thing in my life away, not even for football.

"Family problems, Coach," I reply, lying through my teeth.

"Well, keep the family problems at home from now on. I don't want to see that on my pitch again. You hear me, Cohen?"

"Yes, sir."

"I can't hear you. Let's try that again. I said, do you hear me, Cohen?" Coach asks, raising his voice and looking me straight in the eyes.

"YES, SIR!" I shout, staring right back at him.

"Good. Now get out of my office. Oh, and you're benched next game until you can prove you're worthy to be on my team." I don't argue. I knew that was going to happen. I can cope with being benched for one game. After I've sorted Maisie out, I'll be back in the game. I'm the captain, for fuck sake. They need me. I grab my bag from the floor and walk out, shutting the door on my way. Checking the time, I see it's just now eight. Maisie shouldn't be in bed yet.

As I cross the parking lot, I see Tiffany standing by my Ducati. Aw fuck. I'm not in the mood to deal with her. Make it short and sweet. "Hi, Tiff. Have fun at the game?" She always comes to every game. She says it's to cheer me on, though I think it's just to keep an eye on me.

"Hey, Jesse. You were amazing tonight. Looked really hot out there," she says, leaning on my bike and twirling a strand of her blonde hair. I used to wrap that hair around my hands, but it now does nothing for me. I'll be happy if I never touch her hair again.

"I take it you weren't watching the game then? I played my worst yet," I reply, moving to straddle my bike.

"Well, you looked pretty good to me, but you always look good to me." Eurgh, please. Why did I never see how desperate she is? Maisie would never degrade herself like this. She makes the guys work for her attention. I guess I like the challenge.

"Look, Tiffany. I have somewhere I need to be. Would you mind moving please?" I ask as politely as I can. My patience is running thin now.

"Aren't you going to the after party? I thought I could catch a ride with you? My friends have already left." She flutters her eyelashes at me, hoping to get her own way, I guess. Nope, not going to work with me.

"Sorry. I have somewhere I needed to be like five minutes ago. You're going to have to get a lift from one of the guys inside," I say, revving my engine.

"But..." I don't wait to hear what else she has to say. To be honest, I really don't care. I drive off, speeding down the road. I need to get to Maisie now. I have a feeling that something bad happened tonight. I just hope she tells me what.

****

I think I beat a personal record getting here. It only took me two minutes. Luckily, I didn't get pulled over for speeding. I would have kicked off. I have important issues to deal with.

After knocking on Maisie's door, I wait. Nobody answers, so I knock again, louder this time. Putting my ear to the door, I listen for sounds of movement on the other side of the door. Nothing. I decide to pull out my cell and call her. Listening to the dial tone, I hear a ringing sound coming through the door. I hang up and call back to see if it's her cell. There the sound is again. Yup, it's definitely her cell. My heart jumps in my throat at the thought of something being wrong. She would answer the call if everything was fine. I bang on the door this time. "Maisie, open the door. I need to know that you're okay," I ask frantically.

"Go away, Jesse," she replies, the sound muffled by the door. No fucking way am I leaving.

"No, not until you let me in. I know something's wrong, and I'm not leaving until you tell me what. I'll kick this door down if I have to," I warn. I'm not joking, either. I will kick this door down in the next minute if she doesn't open it.

"Please, just go. I don't want to see you." Ouch, that hurt. I want her to need me. Hearing that she doesn't want to see me practically guts me on the spot.

"You've left me with no choice. I'm kicking the door down in three seconds. One, two…" The door flies open on three.

Maisie stands there with mascara running down her cheeks, her eyes red and swollen. *Fuck!* I can literally feel my heart breaking just looking at her. Whoever has hurt her, I'm going to kill them. I refuse to allow anybody to hurt my Maisie again. I check her out to make sure she hasn't hurt herself. A quick sweeps tells me that's not why she's upset.

"You've seen me now, so you can leave," she says, her voice gruff from crying. She starts to close the door on me, but I put my foot in the way. "Jesse, move your foot. I just want to go to bed." Her eyes are downcast, looking anywhere but at me.

"I'm not leaving until you tell me what's wrong."

"Why do you care so much?" she asks, finally looking at me.

"Why do I care? Isn't it obvious? I like you, Maisie. I like you a hell of a fucking lot, actually. I want to spend time getting to know you better, even though I know you have your guard up. I want to eventually knock that wall down and gain your trust. I know you have no reason to trust me, which is why I want a chance. I saw you return when the game had started, looking like the girl who I first met, like the world had just handed you a huge plate of shit. I want to know who or what took that beautiful smile that I saw earlier off your face. When you opened the door, and I got a good look at your face, all covered with make-up and dried tears, it broke my fucking heart. Please, don't shut me out. I care about you. So much." Fresh tears well up in her eyes. Aw shit. I really don't like to see her cry. "Please, don't cry." I ask. I always seem to make her cry.

"I can't tell you what's wrong," she whispers, looking down at the floor again.

"Of course you can. I want to help you, Maisie. Whatever it is, I'm here for you. Please, don't push me away."

"You can't help," is all she says. I'm getting annoyed now. How does she know that I can't help, if she won't tell me what the problem is?

"Look at me, Maisie." Lifting her head up with my thumb, I hold her head in place, giving her no choice but to look at me. "Just tell me, or at least let me be there for you if I can't help. I don't like seeing you upset. It's tearing me apart not knowing if I can help." Something flashes in her eyes, but it's gone before I can grasp what it is.

"I don't want to talk about it out here. Anybody could hear."

"Well, can I come in then?" She doesn't answer, just stares at me. "Please?" I ask. She doesn't say anything, just steps aside so I can move past. "Thank you," I say.

It's the first time I've been in here. It's pretty bare, just what you're given when you move in, along with her and Chloe's belongings. "So..." I say, not knowing where to start, now that we've got some privacy. "Do you mind if I have a seat?" I ask, pointing to the beds.

"Mine is the one with the purple cover," she says, pointing to the bed on the right.

Sitting down on the edge, I look up at Maisie, standing there awkwardly. My eyes roam down to her lip, which she is biting. I really want to bite that lip. We're alone in her room, and under different circumstances, I would definitely try it on with her. I'm such a jerk. Here she is distraught about something, and all I can think about is getting her into bed. Think about dead puppies. Yup. That worked.

"So do you want to tell me what happened earlier?" I ask, patting the spot on the bed next to me, hoping she will sit down. She doesn't.

"Honestly?" she asks.

"Of course, honestly. I don't want you to lie to me, Maisie," I reply. Why would I want her to lie to me? I just hope she tells me the truth now.

"Ok, but I have to tell you about Monday first." I sit patiently, waiting for her to start. I'm not going to lie. I'm nervous as hell to find out what's wrong. I've never had to deal with these sorts of feelings before. "After I punched you in the face," Maisie starts and cringes, but I just laugh. That was hilarious. "I was on my way to meet Chloe for coffee. Anyway, I go to walk through the door, and your blonde friend… Tiffany, is it?" she asks.

"Yeah, what about her?" I ask, not liking where this is going already.

"Well, Tiffany blocked my path, asking me if my name was Maisie. When she wouldn't move, I said yes. Then, she warned me to stay away from you, or she would make my life hell. I just told her to do her best, and then I walked past her, into Cafe Blanc." What. The. Fuck. I'm so angry right now. Who does Tiffany think she is, telling people to stay away from me, like I'm her property?

"Okay. And I'm guessing today has something to do with Tiffany, as well?" I ask because, knowing Tiff, she doesn't take people not doing as she wants politely. She will seek revenge until she gets her way. That's what happens when you're spoilt growing up. You think everybody will do as you say; everyone except for me, and she knows it.

"Yes, but first you need to know something. I have to tell you before I tell you the rest of the story. I like you too, Jesse, a lot, actually. I know I've been a bitch to you since we met, but I decided to try to let you in and see what happens between us. I don't want to live my life with 'what ifs'. I want to live in the moment and see where life takes me. With you, hopefully." I watch her cheeks go bright red at this revelation. And my heart? I think it just stopped beating. Fuck, I didn't expect that at all. I don't know what to say, so I don't say anything. I reach over, gently rubbing her cheek with my thumb. God, her skin feels so good. It's like silk. Maisie pushes her face into my hand, closing her eyes. She's so beautiful, even with her make-up all over her face. I have to kiss her. Now.

"Can I kiss you? I want to taste you so badly," I ask. Please let her say yes. I need to taste the sweetness of her lips, feel the softness of them pressed against mine.

"Yes," she whispers into my hand. That's all I need to hear. Tilting her head so she's facing me, I stare into her eyes and run my hands through her velvety hair. Moving so that our foreheads are touching, I breathe her in. She smells like strawberries. I take another deep breath, and I know I won't ever get tired of smelling her. Sweeping a loose strand of hair away from her eyes, I lean forward oh so slowly. I want to savor this moment. I'm classing this as our first kiss, except I already know it's going to be amazing. My lips gently graze hers before I pull back, and they're just like I remember, soft and sweet. Going back for more, this time I kiss her a little harder. Maisie responds straight away, letting out a small moan that turns me on so much, while kissing me back in sync, like we've been doing this for years. I pull her closer until there is no space between our bodies, my hands running through her hair, gently tugging. She puts her arms around my neck, gripping for dear life, like I'm going to vanish when she opens her eyes. I'm not going anywhere. I need more. I kiss her harder, our teeth clashing from the force of it. It's still not enough. I don't think it will ever be enough when it comes to her. I'm so hard right now, it's painful. I have to stop before I can't, and we end up doing something she's not ready for yet. Breaking off the kiss takes all the power I possess. She whimpers, opening her eyes. Her eyes are shining, and I'm sure mine are exactly the same. I feel like the luckiest man in the world right now, and it was only a kiss.

"Wow," Maisie says, breathless.

"That's about right." I laugh. My hands are still playing with her hair. "I really want to do that again."

"Then do it..."

"I can't." The throbbing rod between my legs pulses painfully at the thought of kissing her again, reminding me why I can't. Fuck you, self-control.

"Was it not good?" she asks, her confidence disappearing with each second. *Shit. That didn't sound good.*

"God, no. You were better than good. You were amazing. I just have a little problem downstairs," I pause and point to my dick, "and I know that I won't be able to control myself if I kiss you again. Oh, I definitely want to though, Maisie. Don't think for a second that you weren't good enough. This," again I point to my dick, "is proof that you were definitely good enough." She laughs. It's music to my ears, the sound making my body tingle.

"I'll let you off then. So, what does this mean for us now?" she asks, turning shy again. It's cute as fuck.

"Well." Trying to be funny, I get down on to one knee in front of her, holding her hand. "Will you, Maisie, take me, Jesse, to be your boyfriend?" That earns a full on belly laugh from her. I hope she doesn't think I'm just joking, though. I'm being serious, but I thought I would put some humor into it to make the atmosphere not so strained.

"Are you sure?" she asks when she has finally stopped laughing.

"Hell yeah," I reply, giving her a cheeky smile, which she returns, equally as cheeky.

"Then, yes. I would love to be your girlfriend." Picking her up, I spin her around. She squeals in my ear, causing momentary loss of hearing. I don't care. She can squeal in my ear all day if she wants, because she has just made my day. Nothing can get me down now.

I sit her down on the bed and take a seat next to her, suddenly remembering why I came here in the first place. My good mood instantly vanishes; so much for nothing getting me down. "We still need to talk about what happened earlier." I hate to bring it up, but it needs to be addressed. The smile vanishes from her face. I miss it already.

"Oh."

"We have to talk about it, Maisie. I have to know what happened." She starts ringing her hands together, so I put mine on top to stop her. "Don't be nervous. I'm here for you, okay?" She just nods her head.

"When it was half time, I went to the restrooms. While I was in there, Tiffany came in with two of her friends. They knew I was in there. Her friend, Emily, I think, saw me go in there, so they waited. I knew they wouldn't leave until they talked to me, so I left the cubicle, expecting a confrontation like last time. Tiffany had obviously been thinking about what to do to get me to leave you alone. She knows that I'm a nobody compared to her. She started saying how I wasn't good enough for you, and that you deserve to be with somebody like her. Then, she threatened to make me out to be the local whore, saying that nobody would believe me over her. It's true, Jesse. Nobody would believe me. She's a popular senior, but me... I'm just a freshman," she tells me sadly, fresh tears forming in her eyes. Tiffany is a deluded bitch if she thinks that we belong together. Nobody is more perfect for me than Maisie. She's the only one who has ever caught my attention for more than a week.

Wiping the tears from her eyes, I tell her, "Maisie, Tiffany won't do anything. I won't let her. And if she does, then nobody will believe her because I'm more respected than her. I could destroy her in a second, and I will for you, if it means you're protected." I wouldn't even think twice about ruining Tiffany. She's only got where she is because of me. She needs to remember that.

"I don't want you to destroy her, Jesse. I just want her to leave me alone. If I'm going to be with you, I don't want her causing me trouble at every turn. Otherwise, we will never work."

"That's not going to happen. I promise."

"How can you promise me that? She may not listen to you," Maisie says, biting that damn lip again.

Pulling her lip from between her teeth, I rub her cheek, looking into her eyes earnestly. "She will listen to me. I'll give her the benefit of the doubt this time, because you asked me to. By the way, you're too nice for your own good. If she doesn't listen to me, though, I will ruin her, whether you want me to or not. Okay?" She slowly nods her head in confirmation. I'm glad she isn't fighting me on this. She doesn't know what Tiffany is capable of. I'm not going to allow someone special to me to be on the receiving end of Tiffany's wrath. I'd rather die than see Maisie go through pain again.

"Good. Okay, I better go. It's getting late. Thank you for telling me what happened earlier, and thank you for allowing me to be your boyfriend. I promise I'll try to be the best boyfriend I can be," I say honestly, standing up to leave.

Maisie smiles shyly at me, melting my damn heart that I didn't know I had until about three weeks ago. "Please, just try not to hurt me, Jesse. That's all I ask."

Swallowing the rock sized lump in my throat, I reply, "I'll try." I put my hand on the door handle and turn back to face her. "Can I see you tomorrow?"

"I'd like that." I have to kiss her once more before I leave, even if it leaves me in pain on the journey home.

Pulling her into me, I wrap my arm around her waist, the other going into her hair. I can't get enough of the feel of her hair running through my fingers. Leaning forward, I swiftly press my lips to hers, instantly tasting her sweetness. It makes my head spin. I press harder this time, I savoring the feel of her body against mine and her perfect lips pressed against mine, kissing me back in sync. My tongue asks for entry, pushing against her lips, and she willingly lets me in, brushing her tongue against mine. A moan escapes her lips, vibrating in my mouth. It's the sexiest sound I have ever heard. I'll be dreaming about it tonight for sure. My dick pulses against my leg, reminding me to stop before it's too late. Fuck. When did I turn into a ten second man? Maisie does things to my body that I've never experienced before. It's going to be amazing when we finally have sex, if kissing her nearly makes me squirt my load. I just hope I don't embarrass myself when the time comes. Breaking off the kiss, I keep my eyes closed, just breathing her in. I want to engrain her smell into my head.

"Are you okay?" Maisie asks. She must think I'm a weirdo, I internally laugh to myself.

I open my eyes and stare into her beautiful brown orbs. "I'm more than fine. I was just engraining your scent to my memory. I'm not going to lie." I laugh, thinking how creepy that just sounded.

"It's strawberry cheesecake," she replies, laughing.

"Huh?" I ask, confused. Strawberry cheesecake?

"My body lotion. It's strawberry cheesecake scented, just in case you wanted to know."

"And where can I buy this body lotion?" I ask, deadly serious. I'm definitely going to buy it and keep it at my house for when I miss her. Okay... I'm definitely turning into a creep. I need to leave before I start painting my nails with her nail varnish or stealing her clothes, just because they're hers.

"Victoria's Secret." I wink at her, thoughts of her in some sexy ass lingerie running through my mind. "Get your head out of the gutter, Jesse!" she says laughing, swatting at my arm.

"Goodnight, Maisie. Talk to you tomorrow," I say, giving her a final goodbye kiss.

"Goodnight, Jesse," she whispers in reply.

Stepping out the door, I wave, keeping my eyes on her as I walk down the hallway. "Oh, Jesse, please don't say anything to her about it. I just want to forget about it."

I stop walking. "Okay. If that's what you want." I'm still having words with Tiffany. I'll just make sure Maisie doesn't find out.

Only when she closes the door do I turn forward. Maisie really is a dream come true. She's amazing and beautiful, with just the right amount of fight in her. I just hope I keep my promise about not hurting her. I'm going to have to try hard to keep my demons locked inside; way down inside. I don't need my past jeopardizing my future, and I definitely see Maisie in my future.

I hop onto my bike and gun the engine, turning in the opposite direction of home. I have some business to sort out first; business that can't wait any longer. Tiffany needs to be put in her place, and fast. I won't have her hurt a hair on Maisie's head for as long as I live, and the quicker she realizes that, the better for everyone. I promised Maisie I wouldn't destroy Tiffany, but I'm going to give her a little taste of what's to come if she messes with the people I care about, promise or not.

CHAPTER SEVEN
JESSE

Once I make it to the beach, I kick the stand down on my bike, getting off on the sidewalk. I don't need to know where the party is set up; the sound of the music helps me navigate there.

Looking around for Tiffany, she's not hard to spot. She's always the loudest, draping over the guys in the team. Usually, it's me, but I guess since I've blown her off, she's had to find someone else. Oh well. Let them have her. I have a beautiful girlfriend now, who is being threatened by said girl.

Being reminded of why I came here in the first place, I spot my target and make my way over. I have to make my point clear the first time and let her know that I mean business. I'm feeling more pissed off by the second, just from looking at her, so this shouldn't be so hard to do. I don't care if I've known Tiffany nearly my whole life. I have somebody who is special to me, who I would protect with my whole heart.

"Tiff, can I have a few words, please?" I ask, standing before her, trying to act calm.

"Course. I'll always have time for you." Somebody pass me a bucket. How did I never see how sickly she is? "What's wrong?" she asks when we're away from everybody else.

"Stay away from Maisie, Tiffany," I say, getting straight to the point.

Putting her hands on her hips, I watch her welcoming mask slip into one of pure evil. It doesn't surprise me; I've seen it before, just

79

never directed at me. "Why do you care so much, Jesse?" Her upper lip curls in disgust. It takes all I have not to laugh at her, but that wouldn't help the situation.

"I'm not going to warn you again. Stay away from her." I don't have to explain why I care so much. That will just give her ammunition to use.

"Jesse, you deserve better than a nobody. I've been waiting years for you to notice me for more than just sex, and then *she* comes along. You've forgotten all about me, Jesse. I can do so much more for you than she can." I seriously think she's insane. If she was my girlfriend, she would probably be sleeping with all of my friends behind my back. I laugh, earning a confused look from her.

"You are seriously insane, Tiff. Don't you realize that if I haven't wanted to be with you before now, that maybe I'm never going to want to be with you? I can't trust you as far as I can throw you, and I could throw you pretty far. Just stop all of this drama and walk away while you still have your friends and social status. If you don't, well, you know I can destroy you. I'll do exactly what you threatened to do to Maisie, only worse. I'll make it so you drop out of college. Do you understand?" I say, my voice cold, held with a warning so that she understands that I'm not fucking around.

She visibly swallows, her body trembling, even though it's warm outside. She casts her eyes down to the ground, trying to regain her composure. I just wait patiently, not moving a muscle. I'm in control here. One movement could break the control that I'm holding over her.

"I said, do you understand me, Tiffany?" I repeat after a few minutes have passed, my voice still cold and void of any emotion. She looks up, staring straight into my eyes.

"Yes, I understand," she replies, wringing her hands nervously.

"Good. This is the only warning I'm going to give you. Don't speak to Maisie. Don't go near her. Don't even breathe in her direction. If I hear that you've so much as given her a funny look, I'll make good on my promise. Now, go back to your party." I watch her turn around, her shoulders hunched, head hanging low. Waiting until she's a few feet away, I dig the dagger in deeper. "Oh, and Tiff?" She turns around. "Have fun." I smile at her, earning a confused look back in return. If anyone were to walk by, they wouldn't think anything was off, which is why I smile at her.

Nobody needs to know about this conversation, not yet anyway. I'll give her the benefit of the doubt for now, but people like Tiffany never change. She's a snake, who when you're not looking, will bite you on the ankles. I'll be keeping my eye on her because, like I said, I can't trust her as far as I can throw her.

Leaving the beach without people noticing me is easier than I thought it would be. Everyone is too drunk to notice, which I'm thankful for, for once.

Straddling my bike, I kick the stand up, starting the engine. I look over toward Tiffany one last time, and notice her staring at me with her eyes squinted. I give her the 'I'm watching you' signal, turn my bike around, and ride off.

I've always known Tiffany's had a crush on me, but I never thought she would threaten girls who I show some attention to. If it were any other girl, I wouldn't have cared, but this is Maisie. She's not like other girls. She's beautiful and kind hearted. I can also see that she's damaged, just like me. Maybe that's why I'm so drawn to her. I know I can't be saved. I'm too far gone, but Maisie... Maisie can be saved. I see it in her eyes when I stare into them. She's just lost, and I'm going to help her find her way back, if it's the last thing I do.

TIFFANY

I knew as soon as I saw Jesse, that the stupid whore had said something to him. Who was I kidding that she would keep it to herself?

I'm not going to lie; Jesse scares the living shit out of me. I've seen him destroy people before and, trust me, it's not pretty. I just never thought I would be on the receiving end of his wrath, especially over *her!* What does he even see in her? She's just a plain Jane; a nobody. The captain of the football team should always be with the popular girl, and that's me, not some new freshman that he met a few weeks ago.

I've been waiting patiently for years for him to notice me, and he has. He's always come to me when he wants something. Usually it's for sex, but he still came to me. It was only a matter of time before his feelings changed for me, and he saw me as a potential girlfriend, instead of a sex partner.

That's all fucked now. That whore has ruined it for me. After tonight, he will never give me a chance, and it's all her fault! That interfering little bitch! I'm seething mad right now.

I was having fun at this after party, at least until Jesse showed up to threaten me. Now, I just want to go home. Not to cry or wallow in my misery; I'm not that kind of girl. I will never subject myself to being that pathetic. No, I'm going home to plot how to ruin Maisie once and for all. I don't care what Jesse said. I can handle him. I'll find something to use against her sooner or later. I just hope it's sooner. I don't have time to waste. I don't want my Jesse falling in love with anybody but me. That's why I have to leave now and get started. I'll just have to be very careful, especially with Jesse watching my every move.

CHAPTER EIGHT
MAISIE

I woke up this morning with a ginormous smile plastered on my face, and nothing is going to remove it. I haven't felt this happy in months, and it's all thanks to my sexy man, my boyfriend. Yes, I said it. *He's my boyfriend!* I want to scream it from the rooftops, letting everybody know that I'm in a relationship with Jesse Cohen, the guy all the girls want, but can't have because he's with me now.

I'm currently getting ready to go out with Jesse this morning. He called about an hour ago, telling me to dress comfy. When I asked what we were doing, all I got in reply was 'it's a surprise'. No matter how much I begged him to tell me, he wouldn't budge. I hate surprises, I always have. I trust Jesse, though, so I know I will love whatever he has planned.

Headphones in, I start applying my make-up. One Direction's Midnight Memories starts playing. I can't help but sing. *Loudly.* I love this song; it makes me happy.

A tap on my shoulder makes me turn around, screaming my head off. My eyes land on Chloe, standing there, laughing her head off and pointing at me.

I take out my headphones, giving her a glare. "Didn't your mother teach you not to sneak up on people like that, Chloe? I think I just had a mini heart attack, you bitch!" I say, holding onto my heart and waiting for my heartbeat to even out. It's beating double time right now.

"Oh, stop being a big baby. I tried getting your attention by shouting your name for the last few minutes, but you were too into your song. But your face was priceless!" she says, another round of laughter hitting her. Her laughter is infectious and, with the good mood that I'm in today, I can't help but laugh along with her. It is pretty funny, now that the shock has worn off.

"Just don't do it again. I think I peed my pants a little. I'm going to have to go change," I say, getting up to grab some new panties. After choosing a white lacy pair, I walk into the bathroom.

"Where are you off to anyway?" Chloe shouts through the door.

"Jesse's taking me somewhere. Don't ask where because he wouldn't tell me," I shout back, pulling my jeans up. As I open the door, I'm met with a confused Chloe. Yeah, I'm not surprised. I haven't had a chance to talk to her since the football match yesterday. I have a lot to fill her in on. "Come sit down. I have a lot to tell you, but I'll have to make it quick. Jesse's picking me up in twenty," I say, looking at my cell for the time.

"Start by telling me why you left the game early? You were fine when you left to get a drink, then when you got back, you looked like someone had kicked your puppy." I tell her everything that happened with Tiffany in the restrooms.

"Who does she think she is? She wouldn't have said shit if I'd have been with you. I'm sorry, Maisie. I take it you didn't listen to her, seeing as you're seeing Jesse today?" she asks, anger radiating from her body.

"That's the thing... I was going to forget all about him. That's why I left early. I couldn't sit there and watch him when I knew I had to give him up. I was going to give him a chance before Tiffany threatened me," I say, remembering how I felt yesterday.

"So, what made you change your mind?" she asks, intrigued.

"Jesse happened," I reply, a smile taking over my sullen face. Chloe doesn't say anything, just waves her hand for me to explain. I explain about Jesse coming over after his match, me explaining everything to him, and how we ended up admitting that we have feelings for each other. The whole time, the smile on my face gets bigger and bigger. I must look crazy.

"Please, tell me that you two are officially a couple now?" Chloe asks, sitting on the edge of the bed in suspense.

"*Yes!*" I squeal, jumping up and down. Chloe joins me, her smile matching my own. This is why I love my best friend. She always shares my enthusiasm.

"Thank God for that. I thought I was going to have to give you an intervention and knock some sense into you," she shouts while continuing to jump up and down.

I get a stitch, so I stop jumping and hold onto my side, trying to catch my breath. "I know, but you know I'm wary from what happened with Matt. But, you helped me see that life is too short and to live in the moment. This is me living in the moment, giving things a go. I just hope it's worth it."

"Oh, babe, it will be. Trust me. Plus, if Jesse upsets you, then he has to deal with the angry best friend. I'll chop his balls off, which by the way, you should have let me do to Matt!" Chloe says, putting her hands on her hips and giving me a stern expression. I just laugh at her. Trust her to bring that up now.

"That's all in the past now. However, if Jesse upsets me, you will be the first person I tell so that you can seek revenge." Chloe's cell phone ringing interrupts us. Looking at the caller ID, I see it's Jake. Interesting... Chloe's just staring at the cell, watching it ring. "Are you going to answer that?" I ask.

Looking up at me, she shakes her head, chucking the cell down onto her bed. "Nope."

"What do you think he wants?"

"I don't know, and I don't care. Shouldn't you be getting ready? Jesse will be here in five minutes," she says, changing the subject. Having known Chloe since I was little, I know it's best to just drop the subject. She will tell me what's going on when she's ready, and I will be here to listen to her when she is.

"Oh crap. Yeah, I have to finish my make-up," I say, scrambling off the bed.

Five minutes later, I'm ready and peaking out the window to watch for Jesse. It's not normal, but I can't seem to get enough of him.

I don't have to wait long. He's literally coming down the road as soon as I reach the window. He is definitely the hottest thing I have ever seen, especially riding his motorcycle. My parents would have a fit if they found out, but oh well. What they don't know won't hurt them.

I grab my denim jacket from my bed, put it on, and pick up my cell. "I'm off now, Chloe. I'll see you later?" I ask, making my way toward the door.

"Yeah, I'll be here," she replies, still staring at her phone. We need to have a girl's day soon. I'm getting worried about her.

My cell rings as I'm making my way downstairs. Jesse. Smiling at the screen, I answer, "I'm on my way down."

"Okay. See you in a minute, pretty lady," he replies, then disconnects the call. I can feel my cheeks heat up from him calling me that. I know I'm not the prettiest girl around. I'm quite plain compared to most girls. I don't think I'll ever understand what Jesse see's in me, but he must see something, so I'm not going to complain.

As I step out into the autumn heat, a breeze sweeps my hair in front of my face, blocking my view of Jesse. Swiping my hair to the side, I take him in. I swear he seems to get better looking every time I see him. How is it even possible? His jet black hair has that 'just got out of bed' look about it, but he pulls it off so well. At least if I run my hands through it, I don't have to worry about messing up his hair. I don't think he's shaved since I saw him last night, either, as he's sporting more stubble than usual. That's going to hurt if we kiss. I'm hoping there's plenty of kissing today. I've been dreaming about his lips pressed against mine, along with other things, all night. Jesse's wearing his usual black leather jacket, but this time, he has on a red tight fitted t-shirt, showing off his perfect pecs. I just want to run my hands up and down them to see if they feel as good as they look! He's wearing his usual dark jeans and biker boots, too. All that's missing are his yummy tattoos. I'm turning into a pervert, but I don't care. When your man looks as good as him, it's hard not to look and think dirty thoughts. I stop in front of him and look up, smiling. Cheesy much?

"Do I meet up to your standards?" he asks, a dimpled smirk on his face. *Busted!* I feel a blush creeping up my neck for the second time in the last five minutes. I've never blushed so much in life before. Damn you, Jesse, and your hypnotic powers!

Trying to act indifferent, since the redness now covering my face gives me away, I say, "Mostly yes. However, it would be nice to see your tattoos once in a while." I hope I sound confident. I sure don't feel it, though.

"If you're lucky, you may get a peak later." He winks, holding out his hand.

"I hope I'm lucky then." I wink back, placing my hand in his calloused ones. I wonder what he does that makes them like that.

Maybe he plays the guitar? Jesse laughing shakes me out of my thoughts. I seem to be day dreaming a lot lately too. Damn him for that also. "Where are we off to?" I ask, changing the subject.

"I thought we'd take a walk down to the beach and have a picnic there. The weather's not too bad today, so I thought we'd make the most of it while it lasts. Is that okay?" he asks, looking unsure of himself.

"It sounds perfect... I've never had a picnic on a beach before with anyone except my family and Chloe," I reply, smiling up at him. He returns the smile, melting my heart. He really does have a beautiful smile. I could stare at it all day if he let me.

"Well, let's go then. This way, m'lady," Jesse unstraps a basket from the back of his bike, spins me around, and then we head in the direction of the beach. The smile that I woke up with is still in place, except now it's bigger, all thanks to the amazing man next to me.

****

Jesse picks out the spot for us to sit. I don't mind. He said to me on the way here that this is a date, and he wants it to be perfect. So far, he has been true to his word, and we've only been walking.

He sets out a checkered blanket, which by the looks of it has seen better days. Making myself comfy, I slip off my sandals, close my eyes, and let the sun do its magic. This is heaven. I love the beach, being from San Francisco, but they don't make guys like Jesse back home. Being with him makes the experience all the more amazing.

"You look like you're enjoying yourself," Jesse says from beside me.

Opening one of my eyes, I sneak a look at him, seeing an amused expression on his face. "I love the beach. I haven't had the chance to come here yet, so I'm making the most of it."

"I chose well then. I'm glad. I was pretty nervous this morning, thinking that you may not think it's very adventurous," he admits honestly. I didn't think guys like him got nervous. You learn something new every day.

"This is perfect. Thank you."

"Are you hungry?"

As if on cue, my stomach rumbles, reminding me that I haven't eaten today. "I'm starving."

"Good. I bought a lot of food, since I don't know what you like. We have ham sandwiches, sausage rolls, strawberries, grapes, potato chips, chocolate, and water," he says, pulling the items out.

"You're in luck. I love all of that."

"I thought we could be romantic, feeding each other strawberries like they do in the movies," Jesse says laughing, a blush creeping up onto his cheeks. I laugh along uneasily. "We don't have to if you don't want to. It's cheesy, I know." Now I feel bad. I've probably made him think that I'm laughing at him.

"I'd love to. I've never had someone feed me strawberries before. Well, if you don't count my parents when I was a baby, I haven't, so you'll be the first." A smile takes over his face, and it's contagious.

"I'm glad that I'll be your first then."

Passing me a sandwich, we eat in silence. It's not awkward, but more peaceful. It doesn't feel like we have to say anything to fill the silence, either. We're content with just looking at the ocean.

Between the two of us, we ate nearly all of the food. Well, Jesse did, but I'm so full, I feel like my stomach is about to explode. Lying down to get comfy, Jesse leans over me, blocking the sun.

"Have you got room for strawberries?" Oh God, I forgot about them. If I say no, he's going to think it's because I don't want him to feed them to me. I'm going to have to eat them. Eurgh. But for him, I will.

"Okay, but only a few, though. I feel like I'm going to explode into a million pieces."

"You've hardly eaten anything."

"I don't usually eat much," I say, feeling insecure. Since my break up with Matt, I've lost my appetite, causing me to lose a few pounds. I could afford to lose that weight though.

"I'll make it my mission to get you to eat properly then." I put my arms around my stomach, closing in on myself. He must have noticed because he adds, "Not that you need to put any weight on. You're perfect just the way you are. I just don't want you to starve yourself."

"I'm not," I reassure him. I need to change the topic and fast.

"Do you have any brothers or sisters?" I ask the first thing that pops into my head. Besides, I haven't heard him mention his family before. I don't really know that much about him actually...

"No. It's just me and my mom," he says, popping a strawberry into my mouth.

"Mmm." Did I just moan out loud?

"God, that noise... It does things to a man, Maisie. You're going to have to excuse me." Oh, how embarrassing. He rearranges himself through his jeans, and I look away, embarrassed. It's not like I've never seen a guy rearrange himself, but with Jesse, I don't feel like I should be looking right now. I can't explain it. I turn into a frigid mess around him.

"I'm sorry." Playing with my hair, I wait a few more seconds before turning back to face him. All clear. Thank God! "So your dad doesn't live with you?" I know I shouldn't have asked it as soon as I see Jesse's face go void of any emotion. Stupid, stupid, stupid me. I should learn to keep my big mouth shut. "I'm sorry. You don't have to answer that if you don't want to."

"My father is a pathetic piece of shit. If I never see him again, it will be too soon," he says, packing the food away. He doesn't say anything else, and neither do I.

I think I've ruined our date; me and my stupid mouth. The topic of his dad must be a touchy subject. At least I know now, and if he ever wants to talk about it, I will be here to listen. I don't expect it to be in the near future, though by the way he's acting.

I help Jesse pack the food away, not knowing what else to do, and spy the strawberries. Picking one up, I hold it out toward his face, waiting for him to notice.

"What are you doing?" he asks, still looking distant. I hope this works. Fingers crossed.

"We never got to finish the rest of the strawberries. I thought I'd feed you and try to be romantic this time. How about it?" Please say yes.

Laughing, he opens his mouth. I place the strawberry onto his tongue. His lips come down around my fingers before I have a chance to pull them out, and he sucks and licks the juice off of them. I watch my fingers in his mouth, and my breath becomes labored. I can hardly breathe from being so turned on right now. His hot tongue feels so good swirling around my fingers. I can feel my panties getting wetter by the second. I wouldn't be surprised if I combusted on the spot from the intimacy.

Jesse pulls my fingers from his mouth, placing them back in my lap. I'm disappointed. I didn't ever want that to end. I'm caught by surprise when he grabs my face in both of his mammoth sized hands, staring at me, his breathing also labored. I must have affected him as much as he affected me.

"Your eyes look so beautiful right now, clouded with lust," he whispers. I'm sure they are. I'm sure if I did drugs, this is what being high would feel like. I'm high on Jesse. He's my drug, I'm sure of it. He rests his forehead against mine, continuing to stare into my eyes.

"Are you..."

"Shhh," he says, stopping me mid sentence. Inching forward, his lips lock onto mine in a gentle caress. Fireworks go off in my stomach from the contact.

"You." Kiss. "Are." Kiss. "So." Kiss. "Beautiful." Kiss. I love it when he calls me beautiful. His tongue asks for entry, pushing against my lips. I let him in. He tastes so good, just like I remember, and a moan of satisfaction leaves my mouth. One of his hands leaves my face, tangling into my hair and pulling a little roughly. It turns me on more. I wrap my arms around his neck, trying to get as close to him as possible. It still isn't close enough. I turn so I'm straddling his lap. He leans back, taking me with him, his other hand moving to my hips, running up and down my clothed body. I've never hated clothes so much in my life. Before I know it, we're all lips and clashing teeth, trying to get more of each other. I can feel his cock pressed against my leg, digging in, making itself known. God, I want to become acquainted with it so much. I'm sopping wet. I'm sure he can feel it seeping through his jeans. I'm so turned on. I don't even care about modesty right now.

I need to feel his hair running through my fingers. *Now.* Placing my hands on his head, I run my fingers through his hair, gently tugging at the ends. A moan leaves his mouth, reverberating in mine. Boldness over takes me, and I tug harder, earning another moan from him. He must like it rough. I can do rough. I hope. Jesse moves his hand from my hips, running them down my body and squeezing my bottom. I instinctively grind on him, his hardness rubbing my throbbing clit through our clothes. It's a welcome pain. I grind again, trying to release some tension, both of us moaning in union from the movement. I can't stop now. I need to find my sweet release. I won't take long, either. I'm pretty close already. I carry on, moving faster and trying to hit the spot. Our lips kiss in unison with my grinding.

I can feel the storm building up in my stomach, getting stronger and stronger with every stroke. *"Oh God, Jesse!"* I moan, my orgasm hitting me full force. I scream from the intensity of it. Jesse muffles my screams with his mouth, which I'm thankful for. I carry on riding out the last of my orgasm, my body shaking.

"Maisie," Jesse grunts out, digging his fingers into my jeans. I rest my head on his shoulder, both of us panting and trying to catch our breath.

Coming back down from my high, embarrassment starts to settle in. Oh God, what have I just done? I can't even look at him right now. I'm so embarrassed! "I'm sorry," I mumble into his shoulder.

"Hey, what are you apologizing for?" he asks, playing with my hair.

"For what just happened. It shouldn't have happened." Regret swallows me whole. He's going to think I'm a slut now. We've only been a couple for a few hours, and I've already gotten off.

"Maisie, look at me." Lifting my head, I look into his contented eyes. I wish mine still looked like that. I'm sure mine have guilt written all over them now. "You have nothing to be sorry for. Don't be embarrassed, okay? That was the hottest thing I have ever seen. I want to see it again sometime, but only when you're ready. I'll wait however long it takes, because I know that when the time comes, it will be mind blowing. But don't you dare apologize. I should have stopped you, but I was too far gone as well. I should be the one apologizing." What do I say back to that? Had we not have been in public, I probably would have just had sex with him. I'm not ready for that, though, so I thank the heavens that we were out in public. Wait... We're out in public! *What was I thinking?* I look around frantically, checking to see if anyone saw. The coast is clear now, but that doesn't mean somebody didn't see! "Don't worry. I was keeping an eye out. I don't think anybody saw." I hope he's right.

Ringing distracts me from my thoughts. Jesse pulls out his cell, looks at the screen, and sighs. "Hello," he answers, still playing with my hair. "Okay, I'll see you in twenty." He sighs. "I'll try and be as quick as I can." He hangs up the call, putting his phone back in his pocket.

"What's wrong?" I ask, looking up at him from where I'm resting my hand on his chest.

"I have to go. I have to go sort something out for my mom."
That vacant look has returned to his eyes. I hate seeing them so
emotionless. Whatever his mom is wanting isn't good.

"Do you want me to come with you?" I ask, trying to be
supportive. If it's bad, I don't want him to have to go through this
alone. He has me now, and I plan to be there for him.

"No, I need to do this alone. I'll walk you home, and then I
have to go. I'm sorry I have to cut our date short," Jesse says,
disappointment flashing in his eyes.

"It's okay. Come on. Let's get the rest of the stuff packed up
then." I get up and straighten my clothes out. We don't talk while
we pack up. Whatever is going on with Jesse is distracting him. I
wish I could help. It breaks my heart seeing him like this.

When we're done, we walk back to the dorms, holding hands in
silence. Today replays through my mind.

****

"I'll call you tonight," Jesse says when we make it back to the
dorms.

"Okay." I don't want him to leave, but he has to.

"We'll do something else another day. Again, I'm sorry for
cutting it short," he says, strapping the basket to his motorcycle.

"That sounds great. I'll see you soon then." I stand awkwardly,
waiting for him to finish what he's doing.

He turns around, pulling me flush against him, and gives me a
chaste goodbye kiss. Even from the minimal contact, fireworks go
off in my stomach. Will he always have this affect on me? I hope
so.

"Go on in. I'll wait." He smiles his dimpled smile at me, causing
my heart to melt to a puddle in the parking lot. Damn dimples;
they get me every time. Smiling at him, I leave the confines of his
body and walk to the door. I look back one last time because I
can't get enough of my beautiful boyfriend, wave, and then walk up
the stairs.

I hear his motorcycle ride off into the distance, and I suddenly
feel incomplete. It's like he's taken a piece of me with him, most
probably my heart. I know I'll only ever feel whole while I'm with
him, and that's a scary thought. I don't want to dwell on it right
now, though. I'm too happy, and it's all because of the guy who's

just rode off on his motorcycle; the same guy who was romantic, taking me on a picnic and feeding me strawberries today. Do they really make guys like him, or is he too good to be true?

With a cheek aching smile on my face, I open my door, expecting Chloe to badger me for details. I don't see her anywhere. Maybe she's in the bathroom. "Chloe?" I shout. Nothing but silence greets me. Hmm.

Something white catches my eye on my bed. Picking it up, I see it's a note from Chloe.

Gone out with Evan. I'll be back after dinner for the deets!
Luff ya xxx

Well, that explains where she is. I kick my shoes off, lie on my bed as I put in my headphones, and replay today's events for the hundredth time in the last hour. If this is how Jesse makes me feel after a day, I don't ever want to be without him. I feel alive because of him. He's my savior.

CHAPTER NINE
JESSE

I was having the perfect day with Maisie. She was letting her guard down, allowing me in. She even allowed me to see a side of her I didn't expect to see yet. It was the most beautiful thing I have ever witnessed; Maisie, coming undone on top of me, just from grinding against my clothed body. I've never experienced something so sexy in my life. I know that image will be going into the wank bank for a rainy day.

When she mentioned my dad, the anger I feel when I think about him resurfaced. I know I shouldn't have taken it out on her, and I feel shitty because of it, but that's how I cope with the topic. I close myself off and don't allow any space for more questions. It's the best way. Maisie doesn't need to know about what makes me damaged. She'll go running for the hills if she finds out, I don't want her to know yet that I might not be able to give her the future she deserves, the comfort and safety most relationships have, all because of my tainted past. But I vow to try to be the best boyfriend I can to her. I just hope my past doesn't come crashing down around my happy charade.

It seems that my good friend fate is out to get me, though. I know I'll never be allowed to be happy for long. Fate doesn't allow me to. She likes to come and kick me in the ass as soon as something good comes into my life. It's the way it's always been, and I'm sure it always will be. My mom called me just after my intimate moment with Maisie. I knew as soon as I saw that my mom was calling, that something was wrong. She hardly calls me when I'm out, as I'm usually busy, which means she only calls in an emergency.

When I answered the phone, she sounded so distressed. Since my dad fucked us over, my mom hasn't been the same. She's always jumpy and hardly ever leaves the house except to go to work. I've tried to help, tried to make her into the woman she used to be before my dad got bad, but there's only so much I can do. She refuses to get counseling, which I think would really help her to move on with her life. So many times I've had to go to her in the middle of the night because she's screaming and shaking from her nightmares, and it breaks my heart every single time. She's just a shadow of the woman I once knew. I won't allow her to be like this forever, half a person, just because of my pathetic, piece of shit father.

Apparently, my dad's been phoning the house all morning. My mom hasn't answered, as I've told her not to. I'll deal with him. I have been for the last five years. She doesn't have any idea, and I'm not about to tell her. If I give my dad money, I can get him to leave us alone. It's never for long, but it keeps my mom safe. I work hard to pay for his habit, and I'm ashamed to admit that, but I have to keep my mom safe. It's the least I owe her.

That's where I'm headed to now, to sort out my *dad*. I'll pay him off, and then go and sort my mom out. I have to calm her down and reassure her that we're safe.

Pulling up outside my dad's trailer, disgust washes over me. This place is a dump. His trailer is all rusty, the door hanging on its hinges. He should spend some of the money I give him on tidying this place up, but I know that would be pointless. This place is too far gone to repair. I'm surprised it's still standing.

Opening the screen door, not bothering to knock as he won't answer, I walk into what he calls the living room. Eurgh, it smells like mold in here. My nostrils should be immune to the smell, but it gets me. Every. Fucking. Time.

"Drew?" I shout, calling him by his first name. He doesn't deserve the title father.

"I hope you've come here to bring me my money," he slurs, coming around the corner. He looks a state, worse than when I saw him a month ago. I don't even know how that's possible. He must weigh just over a hundred pounds now. Long, greasy hair frames his withdrawn face, which I'm surprised I can see with the beard he's sporting. Apparently, I looked the spitting image of Drew when I was younger, just with my mother's eyes. Drew's are blue, not brown.

"I came to give you some of *my* money, so you will leave my mom alone. I've told you not to pester her, and in return, I keep your habit fed. Don't call her again, Drew." My voice sounds deadly even to my own ears. That's the effect he has on me.

"I'd leave your mom alone if you brought the money on time. You're a day late." I hardly understand what he's saying because he's slurring so bad. He leans against the wall, arms crossed, trying to focus on me.

"I've brought you the money now, haven't I?" I throw the money down onto the sticky coffee table.

"Good. How is your mother anyway? She still a dirty whore?" he asks, laughing. I clench my fists. I won't hit him. I'm nothing like him.

"You have no right to talk about her. Don't even think about her," I hiss through clenched teeth.

He's still laughing. "She always was a good for nothing slut. The only reason I married her was because of you. I didn't want my first born being a bastard child. I told her to get rid of you. She wouldn't listen, though, the stupid slut." I feel my temper rising with his every word. Why do I still give him money? Oh yeah, because he will go to Mom otherwise. Fuck sake. "I didn't want you. I didn't want to give my life up and have a child with her. She was only good for one thing, and she wasn't even good at that. You and that stupid whore made me who I am today. It's all your fault, which is why you pay for my habit. It's the least you owe me, you worthless piece of shit." He's spitting by the end of that. Wound him up thinking about his past, did it? Why can't he ever take the blame for the mistakes that he's made? My mom loved him with everything she had, though; I've never been able to understand why.

I've had enough of his shit now.

"Shut the fuck up, Drew. You fucked yourself up, nobody else, so start realizing that. I'm done here. This is the last bit of money you're getting from me ever again. Clean yourself up and go get a job like normal people. And don't even think about going to see my mom for money, or it will be the last thing you'll ever do." I'm getting out of here before I do something I probably won't regret, but he isn't worth the jail time.

I'm at the door when something hits the back of my head. A beer can. Typical. I stand still, trying to calm down. "I'll see you soon, Jesse." With that, I leave.

What my mom saw in that, I don't think I will ever know. I just hope I don't end up like him. He always tells me I'm more like him than I think. It's true. I am like him. Where women are considered, it's true. But I will never become an alcoholic, throwing away everything good in my life. All I have to make sure is that women don't come between me and Maisie. That will be the ultimate test. My dad failed, but I'm not going to end up like him if I have anything to do with it.

Driving away on my bike, I'm glad to see the back of the trailer park. I have more important things to do now. I have to make sure Mom is alright, and then I need phone my beautiful lady.

****

The lights are off when I pull up outside my house ten minutes later. Not a good sign.

I run into the house and sprint up the stairs. That's where she usually is when Dad calls.

"Mom?" I ask, stepping into her room. Nobody replies. "Mom, are you in here?" I ask again. Come on. Answer. A sniffle answers in response. My head snaps in the direction of her closet. There it is again. Running over, I pull the doors open, my eyes landing on my mom curled up in a ball, looking a wreck. I bend down and pull her into my lap as I rub her hair. "Hey, it's okay. I've got you now. Nothing is going to happen to you." She doesn't reply, just carries on crying. Fuck! I hate my dad for still affecting her this much. "It's okay. I've got you," I reply over and over again, until she calms down.

It takes half an hour to calm her down fully. This is one of the quicker times. Sometimes it takes hours. I don't ask where she goes when she's in this state. I already know. Bringing it back up will just cause another episode. I made that mistake once before. Never again.

Leaning back, I look at my mom. "Come on. Let's go downstairs. I'll make you a coffee." I stand and pull her up with me.

Downstairs, I make the coffees then sit down opposite her at the table. My usually well kept mom is currently a mess of tangled hair and running make-up. It's painful to see her looking like this. I love my mom more than anyone. There is nothing that I wouldn't do for this woman; the woman who brought me up, trying to give me everything I needed, even if she didn't have the money as Drew would take it all. If she had to work an extra job, then she would just to provide for me. That asshole sure didn't. It was left up to my mom to provide for all three of us. I will be forever in her debt.

"I've got something to tell you, Mom." I know this revelation will make her happy. It's all I've got at the moment, and even though I didn't want to tell her yet, I have no choice. I need to see that beautiful smile back on her face.

"What is it, sweetheart?" she asks, her voice cracking from all the crying.

"I've finally got a girlfriend. She's amazing, Mom. You'll love her," I say, a smile taking over my face just at the thought of Maisie. She's already making me act like a lovesick fool.

"Oh, Jesse, that's wonderful. I'm glad you've finally found someone. I was getting worried that you never would." Her eyes cloud over, probably thinking that it's her fault that I'm the way I am. I need to stop her thought train fast.

"Hey, stop that right now. Stop your thoughts from going down that route. It's no one's fault but mine for the choices I've made in the past. If it's anyone else's fault, it's Drew's. I thought that because it's in my DNA, that I would end up like him. Somewhere in my brain, I still do, but Maisie is amazing, Mom. I think she's the one. I mean, I've only known her for a few weeks, but no girl has ever grabbed my attention for more than a few days, let alone made me feel this way. For her, I want to be a better man. I'm trying, Mom. God, I'm really trying. I just hope I don't end up hurting her. She's been hurt enough as it is." My mom's eyes gloss over, and panic spreads through my body. "Did I say something wrong?" I ask quickly.

She shakes her head. "No, darling, you didn't say anything wrong. I'm just so proud of you right now. I have faith that you won't end up hurting her. You're protective of the people you love. You won't let any harm come to her, even from yourself. You're nothing like your dad, Jesse. I just wish you would start realizing this. You are the kindest man I know, even if you haven't always treated the ladies right. But to your friends and family, you are the most thoughtful and kindest man. I'm proud to call you my son. Every day, you make me proud, and I'm sorry that you have to deal with my silliness." I'm about to reply when she holds her finger up, asking me to hold on a second. So I do. She's obviously thinking about something. She gasps, scaring the ever living shit out of me.

"Fuck, Mom! You scared me to death."

"Language, Jesse. You were with her today, weren't you?" She looks at me expectantly. I can't lie to her. She always knows.

"Yeah," I say with a sigh.

"Oh, Jesse, why didn't you tell me? I would have dealt with this myself," she says, getting flustered.

"Mom, it's okay. You know I'll always come to you if you need me. You're my number one priority," I reply honestly.

She shakes her head in disgust at me. "No, Jesse. I *was* your number one priority. You have someone else to give your attention to now. I won't jeopardize your relationship. You're happiness is far more important to me. Don't be doing that again, okay? If I call you, just tell me that you're with her. I will be fine," she says adamantly. There's no point arguing about it because she won't listen. I just nod my head. I will never stop being there for my mom. I'd never forgive myself if something bad were to happen to her. "So when am I going to get to meet her? Maisie is it?" she asks.

"Yes, her name's Maisie. We've only been together since yesterday, but it feels right, you know?" She nods in understanding. "Maybe next week, though. I have to ask her first."

"Oh, yes, of course. Well, just let me know. I'll cook us something for dinner," she says, a warm smile on her face.

"I will, Mom," I reply, smiling at her.

"Do you want dinner? It's getting late, and I'm sure you're hungry. Let me see what we have that's quick and easy." She gets up from the table, making her way over to the freezer.

"Mom, do you just want to get take-out? It'll save on washing up, and it's easier."

"Yes, okay. Chinese okay?" she asks, pulling out the menus from the cupboard.

"Chinese sounds great. You order. I'm just going to call Maisie. I said I would call her tonight."

"Okay. I'll call you when it's here."

Lying on my bed, I dial Maisie's number, waiting expectantly to hear her voice.

"Hi," she answers. My stress from the last few hours instantly disappears at the sound of her voice.

"Hi. You okay?"

"I am now. You?" she breathes into the phone.

"I am now." Maisie's like my stress release, and she doesn't even know it.

"Was everything okay in the end? I was worried about you." The last thing I want is for her to be worried about me. I bet she's been going crazy, getting herself worked up, wondering what is happening. I need to make it up to her.

"Everything is fine. I just had some family business to sort out. You don't have to worry about me. I'm a big boy, remember." She laughs her magical laugh down the phone, and my stomach does somersaults from the sound.

"I wouldn't know," she says cheekily. It makes me laugh.

"You will one day, baby. You just wait. You won't know what's hit you," I drawl down the phone, earning a gasp. Oh yeah, she's speechless. One nil to me.

"You are so cocky, Jesse. It's unreal. And who's to say I want to see it one day?"

"Touché, my little firecracker. However, I guarantee you will sooner or later. I'm hoping for sooner. I'm not going to lie. After today's little taster, I can't wait for the full package experience." Maisie gasps again, and I just laugh. I love winding her up.

"For that, you're never getting the full package experience," she states matter-of-factly.

"I'm joking. I said I'd wait however long it takes until you're ready, and I meant it, Maisie. I'll wait forever if I have to," I say honestly. And I would. Even if I die before I get a taste of her, I'll die a happy man because I got to spend time with the most amazing woman. And she's all mine.

"Thank you, Jesse. It means a lot," she replies solemnly.

For the next half hour, we talk about everything and anything. We never run out of conversation. It flows easily. We laugh a lot and even have a few serious conversations.

I hear my mom shout that dinner's here, reminding me that I have to ask Maisie. "I told my mom about you. I hope you don't mind."

"Of course not. What did she say?" Just come straight out with it. The worst she can say is no, right?

"She's over the moon, actually. She didn't think I'd ever get a girlfriend." She laughs at that. I knew she would. "She wants to meet you."

"When?"

"Next week. You don't have to if you're not ready. I just thought I'd ask." I hold my breath waiting for her reply.

"I'd love to." I release the breath I had been holding. Thank God she agreed. Mom is going to be so happy. Now, I get to let my two favorite ladies meet each other.

"Great. I'll let Mom know. She said she'll cook something for dinner, so make sure you don't eat after lunch. She makes big portions."

"Ok. I'll let you go then. I'll talk to you tomorrow. Night, Jesse."

"Sweet dreams, Maisie." I disconnect the call and look up at the ceiling. I miss hearing her voice already. I'm falling for her *hard*, but right now, I don't even care because I'm happy, all thanks to the beautiful, little Maisie.

"Jesse? Dinner's getting cold," Mom shouts again. I better go and tell my mom the good news. She's going to be ecstatic.

CHAPTER TEN
MAISIE

I've been in a relationship with Jesse for a week now. It's been the best week of my life. We've been hanging out, going down to the beach, or sometimes he comes back here and we watch a movie. Jesse and Chloe get along, which is a bonus. Chloe never used to really like Matt, just put up with him for my sake. Jesse and Jake were already friends, so I didn't have to worry about that. Jake gave him the big brother talk, which I expected would happen. I laughed in Jake's face when he said he would hunt Jesse down and beat the ever living shit out of him. Jake wouldn't stand a chance against him, but I appreciate his concern for me. I really do.

Today is the day I've been dreading for the last week. I'm meeting Jesse's mum. I know I told him I was fine with it, and I am. However, we've only been together for a week. I didn't meet Matt's mom until we had been dating for three months. This is pretty fast for me, but it means a lot to Jesse. For him, I would do anything.

My clothes are thrown across my bed, and I'm standing next to it, getting frustrated. I don't have a clue what to wear. Nothing I have seems good enough for meeting Jesse's mom. Where's Chloe when I need her? She's good at this sort of thing. She would have an outfit picked out in minutes. Me? I've been staring at my clothes for the past twenty minutes and still haven't come to a decision.

I'm going to have to cancel if I can't put something together in the next ten minutes. Jesse's picking me up in an hour, and I still have to shower. Today is not my day, it seems!

"*Fuck sake!*" I scream out loud.

"For all that is holy, what on earth are you screaming about?" Chloe asks as she comes through the door.

"Thank God you're here. I'm having a disaster," I say irately.

"Why are your clothes all over your bed? You having a clear out, because there may be a few things I want to pinch if you are." At this rate, she can have all of my clothes.

"No, I'm not having a clear out. I'm meeting Jesse's mom today, and I have nothing to wear. I'm going to have to cancel," I say, throwing my arms out to the side in frustration. She just laughs at me, so I crunch my eyes at her, letting her know that I'm not amused.

"Okay. You're not going to cancel. I'll help you. Let me see what you have." She stands next to me, looking down at the options. "Well, you can't wear this or this," she says, throwing some of my old sweaters and jeans on the floor.

"See… I have nothing to wear. What am I going to do, Chloe?" I whine, putting my head in my hands.

"Oh, stop being so dramatic. You have tons of clothes. Plus, if you don't want to wear anything here, you can always borrow something of mine," she replies, lifting her eyebrows at me. Why didn't I think of that? We've always shared clothes. I blame it on the nerves. It's making me lose my mind.

"Thank you. Can I see what you have?"

"Of course."

I spend the next ten minutes looking through her clothes and trying to find something to wear. In the end, we decide on a simple white sundress that has a daisy pattern and my blue Mary Janes. It's perfect.

"You're a life saver, Chloe. What would I do without you?" I ask, giving her a hug. I truly would be lost without her by my side.

"Be half of the person that you are now," she says, laughing.

Laughing too, I say, "Probably. Okay, I've got to jump in the shower. I'll see you in ten." I make my way to the bathroom, get undressed, and jump into the shower.

I'm out and ready within twenty minutes. That's a record, I'm sure. Checking the time, I see that I have thirty minutes until Jesse picks me up. I'd rather just get this over and done with, as my nerves are building up, but they probably aren't ready for me yet. I need something to keep my mind off of it, and I know the perfect thing. Chloe is lying on her bed, texting Evan probably. I'll ask how that's going. "So… How are you and Evan?" Chloe looks up from her cell, a confused look on her face.

"Huh?" she asks, sitting up and putting her cell down on the bed.

"I asked, how are you and Evan?"

"Oh, yeah, we're good," she replies vaguely, shrugging her shoulders. That doesn't sound good.

"Just good? You don't seem too happy to talk about it," I say, trying to dig for information. Hopefully she'll give me some. Chloe is usually quite secretive and likes to keep things to herself, and usually I don't push because she always tells me eventually, but this is different. I don't think she's happy. She's just lying to herself that she is to take her mind off of Jake.

"What do you want me to say, Maisie?" she asks defensively. "Does he make me happy? Yes. Do we have a laugh together? Yes. But do I see him as a long-term boyfriend? No, I don't think I do, and you know why. Your fucking brother won't get out of my Goddamn head. I just want to feel loved and be happy. Evan gives me that, Maisie. Is it so wrong for me to be happy for once?" Tears well up in her eyes until she's crying. Dammit, Jake. I knew this would happen. I knew one of them would get hurt eventually, and it seems that it's Chloe. She puts on a tough image, but she's not. She's not tough at all, and it breaks my heart because I can't do a damn thing about it. I can't tell my brother to pull his head out of his ass and sort his act out. He's nineteen, for crying out loud. And the sad thing? I don't think he will realize what he could have had until it's too late. Chloe won't wait around forever; she's making that clear now, but she's doing it the wrong way, settling for second best when she deserves the best.

Rushing to sit next to her, I pull her into a hug. "No, it's not wrong for you to be happy, Chlo. But you shouldn't settle for the first person that makes you happy. You should settle for someone who treats you as his world, and you treat them back the same. You may feel like that won't happen, but it will. I promise. Look at me and Jesse. I didn't think I'd ever meet someone I could trust again after Matt, but I have, and you will too. So please, don't settle for anything more than the best."

She sniffles, wiping her nose with the back of her hand. "You're right. I think I need to end it with Evan then. I mean, he's a really nice guy, but he's not for me." In other words, he's not my brother.

"I think it's for the best, Chlo." My cell rings, distracting me from what I was going to say. Jesse's calling. "One minute," I say to Chloe, answering the phone. "Hi."

"Hi, sweetheart. I'm downstairs." Just hearing his voice brings a smile to my face.

"I'll be down in a minute. Just talking to Chloe."

"Okay. See you in a minute." Disconnecting the call, I look at a Chloe. Her perfectly made up face now has make-up smeared all down it.

"I take it Jesse's downstairs?" Chloe asks, reaching for the tissues and blowing her nose.

"Yeah, he is. I don't want to leave you when you're like this, though." I want to be there for her like she is for me.

"Don't be silly. I can look after myself. You go have fun with your boyfriend," she says, trying to smile for my sake. I can see right through it, though.

"I won't be back late. Then we can talk about this more if you want?" I say, picking up my denim jack.

"Yeah, okay. You better go, or you're going to be late," she says, pushing me toward the door. I laugh at her eagerness to get rid of me.

"See you later," I say, walking down the hallway.

"Have fun!" she shouts down the hall, closing the door behind her. Now that I haven't got anything to focus on, my nerves are back full force. My body is shaking, and my palms sweating when I open the door downstairs and step out into the breezy air. At least if I do sweat from nerves, the breeze will be able to dry it. Not a very lady like thought, but it's all I have right now.

"Hey, hey, sexy!" Jesse catcalls out loud. Damn him. Now, I'm bright red as well as sweaty.

Jesse is standing in his usual spot, leaning against his bike, but something's different about him... He doesn't have his leather jacket on. He has a red and white flannel shirt that is unbuttoned, showing the white top underneath. Everything else about him is the same, but my heart still beats fast like that first time I saw him.

Snapping out of my Jesse haze, the heat in my cheeks reminds me of what he's just done. I give him the stink eye, take the helmet from his hands, and climb onto his bike, ignoring him the whole time.

"Are you ignoring me, firecracker?" he asks, standing next to me and laughing. I don't find it funny right now. Usually, I probably would, but my nerves are making me tense.

"Yes," I say, still not looking at him.

"I'm sorry if I embarrassed you," he says, touching my arm. My bad mood instantly vanishes, just from his touch. It's like he has magical powers. He probably does. Feeling bad about the way I acted, I take the helmet off so I can see him better.

"No, it's okay. I'm just nervous to meet your mom. I shouldn't have taken it out on you. You were only joking around." I give him a smile to let him know I'm sorry.

"Don't be nervous. I know it's scary meeting the parents, well, in my case, parent, but my mom is excited to meet you. She's not scary. Trust me. She's the most amazing woman, and you will love her. I know you will. If you're not ready for this, though, just tell me. I can explain it to my mom," he says seriously, tucking a loose strand of hair behind my ear. I lean my face into his palm, reveling in his touch.

"No, I want to meet your mom. I'm just scared. I'm sure as soon as I meet her, I will be fine. Come on. Let's go before we're late," I say, moving my head from his palm. I miss his touch straight away.

"As soon as I do this," he says, moving forward and placing a kiss on my lips. Oh God, I've missed his kisses. I just saw him yesterday too. The kiss ends way too soon and, before I know it, he's moving to straddle his bike and wrapping my arms around him. If I could have my way, I'd kiss him forever. His lips are so addictive. At least, I still get to touch him. Feeling his ripped abs through my hands, I sigh in contentment. He is my home. I feel whole again, now that I'm with him.

****

All too soon, we're pulling up outside a two-story house. I'm guessing this is Jesse's home. It's nice looking, not too huge or too small. It's just the right size for the two of them. They obviously take good care of their home, as the garden has been decorated beautifully. Flowers of all colors are spread around the outside of the grass.

"Welcome to my humble abode," Jesse says, pointing me in the direction of his home.

"It's beautiful," I tell him, and I mean it. I can see myself living in a house just like this when I'm older.

"Come on. Mom's probably got dinner ready," he says. He grabs my hand, and we walk toward the front door.

It opens just as we reach it. Standing there is a woman roughly the same height as me, who looks to be in her forties. I'm guessing it's his mother. She has brown hair shaped in a bob, dark brown eyes with flecks of gold, and gentle facial features. I wouldn't be able to tell that this is Jesse's mom if it wasn't for her eyes. They are the spitting image of Jesse's. It calms me instantly, looking into eyes like the ones I love so much.

"You must be Maisie. Aren't you just beautiful?" she says, pulling me into her embrace. I awkwardly hug her back. I'm not used to this sort of affection from strangers. As I pull away, I try to smile my bravest smile, though I'm sure I just look deranged.

"That is me," I say, laughing awkwardly. Why the hell did I just say that? Obviously, I'm Maisie. I'm such an idiot.

"Come on. Let's get you inside. Don't want you standing here all night," she says, obviously ignoring my stupid comment. Great first impression, Maisie.

Jesse's mom shows me to the couch, where I awkwardly sit down on the edge.

"You have a beautiful house, Mrs Cohen," I say, trying to show her that I'm normal.

"Oh, please, call me Anna," she says, waving her hand in the air.

"You have a beautiful house, Anna," I say, testing her name out. I'm sure I will get used to it after a while.

"Thank you. Jesse helps keep it maintained. He's such a good boy." I can see pride beaming in her eyes as she talks about her son. She obviously adores him. It's a lovely thing to witness. Looking over at Jesse, I see the same look in his eyes, directed at his mom. I knew they were close, but this proves just how close they are.

"Yes, he is." I smile at Jesse. My earlier nerves have vanished.

He was right. I already love his mom, and I've only been here five minutes. I don't know what I was worrying about.

"I hope you like spaghetti and meatballs. I know it's not very adventurous, but it's my specialty," Anna says, standing up and walking into the kitchen.

"I love spaghetti and meatballs. Thank you."

Jesse moves to sit next to me, squeezing my leg in comfort. I smile over at him, thankful for thinking about me.

"You were right. I love your mom already," I tell him honestly. A smile lights up his face.

"I'm glad. It sure does make things a lot easier. Could you imagine if you hated each other? I'd be torn." We both laugh at that. The image going through my head is hilarious; me and Anna using Jesse as a human tug of war, fighting for him.

"I just had an image of me and your mom using you as a human tug of war," I say, still laughing. That just makes Jesse laugh harder.

"You come out with the most random things. It's why I love you, though." My laughter dies on my lips. Did he just say that he loves me? He couldn't have. I must have misheard him.

"You l-l-love me?" I stutter out. I think I must be in shock. We've only been together a week. He can't love me yet.

His face pales at my question. He must have not have realized what he said. "Oh shit. I didn't mean for it to come out this way. I was going to wait a little longer. I know we've only been together a week, but yes. I do love you. I've loved you since the moment I first saw you on the sidewalk."

"Oh…" I say, not really knowing what to say back. I don't know if I love him yet. It's too soon.

"You don't have to say it back. Like I said, I was going to wait, but you know now." I can't swallow with the mammoth sized lump which has lodged itself in my throat. *Fuck, fuck, fuckedity, fuck.* What do I say now? Can I just run out of the house, all the way back to the dorms, lock the door, and never leave? I really feel like doing that right now, but running doesn't solve anything. I've learnt that the hard way.

"I'm not ready yet," I whisper, looking anywhere but into his eyes.

"And that's okay. I didn't expect you to say it yet anyway. Let's go see if my mom has finished dinner yet," Jesse says, standing up. He grabs my hand, and we walk into the kitchen.

I'm thankful for the distraction. That conversation was intense. I love you is the last thing I was expecting to hear him say, but he always shocks me because he's always unpredictable. Now things are going to be awkward between us.

"Dinner's nearly ready. Sit down if you would like," Anna says, pointing at the ready made table. I need to keep busy to distract myself. Plus, I can't look at Jesse right now. I'm too shocked.

"Do you need help with anything?" Please say yes.

"You can dish up the spaghetti while I finish off the sauce, if you want." Anna says, smiling at me. Thank you, God.

"Okay." I pick up the saucepan and dish the spaghetti evenly onto the plates.

I can't hide from Jesse forever. Eventually, we are going to be alone and will have to address the situation. I'm just not ready yet. I'll think about that when we're alone later.

JESSE

Why the fuck did I have to open my big mouth and say I love you? I knew she wouldn't be ready to hear that, but I wasn't thinking and just said it. I'm such an asshole.

Since I said it, she's been keeping her distance from me. I'm sure my mom can sense the tension between us, but if she does, she isn't saying anything. I just hope it doesn't ruin us. I can't lose her, not now. I've got a taste of what it feels like to love someone, and I don't want to lose that feeling. I especially don't want to lose Maisie.

After Maisie helped my mom serve up dinner, we sat down at the table, the conversation flowing easily. I knew they would get on, and they have. It makes me happy to see the two most important people in my life getting along, laughing and joking with each other. It's like they've known each other for years. I can tell my mom loves her just as much as I do. She's a very loveable person, which is why I fell in love with her so quickly.

After dinner, Maisie offers to help Mom wash up the dishes. Thankfully, Mom shoos her away, saying that we have a dish washer, so it won't take her long. I see Maisie's face fall, and it makes my heart break. She clearly doesn't want to be alone with me. I need to sort this out, and fast. The last thing I wanted to do was scare her, but I have. I'm so pissed with myself.

I have a few minutes to sort it out with her before my mom comes back in. Plopping down on the sofa next to her, I turn her head to face me, giving her no choice but to look at me. "I'm sorry. I shouldn't have said it, but I can't take it back now. Please, don't be upset with me. It's breaking my heart here, Maisie. Please forgive me?" I say, my eyes pleading with her to forgive me. She doesn't say anything, just carries on staring and occasionally swallowing. I've really fucked up, haven't I? "Please?" I try again.

She blinks at me a few times. It's fucking adorable. I don't want to not be able to look into her eyes again or witness her quirky behaviour.

It feels like minutes pass, when it's probably only seconds, before she finally speaks. "Okay," she whispers. Did she say okay?

"Sorry?" I ask, hoping she will repeat it louder this time. I want to be sure that my ears aren't playing tricks on me.

"Okay. I forgive you," she says louder this time. I think my heart just stopped beating. Thank fuck, I'm not going to lose her. I want to shout from the rooftops right now. Instead, I grab her face, kissing it all over. "Thank you." Kiss. "Thank you." Kiss. "Thank you." Kiss. I repeat this over and over again. This makes her laugh. God, I've missed her laugh. It's been an hour since I've been able to hear it because of my actions. I never want to go that long without hearing that sound again.

Coughing to my right stops me mid kiss. My mom is standing in the doorway of the kitchen with a shit eating grin on her face. She's never seen this side of me before, so it must come as a shock; a good shock, though, it seems.

"Don't mind me. I'll go back into the kitchen if I'm interrupting," she says, trying not to laugh.

"It's okay. Everything is sorted now," I say, being vague. I'm sure my mom understands what I mean, but I don't want Maisie to think she was too obvious with her being distant from me.

"Maisie, would you like to see some baby pictures of Jesse? He was the most adorable baby." Oh shit. I was hoping she wouldn't get them out. She has a few of me nude in the photo albums. Now, Maisie's going to see my cock, albeit my baby cock, though she should see what it looks like now before seeing what it used to look like. The photos won't give her a good impression.

"Do we…"

"I'd love to," Maisie says, interrupting me. Fuck. Do I have to stay here and watch her witness this?

"Great! Let me just go and get them." My mom goes up the stairs to retrieve them from her bedroom.

"This is going to be embarrassing," I mumble into my hands. A hand touches my back, startling me.

"It can't be that bad, can it?" Maisie asks quietly into my ear. God, she's stealthy. I didn't know she was right next to my ear. I usually hear everything, meaning nobody can creep up on me. I'm going to have to be extra careful with Maisie. She seems a pro at it.

"Oh, you just wait," I say vaguely.

Mom saves me from having to explain. Maisie's going to see them anyway, and then she will understand why I'm acting like I am. I can't stay here to watch. I have to get out of here.

Standing up, I stretch, showing off my abs on purpose. This will remind Maisie how much of a man I am now. Looking at Maisie, who is trying not to stare at my abs, I lean down and wink at her. Her cheeks flame red instantly. Oh yeah, she likes what she sees alright.

Leaning close to her ear, I whisper so only she can hear, "If you're lucky, I might let you have a touch later." I hear her swallow in response. She's affected alright. Standing up straight, I wink at her again, a smirk playing on my lips. "I'm going outside. I have a call to make." I don't wait for a reply from them. Stepping out the front door, I leave a flustered Maisie with my mom. I'm such a jerk, but I love it, and so does she.

I have about ten minutes to spare. Might as well give Brandon a call. We haven't seen each other much recently, since I've been with Maisie. I feel bad as we usually see each other every day. We're usually inseparable, but since Maisie came along, I've sort of ditched him. I'm a shitty friend.

Pulling out my cell, I dial his number and wait for him to pick up.

"To what do I owe this pleasure?" Brandon answers, sarcasm dripping from his voice. I deserve it.

"Just calling to see how my best bud is?"

"Oh, so you remember who I am now, huh?" I deserve that one too.

"I'm sorry I haven't really spent time with you for a few days, but I have other commitments as well now," I reply.

"A few days? I haven't seen or heard from you for a week. The only time I see you is at practice, and that's because you have to be there." If he's trying to make me feel shittier than I already feel, it's working.

"I'm sorry, Brandon, I really am. Do you want to do something tonight? I could come round for a few beers?" I say hopefully.

"Aren't you going to be too busy with your new piece of ass?" Brandon says, venom dripping from his voice. He's just over stepped the mark.

Starting to see red, I say in my most deadly voice, "Don't you dare talk about Maisie like that. She's not just some piece of ass. She's my girlfriend. I'll beat the shit out of you if you talk trash like that about her again, whether you're my friend or not. Got it?"

"Whoa, chill, will you? You're really serious about her, aren't you?" he asks surprised.

"Yes, I am. She's the one, Brandon. I've never felt this way before." I sound like a woman. I don't care, though. It's the truth. I'll tell the whole world if I have to.

"Wow. I never thought you'd settle down. No offence," he says. No offence taken. I never thought I'd settle down either. "Well, I'm happy for you then, bro. At least I know you're not just ditching me just to get laid." We both laugh at that.

"So, how about those beers tonight?" I ask again.

"Yeah, that's cool. Mine at say nine?"

"I'll be there. Get them in the fridge, so they're nice and cold for me." There's nothing worse than a warm beer.

"Got it, boss. Until later," Brandon says, ending the call.

They must be done by now, I think as I put my cell phone away. I'll give it a few more minutes, just to be safe.

Making my way back into the house five minutes later, I hear laughing. Maybe they aren't done yet. Fuck. I'll just have to brave it out then. "What are you two laughing about?" I ask, entering the living room. I don't see any photo albums out, which is a good sign.

"Oh, your mom was just telling me some funny stories about when you were younger," Maisie says, laughing all over again. That's probably worse than the photos. Damn it, Mom!

"Oh yeah? What story did she tell you?" I ask, hoping that it's nothing too embarrassing. Knowing my mom, it's the most embarrassing story she has.

"I was telling Maisie about that time when you went up to some lady in the supermarket and put your head up her skirt because you thought it was me," My mom says, a cheeky smile on her face.

Yeah, that was the story I was dreading. I was four years old, okay! It's not a crime at that age. Plus, she really looked like my mom. Any child would get confused and do the same. Well, maybe not stuck their head up her skirt.

"To my defense, that woman really looked like you. Plus, I was four, Mom. It was easy to get confused," I say, defending my innocent young self.

"Aw, don't worry, sweetie. That was the cutest thing you've ever done. Though, I never really understood why you always wanted to put your head up my skirt? You started liking the ladies young," My mom says as her and Maisie both laugh.

"Maybe I just wanted to go back to a safe place, however disgusting that is," I reply, shuddering at the thought of going back up my mom's vagina. I think I'm going to be sick.

"Well, you could have tried, but you wouldn't have fit."

"Eurgh, Mom, please. Too much information," I say, blocking my ears. Now, I'm even acting four years old. I need to leave ASAP.

Maisie has a glow on her face that I haven't seen before. She's looking at my mom with pure adoration in her eyes. I knew they would get along well, and it makes me so happy that I was right.

I hate that I'm about to take Maisie home, when she's obviously enjoying herself, but it's getting late, and I need to leave before Mom starts telling even more embarrassing stories. It's bound to happen. "I hate to break story telling time up, but it's getting late. Are you ready to go home, Maisie?"

"Yeah, I guess I should get back. I need to check on Chloe and get some assignments done." Standing up, she walks over to my mom, who is now also standing. "Thank you for dinner. It was lovely, and it was lovely meeting you. I've had a really nice time," she says, giving my mom a hug.

"Anytime, sweetie. Come by whenever you want, even if Jesse isn't here. I would love to see you," my mom replies, letting go of Maisie.

I'm just standing off to the side, my hands in my pockets.

"I would love to. I'm sure you'll see me sometime next week. You can't keep me away if you make me meatballs again," Maisie says laughing. Yeah, my mom makes the best meatballs around. They're bound to bring Maisie back. They always have Brandon.

"You can count on it," My mom replies, walking us to the front door.

"Bye, Mom. I'll be back later. I'm going to see Brandon for a bit after I've dropped Maisie off, so don't wait up." Giving Maisie my helmet, I straddle my bike, waiting to feel her warm hands wrapped around my body. It's a feeling I always look forward to when she climbs on my bike. It always makes me imagine millions of different places that she could put her hands on my body. I can't wait for the day that she finally does. It's all I dream about these days. I have to go slow with her, though. She's told me that she's not ready yet, and I'm not going to push her, but I can still fantasize.

We pull out of my drive, and I head toward my usual destination these days; the dorms.

****

"I forgot to tell you earlier that you look beautiful," I say, brushing a loose strand of hair back behind her ear from where the helmet messed it up.

"Thank you," she whispers. "You don't look too bad yourself." Damn right, I don't. I'm a good looking guy, and I know it, but it's nice to hear it from her.

"I know," I joke, getting a punch in the arm at my cockiness. "I'm joking, but thank you for today. My mom really likes you." I brush my thumb over her cheek, feeling her silky smooth skin beneath by finger.

"I really like your mom, too. I'd best let you go then. Brandon's probably waiting." She steps away from my touch, making me instantly miss her warmth.

Pulling her back into my hold, I kiss her with everything that I am. I'm trying to express how much I love her with this kiss, instead of saying the three dreaded words. They've done enough damage today already.

Deepening the kiss, I bend Maisie back, one hand in her hair and the other holding the bottom of her back. She lets out a small moan, which goes straight through my body and straight to my dick, making him stand up to attention. Every. Single. Time. She has a huge effect on my body.

Tugging her hair, I am welcomed with more moans from her.

Damn my traitorous body. I'm going to have to stop before I explode right here in my pants. Begrudgingly breaking the kiss, I rearrange myself, as right now, he's in so much pain.

"Goodnight, my beautiful Maisie." I touch her lips with my thumb for one last touch, and then pull away.

"Goodnight, Jesse." She turns, heading toward the dorms. She really looks perfect from behind. I'm so lucky to call her mine. I just hope she returns my love eventually.

MAISIE

"Oh, Jesse?" I shout, turning to look at him. I have to tell him before he leaves. He looks at me expectantly, waiting to hear what I have to say. He won't be expecting this though. "I love you too, by the way." With that, I walk through the entrance and up to my room.

I was thinking while I was looking at baby photos of Jesse, and I realized that I do love him. I hate not hearing from him for hours. I hate not being able to see him every day. I hate it as soon as he goes home. I hate it when we aren't touching. I hate thinking about never being able to kiss him again. There are many more things that I hate too. It was then that I realized that I didn't want to be without him. Also, when I was looking at the baby photos, I could just picture a baby who looks just like Jesse running around, except the child was mine and Jesse's. To say that scared me is an understatement, but it also made me realize, again, that I love him if I can picture him in my future. I had to let him know before he went away thinking that it was just one sided. Because it's not. I feel exactly the same as he does.

Feeling lighter now that I've got that confession off of my chest, I walk toward my door, my key at the ready. I'm about to put the key in the hole, when I hear raised voices on the other side of the door. Putting my head to the door, eavesdropping, I hear a high pitched voice shouting and a male voice also raised. It sounds like Jake. Why would he be having an argument with Chloe now?

I try to listen to what is being said. Maybe I can get some insight into what is going on. I know I shouldn't, but I need to know what's happening.

"You can't tell me what to do anymore, Jake! I needed you months ago, but you chucked me away like yesterday's trash. So why would you want me now? Actually, save it. I don't want to hear your lies. Just get out!" Chloe shouts. What does she mean, she needed him months ago? Why would she have needed him?

"Chlo, please listen to me," Jake pleads, his voice softening.

"GET OUT!" Chloe screams at him. I think it's time for me to go in before he gets killed.

Opening the door, I see Chloe standing by the bathroom and Jake pacing the floor. The tension is so thick in here. I could cut it with a knife. It always seems to be this way around them lately.

"Jake, I think you best leave," I advise, raising my eyebrows in warning that he better not fight with me on this one.

"Not until Chloe listens to me," he refuses, crossing his arms over his chest. He's such a stubborn fool.

"GET OUT!" Chloe screams, making my ears ring. Jesus Christ, that girl has a healthy set of lungs on her. In all of our years of friendship, I have never heard her scream like that, not even to her family, and they annoy the hell out of her.

"Fine. Fuck this shit. I'm out of here. You know where I am if you want to listen to what I have to say, Chloe," Jake says, slamming the door behind him.

Chloe breaks down as soon as he leaves, crumbling to the floor with big fat ugly tears rolling down her cheeks. What the hell has he done to her?

Rushing over to her, I assume the same position as earlier. It's like déjà vu. "Do you want to tell me what that was all about?" I ask.

"It was nothing." She sniffles, wiping her face with her sleeve. Is she kidding me?

"It didn't look like nothing, Chloe. When are you going to tell me what's really going on between you two?" I ask, getting frustrated. She always dodges the questions or refuses point blank to answer me. I'm fed up with the secrets now. We're supposed to be best friends, but how can we be when she doesn't confide in me?

"Just drop it, Maisie," she spits out, giving me a filthy look.

"Do you know what? I'm done, Chloe. How the hell do you expect me to be there for you if you won't fucking tell me what's wrong? Until you feel ready to tell me, keep your problems out of my sight. I don't want to see or hear it," I say, shutting the bathroom door behind me.

I know I said I would be patient with her, but I can only put up with so much before I run out of patience, and I've just ran out. I'm not getting involved anymore. She can deal with this by herself.

CHAPTER ELEVEN
CHLOE

Had I just answered when Jake called earlier, I wouldn't have had to deal with him tonight.

They really need to invest in peepholes for the doors in the dorm rooms. I thought it might have been Maisie knocking, having forgotten her key. It wasn't. When I opened the door, I was faced with a red faced Jake. He didn't wait for me to invite him in, which I wouldn't have done, as I wasn't in the mood for his shit today. He just barged straight past me and sat on my bed.

He'd found out about me and Evan. He was fuming, telling me to end it with him. I was going to end it with Evan, but now, I think I might keep seeing him just to piss Jake off. I like Evan. I really do. I even have feelings for him. The problem? He just isn't the jerk that has caused me problems since I was younger.

Every time I try to move on, Jake comes back and ruins my progress. It's like he wants to see me miserable.

Last year, I really thought I had a chance, that he had finally realized that he loved me back, and that we would become a couple. Who was I fooling? He isn't a one woman kind of man. He gets bored after a few weeks.

The thing is that I have loved Jake Peterson ever since I can remember. He's it for me, and no man has ever been able to compare to him. I mean, I've hooked up with guys, but they were never boyfriends. I've never wanted anyone else if I couldn't have him, but you get tired of waiting for someone who doesn't want you back. So this time, I've tried to move on. Evan may be his best friend, but he makes me happy. He takes my mind off of Jake. I know it's not fair to Evan, but I am so fed up with feeling like I'm only good enough for one thing. With Evan, it's different. We haven't had sex yet, so I know it's not about getting his kicks. He actually likes me for me. This is the kind of guy I need; someone who will make me feel treasured and loved, not make me feel like a sex object like Jake always has. To him, I've only ever been good enough for that. He made that perfectly clear a few months ago.

Since then, we just haven't been the same. I snap at him constantly. It's my coping mechanism for what happened. Does it make me feel better, though? No, it doesn't. It makes me feel worse. Sometimes, I think it would be easier if we never saw each other again. It's impossible when your best friend is related to the man you love, though.

Evan was my fresh start. I was really trying to project my feelings from Jake onto Evan, but like always, Jake won't let me. He always worms his way back in, controlling my life by stopping me from forgetting about him.

I've had enough of it now. I'm letting him go once and for all. It's not doing me any good hanging onto false hope that one day he might want me the way I've always wanted him. Waiting for Jake to realize that is like waiting for rain to fall in the middle of a drought. It will just lead to disappointment.

So I let him know that, which lead to him spouting off lies about how he loves me and not to give up on him just yet. I just laughed in his face. How long does he expect me to wait for him exactly? Until I'm dead? I don't think so. I've heard this from him so many times before. I could probably recite what he is going to say before he even knows he's going to say it. He's predictable, and I'm fed up with it. I'm not the naive little girl that I used to be anymore. I am a woman who deserves better than what she's been getting. I need a man who can give me the whole of him, not just bits and pieces when he feels like it.

I should have moved on months ago when Jake proved to me that he was no good. He left me all by myself when I had no one to turn to. He should have stood by my side, been a man about it. Instead, he ordered me around, and then didn't speak to me for months. He left me to pick up the pieces all by myself. I'm scarred because of him. I vowed that night never to forgive him. The first time I saw him again was at his house the night Matt cheated on Chloe. I thought I had finally moved on. One look was all it took for me to be reminded that I was far from over him, though. I didn't see him again until his party the other week. It was then that I finally forgave him.

I was such a stupid bitch. I realize that now. He only cares about himself. He doesn't care about me. He never has, especially not five months ago.

After his performance tonight, I swear to God, I will never forgive him for the emotional scars he has left me with.

CHAPTER TWELVE
JESSE

Maisie told me that she loves me last night.

Maisie. Loves. Me!

I was so worried when I told her that I loved her, thinking I had ruined everything. Her face was so scared at the time. I never expected her to react like that.

So, to hear her say those three little words that mean so much back to me made my heart soar. She didn't even give me time to reply. She just carried on walking. It's a good thing too because I was speechless. I've never been speechless before in my life. That is just another skill that Maisie has that nobody else does.

I woke up this morning with a banging headache. I'd had way too many beers at Brandon's. I was celebrating, though. I celebrated knowing that she feels the same way I do. I never told Brandon this, of course. I already sound like a pussy when it comes to Maisie, and I don't need to sound like more of one.

This morning, I'm paying for it though. Big time. Plus, the sun is out, so that doesn't help.

I soon forget about my killer headache as I remember Maisie saying she loves me. She's like a painkiller. Just thinking of her can help erase any pain.

My stomach rumbles painfully, reminding me that I haven't eaten anything since dinner last night.

Going downstairs, I see my mom sitting at the table reading a book. She's always reading.

"Hey, Mom. What'cha reading?"

"Jesse, you scared me half to death," she says, hand on her heart.

"You must have been really engrossed in your book then. I wasn't even quiet coming down the stairs," I reply, laughing at her face, which is still in shock.

"I was engrossed. I'm reading a new book called 'Silver Lining' by EJ Shortall. She's a new author, and so far I'm really enjoying her novel. Well, I was until you distracted me," Mom says, giving me her 'I'm not impressed' look.

Laughing, I move toward the pantry to get some cereal. "Don't mind me. I'm just getting something to eat, and then I will be out of your hair." I give her a salute, proceeding to pour my cereal.

My cell phone is ringing when I walk into my room. Putting my cereal down on my desk, I see its Maisie calling. "Hey, firecracker," I answer, smiling.

"Hey yourself," she replies.

"What's up?"

"Can I see you today, please? I need to get out," Maisie pleads. I thought she was spending the day with Chloe?

"Of course you can, but what happened to spending the day with Chloe?" I ask confused.

"Oh, I'll tell you about it when I see you. It's a long story. Right now, I just can't talk to her, and being in my dorm all day means I have to look at her miserable face," she says, getting agitated.

"I'll be over in about an hour." That will give me time to eat, shower, and get dressed.

"That's perfect. Thank you, Jesse. I'll see you then. I love you." That knocks the wind out of me. I don't think I will ever get tired of listening to her saying that.

With the biggest smile ever to grace my face, I reply, "I love you too, firecracker. See you in an hour." Hanging up the phone, I jump, fist pumping the air. I don't care if people looking into my window think I'm a weirdo. My girl just willingly told me she loves me. *Again.*

Turning my iPod speakers on, 'Happy' by Pharrell Williams starts playing. It's the perfect song for the mood I'm in right now.

Practically skipping into the bathroom, I quickly jump into the shower and wash away the remnants of beer stuck to my skin, still singing loudly. The neighbors are going to wonder what's going on with the racket I'm making. I'm not fazed. Nothing can bring me down from this high that I'm on.

"Mom, I'm off to see Maisie," I shout into the kitchen forty-five minutes later.

"Okay, sweetie. Have a lovely time." I rush out of the house and jump on my bike, then head off to pick up the woman that I love. That's right, I said it. I love her!

****

Maisie's already waiting downstairs for me when I pull up next to the sidewalk. Staying on my Ducati, I pull her into my embrace, inhaling her strawberry scent. I'm home.

"You okay?" I ask gently in her ear.

"I am now," she whispers back, her breath against my skin causing goose bumps to surface. I shiver from the action.

"Want to go for a coffee? Then you can explain what's happened." Unwrapping myself from her body, I pass her the helmet.

"Do I have to wear this every time?" she asks with a disgusted look as she lifts the helmet in the air.

"Yes, you do. If anything were to happen to you because you weren't wearing that, I would never forgive myself. So, for my peace of mind, please don't fight me on this, and just wear it," I say exasperated. My life wouldn't be worth living if Maisie wasn't in it. I shudder just thinking about it.

"Okay, Mr safety. Maybe you should invest in another helmet then. I don't want anything to happen to you, either. That way, both of our consciences are clear," she says as she puts the helmet on, then climbs on behind me.

As soon as she touches me, I feel a shock go straight through my body. I'm just so in tune to her touch, the smallest contact sends tingles through my body.

"Hold tight, baby," I say as an excuse to have her closer to me.

Starting the throttle, I ride down the road, taking extra care of the careful package holding onto me.

****

"So what happened last night then?" I ask, setting our lattes down on the table, and then shift into the booth opposite Maisie.

She fiddles with the wrapper on her cup for a few seconds before answering me.

"Jake and Chloe have always had a thing for each other, ever since I can remember." That's news to me. She doesn't seem like his type. He always goes for brunettes or red heads, hardly ever a blonde. Though, I could feel the tension between the two at his party. Interesting. "As you know, Jake hasn't had a girlfriend before, which means he's never given Chloe a chance." I nod my understanding. "They've always gotten along throughout our childhood, been friends and didn't let the feelings become a problem, until about a month ago. Chloe hadn't spoken to Jake for nearly four months. Now, every time they are near each other, they argue, giving smart comments to each other. I mean, they used to joke around when we were younger, but not to this extreme. Chloe started dating Evan to try to move on from Jake. I told her to tell Jake, so he wouldn't find out from somebody else, but she didn't listen. Then yesterday, before you picked me up, she cracked. I talked to her, and she decided to end things with Evan. Then last night, when you dropped me off, I heard raised voices coming from my room. Jake and Chloe were arguing. I know I shouldn't have, but I needed to know what was up between the two of them, so I eavesdropped." I raise my eyebrows, feigning disgust. "Don't look at me like that. It was important!" Maisie says, pouting. I so want to kiss those lips right now, but it's not the right time.

"I'm joking with you. I would have done the same. So, what were they arguing about?"

"Chloe started going on about how Jake didn't want her months ago, so why would he want her now? Then she started screaming for him to get out. That's when I barged in, asking Jake to leave. He did after a while. When he left, Chloe broke down like I've never seen her do before. I'd had enough of them arguing at that point, and never being told what's going on between them, so I told Chloe to just tell me. She told me to leave it, so I said that I'm done. How does she expect me to be there for her, if she won't let me, Jesse? I don't want to have to choose between my brother and my best friend. At this rate, I'm going to have to. We haven't spoken since last night. We're both ignoring each other, which isn't hard, seeing as Chloe won't get out of her bed. It's one o'clock in the afternoon, and she won't leave the confines of her comforter. Something has happened between them. I just don't know what." By the time she's finished explaining what happened, she's furious all over again.

I don't know what to say, really. I'm as clueless as she is, except I didn't even know that they liked each other. I mean, I saw Jake constantly looking at Chloe and Evan the other week at his party, but he didn't make it so obvious that he was jealous. From what Maisie has just told me, though, he obviously was.

"Maybe I can talk to Jake? We may not seem that close, but he does actually tell me quite a bit," I say, trying to be helpful.

Sighing, Maisie rubs her hand down her face. She looks exhausted now that I'm paying close attention. "It can't hurt to give it a try. I just hate seeing Chloe like this. She's usually so hard headed. She doesn't give a shit about anything. I'm not used to seeing this side of her, so something bad must have happened."

"Well, I can only try, right? And if he won't spill, then I'll beat it out of him. How does that sound?" I ask, trying to lighten the atmosphere. It works. She laughs so hard her eyes water.

"He wouldn't have a chance at fighting back." That is very true. I don't say that though. I just laugh. I don't want to blow my own trumpet. "It does sound very appealing right now. He's obviously done something to hurt my best friend. Can I think about it and let you know?" Maisie asks seriously.

"Maisie, I was joking, baby. I'm not going to beat your brother up. I'm a nice guy," I say, laughing at her seriousness. Bless her. She's really protective of her friend, so much so that she would have her brother beaten up.

"I'll find someone else to do it then. That boy really does need some sense knocked into him." She crosses her arms over her chest, letting out a huff.

"Come on. Let's go to my house and watch a movie before you try and find a hit man." I'm not joking anymore. The way she's acting, it could be possible. Remind me never to upset her.

MAISIE

Heading toward the doors of Cafe Blanc, Jake walks in with Evan. I'm surprised he's still hanging out with him after what he found out. Well, I'm guessing he found out after what happened last night.

Maybe I can shed some light on what is going on.

Standing in front of him, so that he can't move unless he walks around me, I cross my arms, letting the anger that I'm feeling shine through. He needs to know that I mean business. Jake knows I don't let anybody fuck with my best friend, and he is no exception. In fact, he will feel my wrath more because he's my brother. I don't expect this kind of shit from him.

"You alright, Maisie? You look a little pissed off." Yeah, I wonder why, dick weed!

"Do you really have to ask me why I'm pissed off?" I ask disgusted.

"Not here, Maisie," Jake hisses.

"Yes, right here, you piece of shit. Nobody messes with my best friend," I answer back, standing my ground.

"I'm going to get our drinks," Evan says, walking off, not waiting for a reply. Jake and I are in the middle of a staring contest right now. I'm not going to back down, so he better start explaining.

"Fine. Let's go outside so that the whole room doesn't listen." Turning around, Jake heads outside with me following closely on his heels.

"Maybe you should ask Chloe," Jake says when we are safely away from prying ears.

"I have, but she never tells me anything when it comes to you. I'm sick of this, Jake. I refuse to choose between the pair of you if it comes to it." My heart sinks at the thought of it. I wouldn't know who to choose. It should be easy. You're supposed to always choose your family, but Chloe is family to me. She's the sister I never had.

"It won't come to that, Mais. I promise." He looks regretful. Good, he should. This is just as hard for me as it is for them, just in a different way.

"How can you promise me that, Jake? You can't. You never know what will happen in the future." How do I make him see what it's like for me? He doesn't understand. He's a guy. They don't have problems like this. They just have a fight to get the anger out of their systems. I wish it was that simple for us girls.

"You're right. I can't. I'm sorry, Maisie," he says, looking apologetic. He should have thought about that months ago before whatever happened.

"Are you going to tell me what happened?"

"Some of it is up to Chloe to tell you. What I can say is that we started sleeping together about seven months ago." He shrugs his shoulders like it's no big deal. It is a huge deal.

"*What?* Why didn't Chloe tell me this?" I feel like there's a lot she's been keeping from me. This is vital information, and she didn't tell me.

"Because I asked her not to. I didn't want anybody knowing, Maisie."

"Why not? You usually like telling everybody your business. Don't answer that, actually. So what happened then?"

"I stopped sleeping with her five months ago," he says, casting his eyes to the floor. Hmm…

"And why did you do that? Get bored, did you? Though, I have to say, two months is a long time for you to keep the same sexual partner. I thought you only went with the same person once. I'm surprised," I say, disdain dripping from my voice.

"That's enough, Maisie. Now isn't the time for this. Come on. Let's go to my house." I'd forgotten that Jesse was listening. He holds my hand, trying to pull me away. He succeeds, of course.

"This isn't over, Jake Peterson," I warn, staring at my brother one last time. "You can stop dragging me now, Jesse."

"I will when we are on my bike and on the way to my home," he says, leaving no room to argue.

Deep down, I'm glad that Jesse pulled me away. I would have regretted not confronting Jake in private. I'll thank him later, but right now, I'm too pissed.

"Get your pretty little behind on that seat," Jesse commands, patting the seat.

"Yes, sir," I reply, obeying.

"Good girl." I laugh at his sarcastic praise.

The whole way to Jesse's house, my mind keeps wondering what happened after they stopped sleeping together. I know I'm going to have to talk to Chloe about this. I'm just not looking forward to it.

****

As we step into Jesse's house, the comforting smell that I smelt yesterday hits my nose. It smells like cinnamon, maybe from a candle or scent sticks. I'm not sure. All I know is that I feel at home.

Jesse's mom is sitting on the sofa, a book in hand. She looks relaxed. I wish I could say the same for me. I'm all knotted up. If I had the money, I would be paying for a massage right now.

"Oh, hello, Maisie Love," Jesse's mom says, putting her book down to make her way over to me. "You look beautiful, dear. Please excuse my relaxed state of PJs. It's Sunday, which means it's PJ day for me," she says, pulling me in for a hug.

I don't usually like hugs from people I don't really know, but Anna has made me feel so welcome. I love her already.

"Nice to see you too, Mom," Jesse speaks up from next to me.

"Oh, Jesse, you know I love seeing you. Stop being so silly," Anna says, swatting his shoulder lovingly.

"I'm going to get a drink. Do you want one, Firecracker?" he asks, looking at me expectantly.

"Water's fine, thanks." Turning back toward Anna, I say, "I don't mind. I wish I had brought my PJs. Then I could have relaxed with you." She laughs at that. "Are you reading anything good? I finished my book the other night, so need a new one. Do you recommend any?" I love reading just before I go to bed. I've lost count of how many book boyfriends I have; there are just too many. I especially love my cowboys, but a good CEO is a close second.

"It's a debut novel that just came out called 'Silver Lining' by a new author named EJ Shortall. I'm loving it so far. I only started it last night and am already over half way through. I truly do recommend it if you love a good CEO story. I wouldn't mind one night with a CEO, especially one like the ones I read about." Anna winks at me, making me laugh. Who would have thought she had a dirty streak?

"Oh, mom, please. Too much information," Jesse says, choosing the wrong time to come into the living room. He looks quite pale from what he just heard his mom saying.

"Oh, Jesse, stop being such a prude. Just because I haven't had sex in long time, doesn't mean I still don't know how to get down and dirty. I'm just saying, I could probably show these CEOs a thing or two." She puts her hands on her hips, acting all serious. I can't help but burst into laughter.

If Jesse looked pale before, he looks ghost white now.

"I think I'm going to be sick. Excuse me, please, while I go and throw my guts up into the toilet." He shudders before leaving the room. I think it's for the best. No child wants to hear their parents talking about having sex. I'm no exception. However, this is Jesse's mom, not mine, so it's comical too me.

"Poor boy. Anyway, as I was saying, yes, I think you will enjoy it. You can borrow it after me if you would like. I'll probably be finished by tonight. I can't seem to put it down." With that, she sits back down, the book in her lap.

"That would be great. Thank you. Well, I'll leave you to fantasize. Happy reading."

Walking into what I'm guessing is Jesse's room, I take it all in. I've not been in here yet. When I came over yesterday, we stayed downstairs.

He has cream colored walls, with shelves holding trophies; football trophies from what I can tell.

A navy blue comforter adorns his double bed, which is in the middle of the back wall. There is also a dark wood wardrobe and a desk with a laptop sitting on top. I thought his room would have been darker, going by the clothes he usually wears.

"Do you like my room?" Jesse asks from behind me. I jump. I was so engrossed in taking everything in that I didn't realize he wasn't in here.

"Jesus Christ, Jesse. Will you stop creeping up on me? Remember what happened last time you did that? I don't want to have to repeat it," I tell him seriously. He just laughs at me. "Don't test me, Jesse. I will do it again," I warn.

"Sweetie, give it your best shot." He crouches down so that he's eye level with me, daring me to do it again. Fine then. If he wants me to so badly...

I pull my arm back and swing it forward, aiming for his nose. He captures my hand before I ever have a chance to make contact. Fuck. His reflexes are fast.

"It's a good thing I'm fast. Remind me never to dare you again. You're in trouble now, though, for trying to ruin my pretty face," he says chuckling.

Next thing I know, I'm lying down on my back in the middle of his bed. Wow, that was fast. Jesse pins me down beneath him, and then starts tickling me. No. Anything but this. I'm so ticklish. *"Jesse! Stop!"* I scream, squirming and trying to get him off of me. It's no use. He's like a huge brick above me.

"Jesse, please. I'm sorry!" I'm laughing so hard now that my eyes are watering, probably ruining the small amount of make-up that I have on.

"This is your punishment. Will you do it again?" he asks, staring into my eyes. God, he's so beautiful, especially with the carefree look he has on his face at the moment.

"No, I won't." I'll say anything right now to get him to stop. As soon as he does, he's getting it.

"Can I trust you?" Jesse asks, raising his eyebrows. He's in trouble as soon as I'm loose.

"Yes, Jesse," I answer in my most trustworthy voice.

As soon as he lets go of me, I start tickling him. He doesn't even react. Oh no. I've got a boyfriend who isn't ticklish. What am I going to do now when he decides to do it to me?

Trying another tactic, I go for his pressure point next to his collar bone. I don't even get near it before Jesse starts his torture again. *"Jesse, stop! I'm sorry. I really am."* I'm going to pee myself if he doesn't stop. *"Stop! I'm going to pee myself. Get off of me!"* I use all of my strength trying to push him off, but he doesn't budge. Dammit. I'm going to pee myself in the next ten seconds if he doesn't stop. *"Seriously, get off of me."* I'm still laughing, so he's not going to take me seriously. I wish I wasn't ticklish.

"If I stop, you'll just attack again," he says laughing.

"I won't. I have to pee," I beg. "Please, let me go."

"Okay." He gives up, lying down on top of me.

What did I need to do again? I can feel the hardness of his body pressed against mine, robbing me of all thoughts except dirty ones.

I'm panting loudly beneath him, partly from laughing so much, but also from the contact we have right now. Staring into his eyes, I see he's staring at my lips. I unconsciously bite my lower lip. This makes him groan.

"You have no idea what you biting your lip does to me, do you?" Jesse asks, growling. I have a pretty good idea, but I'm going to act clueless.

"No. What does it do, Jesse?" I ask innocently.

"This," he growls, smashing his lips against mine roughly. I'm too turned on right now to care about the pain.

His tongue seeks entry, so I let him in.

"Mmm," I moan into his mouth.

Tangling my hands into his hair, I deepen the kiss. I love the feel of it running through my fingers.

"Jesus, Maisie. I'll never get enough of you," he says into my mouth, still kissing me. He's such a talented kisser.

"I'm all yours," I reply boldly.

I need more of him. As if hearing my thoughts, Jesse's hands wonder down my body, resting on my bum. He gives it a little squeeze, being gentle. I don't want gentle right now. I need rough Jesse.

"Jesse, please," I beg, lifting my hips up. I need him to touch me more.

"What, Maisie? Tell me what you want," he whispers, starting to nibble my ear.

"Oh God. So good," I moan, loving the warmth from his mouth on my ear. It sends tingles all the way to my sex. I'm so wet right now. My panties are probably soaked from my juices.

"What do you want, Maisie?" He grinds his hips into my sex, sending another wave of tingles through my body.

What do I want? Am I ready to have sex with him? Do I want to have sex with him?

Right now, yes I do. Will I regret it later? I don't think so. This is the man I love. I'm ready. "I want you, Jesse," I moan out as he grinds his hips again.

Hell yes, I am ready if he has this effect on me already. We're hardly doing anything, and I'm close to climaxing.

"Where do you want me? Here?" he asks, his hands rubbing over my aching breasts. My nipples harden instantly, straining painfully again my bra. "Let's get this off." He pulls my t-shirt over the top of my head in one move, leaving me lying in just my white lacy bra. "Hmm. So. Beautiful," he says, between kissing the top of my breasts. "Can I take it off?"

I nod my head yes. Leaning forward, he unhooks the clasps one handed. He's obviously done this before, but now isn't the time to dwell on that. I don't want to be distracted from the trance that we are in.

Jesse lowers his head, his hot breath tickling my hard nipple. His tongue snakes out, swirling around my left nipple, getting a taste.

"You have such perfect breasts. Just the right size." He cups them to demonstrate what he means, his cold hands causing goose bumps to surface on my breasts. His lips lock on my right nipple this time, sucking, while his fingers pinch my other one. "Mmm, you taste so good, baby," he muffles.

"Ohhhh," I moan from the pleasure and pain that he is giving me.

He bites my nipple, causing me to cry out, before moving to give the other one attention. His fingers replace his mouth, rubbing my stinging nipple. He repeats the process again, causing me to get more and more worked up. I'm a mess of grinding hips and panting breaths right now.

"You look so sexy squirming underneath me." I haven't been able to look into Jesse's eyes yet, and now that I have... Oh my God, they are clouded with lust. It's such a turn on. I'm sure mine look exactly like his do right now.

"I need more. *Please,*" I moan, needing to feel more of what he has to give.

He chuckles at my impatience. "Stop rushing me. You will get more. Oh baby, trust me. You will get more, but I want to savor your body. I want this engrained into my memory forever." That has to be the hottest thing anybody has ever said to me. I nod my head in understanding, watching him move down the bed as he starts to pull my yoga pants off.

After throwing my yoga pants onto the floor, Jesse surveys my body from head to toe, an appreciative look on his face. I wish I could see and feel his body. "Take your shirt off," I order, leaning on my elbows to get a better view of him.

"Yes, ma'am," he replies, saluting me.

He lifts his t-shirt up over his head in one swift move, chucking it on the floor next to my clothes. "Now your jeans."

When he's taken his jeans off, I curl my fingers at him, demanding him to come here. I've never been bold in the bedroom before, but with Jesse, I feel comfortable. A side of me I never knew existed is shining through.

Feeling Jesse's rock hard abs on top of me, I run my hands down his back, getting acquainted with the contours of muscles there. He really is a fine piece of art. If I had to define perfection, Jesse would be it.

We roll so that I'm on top, and I run my hands down his

stomach, stopping at the waistband of his boxers. There's time for that later. Right now, I need to do something that I've wanted to do for weeks.

Leaning down, I keep eye contact with Jesse while running my tongue down his chest to his boxers. "Mmm," I moan, the taste of him on my tongue.

Jesse returns his hands to my breasts, fondling them, while I move to lick his nipples. He pinches my nipples, the pain making me bite down on his.

"Jesus," he hisses. I laugh. "Get on your back. You're in trouble now."

He rolls me back over and traps my hands above my head with one hand. I try to break free, but he's far too strong. His other hand runs down my body, heading south, until he touches the waistband of my lace panties. He doesn't do anything, just lingers there, torturing me. I lift my hips up, letting him know that I want him to touch me, and he does. One finger slips in, moving in and out slowly. The whole time, our eyes are locked in a trance. He slips another finger in, his thumb starting to rub my clit. "Oh God," I moan, close to climaxing already. His fingers are magic. He's hitting the spot perfectly.

I can feel the slow burn of my climax starting. My body is trembling already.

"Come on, baby. Cum for me," Jesse whispers. That's all it takes. My body convulses from the power of the orgasm tearing through me. I scream from the pure pleasure that his fingers are making me feel. His lips come crashing down on mine, silencing my screams, his fingers working out the last few tremors.

As I catch my breath, I look into Jesse's lust filled eyes.

"That is the hottest thing I have ever seen, baby."

Looking down between us, I see his hard length straining against his boxers. I need to sort that out for him. Licking my lips from the thought of his cock in my mouth, I lean forward, putting my hand down his boxers and freeing his hard length. Jesus, it's huge. I don't know if I can fit all of it into my mouth, but I'm damn well going to try.

I stroke him a few times, and then push Jesse onto his back, trying to get a better angle. "Your turn now," I drawl, starting to pump his cock.

"Mmm," he moans, closing his eyes.

Still stroking him, I lean forward, putting my mouth around the head of his cock. His eyes startle open, staring at me. Swirling my tongue around his head, I lick off his pre-cum. He tastes amazing, not too salty.

I've never liked giving head, but doing it to Jesse, and seeing the pure pleasure on his face, is making me even wetter.

I start moving my head up and down in a slow rhythm, taking his length into my mouth the best I can. Relaxing my reflexes, I fit most of it in.

"*Stop!*" Jesse says suddenly, lifting my head up. Did I do something wrong? Oh no. I did, didn't I?

"Did I do something wrong?" I ask, voicing my thoughts. Feeling insecure, I try to cover myself up with my hands as best I can.

"No. God no. I'm just close to coming. I'm not ready yet. Trust me. You did nothing wrong. The opposite, actually." I release the breath I had been holding. "I want us to finish together. If you're ready, that is?"

Am I ready? God, yes, I am ready.

Nodding my head, I lower my hands, baring my body to him. Excitement flashes in his eyes just before his lips tenderly touch mine. Jesse lowers me down gently onto my back, his hands running down my body. Oh so slowly, he takes my underwear off, then stands up and takes his own off, the whole time his eyes never straying from mine.

Seeing him standing there in all of his naked glory, I take him in, memorizing every inch of his body; the way his tattoos curl around his arms onto his chest, the dark hair on his stomach leading to his manhood, his delicious V muscles. I take everything in. He really is a fine piece of art. No wonder the ladies love him. He is perfection.

"Is it up to your standards?" Jesse asks, distracting me from my perusal.

"It's better," I whisper honestly. I've only ever seen one man naked before, and he has nothing on Jesse. Jesse puts other men to shame, I'm sure. "Come here. I need you." I curl my fingers at him, and he walks toward me. His body completely covers my tiny size. I feel his cock dig into my leg, reminding me what is about to happen. Butterflies start up in my stomach. I'm nervous now. I've only ever had sex with one person before. Matt.

"Are you sure you're ready to do this?" Jesse asks again. I nod, my throat too dry to speak. "I don't want you regretting it tomorrow. You're definitely sure?"

"Yes, I'm sure," I whisper. I give him a little smile, letting him know that I'm okay with this. I'm ready.

Feeling him at my entrance, I open my legs, making it easier for him to slip in. He slides in slowly, filling me inch by sweet inch.

"Are you okay?" I nod, letting him know that I am. It hurts a bit, though, as I'm not used to this size.

When he's all the way in, he stills, giving my walls time to expand around his impressive length.

"God, baby, you're so tight."

I lift my hips, letting him know that I'm ready. Jesse starts off slow, hitting my sweet spot every time. "Oh, Jesse," I moan from the pleasure he's giving me.

"You're mine now, baby. There's no going back. This pussy is mine," he pants out, his thrusts getting harder and faster.

"Yes," it's all I can say through my moans.

"Say it. Say this pussy is mine." He thrusts into me hard, knocking the wind out of me. I cry out, grabbing the sheets. "Say it," he demands, thrusting into me hard again.

"YES! THIS PUSSY IS YOURS!" I scream as his thrusts get even harder and faster.

"Good," Jesse replies, satisfaction on his face. I can't imagine giving myself to anyone else. I've never felt such pleasure before. I didn't even know you could feel this. Jesse has shown me new heights tonight.

I need to touch him. Letting go of the sheets, I wrap my legs around his waist, allowing him in deeper. Oh God, I can't take this much longer. I run my hands down his back, grabbing onto his tight bum and digging my nails into it.

"That's it, baby. Harder," Jesse growls into my ear. I dig deeper, bringing him closer to me.

That slow burn is building again. I don't know if I can go through that again just yet. It's too strong. My walls tighten around his cock. I'm so close.

"Come on, baby. Milk me. I can't hold on much longer, baby," he groans, pumping so fast my head hits the headboard. I can't feel the pain over the immense pleasure that is about to tear through my body.

"JESSE!" I scream, the orgasm tearing through my body more powerful than the last one.

"MAISIE," Jesse moans loudly, climaxing at the same time. I feel him release, my walls milking him of his juices to the last drop. He collapses on top of me, his sweaty body sticking to mine and both of us panting for breath.

When we have finally caught our breaths, I sigh contentedly.

"I love you, Maisie," Jesse says, lifting his head from my chest to look into my eyes. My heart melts hearing him say those three little words.

"I love you too, Jesse," I reply, pushing his hair out of his eyes.

"Let me go and get you a towel to clean yourself up." He pulls out, standing stock still at the end of the bed and looking down at his cock soaked in our juices.

"What's wrong?" I ask at the scared expression on his face.

"I forgot to put a condom on. *Shit!* I've never forgotten before," he says, running his hands through his hair in frustration.

Swiveling around on the bed, I stand up and make my way over to him. "It's okay. I'm on the pill. I have been for the last three years, and I got checked out when my relationship ended. I'm clean."

"I'm clean too, by the way. I get checked out all the time," Jesse says, looking relieved. "Come on. Let's get you cleaned up." He takes my hand and leads me into his bathroom.

For the rest of the afternoon, we watch films while cuddled up in his bed.

When I arrive home later on that night, Chloe is absent, so I climb into bed, feeling a twinge of pain in my sex that reminds me of the best sex of my life with the man I love. I fall asleep with a smile on my face.

CHAPTER THIRTEEN
MAISIE

Jesse and I have been together for nearly two months now. It's been the best two months of my life. I see him mostly every day, except when he has work or football practice, or if I have too many assignments to do. So this week is going to be hard.

I'm going home to see my family for a week as it's Thanksgiving.

Don't get me wrong; I'm stoked to be seeing my parents for the first time in nearly three months, but I'm really going to miss Jesse. I wish he was coming with me, but he doesn't want to leave his mom all on her own. I understand. I really do. Thanksgiving isn't a time for being alone. It just sucks ass.

Chloe and I haven't really spoken since our disagreement. We're just going about the motions, living together but not spending time together like we used to. She's really withdrawn into herself. She's often out doing God knows what, then returning home really late at night usually so intoxicated that she can hardly walk. I've tried talking to her about it, but she just ignored me and went back to sleep. I don't know what else I can do.

I offered her a lift home to see her parents, but she declined, saying she wants stay on campus. Her mom is going to be really upset that she isn't coming home. I'll probably pop over to see her. Maybe if I tell her mom how she's behaving, she can knock some sense into her. I just want my best friend back.

I put some of my belongings that I'll need for the week into the trunk, and then get into my car and start the long journey home.

****

Eight hours later, I'm parked outside my parent's house. The journey took two hours longer than usual. I guess everybody is going home to their families for the holidays.

Jake's truck is already in the drive. He must have left early to beat the traffic.

As I get out of the car, the front door opens, and my mom comes bursting out and running down the drive to pull me into a tight hug. I inhale her familiar scent. I've missed her so much. I hug her back just as tightly, and tears gather in my eyes; happy tears at seeing my mom again after nearly three months of being apart. We've never spent this long away from each other before.

"Hey, Mom," I say, sniffling into her ear.

"Oh, sweetie, what's wrong?" she asks, pulling back to inspect me. "Has something happened?" She's panicking now.

"Nothing's wrong, Mom. I'm just so happy to see you, is all. I missed you and Dad." I give her a smile to let her know that I'm okay.

"Oh, we missed you too, darling. So much. Come on. Your dad is excited to see you. He's been worried about his little girl. It's been driving me insane," she says, rolling her eyes as she leads me into the house.

Closing the front door behind me, I inhale the familiar scent of my childhood home. It still has that vanilla smell from the air fresheners my mom uses. I smile, happy to be home.

"Is that my pumpkin?" my dad asks, coming out of the kitchen wearing an apron, a big smile on his face.

I rush over to him and wrap my arms around his six foot two frame, feeling like I'm a four year old again. I've always been a daddy's girl, and that's never going to change. I inhale his earthy scent, it reminding me of so many wonderful memories. To a girl, there's nothing like the smell of your daddy. It's safe and warm.

"I've missed you, Daddy," I mumble into his chest. My damn tears have started up again now. It's a good thing Jesse didn't come. He would be laughing at how I'm reacting. Anyone would think that I haven't seen them for years, instead of just a few months!

"I've missed you too, baby girl. How's college?" Dad asks. I step out of his embrace.

"It's really good. My classes are going well," I reply vaguely.

"Made many friends?" We move into the living room. He knows that I've always found it hard to make friends. I can't tell him about Jesse, though. He's so protective of me, especially after what Matt did.

"No. I've been busy with my assignments," I lie through my teeth. I hate lying to my parents, but in this case, it's necessary.

"Maisie, you have to make friends. You can't just hang around with Chloe. College is all about new experiences and having a little fun. You can't be holed up in your room twenty-four seven. I'm sure Chloe has made new friends. The longer you leave it, the harder it will be, as everyone will already be in groups," Mom says worriedly.

"She hasn't made friends because she's always with her boyfriend," Jake says, coming around the corner. *Fucking hell*...Why did he have to open his big fucking mouth? As I shoot daggers at him, which right now I wish could kill, he sits down in the chair opposite me, a smug smile on his face. Oh no. If I'm going down, he's going down with me.

"Jake was sleeping with Chloe," I spit out, the smug smile now on my face, and the daggers now shooting out of his eyes. Take that, fuckwit!

Mom and Dad repeatedly look between us, their mouths hanging open. The silence lasts for what feels like forever. I guess it is a lot for them to take in. I just hope they choose to question Jake.

Their gazes finally land on me. Oh shit. This isn't good.

"What's your boyfriend's name, and where did you meet him?" Dad finally asks, his expression hard.

"His name is Jesse, and he's in my English class," I reply, treading carefully. I look at Jake, conveying with my eyes for him not to say anymore. I don't need him blabbing about Jesse's past. That will not go over well with my dad.

"Right... And how long have you two been together?"

"Nearly two months." I smile, thinking about our time together.

"Is he your age?" My Dad's eyes are squinted, probably deep in thought.

"No he's in Jake's year. They are friends. Tell Dad, Jake." I give

Jake a look, warning him to say only good things. He has the power right now, and I don't like it one bit.

"Yeah, he's a cool guy, Dad. We've been friends since I first started college, and from what I can see, he really cares for Maisie. I know you're thinking about what Matt did, but trust me, Jesse's nothing like him. I wouldn't let him near Maisie if he was." My dad nods, obviously trusting Jake's opinion. I thank Jake with my eyes for not saying anything that would get Dad riled up.

"Okay. When am I going to meet this Jesse?" Not anytime soon, I think.

"Erm… I don't know, Dad. He's pretty busy." No he's not. I just don't want you to give him the third degree. I had to watch my dad give Matt the third degree, and it was so embarrassing. I expected him to run a mile and never look back, but he didn't. I wish he had now, though. It would have saved me from a lot of heartache in the long run.

"Sweetheart, why didn't you tell us you had a boyfriend?" my mom pipes up, looking distraught that I hadn't confided in her.

It's not my mom that I was keeping this from, but my dad. I mean, I love him to pieces, but he's just too overprotective sometimes. I knew my mom would tell him, hence why I didn't tell her.

"I'm sorry. I really am. You know what Dad is like, though. No offence, Dad," I apologize, looking at my dad. "He would have gone all protective daddy bear on me, Mom. I didn't know how long Jesse and I would last either, so I needed to make sure first before I told you both. I really do love him, Mom. He's completely different than Matt. He cares about me, always puts me first, and he listens to me when I need someone to talk to. You will both love him. I know you will. Plus, he's not bad on the eyes either." I laugh, winking at my mom. She chuckles.

Facing my dad, I see no emotion on his face. "I promise you will love him, Daddy. I'll let you meet him soon, okay?" I give him a smile, letting him know that I'm happier than I have been in months.

"Come here, pumpkin," my dad says, his arms stretched out wide. I walk into them and feel safe. "As long as you're happy, then I'm happy. But you let Jesse know that if he so much as hurts a hair on your head or makes a tear fall from your eyes, I will kill him, and that's a promise." I chuckle because I know that isn't just a threat.

"I will tell him, Daddy," I pull away from his embrace and see my mom smiling.

"Come here, baby girl." She also gives me a hug. "I'm so glad to see the shine back in your eyes again. I missed it," she whispers into my ear. I nod, too emotional to talk right now. I know if I do, I will probably cry. "Sit down, and I'll go make us all a coffee."

She comes back in a few minutes later, coffees all made. I sit quietly, waiting for what is to be said next. We have a lot of catching up to do.

"Wait... Did Maisie say that you were sleeping with Chloe, Jake?" My mom asks, remembering what I had said. Jake sinks back into his chair. Shit. There's no hiding from it now, buddy. You're the reason my best friend has closed in on herself!

"You best start explaining, Jake," Dad pipes up after a few minutes of silence.

There is so much tension in the room right now. Jake will probably want me to bail him out of this, but he's on his own. I know he helped me, and I'm thankful for that, but this is my best friend he's fucking with. I have to pick my battles. This is one of them.

"This doesn't leave this room. Understood?" he finally pipes up. We all nod in response, eager for what he is about to say. If he's spilling his feelings, I'm listening intently. This doesn't happen often.

"Well..." He starts, and then swallows loudly before continuing, "Chloe and I started sleeping together about seven months ago. I ended it five months ago." His voice changes at the end. I swear he sounds upset. He can't be, though. Jake doesn't get upset over girls. Even if he has always had a soft spot for her, it's not his motto to show feelings. More like love em' and leave em'.

"Why did you end it?" my mom asks. That's what I want to know too. Good thinking, Mom!

"I can't tell you why," he sighs, exasperated.

We all look at him expectantly. That isn't going to cut it, especially now that I have a bigger team on my side. My parents love Chloe as if she were their own. If Jake hurts her, they will skin him alive.

"Jake..." my dad warns, getting frustrated.

"Fine. I'll tell you. I got bored of her. It was exciting at first, but it got old very quick, so I ended our arrangement. Happy now?" He rises abruptly from his chair, walks out of the room, and slams the front door behind him.

We're all left speechless.

"What the hell just happened?" I ask my gob smacked parents, confused.

"I don't have the slightest clue, but when I get hold of your brother later, I'm chopping his dick off. If he's going to abuse it, he's going to lose it. I'm allowed to decide that because I graced him with it," Dad says matter-of-factly. Mom and I burst out laughing at his seriousness. "But on a serious note, how's Chloe? When we've spoken, you haven't really talked about her."

Maybe they can tell me what to do to help. I don't know what to do anymore. All I know is that I can't leave Chloe alone any longer. She's changing, and not for the better.

"She's not good. We had a disagreement one night when I heard her and Jake having an argument. I asked what was going on, and as usual, she dodged the question. I'm fed up with trying to help. I don't know how to help when she won't tell me what's going on. Since then, we've been keeping our distance from each other. She's gone all day, and if she returns, she's usually drunk. She's a mess. I miss my best friend," I say, trying to keep the tears at bay.

Now that I've said it out loud, it's bad. It's really bad. I can't let Chloe keep on doing what she's doing. She's deteriorating before my eyes, and I've just stood by and let it happen. I'm such a shitty friend. She's always been there for me. I should have done the same. She would have told me when she was ready. I just needed to be patient.

"You know Chloe, baby girl, and she will tell you when she's ready. I know it's frustrating because you want to help her, but maybe she doesn't want help right now. Whatever is going on, she obviously doesn't want to burden you with it. We all know that you've had your own problems to deal with recently. She was probably thinking of you," my mom says soothingly.

They always know the right thing to say.

"I hope so, Mom. If not, then I'll send her to you? You two can knock some sense into her." They laugh because they know I'm being completely serious. If anyone can knock some sense into Chloe, it's my parents. It's a gift they have.

"Of course, sweetie," my mom replies for both of them.

"Okay, I'm going to pop to the store. Do you two need anything?" I ask. I desperately need to get out right now. I need a breather from the twenty-one questions.

"No, we have everything. We'll see you soon," my mom replies.

I get my car keys off of the side table, and then walk out the front door, to my car.

****

After parking outside the local store, I walk across the lot. I hope I don't bump into anyone. The last thing I want to talk or hear about is Matt. I've not spoken to any of my old friends since that frightful night, and I plan on keeping it that way. The only true friend I had was Chloe, and I pushed her away. I intend on sorting things out with her when I return to campus.

The bell on the door rings as I step inside, and the familiar smell of hot dogs graces my nostrils. I never thought I would be so happy to smell it. I used to hate the fact that it always stunk of hot dogs in here.

As I go over to look at the magazines, Mrs Jenkins, the old lady who owns the store, waves at me. "Maisie, dear, how lovely it is to see you. How have you been?"

"I'm doing well. How are you?" I reply.

"Oh, you know, the same. I'm not getting any younger, dear. I should be retired, but seeing faces like yours every day makes me want to carry on working. I've missed seeing you around. Tell me. How's college?"

Mrs Jenkins is nearly eighty years old. She's run the local store for as long as I can remember. When I was younger, she used to give me free candy, and then when I got older, she gave me a part time job. I really look up to her. She's had a tough life. Her husband and children died in a car crash, and she's never moved on. She just carries on running the family store by herself. I used to keep her company, but now, I don't think she has anyone. I'll need to spend some time with her while I'm home.

"Oh, I love college. My classes are fantastic."

"You've got that glint back in your eyes, sweetheart. Is there a special somebody who's put it back there?" This woman is too smart for her own good. She never misses a thing.

With the biggest smile on my face, I tell her, "Yes, actually, there is. His name is Jesse."

A smile takes over her face too. "Oh, that's wonderful, dear! You deserve someone who obviously makes you happy. Have you got a picture of him that I could see?"

I take out my cell phone and scroll through my pictures until I find one that I took of us the day we first made love. Showing her my phone, I watch her expression.

"He's a bit alright, isn't he?" she says, winking at me. "If only I was fifty years younger." That causes me to laugh. Hard.

Under the sweet little old lady act, there's a woman with a lot of fire still. Mrs Jenkins isn't immune to a good looking guy. I remember from when I worked with her. If a good looking guy came in, she would flirt with them. I used to look forward to those days; it was entertaining to watch.

The bell on the door rings, signaling someone entering. Putting my cell phone in my pocket, I look up to see who it is. The smile falls from my face the second my eyes land on Matt. I stand stock still, stunned into silence. He looks as clean kept as ever with his tidy hair and expensive clothes. He hasn't changed a bit.

What surprises me the most, though, is that I feel nothing when I look at him. My stomach doesn't do a little summersault like it used to, and my heart doesn't skip a beat. Now, he's just like any other person.

I haven't seen him since I walked out of his party. He tried to come to my house to see me before I left for college, but thankfully, my dad wouldn't let him in.

Now I have Jesse, the best looking and kindest man I have ever known. Matt doesn't have anything on Jesse. If I had to compare the two, Matt is mediocre. My skin is crawling just looking at him after all this time.

"Maisie, I didn't know you were back," Matt says, breaking the silence.

Swallowing, I say, "It's Thanksgiving. Of course I came back." It comes out as more of a croak. I need a drink.

"Of course," he replies, staring at the floor. "It's good to see you. You look like you're doing well." Yes, no thanks to you, fuckwit, I think.

"That's what moving away does. No drama, nobody who knows you. I started over again," I tell him honestly. His face falls at that revelation. Turning back to Mrs Jenkins, who's silently watching the scene play out in front of her, I tell her, "I'm going to head home now, but I'll come back to see you before I leave. It was nice to see you."

"You too, dear. Make sure you do come back to see me. Oh, and ignore him. You have an incredible man now. Matt is your past. Don't hold on to those of your past. They are there for a reason. Let go and focus on what Jesse can offer you in the future," she says just loud enough for Matt to hear. She sure is a wise woman.

Ignoring Matt on my way out, I walk to my car.

"Maisie, wait," he shouts, running toward me. Fuck. I was so close. Now I'm going to have to talk to him. I have nothing else to say that I haven't already said.

I feel him stop behind me, but I don't turn around. Maybe he will take the hint.

"I just want to apologize, again, for what happened. I'm so sorry. I regret it every single day. I miss you, Mais," he says sorrowfully.

"You're forgiven," I reply bluntly.

"Well, I don't forgive myself. I never will. You were the best thing to ever happen to me, and I lost you." I can't bear to hear this anymore. Why does he have to drag up old demons?

I turn to face him, seeing him with his head held downwards in sorrow.

"Look, I have to go, but just forget about it. I have. You will never move on with your life if you keep holding onto the past."

"I overheard Mrs Jenkins in there. I take it you have a new boyfriend then?" Matt pipes up, just as I'm about to spin back around.

I knew as soon as Mrs Jenkins said it, that Matt would hear. Who was I kidding, hoping that he wouldn't ask? I'm not going to tell him, though. He has no right to ask anymore.

"It's none of your business if I do or don't have a boyfriend, Matt," I reply, my voice filled with finality. Of course, he's never listened to me before, so why would he now?

"It is my business, Maisie," his voice, which is filled with disgust, matches the look on his face.

"How the fuck is it any of your business, Matt? You were the one who cheated on me, remember? You chucked us away when you decided to go elsewhere. You lost the right to know anything about what I do that night. This conversation is over. Goodbye, Matt."

I have to leave right now, or I will lose my temper. How did I ever find him attractive? People always told me that he was controlling when it came to me, but I never believed them. I couldn't. I was blinded by what I thought was love for him. I realize now that it wasn't really love, though. It was just a silly high school crush. I love Jesse more after two months than I ever loved Matt in the four years we were together.

"You're just a dirty whore, Maisie. It didn't take you long to move on at all. We were together for four years! How can you move on in five months?" His nostrils flare like they always do when he gets angry.

Did he just call me a dirty whore? Oh, hell no. I'm not having that.

Moving to stand right in front of him, I poke him in the chest and hiss at him, *"Don't you dare call me a dirty whore! I wasn't the one who ruined our relationship, Matt. You did when you slept with Megan. So yes, I've moved on. I wasted five months of my life living through the motions, and then Jesse came along and helped me get out of the big black hole that I thought I was trapped in. So sue me for finally having a life."* Shit, I just told him Jesse's name. Oh, it's not like he's going to hunt him down and beat the shit out of him, is it? Might as well just tell him.

"And I apologized for that!" Matt shouts, exasperated. "So his names Jesse? How did you meet?" He's now as cool as a cucumber. How does he switch moods so quickly?

"Yes, and if you must know, he's in my English class." I put my hands on my hips and sigh.

It doesn't look like I'm getting home any time soon. Matt obviously has a lot of questions to ask. Well, if he's going to be nosey, I'll give him what he wants. I doubt he will be happy about it, but if he doesn't want to hear it, then he shouldn't ask.

"So he majors in English?"

"No, he's the captain of the football team. You know how I've always liked sporty guys," I tell him, trying to gauge his reaction. He bristles at that. Good. That will teach him.

"Yeah, I do," he says quietly. "How long have you been together?"

"Nearly two months. Are we nearly done here? I have things to do," I say.

"Just one more question, and I want you to be honest with me, okay?" he asks, looking me straight in the eyes. It's making me nervous. They are the eyes that I used to spend hours staring into, but now I can barely stand to.

I nod my head, waiting for him to spit it out.

"Have you had sex with him?" he finally asks.

Did he really just ask me that? Who goes around asking their ex if they've had sex with their new boyfriend? He isn't going to like my answer. However, he wanted the truth, so I'm going to give it to him.

"Yes." I don't hesitate to answer. I'm not ashamed. My first time with Jesse was the best I've ever had. He knew what he was doing. He showed me love the whole way through, catering to my needs, spot on. A smile appears on my face from rethinking back to that night. I've engrained it to my memory.

"Of course you have, and by the smile and the dazed look in your eyes, I'm guessing you're imagining it right now. Well, it was nice to see you again, Maisie. Have fun back at college with your new boyfriend." With that, he walks off to his car, which is parked on the other side of the parking lot.

Had I known that would piss him off, I would have told him about ten minutes ago. Oh well. I'm not going to dwell on it. There is nothing more that needs to be said between us. I can finally get on with my life, without Matt subconsciously entering my mind and trying to destroy it. Old demons are put to rest now.

With a smile on my face, I hop into my car, turn on the radio, and head back home.

CHAPTER FOURTEEN
MATT

When I headed to the store, the last person I thought I would bump into is Maisie. I haven't spoken to her since the night I made the biggest mistake of my life. That night still haunts my nightmares.

The night of my party, Maisie and I had an argument. Over what I can't remember now, all I know is that it had something to do with Chloe. I hated that bitch. She always got in the way of my relationship with Maisie. The only reason I put up with her was because she was Maisie's best friend. I tried to subtly keep Maisie away from her. She was bad news, constantly sleeping with guys, partying all the time, and she was generally just a loud mouthed bitch.

Anyway, after the football match, that we won, I went back to my house and started drinking before everyone was due to come round. By the time people started arriving, I was completely shit-faced.

When Megan tried it on with me, I stupidly said yes when she asked if I wanted to sleep with her. She's always had a crush on me for as long as I can remember. I've never been interested in her, though, as I've always only had eyes for Maisie. No way would I usually choose Megan over her, but I was intoxicated. You know what men are like when they've got a load of alcohol in their system. They fuck anything and everything. I'm no exception. However, usually I had Maisie with for when I need to let loose.

She wasn't there at the time, and to be honest, after our fight earlier, I doubted that she would turn up. So I went for it. I risked everything for a lay that wasn't even very good.

When I saw Maisie standing in my bedroom, watching the whole thing play out in front of her, my heart literally dropped into my stomach. I sobered up instantly. It was too late, though, because she had witnessed my betrayal. I knew that was the end of us straight away, but I had to at least try to salvage our relationship.

Maisie was it for me. She was who I saw spending the rest of my life with. All of that disappeared the minute I saw her face. She looked so heartbroken. I see that face every night in my dreams, except it's not a dream. It's a fucking nightmare, and it plays on repeat every night, taunting me with what I fucking lost all because of one stupid fucking decision.

Maisie told me never to contact her again. I couldn't do that, though. I had to see her, to try to sort our relationship out. If she never forgave me, then I would have to live with that for the rest of my life.

I went to her house every day for the next three months, to no avail. Her dad wouldn't let me past the front door. I'm surprised he didn't kill me for what I did, actually, though he wasn't too pleasant whenever I saw him. I wasn't giving up on her, though. No way.

I heard she had left for college when I started at the local one that we were both supposed to attend together. Someone from out graduating class told me. I was so pissed off at myself.

Anyway, I didn't hear any news on her for months, until about a month ago. Some girl called Tiffany added me on Facebook. I'd never heard of her before, but she looked pretty hot if her profile picture was anything to go by, so I clicked accept. A message came through straight away, asking if I knew a Maisie Peterson. My heart dropped, wondering if something bad had happened to her. When I replied yes, Tiffany asked how I knew her.

She told me that Maisie was dating someone named Jesse Cohen, that Maisie stole him from her. When I didn't reply, she said she wanted my help. She wanted me to help her get Jesse back. I didn't know who this girl was. She could have been bullshitting, for all I knew. Plus, the Maisie I knew wasn't like that. She must have had the wrong person. I told her I would let her know.

When Maisie let slip her boyfriend's name, I knew that Tiffany was telling the truth.

She had finally moved on, forgetting all about me. Maisie isn't supposed to be with anyone but me. She is it for me, and I won't let anybody else have what I can't.

Back in my car, I watch Maisie pull out of the parking lot. I'm fuming.

Opening up Facebook on my phone, I send Tiffany a message, telling her "It's on."

If I can't have her, then no one else can either, especially not this Jesse guy. I'm going to do whatever it takes to get her back where she belongs, which is with me.

CHAPTER FIFTEEN
JESSE

It's Thanksgiving today, a day to celebrate and spend with family. I never enjoy it, though. What's there to enjoy when it's only me and my mom? Don't get me wrong; she goes all out trying to make it special for us. It just gets lonely, you know? Most people are surrounded by their huge families, but not me.

Also, I miss Maisie so much. I haven't seen her for three days. It's not very long to most people, but to me? It's been the longest three days of my life. We usually spend most days together, and that's how I like it.

I miss staring into her chocolate colored eyes while I make love to her. I miss holding her in my arms, when we're all worn out, trying to catch our breath. I miss the way she blushes when she's uncomfortable. I miss all of that.

We've been talking on the phone every night until one of us falls asleep, which is usually her, but it's just not the same as seeing and talking to her in person.

I've decided to sleep in this morning, so I don't have to spend as long being bored and missing her.

After getting a shower and getting dressed, I head downstairs to see if Mom needs any help. I'm just about to walk into the living room when female laughter, that isn't my mom's, stops me in my tracks.

It can't be. I must be hearing things that I so desperately want to hear right now. Maisie's in San Francisco with her parents, so she can't be sitting in the other room. She would have come upstairs to see me if that was the case. Wouldn't she?

I walk into the living room and stand still at the sight of Maisie sitting with my mom on the sofa. I'm shocked, to say the least. I seriously thought my ears were playing tricks on me.

Maisie breaks the silence first by saying, "Hi." She stands up from the sofa and slowly makes her way toward me.

I still don't reply. I still feel like I'm dreaming. She isn't really here, not when she could be with her family. I close my eyes and pinch myself to wake up. *Ouch, that fucking hurt.* I open my eyes and stare straight into the ones I have dreamt about endlessly for the last three nights. I blink a few times, double-checking that she's really here and that I'm not dreaming.

"I'm really here, Jesse," Maisie says, chuckling at my reaction.

I register what she's saying, processing everything carefully. Yup, she's definitely here. I scoop her up into my arms at the speed of light, and then kiss every inch of her face. Her strawberry scent wafts up my nose. *Mmm, I've missed that smell.*

"*Jesse, put me down!*" she chuckles into my ear. I've missed that sound too. I've just fucking missed her so much. I never want to go that long without seeing her again. Next time, I'm going with her.

"Nope, not going to happen, Firecracker. I'm never letting you go again."

"You two go upstairs and catch up. I'm going to prepare lunch," Mom interrupts, shooing us away.

She doesn't need to tell me twice. I spin us around and smack Maisie's ass, causing her to screech, as I take the stairs two at a time.

I gently lie her down in the middle of my bed and climb on top of her. My arms framing her head, I stare into her beautiful brown eyes. I could seriously look into them forever. They are hypnotizing. They are the window to her soul. I can always tell if something is wrong just by looking into her eyes, and right now, there is something wrong. She's missing her usual glint.

"I thought you were spending Thanksgiving with your family?" I ask, treading carefully. If I ask correctly, she may tell me. Then again, she might not. She still hasn't told me about what happened in her past to make her so wary of men.

"I just missed you. Plus, it wasn't like my family was going to be lonely without me. My grandparents are down for the week, and my aunt and uncles are coming down today. There are plenty of them to fill my place," Maisie replies, giving me a warm, loving smile. I'm not buying it. I believe that she wanted to see me, but would she choose me over her whole family? No. Something happened.

"Did something happen, Maisie?"

She averts her eyes from me before answering, "No, nothing happened."

Gently taking hold of her face, I hold it in place. She still doesn't look at me, though. She really isn't good at lying. "Maisie, baby, look at me, please," I ask calmly.

She begrudgingly looks at me. "Tell me what happened, baby,"

"Nothing happened, Jesse. Just drop it already." Maisie pushes against my chest, and I move willingly. She obviously needs her space right now. I'm not giving up that easily, though. We aren't leaving this room until she has spilled what happened.

"No, Maisie, I won't drop it. You never want to let me in. You always want to keep everything to yourself. We are in a relationship, aren't we?" I ask, putting my hands on my hips. I don't know where else to put them. I've never been in this situation before with all these feelings and shit. It's not me.

She stops her pacing and stares at me all wide-eyed. "Of course we are. Why would you say that?" She sounds all worried.

"Well, act like we're in a relationship then, Maisie. People in relationships share their problems with each other, not keep them bottled up. We won't work if you do that. I *want* to be there for you. I can't if you don't let me in, though. You have to decide if you want us to work." I turn, heading for my bedroom door. I'm the one needing space now. This isn't how I expected things to go when I next saw her. I was going to carry her up to my room and fuck the living shit out of her. Maybe I should still do that. It might make her remember what she has.

"*Jesse, wait!*" Maisie shouts desperately, stopping me in my tracks.

I turn around to face her, waiting for her to continue. Wringing her hands, she doesn't say anything for a few seconds. I'm about to turn back around when she blurts out, "I caught my boyfriend cheating on me."

I'm shocked into silence. Why would anyone cheat on Maisie?

If anyone could be close to perfection, it's Maisie. She's the sweetest, kindest person I know. I'm lucky to have her. Hell, anybody would lucky to have her, and that fucking dick went and ruined it, messing her up in the process. No wonder she has trust issues. If I ever see that fucker, I'm going to punch him straight in the face for hurting the best girl in the world. Then, I'm going to shake his hand and thank him for fucking up, because if he hadn't, I probably wouldn't have had a chance with her.

I'm about to speak up when Maisie continues, "I was supposed to meet him for a party at his house after a game. We'd had an argument earlier in the day because I said I was arriving with Chloe. Anyway, when I got to the party, I couldn't find him anywhere. I found one of his friends, who told me he was probably upstairs as he'd already drunk a lot. So, I went upstairs to try and find him. I was about to walk into his room when I heard a girl moaning, so like an idiot, I listened. She said his name. I had a feeling that he was in there, so I walked in to confront them. Matt was fucking a girl named Megan. That girl had been trying to split us up for years, and she'd finally succeeded. He came groveling as soon as he was dressed, saying he was drunk and he was sorry. I haven't spoken to him since." When she's finished, she starts laughing hysterically.

I'm confused. Why is she laughing? She's finally explained why she has trust issues, and now she's laughing.

I watch her for a few minutes, trying to understand what has just happened. She doesn't calm down. "Maisie, why are you laughing, baby?" I ask.

She looks at me and replies through her laughter, "Oh, it's just funny, isn't it. Don't you think?" I think she's gone crazy.

Pulling her to the bed, I sit us both down. "I'm really confused right now, babe. Care to explain what's funny?" I'm sure my eyebrows are at the top of my head right now.

"I was so upset when Matt did that to me, but when I saw him the other day, I felt nothing but disgust. You should have seen his face when he realized he has no effect on me anymore." That's why she came back. She may act like she doesn't care, but deep down, she's ruffled. She wouldn't be here if she was okay with it. She stops laughing, staring at me seriously. "You wanted to know why I came back?" I nod my head. "I came back because it was digging up the past, a past that I don't want to remember anymore. Bumping into Matt helped me realize that."

"Baby, you can't not go back home because of something that happened in the past. That's not moving on. I'm proud of you for facing this Matt guy, really I am, except you're parents live there too, baby. You're going to have to go home from time to time. If you want, next time you go home, I'll come with you if it will help."

I'll go anywhere she asks. This way, I won't miss her when I have to go days without seeing her. I might get her attached to my hip, so we'll have to be together all the time. If only…

"I would love that. Oh, and by the way, my parents want to meet you. Jake told them I had a boyfriend, and I got the third degree from my dad, but luckily, Jake spoke highly of you. I was thinking about going to see them in a few weeks, since I left early today. Would you come with me?" she asks sweetly. How could I say no to that?

I'm scared shitless deep down. I've never done the whole 'meet the parents' thing before. I can only give it my best shot and hope they like me, right?

"Of course, baby. I'd love to meet them." I give her my best fake smile. Luckily, she buys it. I've got a lot of preparing to do for this. *Shit!*

She's biting that damn lip of hers again. My cock springs to life just from that little action. Fuck. I need her. Right. Now. Growling, I jump on her and push her onto her back. Smashing my lips against hers, I kiss her. Hard. I kiss her like a starving man. I've been starved of her sensuous lips for days now. My tongue seeks entrance, and she willingly accepts.

"Mmm," she moans, the sound vibrating straight through my body.

She grinds her hips, her clothed pussy brushing my cock. Sitting her up, I take her top off in one swift move, exposing her beautiful hour glass figure to me. I'll never get enough of her body. Her pink, lacy bra comes off next, leaving her pert breasts rising and falling with her breathing. I need to taste them. Sucking her nipple, her sweet taste fills my mouth.

There's time for foreplay later. Right now, I need to be inside her.

I stand and rip my clothes off in record speed, while she takes off her remaining clothes.

Lying Maisie back down on the bed, I gently lay on top of her smooth warm body, everything touching in the right place. Her hard nipples graze my chest. My pulsing cock rests perfectly in her wet folds.

Staring down into her lust filled eyes that I love so much, I gruffly tell her, "This is going to be hard and fast."

I don't wait for her reply. I hike her legs up around my waist, holding one up with my hand, and then in one swift move, I enter her completely. Jesus! She's always so tight.

Holding still to let her adjust around my man hood, I slowly kiss her. God, I'm going to cum before I've even started moving at this rate. I break the kiss and start to move my hips, watching my rock hard cock moving in and out of her sopping cunt. My cock is dripping more and more the longer we go.

"Oh, Jesse," Maisie moans, arching her body off the bed.

"I've missed you so much, baby," I tell her, speeding up my tempo.

She meets me thrust for thrust in perfect sync, pushing me closer and closer to climax. She feels so good, like a tight glove around my dick. Her moaning becomes more frantic. She's close. Oh so close. I can already feel her walls tightening, getting ready to milk me dry.

Lifting her legs up higher, I drive in deeper. "Come on, baby," I tell her. I don't know how much longer I can hold on. Maisie always feels so fucking good.

"Oh God, Jesse." Maisie's walls grip me like a vice as her orgasm hits, her juices washing all over my cock.

That's all it takes; I'm a goner. "*Fuccccccccck*," I groan, pumping a few more times.

I collapse on top of Maisie, our sweaty bodies sticking together, and we both lay there trying to catch our breath.

Smoothly rubbing her soft skin, I tell her, "Every time with you feels like the first time."

I don't risk looking at her. This is tough territory for me. She sighs softly, my head rising and falling with her breathing. "I know what you mean. Every time gets better and better."

I don't reply. I don't need to. She just summed it up. I continue on rubbing her soft skin, loving the feel of her beneath me. I could lie here like this forever, not a care in the world, just us two and these four walls.

Unfortunately, life isn't like that. I have a mother downstairs waiting for us.

After pushing myself off of the bed, and instantly missing Maisie's body heat, I begrudgingly put my clothes back on. "As much as I would love to stay in bed with you all day, darling, my mom is waiting downstairs, and if dinner is ruined because I couldn't keep my dick in my pants, she will kill me." Maisie laughs at me, still not making any attempt to move. Damn it. She's still spread eagle, my semen coating her entrance. My cock gets hard again just at the sight of her like this.

Mom is waiting downstairs. Mom is waiting downstairs. Mom is waiting downstairs. After giving myself a pep talk, I shake my head to clear the dirty thoughts that are running wild right now.

"I'm going to go downstairs to help Mom," I say, looking anywhere but at her. I can't right now, or we will never leave this room, my mom be damned. She will have to drag me out of the room.

"Why aren't you looking at me? Have I done something wrong?" she asks worriedly.

Shit. She's got the wrong idea.

Still not risking looking at her for my own sanity, I tell her honestly, "No, baby, you've done nothing wrong. If I look at you right now, we will never leave this room. I will fuck you all night long, until you can't walk anymore. That, baby, is the reason I can't look at you right now. I'll see you downstairs. I need something to take my mind off of my dirty thoughts right now. Maybe cutting some vegetables will help."

I close my door behind me and shrink back against it, closing my eyes, and release a big sigh. What is Maisie doing to me? I'm insatiable when it comes to her. If I had my way, and I could go that long, I would be inside of her for twenty-four hours straight. Unfortunately, I think my dick might fall off if I could. Maisie's definitely going to be the death of me.

****

Lunch is so delicious and just what I needed after my strenuous session with Maisie earlier. Luckily, Mom always makes enough to feed ten people, so I get seconds and plan on having more for dinner. I'm a growing man. It's allowed.

Usually, Thanksgiving is just another day for me. I'm not

usually thankful for anything. I'm not ungrateful or anything, it's just I've always been dealt the shit cards for as long as I can remember. Today always makes me remember what I went through as a little boy. This year, though, is different.

Today, I have Maisie. I have the most beautiful girlfriend who decided to spend today with my mom and me, instead of her own family. She's selfless, and I admire her so much. From what she's told me, she's been dealt the shit cards too recently. She is so strong, though. She just doesn't realize it yet. I'm going to help her realize it. I'll spend the rest of my life making her realize how strong she is, and I won't even care. I'll be one happy man if I get to spend the rest of my days with Maisie. She really is one in a million.

Mom is really happy today, as well. Usually, we have lunch, watch a few movies, and then go to bed. It's a hard day for her. She always tries to make it a special day for me, and I appreciate it, but sometimes, no matter how hard you try, bad memories just won't go away; For either of us.

So it's nice to witness my mom enjoying herself for the first time in I don't know how long. She adores Maisie and views her as her daughter after only a few short weeks. I've already had the third degree, not to mess it up, to make sure that I treat her properly, and not to hurt her. She threatened to chop my balls off if she ever finds out that I've ruined the best thing to ever happen to me. The thing is, I'd probably do it to myself before she could. I realize how special Maisie is. I'm just thankful that my mom sees it too and treats her as part of the family.

After lunch, I clean up while they put a movie on. It's routine; Mom cooks, and I clean up.

Now, we are all sitting on the sofa, Maisie's cuddled under the crook of my arm, and we're watching 'Dirty Dancing'. Not my choice of film, but hey, my ladies are happy. That's all that matters. Plus, I'm not going to lie; I have a bit of a man crush on Patrick Swayze in this movie. That guy is talented.

Looking down at Maisie, just to get a peak of her perfect face, I see a slight smile playing on her lips. She's so engrossed in the movie that she doesn't notice me staring at her. She really is adorable. I don't want to embarrass her, so I leave her be, taking little peaks throughout.

****

"Jesse, Brandon's here," my mom shouts upstairs.

Fuck. I completely forgot that he was coming over. I've been so wrapped up in Maisie being home, that I forgot about everything else.

Maisie looks at my face and laughs.

"You forgot he was coming, didn't you?"

"Yes. Fucking hell. Now I'm going to have to get drunk," I reply, shaking my head.

"Why on earth would you have to get drunk? Just have a few," she replies, confused.

"You obviously don't know Brandon. You can't just have a few with him. You have to get completely obliterated. I apologize in advance for what I do. I can't be held accountable for my drunken actions." I cringe at the thought of what I could possibly do. I'll most probably end up pissing her off.

Giving me a stern expression, she replies, "Leave it to me." She gets up from the bed and walks to my bedroom door, giving me a wink before strutting down the hallway, her luscious hips swaying with every step. Damn it. She's made me get a boner just from watching her. I'm going to have to wait a few minutes. Otherwise, I'm going to jump her bones, and I don't care who sees.

Think of dead puppies. Yup, that works.

"Hey, bro," I say to Brandon when I'm finally downstairs.

Giving our usual fist bump, he replies, "I didn't think you were ever going to come down. I've started without you." He holds up his half empty bottle of beer. He doesn't waste any time does he.

"Sorry, had something to sort out. Pass me a beer then. I've got some catching up to do." he passes me a beer, and I gulp down half the bottle in one go. Man, this is some good shit.

"We'll be in the living room if you need us," my mom says, taking Maisie with her. I can see the worried expression on Maisie's face. She's never seen me really drink before, so she doesn't know what I'm like. She's only got her experience of her ex. I'm not like him, and besides, there are no girls here, and I don't swing for the same sex.

Taking a seat at the table, Brandon fiddles with the paper on his bottle as I take the seat across from him. He only ever does that when he has something to tell me.

"Just spit it out, whatever it is that you have to tell me," I tell him when he makes no move to speak.

"When you left last night, Tiffany rang me up," he says, looking at me and trying to gauge my reaction. He isn't going to get one. I don't give two fucks about her.

"And you're telling me this because...?" I trail off, wondering where he's going with this. I never told him what Tiffany did to Maisie. He probably thinks we are all okay. I'm going to try to keep it that way if I can. Maisie doesn't need any drama.

"I'm telling you this because she was completely out of it, Jesse. I mean, she's always liked to drink, but I've never seen her this bad." Worry lines his face. I don't know why he's worried. He hasn't ever been able to stand her.

"Well, did you sort her out then?" I ask.

"Yeah, I did, but why the fuck is she calling me for? That's usually your job." I shrug my shoulders in reply. I really don't want to hear any more of this conversation. Just thinking about her makes my blood boil. "What do you mean?" he asks, mimicking my shoulder shrug.

"It means, I don't know why she didn't call me, and to be honest, I'm glad she didn't. I've had enough of her shit to last me a lifetime. If I never hear from her again it will be too soon. Now, did you come over to bitch about Tiffany or to relax and have a drink?" I ask, hoping he takes the hint and changes the subject.

Luckily, he gets it and doesn't mention anymore on the topic.

"You heard anymore from *you know who*?" Brandon whispers so that no one over hears.

Rolling my eyes, because his topics of conversation tonight are killing me, I answer, "No. I told him I was done, and so far, he's not been back in contact. It's only a matter of time, though."

"Are you sure you don't want me to get someone to get rid of him for you? You know that I know people, Jesse," he says seriously. He reminds me of this every time shit goes down with my dad. As much as I hate him, I don't want to see the fucker dead. I just wish he would disappear from our lives.

Laughing at him, I say, "Thanks for the offer, but my answer is still the same." I take a gulp of my beer to wash down the anger tingling my body at the thought of him. Two conversations about people that piss me off so far, what's next?

"I'm still going to keep asking you. One day you might change your mind," He wishes. Brandon hates my dad just about as much as I do. He's witnessed firsthand what my dad is capable of, which is why he's always had my back and is my brother.

For the next hour, we only talk about funny topics, mostly about the latest chick he's banging. He's as much of a whore as I was. Now that I am a taken man, I am going to live vicariously through his life. I don't need to sleep with a different girl every night. Maisie is more than enough for me, but it's funny to hear his stories.

Five bottles of beer down, Maisie comes into the kitchen to join us.

"Hey, baby," I say, pulling her down into my lap. I've missed her for the last hour, even if she was in the room next door.

"Hi," she replies, smiling her adorable smile that lights up her whole face. I need to kiss her. It's been too long.

Gently guiding her head toward mine, I place my lips over her soft, sweet ones, savoring the feel of them.

Gagging noises pull me out of my sexual induced haze. Brandon is sitting there pretending to be sick from the sight of us. I lean over the table and punch him in the arm for being an ass. Maisie just laughs at him.

"Hey, fucker, knock it off," I warn him, trying to keep a straight face. All I want to do is laugh at him for being such a dick.

"Man, I don't want to see that shit. Please save it for the bedroom," he replies, waving his hand in the air.

"No such luck, man. Her lips are the best thing, and I will take advantage of them," I say, giving Maisie a wink, earning a blush from her.

"I'll be the judge of that. Maisie, give me your lips, babe," Brandon says, puckering his lips ready for a kiss.

No. Fucking. Way. Over my dead body, is he getting to infect my girlfriend's lips.

"You wish, Brandon," Maisie pipes up, laughing at him.

Putting his hand over his heart and gasping, he says, "You wound me, woman. Am I not good enough for you?"

That makes her laugh harder. I laugh too. He really is a joker.

"Jesse is more than enough for me," she says, leaning down to give me a kiss. Perfect answer.

I give Brandon a smug smile. He just smiles back at me, not at all phased that he got rejected.

I only have another two beers over the next hour. After last night, I don't want to drink too much. I don't need a repeat of how I felt this morning. Plus, I have Maisie, and needs my attention. I can't give her that if I'm completely drunk.

We've spent the last hour joking around, Maisie included. She's not really met Brandon until tonight, which is surprising seeing as we've been together nearly two months. They've gotten along really well tonight, though, which I'm glad about. Brandon was jealous of her when we first started dating, but now, I think he realizes why I love her.

"Well, I better be off. I'll leave you two love birds to go have some sexy time," Brandon says, laughing and scraping his chair along the floor.

He's drunk. It's not surprising, though, seeing as he drank the rest of my half as well as his own.

"How are you getting home, bro?" I ask. He better not say he's driving.

"I've got my car. How the fuck did you think I was going to get home?" he asks, raising his eyebrows at me like I just asked the most ridiculous question.

"You're not driving home in this state. I'll take you home, and don't bother arguing with me. I've hardly had anything to drink." I get the keys off the counter. "I'll be back in twenty. Go get into bed. I'll be there shortly," I tell Maisie, kissing her forehead.

"Okay. Be safe, though." She says goodbye to Brandon before walking upstairs.

"Come on then. Let's get you home, so I can get back to my girl," I say, walking out to my mom's car.

The first few minutes of the journey are silent. I'm starting to think he's fallen asleep when he suddenly says, "You've got a keeper there, Jesse. Don't mess it up."

"I know I do. She's the best thing to ever happen to me. I'm trying not to mess it up," I reply honestly. If anyone knows how shit scared I am about commitment, it's him.

"You won't mess it up. Just remember, you're not your dad. And every time that you think you're going to fuck it up, think of her face and never being able to see it again. It will kill you more than you know. Trust me."

Brandon never talks about feelings. Ever. Especially not his own. Which is why I'm confused right now. Is Brandon saying that he knows what it feels like to lose someone you love? He can't, though… He would have told me if that was the case. Wouldn't he?

"Brandon…" I say, not really knowing how to put it.

"Yeah, I've lost the only person I've ever loved before. You wouldn't think it, but I know what love feels like." Shit. He sounds all depressed right now.

"Why don't I know anything about this?" I ask, looking over at him staring out the window.

"No one knows. It's not something I go round broadcasting." He's silent for a few seconds. "You remember when I went to stay with my cousins in Texas last year for a few months?"

"Yeah,"

"Well she was my cousin, Katie's, best friend. I saw her the second I arrived. She was the most beautiful thing I'd ever seen. Bright red hair. The greenest eyes. She didn't look twice at me, though. We all went out one evening, and we started talking. I mean, really talking, none of this shit that I do with the girls down here to get them into bed. I got to really know her. We started spending some time on our own through the months while I was there. I fell fucking hard for her, man. We didn't sleep together until the second month. You know that's not like me. I usually sleep with the girl on the first day. I can remember everything about that night even now. Anyway, just before I'm about to leave to come back here, I go to her house to say goodbye and ask if I can see her again. I was willing to keep going down there to see her. When I got to her house, I saw her in the front yard kissing some other guy. So me being me, I went to confront her. Turns out, he was her boyfriend. I mean, I thought we had something, you know? Anyway, since then, I've sworn off girls. But you, you have a keeper."

Wow… What do I even say to that? We've never been the best with talking about our feelings, but I have to say something, right?

"Don't sweat it, bro. I didn't tell you all of that for you to feel sorry for me. Forget I ever told you that, okay? You know I don't do all that mushy shit." He laughs, but I can tell it's forced.

"Are you going to be okay?" I ask, worried for him. No wonder he's been sleeping around so much more since last year. He's trying to take his mind off the one who got away.

"Don't worry about me. I'm still breathing, aren't I? Plus, there are plenty more fish in the sea, and I'm not ready to settle down yet. I'm a lone wolf, my friend. Now, fuck off and go and make love to your girl." Brandon gets out of the car, slamming the door shut before I can form a response.

He's really shocked me tonight. That doesn't happen often with him. He's usually very black and white. I can't just forget it like he wants me to. He's obviously not handling it as well as he thinks he is. I won't bring it up again just yet. I'll give him time to heal, and then I'll bring it up, and I will question him about it, because now that I know what's happened, I can tell he is spiraling out of control.

****

When I arrive home, Maisie is fast asleep in one of my shirts. She looks too peaceful to wake up, so I carefully get into bed and pull her into my body, resting my chin on her head. Her scent instantly washes away my worries. I'm home now, where I belong, wrapped up with my beautiful girlfriend

CHAPTER SIXTEEN
MAISIE

I've been back at college for a week now, and I still haven't sorted things out with Chloe. I'm scared shitless, if I'm being honest. I was going to talk to her after Thanksgiving, but one day turned into another, then another. A week later, I've still not spoken to, let alone seen her. I wouldn't be surprised if she's moved someone else into the dorms. I know that she would need my permission for that, but Chloe does what she wants. Plus, she's made tons of friends since we've started, whereas I've made none.

I've spent every night since I got back at Jesse's. His mom says she doesn't mind, but I just feel guilty because I'm living there free of charge. I'm not helping to pay for any of the food that I'm eating or the essentials.

Jesse doesn't know it yet, but I've decided to go back to my dorm tonight. I can't avoid Chloe forever. She may not realize it yet, even if everybody else does, but she needs me. I've been the worst best friend. I need to step up to the plate and be there for her. I plan on being true to my word tonight.

After finishing up my classes for the day, I head over to Cafe Blanc. I'm in dire need of a caffeine fix right now. I'm sure that if I go another hour without caffeine, I may just get the shakes. I'm addicted to the stuff. It could be worse, though. I could be addicted to drugs.

My cell phone vibrates just as I'm about to walk through the door. Not looking where I'm going, I pull my cell out, seeing a text from Jesse. As I'm about to open it, someone smashes into me, sending my cell flying through the air and crashing on the floor. A loud crack reverberates through the air. Oh, fuck nuggets, there goes my screen. That's going to cost me money that I don't have to repair it.

"Oops," a high pitched female voice says in front of me.

Seeing who was rude enough to bump into me, I come face to face with the bitch herself. Tiffany. Go figure. Anybody else would have seen me standing there and said, 'Excuse me', or would have at least walked around me to use the other door. Not her, though. She just loves to make my life hell.

I haven't heard from her since she threatened to ruin me at Jesse's football match. I'd completely forgotten about it too, up until now. She must know that Jesse and I are together, especially as they hang around with the same group of people. I'm curious as to why she hasn't made good on her promise?

"Tiffanyyyyyyyy," I drawl, disdain dripping off my tongue.

"Maisie, Maisie, Maisie. You really should watch where you're going, you know. Some people wouldn't be as nice as I was. You're lucky only your cell took the brunt of it. Had it been someone else, it may have been you," she says, trying to sound sweet and innocent. She's anything but. She's the devil. She shakes her head at me in disappointment.

"Well, I must thank you then," I reply sarcastically, rolling my eyes at her.

"That is most certainly my pleasure," she says, mimicking thanking me by taking off an invisible hat.

Why didn't I ever punch her in the face?

Trying to stop myself from making good on that thought, I tell her, "Nice to see you as always, Tiffany."

"I'll see you around, I'm sure," she says, stepping away and waving at me.

I go to retrieve my cell from the concrete, only to watch in slow motion as she purposefully stands on it, the cell cracking underneath her platform wedges. *Fucker!!!* It's definitely broken now. I'm going to have to buy a new one, thanks to her.

She gives me a smug smile, grinding her foot for good measure. Breathe Maisie. Just breathe. She isn't worth jail time. Act indifferent, I tell myself.

Finally, she walks off, flicking her hair over her shoulder and not giving me a second look. If anybody was to walk past, they wouldn't think anything is wrong right now. Inside though, I'm one second away from pounding that bitch to the ground. I've never felt such hatred toward anyone as I do her.

Salvaging the broken pieces of my cell, I take out the sim before chucking the rest in the trash. I definitely need that coffee now.

****

"*She what?*" Jesse asks in disbelief when I tell him what his little bitch of a friend did.

"Exactly what I just told you she did, Jesse. That girl is a psycho. At least I've got a new cell now." I'm still in shock, not because she hurt me, because she didn't. It's just that what she did wasn't necessary.

"I'm going to have words with her. I don't care what you say, Maisie. This has gone too far. She laid low for a while, and now she's starting again. She won't stop. We both know that. I need to make myself clearer this time," he says, lost in thought.

Again? What does he mean, 'again'?

Confused, I ask him what he means. He looks up from the table, obviously not understanding what I just asked. So I ask again. I watch his face drain of color, instantly making me worry.

He takes a hold of my hands, his thumbs rubbing them back and forth. My skin prickles, and my palms sweat in fear of what he is about to tell me. I know I'm not going to like what he is about to say.

"Before I tell you, please don't be mad at me, baby. I did it to protect you." He rushes his words out.

I nod my head. I couldn't talk even if I tried; my throat is as dry as sandpaper right now.

"I know you told me not to say anything to her about when she confronted you, but I couldn't just stand back and watch her destroy you, baby. Because she would have, and I can't lose you. I went to see her after I left here, warning her to leave you alone or I would ruin her. I thought I'd made myself clear, but obviously she needs to be told again, or taught a lesson. I haven't decided yet..." he says, trailing off.

I can't believe it. I trusted him. We'd only been together a few hours at that time, and he had broken my trust. If he's kept that from me, what else has he kept from me? My body visibly shakes, thinking of all the things he could have lied about.

"Hey, calm down. I haven't kept anything else from you. I promise," he says, sounding sincere.

How can I believe him, though? He also sounded sincere when he promised not to speak to Tiffany, and look how that turned out. He went and pissed on our promise.

I frantically shake my head at him. I don't believe him. How can I? He knew I had trust issues. Men are all the same. You can't trust them as far as you can throw them, and for me, that isn't very far.

"H-h-how c-c-could you?" I stutter, my shock flying through the roof right now.

"I'm sorry, Maisie. I really am. You have to believe me, that I did it for your safety," he replies, eyes wide.

My breathing hitches. I can't breathe. *Shit.* I think I'm having a panic attack. My eyes search frantically around, looking for something, anything to help me. I haven't had an episode in so long, not since Matt. I need my parents.

"Maisie, look at me, baby. You need to breathe," Jesse says, suddenly crouching in front of me. I look into his worried eyes, feeling betrayed. This is his fault. I'm like this because he couldn't keep his promise. I knew he was the same as soon as I set my sights on him. I still gave him the benefit of the doubt, though.

Pushing him away, because I can't look at him at the moment, I then put my head between my legs. It's the best thing after a paper bag. Since I don't have one of those right now, this will have to do.

I stay like this for what feels like forever. Eventually, my breathing finally calms down, but I'm covered in sweat.

"Jesus, Maisie. That just scared the shit out of me. Are you okay?" Jesse asks. In my panic attack, I'd become completely oblivious to Jesse trying to help me. Looking at his face reminds me of why I had the damn panic attack in the first place.

My breathing starts hitching again, just from the sight of him. I need to leave before I have another episode. I can't handle another one. I feel drained. I just want to go to my room, sleep, and forget about everything. I'll deal with it all in the morning when I have a clear head. If I discuss it now, I'm likely to make a bad decision that I will probably regret in the morning. It's best if I just leave.

Ignoring his question, I push my chair back, standing up and looking anywhere but at him. "I'm going to be staying at the dorms from now on. I'll see you tomorrow." My voice comes out scratchy from my dry throat.

"Wait..."

I pause, looking at him. He looks so stressed. His hair is disheveled, like he's been running his hands through it for the last fifteen minutes. The lines on his forehead are pronounced from his frowning. I'd make a joke about it if I wasn't so heartbroken right now.

"Will I see you tomorrow?" he eventually asks.

"I don't know, Jesse. I need time to think," I reply honestly. I don't know what the outcome of this is going to be. I don't know if I can ever trust him again. Without trust, there isn't a relationship. It's the key to a successful one.

"Okay," he sighs dejectedly. His shoulders slump, his head hanging low. He looks like how I feel, and I don't know why, but I feel sorry for him. I shouldn't, though, not after what he's done. Except I do. I need to leave before I forgive him without thinking it through.

Not waiting for another word to be said, I leave his house, not once looking back. If I do, I will crumble and forgive him. I can't do that. The last thing I want is to be in relationship that ends in heartbreak. I thought my break-up with Matt was bad. If I broke up with Jesse, it would be heart shattering. I would never find myself again. That's why I need to think before I do something I could possibly regret.

****

I walk into my dorm room for the first time in nearly two weeks and see that the place is a tip. From the looks of it, Chloe hasn't lifted a finger since I left. There are take-out boxes lying over every surface, dirty clothes covering the floor, and neither bed is made, which is strange because I made mine before I left. So that must mean... *Eurghh, seriously, Chloe?* I'm going to have to chuck those sheets now. God only knows what they have seen.

Mentally shaking the disturbing thoughts away, I try to find spaces to walk on that aren't covered.

I try to change my sheets without touching them. It proves to be impossible. Damn you, Chloe. I'm going to kill you when I next see you. It's not a surprise that she's not here. She was hardly here before I went home. I'm going to have to apologize to her tomorrow instead.

Sheets changed, I go into the bathroom to change into my PJs. It's no better in here, either. Oh well. I'll deal with the mess tomorrow. I'm too tired right now.

After climbing into bed, I plug my headphones in to distract me from my disastrous day. The tears come anyway. Jesse betrayed me. It may not have been something big, but he still betrayed my trust. For that, I don't know if I can forgive him...

CHAPTER SEVENTEEN
MAISIE

Ow, shit. My ear really fucking hurts. Why does it hurt? Rubbing my ear, I realize that my ear bud has been digging into it. Now I remember why I don't wear them to bed anymore.

Sitting up, I stretch, feeling refreshed. I check my phone and see that it's eleven am. Wow, I slept for twelve hours straight. I must have drained myself more than I thought yesterday. I also see that I have five texts and ten missed calls. All from Jesse. I'm not ready to reply to him yet, though. He can wait a little longer.

"Nice of you to grace me with your presence," Chloe says sarcastically next to me.

My heart jumping through my throat, I turn toward her serious face, waiting for my heart beat to calm down. I think I might have also just peed myself a little.

This is the first time I've seen her since I went home. Before I left, she looked a mess. And now? She actually looks back to normal. It seems that she's taking care of her appearance again. It's good to see.

"Can we talk?" I ask, facing her. This could either go really well or very badly. Quite frankly, I'm scared shitless. Chloe doesn't forgive easily. I've just never been on this side of her before.

"Sure. Whatever," she replies, shrugging her shoulders nonchalantly.

I swallow the mighty lump that seems to have lodged itself in the middle of my throat before I tell her, "I'm sorry, Chloe. I've been a shitty friend. I should have stuck by you when you needed me, not pestered you. You would have told me eventually. I just wanted to be there for you, like you are for me. You just don't make it easy, is all."

The serious look leaves her face, being replaced with sorrow.

"No. I'm sorry, Maisie. I know you were just trying to help me, and I pushed you away. I wasn't ready to talk about it. I'm still not, but I will tell you eventually. Just not right now, okay?" she asks, begging me to understand.

"I understand," I tell her honestly. And I do. Chloe's always told me what's bothering her when she's ready. I just got stressed out, as it was between her and my brother. I didn't want the drama. However, I still had it, as I made it ten times worse by falling out with her.

"I should have apologized to you the day after, but I just didn't know how to. I was in the wrong, and I see that now. Can we just forget we ever fell out? I miss you, Maisie. I promise I will tell you when I can," she pleads, hopefulness etched on her face.

"Of course we can! I was going to talk to you about it over a week ago, but I was too scared to face you. You're a scary bitch when you want to be, you know?" We both laugh at that.

"I know I'm not the easiest person to fall out with, but I would never black list you, baby girl. You're stuck with me forever. Now, come here. I need a hug. It's been way too long," she replies, holding her arms out for me.

I leap into her arms, and we squeeze each other like we haven't seen each other in years. To us, it feels that long. We usually see each other every day. This is the longest we've gone without talking, let alone seeing each other.

"I'm sorry," we both say at the same time.

As I pull out of the hug, I look around the room, remembering the mess that I walked in on last night. How one person can make so much mess, I don't know. Chloe's never been the tidiest, but this is disgusting. I know I said I would clean it up tomorrow, but I've changed my mind. I'm not touching any of this. I don't know what it's seen.

I stand up, and to drive my point home, I spread my arms out around the room, indicating the mess. "What the hell happened here? It looks like a tornado hit our room."

Sheepishly looking down at the mess, she answers, "Yeah,

about that... I've been too distracted to clean up after myself. And in all fairness, I didn't know when you were coming back. You haven't been here for nearly two weeks."

Touché. Though at the moment, I'm sure even a homeless person wouldn't want to live here. I'm thinking it would have been healthier to stay with Jesse. Or not... I came back here to get away from him for a reason.

My heart aches at the thought of not talking to him today. He really is my whole world. Why did he have to go and do what he did?

I sit down on the edge of my bed, memories flashing through my mind of the things we have done together. We have made so many memories in two months. It could have been so much more. It would be sad to say goodbye to the possibility of not having more. I could have happily spent the rest of my life with him. It's all happened so fast, but I know he would have made me the happiest woman alive. A tear escapes my eye, dripping onto my cheek. This hurts more than I thought it would. I quickly wipe the tear away before Chloe can see it to ask what's wrong. I know that if she asks, I will tell her. I need her help so much more than I realized. She's always given me words of wisdom during my hardest times.

"Chloe, I need your help," I say, beating her to the punch.

The tears are coming down thicker now, blurring my vision.

"Hey, what's wrong? Why are you crying? I thought we were okay?" she asks, coming to sit next to me. Turning to face her, I wipe my eyes to see better, but it's no use. They fill up again as soon as I've wiped.

"We are okay," I say, my voice gruff.

"What's wrong then?

Wringing my hands together, I tell her everything.

When I'm finished, I inhale a deep breath, feeling better for spilling my guts to her. I just hope she can help me. I don't know if she can help with my impending trust issues that I now have, though. No one can help me with that except me. I just don't know if I will ever be able to trust Jesse again.

"Okay, let me get this straight. You're upset with him because he tried to defend you?" she asks, looking confused.

"It's not because he defended me. He went behind my back and confronted her after I told him to leave it. He broke my trust,

Chloe. You know that's a big deal for me, especially after Matt," I reply defensively.

"I'm just trying to help here, so don't get angry with me, Maisie. From what I can tell, he may have broken your trust, but he did it to help you. He wasn't doing it to make things worse. He loves you, Maisie. He's just protecting what is his. Any good guy would do the same, and you know that. Would you rather he didn't say anything to her? Because even I can tell you that she would have done a lot worse than break your cell phone. Don't give up on him because he tried to protect you. You need to realize what his intentions were before it's too late."

See, this is why I need my best friend. She always makes me see sense. If it wasn't for Jesse having words with Tiffany, we probably wouldn't have lasted this long. Tiffany would have found a way to ruin us. Even though she's acting up again, Jesse would nip that in the bud right away, protecting me. He's my savior. I just didn't realize it last night.

I'm such a dumbass.

"God, you're right. You're always fucking right. This is why I need you. I need to talk to Jesse now. I have to apologize for how I reacted." I reach for my new cell. Chloe's hand comes down on top of mine before I reach it.

"You're right. You do need me. Don't call him yet, though. Let him sweat a little bit longer," she winks at me, giving a devilish smile.

"Maybe I will." I put my hand back in my lap, returning her devilish smile. Jesse can wait a little longer. It won't kill him. This way, I can spend some time with Chloe, not worrying because everything will be okay later. I'm not giving up on Jesse. No chance in hell. Tiffany's going to have to do worse than break my cell.

He did a thoughtful thing for me, and I just threw it back in his face. I will make it up to him later on.

For the next few hours, I don't touch my cell phone when it goes off. I leave it; the whole time with a smile on my face because everything is going to be okay.

CHAPTER EIGHTEEN
JESSE

I haven't stopped pacing for nearly the whole day. I didn't get any sleep last night, so today, I'm running on energy drinks and coffee. Lots of it. I've got the shakes because I've consumed so much caffeine.

I'm getting worried. I haven't heard from Maisie since she left my house last night. She isn't answering my calls or texts. If I get her voicemail one more time, it's likely that I'm going to throw my cell at the wall.

I've thought about going to check on her, especially after the episode that she had last night, but she made it clear that I'm not welcome. She needs time to think. About us.

Oh God. When she had that panic attack last night, I felt helpless. It was my fault that she was in that position. If I hadn't have betrayed her trust like that, none of this would be happening. She would be in my arms right now, possibly making love. My idiotic actions may mean that I never get to hold her in my arms again, let alone make love to her.

Damn it. I'm such a piece of shit. I don't even deserve her forgiveness. I'm just like my father; throwing away the only good thing to ever happen to me. I'll never find anyone else like her for as long as I live. Nobody will ever compare to her. She's my perfect girl.

Punching my bedroom door out of frustration, I don't even feel the pain. I'm sure I will later. It doesn't matter, though. I should do

175

it a thousand more times. It's what I deserve after what I've done.

Checking the time for the millionth time today, I see that it's seven. I've still not heard anything from her. Fuck it. I can't stand around wondering what is going to happen. I have to go see her. I have to try and work things out with her.

I spot my guitar sitting in the corner of my room, thinking... It could work. I have to try. It's the only chance I've got at actually winning her back. And if it doesn't work? I don't want to think about that.

Strapping it onto my back, I don't think about it anymore. I'm just going to give it my best shot.

When I finally pull up on the sidewalk outside of the dorm rooms, the nerves kick in. My palms start sweating, and my body shivers, not from the cold but from the nerves. I can't be nervous. I need to be confident. Mentally shaking it off, I pull my shoulders up straight, marching through the doors and up the stairs like a man on a mission. And I am.

I loudly knock on the door and wait patiently for my whole life to answer the door.

CHAPTER NINETEEN
MAISIE

Knock, knock

The sound interrupts our movie marathon.

I pause the movie, and then get up from my bed, dusting myself off. I'm most probably covered in crumbs. Chloe and I have been eating junk food all afternoon. It was deserved after all the cleaning we did.

"Who the hell could that be?" Chloe asks, sitting up and looking at the closed door like she has some sort of superpower that allows her to see through it.

"I won't know until I answer it," I tell her sarcastically.

Still facing Chloe, I open the door. A smile breaks out on her face. It must be someone for her then.

As I turn to see who it is, my chest bumps against a familiar rock hard one. I would recognize that chest anywhere, all muscle and perfection.

I have to physically stop myself from resting my head on his chest and inhaling him deeply. I settle for a discrete sniff. It will have to do for now. I'll take full advantage of him later.

Right now, though, I'm playing cool. For all he knows, I still need time to think. I know it's cruel, but I'm still going to do it. Call it a lesson for hurting me in the first place, even if, in his mind, it was for good intentions.

Slowly dragging my eyes up his body, I notice that he's still wearing the same clothes from yesterday, and they are all crumpled.

His eyes look tired with huge bags underneath them. *Shit. What have I done? He looks a mess.*

He gives me a small smile, like he has no energy for anything bigger. I mirror his smile, not because I don't have the energy, but because I feel like a huge dick right now. He doesn't deserve this.

"Can I come in?" he asks gruffly when I make no move to let him in.

"Yeah… Of course," I tell him, moving out of the way to let him by.

As he closes the door behind him, I stand awkwardly, not knowing what to do now that he's inside. The room seems to have gotten smaller, or maybe I've suddenly become claustrophobic.

I sneak a quick peek at Chloe while Jesse's back is toward me, begging her to help me. The smile that was on her face when I opened the door has been replaced with worry. Every time she's seen Jesse, he's always looked good because he takes care of his appearance. Today? He looks like road kill.

Chloe shrugs her shoulders, as clueless as I am.

Just get on with it and apologize, I mentally scold myself.

"Look, Jesse…" I start, getting cut off.

"Don't talk. Just listen," he interrupts, motioning for me to sit down on my bed.

Obeying his command, I sit down on the edge, watching as he pulls something over his shoulder.

His guitar.

How did I not notice that? I must have been so shocked by his appearance that I failed to notice anything else. Why did he bring his guitar here, though? I've never heard him play it before, even when I've begged him.

He opens his case up on the floor, pulling his guitar out with care. Chloe and I share a look, both wondering what he's doing. He doesn't say one word the whole time, and neither do I. I'm confused as to what's happening right now.

Guitar in place on his stomach, he begins tuning.

It feels like forever has passed when he's finally ready. I'm starting to get fidgety. I can't take my eyes off of the beautiful man in front of me, who by the looks of it, I have destroyed.

"I know I've always said no to playing for you in the past. I just wanted to wait for a special moment, but I guess now is as good as any. I hope you like it," Jesse, says, nervousness seeping out of his pores. I've never seen him like this before. Where is my confident, cocky man?

He starts to strum his guitar, the tune sounding familiar. I can't place the song until he starts singing the first verse.

One Direction - Little things. One of my favorite songs, the words are just beautiful, but it's even better now that Jesse is singing those words to me. And his voice? Wow. He has the smoothest voice I have ever heard. It's beautiful, hypnotizing me. I'm drawn into him, and I can't seem to focus on anything else.

Tears well up in my eyes. He chose a beautiful song to sing to me, letting me know that he loves all of my imperfections.

He stops singing, carrying out the last few notes of the song.

As he places his guitar down on the floor, I wipe my tears away, watching him in silence. Jesse stands up and focuses his attention on me, neither of us uttering a word. I'm speechless. It was the most romantic gesture I have ever witnessed.

"That was so romantic," Chloe whispers, voicing my thoughts exactly.

Jesse blushes from the compliment. I'm sure he's never been called romantic in his life, but for me, he is changing his ways. I have to sort this out.

Swallowing past the emotional lump lodged in my throat, I say, "Come here, you romantic fool!" Jumping up from the bed, my arms wide open, I jump onto his stomach, holding onto him for dear life.

I'm home again. God, I've missed him. It's only been a day since I last saw him. This is how I know that he's the one. I want to spend all of my time with him, hating it if I'm away from him for too long.

Tears stream down my face, soaking his crumpled shirt. They aren't sad tears. God no. They are happy tears; happy that everything will be fine again.

"God, Maisie. I'm so sorry, baby," Jesse says quietly into my ear, his voice filled with sadness and regret.

"Everything is okay now," I console him.

His grip gets tighter, crushing me. I laugh.

"Do you forgive me?"

"Without a doubt. I'm sorry that I didn't see where you were coming from. I was just so pissed that you betrayed my trust that I was too blind to see your intentions." I kiss his neck, giving him

179

more proof that I've forgiven him, but also because I've missed him; mind, body and soul.

"Thank God!" is all he says before his lips come crashing down on mine. I'm ready and waiting for him, though. I kiss him back like a starved woman. I am a starved woman. I haven't felt his lips for twenty-four hours. That's too long if you ask me.

As I run my hands through his already messy hair, he deepens the kiss.

I moan from the pure satisfaction I'm feeling right now.

"Ahem," Chloe interrupts, reminding us that we aren't alone.

I was so in the moment that I'd completely forgotten she was here. Jesse puts me down, his arm going around my waist so that there's still contact.

Looking at her sheepishly, I cringe. "I'm sorry," I tell her, my face burning up. She must have had a show.

Shrugging her shoulders, a smirk in place, she replies, "Hey, as much as I like sex, I don't like to watch other people practically dry humping. I can go out if you want to carry on?"

"If you don't mind?" Jesse speaks up before me.

"No! This is your room too, Chloe. We can leave," I tell her, giving Jesse the stink eye for being so rude.

"No, no, no. It's fine. Evan texted me anyway, asking if I want to come over. I've already told him yes, so he will be here any minute now."

Hmm… I didn't know that she was still in contact with him. I wouldn't, though. I haven't been here for her, so I don't know who she's talking to and who she isn't. I'm not going to lie, but it pisses me off that she's still seeing him when something is going on with her and Jake.

Trying to hold my tongue on that matter, I smile and nod my head. It's all I can manage right now. I need a few minutes to process it. I'll talk to her later when Jesse's gone, just to get some insight on the situation.

As I move to sit on the bed, a horn blares loudly. Chloe jumps up, getting her shoes and jacket. It must be the mighty Evan. Then she's gone, leaving Jesse and I alone to discuss our troubles.

Silence is all that greets us for a few minutes. We're just watching each other, neither of us knowing where to start. The silence is making me nervous, so I bite my lip, giving me something to focus on.

Jesse, growls, his eyes squinting. What is his problem? This only makes me bite harder. I've always had a problem with that. Sometimes, I bite so hard, I cut myself. It's a bad habit, but one I can't break because, most of the time, I don't even realize that I'm doing it.

He jumps on top of me, crushing me and pushing me into the mattress. His lips come down on mine, pulling my lip from between my teeth. His tongue seeks entry, tangling with mine. I lift my hips, rubbing against his hardness.

Our clothes are off in record time, with Jesse resting over me, slowly entering me. It's slow, sweet torture.

Starting off slow, he showers me with love, showing me with his actions how sorry he is.

We're finished all too soon, both of us having a mind shattering orgasm, leaving us breathless. Turning on my side to face him, love overwhelms me. He may have his flaws, but in my eyes, they are what make him perfect.

"Wow," I say, giving him a satisfied smile.

Laughing, he replies, "If that is what make-up sex is like, we should definitely fight more often." That earns a smack from me. It's true; that was probably the best sex we've ever had. If I wasn't so tired, I would definitely be up for a replay.

"We don't need to argue to have amazing sex. It's always amazing. Plus, our arguing doesn't look good on you. You looked like a bag of shit when you walked in earlier," I tell him seriously.

"Geez, Maisie, talk about wounding a guy," he says, feigning hurt. It makes me laugh.

"I'm being serious. Have you not showered or something? I'm guessing you haven't, since you're still wearing yesterday's clothes."

Giving me his are you serious face, he tells me, "I've been too frustrated with myself to do anything but pace my bedroom all day. I'm running on caffeine right now. I'm sure I'm about to zonk out at any minute."

"Aww, my poor baby," I say, stroking his face.

Jesse singing to me earlier pops into my head, changing my train of thought. I melt inside, just remembering it. I smile, hearing his voice in my head, and remembering the way he looked as he played his guitar with so much precision. It was sexy as hell. He is sexy as hell. And he's all mine!

"What are you smiling about?" Jesse asks, distracting me from my day dream.

What is in front of me is just as good as my day dream; Jesse in all his naked glory. Mmmm…

"Hello? Earth the Maisie," he says, poking me in the shoulder. *Shit, I must have zoned out again. Get a grip, Maisie. You've seen him naked before.* I will never get tired of looking at his beautiful body, the body I want to lick all over while running my hands over his hard pecs at the same time.

"Yes?" I ask, shaking my head to rid myself of my distracting thoughts.

"What are you thinking about that is making you smile like that?"

"Oh, just you singing to me earlier," I tell him dreamily. He laughs uncomfortably at me. "Don't be ashamed. It was beautiful, Jesse. The most romantic thing anybody has ever done for me. Don't tell anybody this, *but you sing it better than One Direction.*" I whisper the last part to him, giving him a wink.

"Thank you, baby," he says, accepting the compliment. Good, because I would have fought him on it. "I've been learning that song for about a month now. I was going to sing it to you on our three month anniversary, but I needed to do something to win you back. It was my last resort. Now, I have nothing special for our anniversary."

"It will be special because I'm with you. I don't need songs. They are nice, but I just need you."

"Come here, you soppy fool." Cuddling into him, I listen to the steady rhythm of his heartbeat until I can't keep my eyes open anymore.

CHAPTER TWENTY
JESSE

It's been a week since Maisie and I made up, and we are now stronger than ever. Our trust has spiked to higher grounds. We both realize we have each other's best interests at heart. All in all, we are both extremely happy right now.

Today is the day that I have been dreading for the last week. The day after we made up, Maisie asked if I would meet her parents this weekend. I begrudgingly agreed. This week has been the longest week of my life. I've nearly cancelled a thousand times, and today isn't any better. We're leaving in an hour, and I'm this close to cancelling for real. I feel sick to my stomach with nerves. It's not that I don't want to meet her parents, because I really do. I'm just not sure if I'm ready yet. I have no experience with meeting girls' parents. The only experience I've had is from watching movies. That didn't end well, which gives me a bad omen about today.

I'm doing my usual pacing this morning, waiting for Maisie to come over. My mom keeps looking at me like I've lost my mind. She's been repeatedly telling me 'not to worry' and 'they will love you'. Yeah, she doesn't know about all the things that I've done. To her, I'm the sweet little boy who does nothing wrong; how wrong she is. I know Maisie's dad will be able to see right through me. It's a guy thing. We can spot a dickhead a mile away.

"Jesse, will you sit down, for crying out loud?" My mom scolds, sitting on the sofa trying to read, looking as cool as a cucumber, when I'm anything but.

I don't argue with her, but just sit down, tapping my leg instead.

"And you can cut that out as well," she says, pointing at my leg.

Crossing my leg over the other, I sit forward, staring at her. "Mom, are you sure they're going to like me? You know I've never done this kind of shit before."

"Jesse, will you stop panicking? They will love you, especially when they see how much you care for their daughter. That's all any parent cares about," she says affectionately.

Nodding my head, I look out the living room window, at the empty street. It doesn't help my nerves. Spinning my head back toward my mom, who has just started reading again, I tell her, "I don't think I can do this, Mom. I'm going to have to cancel." I stand up and start to pull my cell phone out of my pocket to call Maisie.

"You will do no such thing, Jesse Cohen! Where is my confident boy? The one who doesn't give a damn what people think about him? Who will try his best to prove his intentions, and who certainly doesn't let people down? I didn't raise this boy who is about to cancel on his girlfriend when she is excited to show you off. Now, sit your ass back down on that couch and watch some damn TV or something. Maisie will be here to get you soon, so sort it out before I slap you." Wow... I haven't seen feisty Mom in so long that it's shocked me.

Staring wide eyed at my mom's serious face as she glares at me, I ask, "Did you just tell me off?"

Nodding her head abruptly, she replies, "Yes, I did, and if I have to do it again, I'm grounding you." Then she gives me a wink.

That's all it takes for me to crack up laughing.

"Well, if I'd have known that was all it took to make you relax, I would have threatened to ground you hours ago. Hell, even last week. You've been nothing but a pain in my ass since Maisie asked you to go with her. I could have strung you up a few times, you know?"

Arghh shit. There goes my good mood within a second. It was nice while it lasted. My face goes flat, my knee shaking again. I check the time. It's only been five minutes since I last checked it. How long is Maisie going to be?

"I'm going upstairs. I can't sit here and watch you anymore. You're getting on my nerves," my mom says, getting up from her seat.

She doesn't understand what I'm going through right now. She's not the guy. She's never been the guy. Parents always love the woman, but never the man. We have to work hard for acceptance.

A car engine makes me stand up abruptly. I race to the window and see Maisie coming down the road.

Quickly getting my overnight bag, I grab my wallet, shouting a goodbye to my mom, and head out the door. I'm in the car before she even cuts the engine.

"Someone's eager," Maisie says, laughing.

She is so beautiful with her hair curly and framing her face today, with minimal make-up on that shows off her flawless features. My nerves instantly vanish being near her. Staring at her plump lips, which are open from her laughing, I sweep her hair behind her ear, and lean my forehead against hers.

I don't make a move to kiss her. Right now, I just need to smell her.

I inhale deeply, so that her sweet scent goes to the back of my nose, and then breathe out a sigh of relief. I don't know what I'd do if she ever changed her body lotion. This is home for me; my safe place, my comfort. I'd be lost.

"Are you okay, Jesse?" she asks, looking at me worriedly.

"Shh, I just need a minute," I reply, taking another sniff.

She doesn't reply, just lets me carry on what I'm doing. She knows me well enough to know when I need a moment to relax.

When I'm calm, I give her a brief kiss on the lips.

"Let's go then, firecracker. To the parents' house we go!" I say in a chanting voice, pointing behind me.

Maisie rolls her eyes at me, reversing out of the drive.

****

"We're here," Maisie says, nudging me awake.

I must have fallen asleep. I'm glad I did. For the three hours plus that I was awake, I was a nervous wreck, hardly engaging in conversation.

"Okay. Just give me a minute to wake up before we go in, please. I don't want to look like shit." She laughs. I would laugh too, but I'm sweating so badly right now. I'm not finding anything funny.

As I take in the house in front of me, it looks huge. It's a normal size, but I feel really small compared to it. I'll feel even smaller when I'm inside.

God, I wish Jake was here. Then I'd have a guy on my side. He's not here, though, as apparently he's had a falling out with his parents. Great timing for that, buddy. I need you!

After staring at the house for what feels like hours, I mentally shake myself. Let's just get this over and done with. What's the worst that could happen? That they hate me? Or they might love me. I just hope it's the latter.

Finding Maisie just staring at me, I give her my bravest smile and say, "Come on then, firecracker. Let's go meet the parents."

She gives me a cautious smile in return, and then moves to get out of the car.

Meeting her at the front of her car, I grab her hand, as we head toward the front door. The door swings open before we have a chance to knock, scaring the shit out of me.

A man around my height but stockier stands on the threshold, looking at Maisie with adoration in his eyes. It's obvious he really loves her, which makes my job of getting him to approve of me harder. *Great.*

I watch him give Maisie a hug before he realizes I'm here.

"I take it you're Jesse?" Wow, his voice is deep; a lot deeper than mine, and that's saying something. His eyes narrow, inspecting me from head to toe.

"Yes, sir," I say politely, smiling and trying to act confident.

Don't let him see your fear. He will thrive on that, I mentally tell myself.

"Nice to meet you, Jesse. I've heard a lot about you," her dad says vaguely, shaking my hand. Hard. Maisie watches the interaction, not saying a word. Wise woman.

I hope they are good things. I nod in reply.

"Let them in for God's sake, Tim!" a woman says behind him, whom I'm guessing is Maisie's mom.

Tim moves aside, letting us in. A woman who looks the spitting image of Maisie, only older, stands in the hallway with a welcoming smile on her face. I instantly feel at ease looking at this woman. She and Maisie could be twins.

"Hey, mom," Maisie says, giving her mom a hug.

Her mom whispers something into her ear, causing Maisie to

blush. God only knows what she said. I'll have to ask Maisie later.

Stepping up next to Maisie, I take hold of her mom's hand, giving it a kiss. It may be old fashioned, but it's causing her to blush. *One point to me!*

"You must be Theresa," I say, still holding her hand.

Next to me, Maisie is standing there trying not to laugh. I'm glad she finds this funny. My mom loves her. She didn't even have to try. I have to try. Maybe not with her mom, but her dad is a different matter. I shiver just thinking about it.

"And you must be the charming Jesse," her mom drawls.

"That I am." I give her a wink, dropping her hand.

Taking hold of Maisie's hand again, I give her a real smile. I like her mom.

"You never told me he was such a charmer, Maisie," her mom scolds playfully.

"You never asked," she replies, laughing at her mom's red face.

Tim coughs behind us, reminding us that he is there. Shit. Maybe he isn't pleased that his wife seems to be affected by me. Even older ladies aren't immune to my good looks.

"Let's go in the living room, shall we? Then we can get to know Jesse better." Tim walks in ahead of us, stone faced, authority seeping out of his pores.

Without even having to say anything, he's been letting me know who is in charge since I walked in. I respect that. If I had a daughter, I would do the same.

"Don't worry about him. He's a big softy once you get to know him," Theresa whispers behind me. I hope she's right.

When we are all comfy on the sofas, I look toward at Maisie. She's sitting there biting that damn lip of hers. Giving her a look, I tell her with my eyes to cut it out. I won't be held accountable for my actions if she carries on, and I'm sure her dad won't be too pleased if I take his daughter on the sofa. I think he might just get his shot gun, if he has one, and kill me.

"So, Jesse," Tim pipes up, starting the conversation. "I hear that you're nineteen and play football. Is that correct?"

"Yes, sir,"

"Please, call me Tim," he tells me, still not cracking a smile. He's going to be a tough one to crack.

"Yes, that's correct, Tim." I tell him, referring to his name like he asked. Now that I've said it, I hope he doesn't think I was being a smart ass.

"And you met Maisie in English?"

No we didn't. We met when I bumped into her on the sidewalk, trying to get a better look at her assets. Though, I won't be telling her dad that, not if I value my life, and I want to make a good impression.

"Yes, I sat down next to her. I thought she was beautiful," I tell him, sneaking a look into Maisie's eyes, asking if I'm doing okay. She subtly nods her head, letting me know to carry on.

Theresa is swooning in her chair from what I've just said about her daughter. She would get along well with my mom. They both seem likes romantics.

"Yes, she is beautiful. Look, I'm going to cut straight to the point because I'm sure you know about Maisie's ex and how he messed her around."

Maisie groans next to me.

Ignoring her groan, he carries on, "I want to make this clear. If you even so much as hurt a hair on her head, or hurt her emotionally... Hell, if you even make a tear escape from her pretty eyes, I will hunt you down and kill you myself. Do I make myself clear?" he finishes, staring me straight in the eyes.

Staring straight back at him, I tell him honestly, "I won't intentionally hurt your daughter. I can't promise that I won't fuck up from time to time, excuse my language, but I love your daughter. The last thing I want to do is hurt her. It would kill me if I did. I want to be there for her and protect her, and I'm trying my best. That's all I can do." I don't blink the whole time. He needs to realize that I'm not giving him some bullshit excuse. I care about Maisie more than anything in this world.

Nodding his head once, he replies, "That's all I'm asking for, son. Welcome to the family." He smiles for the first time.

I breathe for what feels like the first time in minutes. So far, so good; I've been accepted. Now, I have to try and not mess it up. It shouldn't be too hard. I hope.

We spend the next hour getting to know each other, laughing, and joking around. Maisie seems happier than when we first arrived, which is good. I think she was as worried as I was that they wouldn't like me. Now that she knows they do, she can relax. So can I.

"There's someone I want you to meet," Maisie tells me when

her parents leave the room.

"Who's that, baby?" I ask, rubbing her hand in slow circles.

I kept the contact to a minimum while her parents were in here with us. Now that they've gone into another room, I have some making up to do. I was starting to get withdrawal symptoms.

"I used to work in the store down the road. The lady who owns the store doesn't have any family, and I promised to see her every time I came back down. Last time I was down, I only saw her for a few minutes. Plus, I want you to meet each other. She will love you," Maisie says with an affectionate smile on her face.

This lady obviously means a lot to her.

"Of course. Let's go then."

We get up, Maisie lets her parents know where we are off to, and then we drive the short drive to the store.

****

Walking into the store, I'm instantly hit with the smell of hotdogs. My stomach grumbles, reminding me that in my nervous state, I forgot to eat today.

"Maisie, is that you dear?" an older lady says from behind the counter.

"Yes, it's me. I've brought someone for you to meet." She grabs my hand, dragging me toward the lady.

"It best be that hunk of a boyfriend of yours that you showed me last time you were here. Otherwise, I don't want to know," she laughs, sounding throaty.

Giving Maisie a wink, we stop in front of her.

"Good gracious. He is better looking than in that picture you showed me." She fans herself, smiling at us.

"Mrs. Jenkins, this is Jesse. Jesse, Mrs. Jenkins," Maisie says, introducing us.

Taking a hold of Mrs. Jenkins's hand, I give it a kiss. "Nice to meet you."

"He's a gentleman, too. You can't go wrong with one of them," she says, winking at Maisie. "Nice too meet you too, Jesse," she says, blatantly checking me out. "If only I was fifty years younger."

We laugh at that.

"Hey, don't laugh. Just because I'm past it doesn't mean I don't know a good looking guy when I see one."

"Please, stop," Maisie says, full on belly laughing.

I have a smug smile on my face. Hey, don't judge; I am a good looking guy. It never gets old being told it, either.

"I won't say any more, except that you've done better than the last one. I never did like him," Mrs. Jenkins whispers that last part.

That comment stops Maisie laughing straight away. It's still a touchy subject, especially after what happened the last time she was down.

"Come sit down. I'll get us some chairs," she says, pointing to the one that she was sitting on.

"You two stay here. I'll go and get them. Just tell me where they are," I tell her. She doesn't need to be picking up chairs and bringing them down when I can do it.

"Go into that room. It's the staff room. There should be some in there, dear," she says, pointing to a door to my right.

Nodding, I go and retrieve the chairs.

MAISIE

Watching Jesse go to get the chairs, my heart soars with love. He really is so thoughtful, always thinking of others.

As soon as he's out of sight, Mrs. Jenkins starts whispering, "He seems like a nice young man."

I nod, a smile on my face; a true genuine smile. She hasn't seen me smile like this in a while.

"I can tell. You have that smile on your face that I haven't seen in a while. It's nice to see it. You always did have a beautiful smile," she says, smiling, her eyes crinkling. See, what did I just say? It's like she can read my mind.

"He makes me very happy. I love him. I know some may say it's too soon, but I really do. He is the most amazing man I've ever met. He's completely different from Matt," I tell her honestly. I know that, out of everybody, she won't judge me.

"He loves you, too, you know. I can see it in his eyes when he looks at you. He looks at you like George used to look at me. You two have a special kind of love. Don't throw it away, as you may never find another like it."

Before I can reply, Jesse comes back into the room. I wouldn't have known what to reply to that anyway. Plus, how does she know this stuff? I always knew she was wise.

After plopping down in one of the chairs, we spend the next hour with Mrs. Jenkins as she asks Jesse millions of questions. I think she knows him better than I do right now, and that's saying something.

"We best be off. Dinner will be ready soon," I tell Jesse, checking the time. Jesus, it's nearly five.

"Okay. Would you like me to put the chairs back?" Jesse asks Mrs. Jenkins.

"No dear, it's okay. You never know. Someone else might come in to see me for a while," she replies.

That's probably not true, but I'm not going to question her on it. I just hope someone does come in to see her. I hate the thought of her being here all alone.

"You two get off now, before your mom comes in complaining that I'm keeping you hostage," she jokes, shooing us away.

Giving her a hug before I leave, I tell her that I'll come and see her at Christmas. I don't want to leave her alone on a special day, especially when she doesn't have any other family. I'm the closest thing she has.

Jesse gives her a hug after me. "It was nice to meet you. I hope we will see each other again soon."

"Of course we will, dear. You keep yourself safe and look after my Maisie for me, okay?" she asks, giving him a pat on the arm.

"Of course I will."

After saying our goodbyes, we leave the store and head toward out to my car.

"She's sweet," Jesse tells me, grabbing my hand.

Giving him a smile, I tell him, "She really liked you. She was even flirting with you. I've never seen her like that before. It was embarrassing."

"Well, what's not to like? Look at me, baby. I'm a God," he tells me, pointing at himself. Pushing him, I laugh at how big-headed he is. He really does love himself, doesn't he?

I won't admit it, but it's true. Women of all ages notice Jesse. I've gotten used to it now. I've not met one person who is immune to his good looks. Even my mom was swooning at him earlier.

"Who's that standing next to your car?" Jesse asks, looking in the direction of my car with a confused expression on his face.

I turn to see who he's looking at and groan.

Great; just who I want to bump into. Matt…

I wonder how long he's been standing out here. He sure as hell didn't come into the store. I really don't want Jesse and Matt to meet each other. Who's to say what Jesse will do, especially if Matt starts his shit again like he did the other week?

"This is going to be fun," I say under my breath.

Stopping in front of Matt, I don't say anything to him. I just stand still, staring him down and letting him know that I'm not in the mood for him to start shit.

"We have to stop bumping into each other here, Maisie," he says, arms crossed over his chest as he leans up against my car.

Is he being serious? I'm not the one who's been waiting at his car for God knows how long.

Giving him a polite smile, since two can play at this game, I tell him, "We do. So how long have you been waiting for me to get out?"

His cocky smile slips a bit, but he regains his composure quickly. Caught you out, buddy. One point to me.

"Oh, not long," he says, waving his hand in the air nonchalantly. "Are you going to introduce me to your friend?" He looks at Jesse, his eyes sweeping him from head to toe, disgust on his face.

He blatantly knows who Jesse is. I wouldn't be surprised if he's done research on him.

"Yeah, who is this guy?" Jesse asks from beside me, anger in his voice.

I think, deep down, he has an idea of who this is. He just wants to be sure.

Facing Jesse, I introduce them. "Jesse, meet Matt. Matt, meet Jesse."

Jesse nods, holding his hand out for Matt to shake. "Nice to finally meet you, Matt. I've heard all about you."

Matt looks toward at me, narrowing his eyes. Yeah, that's right, buddy. You didn't expect me not to talk about you, did you?

Giving him an innocent look in return, I grab Jesse's hand tighter, silently communicating that I'm uncomfortable.

"Anyway, it was nice to see you again, Matt, but we best be off," I tell him, hoping he takes the hint. He doesn't move. He just stands there, like he has all the time in the world. He probably does.

"Leaving so soon? Why can't I get to know your friend?"

He doesn't really want to get to know Jesse. He just wants to be awkward. If he's wanting to push my buttons, he's doing a mighty fine job of it. This is one of the things I always hated about Matt. If he wants to do something, he will try until he gets it. This is no exception, except this time, I'm not backing down. He has no reason to get to know Jesse. They most probably won't see each other again after today. I hope.

I don't want my past and my future mixing. I left my past behind months ago. I don't need Matt rubbing in Jesse's face that we used to date. Jesse can get very territorial, and I'm sure that will set his caveman side off.

"I don't think that's going to happen," I tell him honestly.

"Why not?" he asks, feigning confusion.

"Because, you don't need to know who I am, bro. We will probably never see each other again, so there's no need to get to know each other," Jesse pipes up, saving me from having to answer.

From the hard look on Matt's face right now, he isn't happy with that answer.

"Because, *bro*, Maisie is my ex, and I want to make sure her new boyfriend is treating her like she deserves to be treated. I don't want her going out with just anybody. She deserves the best."

Ooooh, that is just bullshit. He doesn't care about me or my feelings. He's just caring about himself here, trying to eye up the competition. Well, there is no competition. Jesse wins hands down.

"Well, you should have thought about that before you cheated on her and lost her. I won't be stupid enough to make the same mistake you did. You see, I realize what I have, unlike you. I don't take Maisie for granted. I put her first, protect her, and love her, something you failed to do. I fixed her after you left her broken. She is the most amazing woman I know, so please don't tell me how to look after her. I've done a pretty good job so far, without your help," Jesse replies, starting to get angry.

His jaw his set, pronouncing his square jaw. His eyes are fixed on Matt.

"Come on, Jesse. Let's go. He's not worth it," I say, trying to pull him away.

"Yeah, you listen to her, you piece of shit," Matt says, trying to goad Jesse.

All hope of leaving without a fight is now out the window. Biting my lip, I wait for Jesse to lose his shit. I can feel it coming. Nobody talks to him like that. If Matt knew that, he wouldn't have said it.

"What the fuck did you just call me?" he asks, his voice dangerously cool. That's even scarier than him shouting.

"I said, listen to her, you piece of shit," he repeats sarcastically.

I'm going to punch Matt in a minute. He doesn't know who he's messing with. Jesse will destroy him.

"Matt, leave it," I warn him, giving him an out.

"Don't worry, Maisie. I'm not going to hurt him. Like you said, he isn't worth it," Jesse says, turning to look at me, the cold look being replaced with affection.

That's when I see Matt's fist fly toward Jesse's face out of the corner of my eye. It all happens so fast. I don't even have time to warn Jesse, but he doesn't need warning. He captures Matt's fist, throwing his other fist into Matt's face. A loud crack reverberates through the parking lot. Shit, that has to hurt. I'm pretty sure a bone just cracked.

"Arghhh," Matt shouts, his free hand going to his jaw.

Jesse grabs my arm, moving me to the driver's door.

"Get in the car," he tells me, his voice telling me not to argue with him.

After getting in, I open his door, except he can't get in. Matt is still in the way. Watching from the safety of my car, I see Jesse lean in close, whispering something to Matt.

I can't hear what is being said, but from the looks of it, Jesse isn't being very friendly. I don't blame him. Matt was out of line. He deserved much more than what he got. I'm surprised Jesse only hit him once.

Matt moves away from the car, allowing Jesse to get in. When he's closed the door, I start the engine, leaving the parking lot and Matt behind.

The ride home is silent. Jesse still seems to be angry, his jaw still locked tight from where he's grinding his teeth. Matt really riled him up, and knowing Jesse, he's fighting with himself on turning back around and beating the crap out of him.

Cutting the engine outside my house, I turn in my seat to face him.

"Come on. Let's go inside."

"Wait... He's a douche," Jesse states seriously.

"I know. He was out of line back there, but it's over now, so let's go inside and forget about it, okay?" I tell him.

"What did you ever see in him?" he asks, looking lost in his own world.

Do we really have to talk about this now? It's making me uncomfortable.

Sighing, I tell him honestly, "He wasn't always a douche. When I first met him, he was really nice. He was interested in me. Back then, not many people paid attention to me. I wasn't popular, but I wasn't geeky. I was normal on the social status. So, when he took an interest in me, I felt flattered, and I fell for him. We were together a long time, Jesse. It wasn't until he did what he did that I realized what he was really like. He didn't really care for me. He was popular, could have had any girl he wanted, when he wanted. I was foolish to think that I was ever enough for him. I thought I loved him. Now, I know that it wasn't love. It was infatuation."

He nods, taking in what I just told him. I swallow, praying that he will leave it now.

I'm starting to think that this place is a bad omen. Both times that I've been down, I've bumped into Matt. If my parents didn't live here, I probably wouldn't come back. There are too many bad memories here.

We're silent for a few minutes, just looking out the window. I don't have a clue about what's going through his head right now. I just hope this doesn't ruin us. Matt means nothing to me anymore. I hope Jesse realizes this.

"Come on, then. Let's go and have dinner. I'm starving," Jesse finally says, giving me his usual beautiful smile, dimples and all. It makes my tummy flutter.

Feeling relieved, we get out of the car.

We don't mention what happened at the store to my mom and dad. We just act like everything is okay. I'm thankful that he doesn't mention it. My dad would probably go down to Matt's house and kill him for sure this time.

After dinner, we all go into the living room and watch a movie. My dad has finally warmed up to Jesse, which makes me happy. They seem to be getting along really well, joking and laughing with each other, like they've known each other for years.

Mom and I have been sharing secret looks at each other all

night. We both knew that they would get along. They may not realize it, but we have, after just one day of them knowing each other. They are more alike than they think.

Getting into bed hours later, I wait for Jesse to get out of the bathroom. Noticing his clothes on my bedroom floor makes me smile. I was surprised when my parents allowed Jesse to sleep in my room. I used to have to sneak Matt in through the window. That probably had to do with the fact that they weren't keen on him, but they seem to love Jesse. I'm not going to complain. I'm so happy that they are getting along.

"Hey, what are you thinking about that causes that huge smile on your face?" Jesse asks, startling me. I didn't hear him come back into the room. He just scared the crap out of me.

"Oh, just that I'm happy that my parents love you and are letting you sleep in my room," I tell him as I turn onto my side to face him.

His hair is all wet from just getting out of the shower, his skin all shiny. He looks so sexy when he's just had a shower. I dream about him like that sometimes. He really is an Adonis. My Adonis.

"I'm glad they love me too. Do you know how nervous I was this morning? My mom threatened to ground me because I was getting on her nerves so much. I haven't been grounded since I was fourteen!" he tells me, causing me to laugh.

I can't imagine his mom getting on to him. She's always so relaxed.

"Yeah, you go ahead and laugh." He looks at me with amusement on his face. "It's hard for us guys to meet the parents, especially the dad. When I first saw your dad, I was like, 'oh shit, he's going to kill me'. He looked intimidating as shit!" I laugh harder, full on belly laughs.

Everyone says my dad is scary. I don't see it, but I've never had a reason to be scared of him.

"I can see where you're coming from," I tell him, trying to make him feel better. I really don't see it, but oh well.

"You're so full of shit," he says, jumping on top of me and starting to tickle me. God no. Not this again.

Laughing, I try to catch my breath, while trying to push him off of me. He weighs a ton!

"Jesse, get off of me," I say through my laughter.

"Uhuh. No way, missy, not until you apologize for lying to me."

He starts tickling me harder.

Gasping for breath, I tell him, "I-i-i'm s-s-s-orr-y!" Tears are streaming down my face from laughing so hard. My legs are thrashing around, and my arms try to push him off to no avail.

"You're going to have to do better than that…" he says, laughing at me.

"I-I-I'M S-S-S-OR-R-RY, JES-SSE," I shout in his face.

My parents are probably wondering what the hell is going on up here. I'm surprised my dad hasn't come in already. I could really use his help getting this big oaf off of me right now.

"Better." He stops tickling me, though he doesn't make any move to get off of me. Leaning his weight on his arms, finally allowing me to breathe properly, but now missing his body weight on mine, he stares into my eyes, panting heavily.

Looking back into his eyes, I notice that the gold flecks in his eyes are shining bright. They only ever do that when he's happy or horny. Feeling his hardness digging into my leg, I'm guessing it's the second reason. Leaning up, I press my vagina onto his erection and give him a smirk.

Biting my lip on purpose, knowing it gets him going, I grab my comforter and squirm underneath him.

"Mmm," he groans quietly, just before his lips descend onto mine.

We kiss like we've been starved of each other for days, all lips and teeth. He runs his hands down my body, and then brings them back up to rest on my breasts. As he harshly squeezes them, I let out a hiss. It's a weird combination, pleasure and pain. I've never experienced it before. Usually, Jesse is gentle with me. This is a side of him I've yet to see. I like it.

I slip my top off, and then lie back down in only my PJ bottoms. Jesse goes straight for my naked breasts, fondling and sucking them and still not being gentle. It's such a turn on, though.

Running my hands down his naked back, I feel every hard contour. He really does look after himself. His body is perfect.

I move my hands down and grab his boxer clad bottom, squeezing and pulling him closer to me. That causes him to press into me in just the right spot. I moan loudly.

"Shh, baby," Jesse says, putting his hand over my mouth.

Shit. My parents are downstairs. Should we really be doing this? I'm too far gone right now to care. I need to find release. I'm just going to have to try and be quiet. That's going to be hard.

"Do you want me to gag you?" Jesse says randomly.

I look at him confused. Why would I want him to gag me?

"So you keep quiet. It's the best way," he says, answering my unspoken question.

Do I want to be gagged? I've never done anything like that before. I know it's not exactly spanking and all that shit, but it still scares the crap out of me. What if I swallow my tongue or something?

Then there's this little voice in the back of my head, the adventurous side, telling me to try it. I might like it.

The adventurous side wins. I'm intrigued. Plus, I trust Jesse not to hurt me.

I slowly nod my head yes.

"Are you sure? We don't have to. I was just thinking it would be the best way for you to keep quiet, is all," he says, looking worried.

Placing my hand on his arm, I give him a confident smile. "I'm sure. I trust you, Jesse."

He nods, looking around the room for something.

"Do you have a scarf or something?"

"Yeah, in my closet on the top shelf."

He walks over to my closet and pulls out a pink, wooly scarf. This is the last thing I thought I'd use it for when I bought it.

As he walks toward me, I sit up. He gently puts the scarf around my mouth, tying it behind my head. It's not too tight; just tight enough to muffle sounds.

"Is it alright?" he checks.

"Yeah," I reply, my voice muffled.

Jesse laughs at me as he takes his boxers off. I take in his impressive length, picturing it inside of me. My eyes glaze over. Jesse instantly stops laughing, his eyes also becoming hooded.

He tortures me by slowly crawling over the bed to me, taking his sweet time. If I could pick him up and plop him down on top of me, I so would. Alas, he is far too strong and heavy for me.

I lie on my bed impatiently, and he finally crouches by my feet.

He starts to take my PJ bottoms off, slipping them slowly off one leg, then the other, and then tosses them onto the floor along with my panties.

Taking a hold of my foot, he lifts it up to his mouth, licking from the sole of my foot, up to the top of my leg, stopping just before touching my sacred place. Then he does the same to my other leg. The whole time, he never takes his eyes off of mine. I lick my lips, so turned on and wet right now. I need him inside me. Now.

When he gets to the top of my leg this time, he doesn't stop. He carries on licking until he touches my clit. A shudder runs through my body, and goosebumps cover my skin.

He strokes over my sensitive nub again, causing me to buck underneath him. A muffled moan escapes, being captured by the scarf that's firmly tied over my mouth.

His tongue is relentless, going at impressive speeds and hitting my clit spot on. Every. Single. Fucking. Time.

I'm a bundle of sensitive nerves, squirming, close to climaxing on his face.

Jesse pushes two fingers into my pussy, deeply, his tongue still working its magic on my clit. That's all it takes for my climax to hit a new height.

I fall to pieces, my orgasm tearing through my body. Though I try hard not to scream, a few get out anyway. It's impossible to be silent when I'm having the most powerful orgasm to date.

I dig my fingers into the comforter as I come down from my high, trying to catch my breath.

Jesse moves upwards, resting on my chest. He doesn't give me time to recover fully before he shoves his cock deep inside me in one swift move.

"Jesus," Jesse whispers, allowing me time to accommodate to his lengthy size.

Lifting my hips up, I let him know that I'm ready.

He starts his slow rhythm, building up speed pretty quickly. Digging my nails into his back causes him to hiss. He loves it when I do this. It spurs him on.

I moan as Jesse kisses my neck just below my ear. I love it when he does this. It's my sensitive spot.

Meeting him thrust for thrust, my second climax builds, swirling in my belly and threatening to explode at any moment. I'm not ready. I'm so not ready. I've just recovered from the first one. My body doesn't care if I'm not ready, though.

One more hard thrust is all it takes for my orgasm to make itself known. Immense pleasure sweeps through my body, blinding me for a few seconds and causing me to scream.

Jesse grunts one last time, emptying his seed inside of me before collapsing on top of me.

When we've finally caught our breath, he helps me undo the scarf. I lean up, giving him a passionate kiss on the lips. I missed kissing him during our love making.

I lie back down with my back against Jesse's chest, and a yawn escapes my mouth. I'm so tired after today.

"You're tired. Get some sleep. Goodnight, baby. I love you," Jesse whispers into my ear.

Every time he tells me that he loves me, fireworks explode in my stomach. I love hearing him say that.

Turning my head, I give him a goodnight kiss. "Night. I love you too."

Cuddling into his chest, I sigh, feeling relaxed and at peace. I'm where I'm supposed to be right now; in the arms of the man I love. Nothing feels better than this.

I faintly feel a kiss to my head, and then fall asleep to the sound of Jesse's heartbeat with a smile on my face.

CHAPTER TWENTY-ONE
JESSE

It's Christmas in a few days; that time of the year again where family matters, except usually to me, Christmas isn't that special. I mean, I'm thankful that I have my mom, and we have a nice time, but it's just us. We don't have anyone else to spend it with, just like Thanksgiving.

I have Maisie this year, though we won't see each other. She has to go to her parents', which sucks. I was invited, but I just can't leave my mom by herself. That would be selfish of me, especially when she's always put me first.

So, since I can't spend Christmas with my baby, I'm taking her out tonight. She doesn't know where we're going. I just told her to dress nice and that I will pick her up at seven.

I've booked this posh restaurant that usually has reservations filled for weeks. I took a chance and booked it weeks ago, hoping that we would still be together. I had faith, though, and I was right. I've never been there before, but it has good reviews. We'll find out tonight.

I'm pretty nervous, to be honest, because we're exchanging gifts tonight. I bought her present last week. I asked my mom for her opinion, and she said Maisie will love it. I just hope she's right.

I'm all dressed and ready to leave. I just have to make sure I've got everything I need. I'm wearing a dress shirt for the first time in I can't remember how long. It's suffocating me, but for this place, I have to dress nice. Suffocation, so be it.

Swiping my keys from my desk, I put Maisie's present in my pocket, then grab my leather jacket and head downstairs.

"You look handsome," my mom says, waiting at the bottom of the stairs.

"Thanks, Mom. I feel like a dick," I tell her, making room around my neck to breathe.

"Well, you don't look like a dick. You look so nice. Maisie's going to be speechless when she sees you tonight," she says, giving me a wink.

Yeah, I know all women love a man in a suit. I'm not wearing the suit or tie, just everything else.

After checking myself in the mirror one last time to make sure that I'm good to go, I check the time and see that I'm late.

"Shit. I've got to go, Mom. I'm late to pick Maisie up. If we're late for the reservation, we will probably lose it. I'll see you tonight, okay?" I give her a kiss on the cheek goodbye.

"I'll probably be asleep. You tell me all about it tomorrow."

"I will. Night, Mom," I say before leaving the house and running for my Ducati.

****

Maisie's door swings open just as I'm about to knock.

I'm blown away as soon as I set eyes on her. She looks beautiful, wearing a pale pink sundress with silver heels. She looks like an angel.

"You look beautiful," I tell her when I finally get the courage to speak again. I was flabbergasted for a second there.

"Thank you," she replies, blushing at the compliment.

"Are you ready to go?" I ask, remembering that we're running late.

"Yes. Let me just grab a jacket and my car keys, and we're all good to go."

I'm standing on the threshold, watching her grab everything she needs, not once taking my eyes off the beautiful creature in front of me. She's completely blown my mind.

Closing the door behind her, I grab her hand, and we head toward her car.

I'm driving us tonight. I can't exactly ask her to get on my

Ducati when she's all dressed up. She'd end up windswept.

After helping Maisie into the car, like the gentleman I am, I close her door and make my way to the driver's side.

I adjust the seat so that my legs aren't touching the steering wheel, and then start the engine and drive off toward our destination.

"Can you tell me where we're going to yet?" Maisie asks, giving me the puppy dog eyes.

Damn them puppy dog eyes. She knows they get me. Every. Single. Time.

I won't give in. I won't!

"Oh, no you don't, missy. Face the other way," I scold her, turning my attention back to the road.

"Hmmph," she huffs, folding her arms across her chest.

I laugh at her sulking.

I won't allow her to get what she wants this time. I want tonight to be special. I've been planning this for months now, so I can't let her ruin the surprise. She can do the puppy dog eyes all she wants, but I refuse to give in.

The rest of the drive is silent. Maisie seems to be in a mood with me. She best get over it, or tonight will be ruined.

Pulling into the parking lot fifteen minutes later, I park near the entrance, finally allowing her to see where we are.

"Is this?" she asks when she sees where we are.

"Yes, it is, darling," I tell her, smiling at the megawatt smile that appears on her face.

Maisie told me weeks ago that she wanted to try this restaurant out, but that she couldn't afford to. It is expensive, though nothing is ever too expensive for my girl. I would buy her the world if I could. This is the next best thing. She's been raving about this place. Now, I'm finally making her wish come true. One down, plenty more to come, I'm sure.

"Eeeeeeeeeeeekkk!" she squeals, jumping up and down in her seat, causing me to laugh.

"Calm down or they won't allow us in. This place is for sophisticated people, not common people like us," I say, putting on a common accent and giving her a wink.

"Come on, m'lady. Let me escort you to dinner."

I go around to help Maisie out of the car, and then link her arm through mine.

"Oh, why thank you, kind sir," she replies, playing along with the joke.

After closing the car door, I walk us up to the entrance, where we are soon shown our table.

Maisie gasps next to me when she sees where we will be sitting. I chose the best place.

We're on the veranda, looking out onto the grounds and sheltered by a huge umbrella. A fountain is in the middle of the grounds, lit up and looking incredible in the night time sky. Fairy lights dangle from the umbrella, shining brightly. A single candle sits in the middle of our table, casting shadows. It's simple but elegant. Perfect for Maisie.

I pull out Maisie's chair and tuck her in before retreating to my own.

The waitress hands us our menus, then leaves us alone in the silent night.

It's the perfect night to be outside. Even though it's December, it's not too chilly. There are outdoor heaters as well, which helps. They really thought of everything when designing this place.

"This place is beautiful, Jesse. Thank you," Maisie says, taking my hand across the table and staring at me lovingly.

"You're welcome, baby. You know I'd do anything for you. This is just a tiny step in proving that to you," I say, giving her a warm smile.

"Thank you. You're the best."

I have to kiss her now. I lean over the table, being careful of the candle, and give her a lingering kiss, savoring the feel of her soft, puckered lips pressed against mine. Mmm, heaven.

Breaking the kiss before I get carried away, I sit back down and start looking at the menu.

The waitress comes back over to take our order a few minutes later.

"Are you ready to order?" the waitress asks, pen and paper ready.

"Yes. I'll have the spaghetti Bolognese with a water, please," I tell her. I don't know what half of the things on the menu are, so I'm playing it safe with the spaghetti.

"And you, Miss?" she asks, looking toward Maisie.

"Oh, I'll have the beef stroganoff with a water, please."

"Your drinks will be with you shortly," the waitress says, then takes the menus and leaves us alone again.

"Very adventurous, Jesse. Spaghetti Bolognese. Seriously?" Maisie asks, laughing at my choice of food.

"Hey, I don't know what half of the other stuff is. Plus, this better be fucking good spaghetti for $30. Most expensive spaghetti in the world!" I tell her, feigning shock. I've never paid more than $10 for food. This is new for me, but like I said before, anything for my girl. $30 is a small price to pay for her.

"I'm sure it will be fantastic. Though, I'm sure you do know what some of the other stuff is," she says, still laughing.

"Well, if they wrote properly, instead of using all those fancy words, people might be able to understand what they mean." I probably do know what some of the other stuff is, but when they use all those fancy words, how is a man who's never been to a restaurant like this, or who isn't a chef, supposed to know what it is? I sure don't. I probably never will.

"We'll do some research, so you're not blindsided in case we ever come here again."

Damn, she's already thinking about spending my money when I've not even paid for this meal yet. I have a feeling that I'm going to be doing a lot of extra hours at work over the next few months.

"Are you planning on stealing my money, and then dumping me?" I ask, joking.

Putting her hand to her chest, she says, "Me? Would I do that to you?"

"Would you?" I ask, staring her down.

"You won't know until I steal your money, will you?" she laughs, tipping her head back.

It's good to see her so carefree. Times like this make me realize that love is a good thing. I was just making excuses and protecting myself when I was younger. I'm glad I finally let someone in for once. If it doesn't work out between us, at least I can say I've had the experience of knowing what love feels like. I just hope and pray that it lasts forever.

"Take it. Take it all," I beg her, arms out to the side, baring myself open.

"Maybe another day," she winks.

The waitress comes back with our drinks, the food following not long after.

Tucking into my original choice of spaghetti Bolognese, I moan.

God, this is the best spaghetti I've ever tasted. It's definitely worth the amount of money they are asking for it.

"I take it that you're enjoying it by the orgasmic noises that you're making?" Maisie asks with her fork poised in front of her mouth.

"Definitely. Want to try a bit?" I ask, putting some onto my fork for her.

"Sure."

"Do you want to do this lady and the tramp style or eat it off my fork?" I ask while wiggling my eyebrows up and down.

Laughing, she replies, "I think I'll just eat it off of your fork. It might be frowned upon if we do the other option."

"Touché, baby." Feeding her, I watch her face as she savors the flavor.

"Mmm," she says, licking her lips clean.

The sight of her licking her lips like that makes me hard. Damn it. I swear her lips have magical powers.

I discreetly rearrange myself, trying to make myself more comfortable with the hard rod between my legs, and then try to casually carry on eating.

We eat the rest of our meal while making small talk. Luckily, Maisie doesn't notice that I have a problem downstairs, so I have time to recover.

Feeling full, I lean back in my chair and rub my stomach.

Maisie takes a sip of her drink, her sweet lips around the edge of her glass. Even that turns me on. She doesn't have a clue what she does to me. I'm infatuated by her. Completely.

The bulge in my pocket reminds me that I still haven't given her gift to her. Fiddling around with it in my pocket, my nerves start to get the better of me. I'm not used to buying girls presents yet, though, I only plan on buying presents for Maisie. "I've got something for you. I was going to give it to you on Christmas, but since you're not going to be here, I want to give it to you now." After pulling the square box out of my pant pocket, I gently place it on the table in front of her.

She looks down at it, a nervous smile on her face. "Just open it," I tell her. It's not helping that she's taking her damn sweet time.

She tentatively reaches her hand out, picking the box up.

She slowly unwraps it, and I watch as she lifts the lid and her hand shoots to her open mouth. Is that a good thing, or a bad thing? Fuck if I know. Shit. Maybe she doesn't like it.

"I can take it back if you don't like it," I rush out.

Frantically shaking her head no, tears form in her eyes. Why does this happen every time I get her a gift? Maybe, just maybe, one day I will be able to buy her something without starting the water works. It's very confusing. Does she like it, or doesn't she?

"Are you sure? Because I still have the receipt. Just tell me if you hate it," I ask for reassurance.

Finally removing her hand, she cries out, "No. I won't allow you to take it back. I love it, Jesse. It's absolutely beautiful."

Thank you, God.

"Do you need help putting it on?" I ask, reaching for the box.

I take the bracelet out and clasp it onto her wrist, watching how beautifully it sits.

I'm so relieved that she loves it. When I was looking for the perfect gift, I wanted something that was meaningful to her. I came across the bracelet when I went into Pandora after a whole day of shopping. I knew it was meant for Maisie the second that I set eyes on it.

MAISIE

It's so beautiful. I can't take my eyes off of it. Jesse bought me a Pandora bracelet. It isn't the bracelet that causes the tears to fall. No. It's the charm that he chose. It holds a lot of meaning for us.

Jesse picked out an elephant charm. To most people, it wouldn't be anything special. To me? It's the most thoughtful gift anyone has ever given me. He always seems to do that. He knows me. He knows me really well.

On our first date, when he took me to the zoo, he bought me a stuffed elephant. I cuddle that to sleep every night that I'm not with him. He got it for me because he knew that my favorite animal is the elephant.

And now he's bought me the charm so that I can wear it every day as a reminder.

He truly is the most amazing, sweetest, romantic guy I have ever met, and I love him so much.

"Thank you, Jesse. I love it so much," I try to tell him through my tears.

"You're welcome, baby. Anything for you. You mean so much to me. I wanted to get you the perfect gift, one that would hold a lot of meaning for you. When I saw this, I knew it was the perfect thing to buy you," he says, crouching down in front of me and staring straight into my eyes.

I stare back into his, getting lost. They are such dark orbs, sucking me in. One day, I'm going to get lost in them. I'm sure of it.

"What did I do to find someone as perfect as you?" I ask him dreamily.

"Baby, I think I should be asking you that question."

"No, seriously. I was so horrible to you when we first met. I didn't even give you a chance," I tell him, feeling horrible as hell. He really didn't deserve all the shit I put him through when we first met. He never really did anything to upset me. He just tried to get to know me. I threw him away without a second glance for ages. He never gave up on me, though, and for that, I will be forever grateful.

"Maisie, you only knew me from my reputation. Any normal girl would have done the same, and I don't blame you. Heck, I would have done the same if I was a girl. I'm the lucky one, that you gave me a chance in the first place. I can't promise you that we won't argue because we will. We already have. I can only promise that I will try to be what you need. I will try to give you the world, baby. You have my promise on that. You deserve nothing but the best. You truly are so special to me." Tears stream harder down my face. He really is unbelievable.

I wrap my arms around his neck and sob into his chest, never wanting to let him go. He hugs me back just as tightly, letting me know how much I mean to him through his actions. I do the same back, not being able to find the right words to say to him right now. Nothing I could say would be as beautiful as what he just said to me, anyway.

We stay like this for a few minutes, until people start to stare at us. Pulling away, I wipe my tears and try to make myself presentable.

Jesse sits back down, taking a hold of my hand, not once breaking contact.

"I have your present at your house, by the way. Your mom's been looking after it for me," I tell him with a wink. I knew that he would go snooping around my room, looking for it, so for safe keeping, I asked his mom to hide it. He would never have thought I'd ask her for help.

"You sneaky woman! No wonder I couldn't find anything. I thought you might have forgotten to get me something," he tells me, pulling a sad face.

I laugh. "Seriously? Why would I forget to get you anything, you silly man?"

"Well, when I couldn't find anything, I thought that was a possibility. Or that maybe you were really good at hiding things. I never thought you would team up with my mom," he says, squinting at me.

"That's exactly why I asked her," I tell him, a smug smile of achievement on my face.

"Well, let's get the check and go home, so I can open my present," Jesse says, acting like a little kid.

My present to him probably didn't cost as much as the bracelet did. It probably isn't even as thoughtful. I just hope he likes it as much as I love my present.

After paying the check, we take my car back to his house.

"So where is it?" Jesse asks as soon as we walk through the front door.

"Give me a chance, will you?" I ask, chuckling at his eagerness.

"Fine," he huffs, crossing his arms like a four year old boy who hasn't gotten his way.

Upstairs, I tell Jesse to wait, and then knock on Anna's door before walking in.

She's lying in bed, looking comfy and reading another book. That woman is always reading.

"Hey, don't mind me. I just need to know where you put my present for Jesse." I tell her.

"It's on the top shelf in my closet. Has he given you your present yet?" she asks, a huge smile on her face.

I'm guessing she knows what he bought me then.

Not trying to hide the smile on my face, I show her my wrist. "He did."

"It's beautiful, isn't it? He told me why he chose an elephant. Who knew my son could be so romantic?"

We both laugh at that.

"Hey, I can hear you, you know!" Jesse shouts through the

door.

"Good!" Anna shouts back, giving me a wink.

They both love winding each other up.

After fetching the present, I turn back to Anna. "I better give this to him. He's been acting like a kid for the last half hour," I say, rolling my eyes.

"Yeah, he tends to get like that. Good luck."

Leaving the room, I ignore Jesse standing in the hallway and make my way to his room.

"Sit down," I tell him, pointing toward the bed.

"Yes, ma'am."

I've never been so nervous to give someone a present before. Matt and I always told each other what we wanted. Jesse gave me no ideas whatsoever, even when I begged him, so I thought out of the box.

Pacing in front of him like a caged tiger, I tell him, "It didn't cost as much as the present you bought me, and it's not as thoughtful. I didn't know what to get you, but I tried my hardest. I just hope you like it. If you don't, then I'll take you to choose something."

"Calm down," he laughs at me. "I'm sure I will love it. Now, pass me my present." He snatches the present out of my hand and gets it unwrapped before I've had the chance to blink.

Biting my nails, I watch as he inspects it. I made a collage of photos of us since we starting dating. At the time, I thought it sounded so cool, like the perfect gift. Now? I'm not so sure. It seems pathetic.

"Do you like it?" I ask nervously when he still hasn't spoken a few minutes later.

"Like it?" he asks, finally looking at me. His face doesn't give anything away. Crap… He hates it.

Subtly nodding, he answers, "I don't like it." My heart feels like it's just been crushed. "I love it, baby."

I check to see if he really means it, or if he's just saying that to spare my feelings. He's smiling at me. It's a proper smile, too. My mood lifts, happy that he actually likes what I got him.

"I thought you hated it. You didn't speak for ages."

"I was looking at all of the photos, remembering the memories that go with them. That's why. Why would I hate it?" he asks, genuinely looking confused.

"I already told you that it didn't cost nearly as much as what you got me, and it's not even nearly as thoughtful."

Jesse taps the space next to him, telling me to sit, so I do.

"I don't care how much it cost, babe. This is special to me. There are so many memories wrapped into one present. If anything, this is more thoughtful than what I got you. It doesn't matter about price, as long as we both love what we got. You love your gift, right?"

"Of course I do," I tell him, holding my charm in my hand.

"And I love what you got me. That's all that matters."

"You're right."

"Now, come here and give me a hug and remove that frown from your face. Your face is too beautiful to look like that." He sets his present on the bed and opens his arms wide for me to enter.

Wrapped in his embrace, I exhale, feeling like the happiest girl. My charm glints off the light from the room. I really do have the best boyfriend. He gets me more than anybody ever has. I never want to lose him.

"Let's get an early night. You have a long drive tomorrow," Jesse, says, reminding me that I'm leaving him. Again.

I begrudgingly agree with him, so we get changed and get into bed.

We recap memories from the photo frame that I got him until I can't keep my eyes open anymore. Arms wrapped around Jesse, my head on his chest, the sound of his breathing is a lullaby, sending to me sleep.

CHAPTER TWENTY-TWO
JESSE

Waiting to see Maisie again after the Christmas break was the longest week of my life. It's also the longest we've been away from each other.

We talked on the phone every day, and texted when we weren't on the phone, but it still didn't help me to not miss her.

I spent my days at work, football practice, and seeing Brandon. I'm not going to lie; I got drunk a couple of times, resulting in drunken calls to Maisie. Some of the stuff that she told me I'd said was embarrassing. I can't even repeat it.

Christmas day was the same as always. Mom and I opened presents in the morning. I helped prepare lunch, and then we sat down and ate until we couldn't eat anymore. We spent the rest of the day watching crummy Christmas TV.

That was two weeks ago.

Everything has been going smoothly since then. Maisie and I are going strong. Mom and I are getting along well, and she seems to be getting better. I just have this terrible feeling that everything is about to turn to shit. Call it a bad omen. Things in my life can't be good for long. Two weeks is too long in my life. I'm just patiently waiting for the other shoe to drop, and it will. I can feel it in my bones. It's just a matter of time.

I finish classes early today, so I'm heading home to wait for Maisie, who is coming over when her classes are done in an hour.

As I pull into my drive, something feels off.

Inspecting the area, my eyes land on the front door, which is standing wide open. It shouldn't be open... Mom always makes sure that the door is locked after I leave, and she hardly ever leaves the house, unless it's shopping day or she has work. She has neither of those today.

Cautiously walking to the front door, and trying not to make my presence known, I listen for any sounds.

Nothing.

Shit. I need a weapon. Choosing the nearest thing that could possibly do damage, I pick up one of Mom's umbrellas. It will have to do.

"Mom?" I whisper, thinking she might hear me if she's hiding.

When I step into the living room, the umbrella falls to my side.

I don't have to look any further for my mom. She's in the corner of the room, unconscious and covered in blood. The man accountable for it is sitting on the sofa, one leg crossed over the other, looking relaxed.

"Good afternoon, Jesse," he slurs.

I'm going to fucking kill him. I rush over to my mom and check to see if she's got a pulse. I feel a faint one. Thank you, God. I can't lose my mom.

"What the fuck have you done to her, you piece of shit?" I growl, my voice sounding deadly even to my own ears.

"Oh, nothing that silly cunt didn't deserve," he says, dismissing my mom like a piece of trash.

"*Don't you dare talk about her like that,*" I warn, my temper about to explode.

"You've always been a mommy's boy. I'm surprised you're not gay," he laughs, the sound glaringly out of place in the quiet room.

"Why are you here?"

Drew stands up, closing the distance between us. God, he reeks of alcohol. There's only one reason why he came here. I just want to hear him say it.

"I came here because you stopped giving me money. Didn't you, you little cunt?" He doesn't wait for me to answer. "I need to find money from somewhere, and I knew with a little persuading that your mom would hand some over, except she fucking passed out before she could tell me where the money is. So, I guess you'll just have to tell me. Where is my money?"

He's all up in my face, breathing his smelly breath over me. I'm disgusted that I share DNA with this guy. After checking to make sure Mom is okay, I turn back toward my scumbag of a father.

"Get. Fucked," I tell him, spitting the words in his face.

He isn't getting another dollar out of me. I'm done helping him. He's never done anything for me, so why should I carry on helping him?

"I don't think you heard me. Where is my fucking money?" he shouts, getting red faced.

Oh, this is going to be funny. Does he seriously think he can take me? I'm much stronger than he is now that I'm not an innocent child. I'll have him knocked out in one punch.

"And I don't think you heard me. I said, Get Fucked," I tell him calmly, which just riles him further.

"What's going on?" Maisie's scared voice asks from behind me.

Wait. What? She isn't supposed to be here for another half hour. I have to get her out of here before my dad finds out who she is. He'll destroy her if he can. I won't give him the opportunity.

Not looking at her, keeping my eyes on Drew, I tell her sternly, "Maisie, leave."

Drew is checking her out. Dirty fucking pervert. My temper rises to new heights. *Get your fucking filthy eyes off of my girl.*

"Maisie, leave. NOW!" I shout. I don't have time for this. She needs to listen to me and leave. I don't need her seeing my demons come to life. I've been protecting her from this since I met her. I need to keep protecting her from this.

"Now, that's no way to talk to this beautiful lady, is it, Jesse?" my dad slurs, trying to act charming and giving Maisie a sickening smile.

Maisie doesn't reply. I know the moment she spots my mom in the corner of the room by the loud gasp that she makes.

Then she's running toward me and checking my mom over.

No way am I going to be able to get her to leave now. She loves my mom too much to just leave her.

"What have you done to her, you monster?" Maisie screams at Drew, tears streaming down her face.

He best be careful how he replies.

"Just leave her. She'll be fine. Come and introduce yourself to me, sweetheart."

Maisie flinches and looks at Drew's outstretched hand in

disgust.

"Don't even think about it," I warn him, taking a step to my left to try and hide them from his view.

"She's awful pretty, Jesse. Why don't you share her with me?" he sneers at me, licking his lips.

That's it. He's gone too far now. Nobody talks like that about MY girl.

Leaping forward, I uppercut him straight in the nose, causing him to stumble back onto the sofa.

God, it feels good to finally do that. I've waited years to give him a taste of his own medicine.

"Is that all you've got, you pussy?" he goads, holding his nose. "Maisie needs a real man, not a fucking queer like you."

"Jesse, don't list…"

I don't hear the rest. I'm seen red for the first time in a long time. And the great thing is that the reason for that is sitting right in front of me. I can finally take my anger out on him.

Pouncing on top of him so that he's trapped under my weight, I punch him over and over again, the whole time replaying the times that he beat my mom, until he stops struggling.

Screaming is going on in the background the whole time, though I don't know where it's coming from. I'm only thinking about one thing; destroying this man who has destroyed my mom and me time and time again. I have to get rid of him once and for all.

Something tugs on the back of my shirt, ripping me off of Drew.

My fist poised in the air, I spin around, coming face to face with Brandon.

I immediately drop my arm, collapsing into him. That's when the tears start falling down my face.

What the fuck have I done? I'm as bad as him. This is what he wanted. He wanted to prove that I'm just like him, and I gave him what he wanted.

"It's okay," Brandon says, rubbing my back.

It's not okay. I'm a monster. I knew I was. I was just waiting for it to show itself.

"I'm the same as *him*, Brandon," I cry.

"No you're not, buddy. This isn't your fault, okay? Go and check on your mom. I'm going to check on Drew."

Looking to the corner of the room, I'm met with a wide-eyed Maisie, who's still holding my unconscious mom. She looks so scared right now. I don't blame her. I'm scared of what I've just become too.

I can't go over there knowing I put that look on her face, so I stand where I am.

"He's breathing," Brandon says.

I don't feel relief hearing that he's still alive. I feel disappointment. He doesn't deserve to live. At least if he was dead, my mom would be able to live her life without fear.

"I need to finish him off," I say to no one in particular.

"NO!" Maisie shouts.

No matter what she says, she isn't going to change my mind. The world will be a better place without him. And me. I'll probably get sent to jail. That way, I won't be able to hurt Maisie or anyone else.

Ignoring her, I take a few steps toward him before, Brandon comes crashing down on me, pinning me to the floor.

"Get the fuck off of me, Brandon," I warn, my voice deadly. I'm in no mood for him to interfere. How the fuck did he get here anyway? I didn't call him.

"No. You're not going to end up in jail. I won't let you. Your mom and Maisie need you. Stop being selfish." It feels like he's just slapped me across the face with his words.

Selfish? I'm trying to protect them from me. I'm only going to end up destroying them. It's inevitable, especially now that the beast has been unleashed. I'm a ticking time bomb.

If I say I'm going to go after Drew, there is no chance that Brandon is going to let me go. I'm going to have to play along. I'll wait until they've all gone before I make my move, even if I have to finish him another day. I will do what I have to do.

"Fine. I'll leave it. Just get the fuck off of me." I relax my body, showing defeat.

"You better not be messing me around, Cohen," he warns in my ear.

"I'm being serious. I'm not going to do anything."

He eventually gets off of me, allowing me to get up.

"Jesse, she's waking up," Maisie says worriedly.

Rushing over, I fall to the floor next to my mom. Her eyes are fluttering open, though I'm sure they are going to be painful. She has two black eyes. Fucker really did a number on her this time.

"Jesse," she says hoarsely. Her eyes are barely able to open from the bruising.

It hurts like hell to see my mom like this again.

"I'm here, Mom," I reassure her, holding her hand.

"Y-y-your d-d-dad," her eyes start looking around frantically, her body shaking with fear.

"He's not going to hurt you anymore," I tell her, looking her straight in the eyes.

Her body relaxes, her eyes closing again.

"Thank you," she whispers before her breathing evens out, and she's falling asleep again.

"Brandon, a word please," I say, nodding my head toward the stairs.

"Okay," he replies, following me. Maisie stays with my mom.

"I need you to get Maisie out of here. She's seen enough," I tell him, leaving no room for questions.

"She isn't going to go willingly, bro," he states.

"I know," I agree, nodding my head. "You're going to have to do whatever it takes to get her out, even if that means tossing her over your shoulder and not letting her leave your car. Can you do that for me?"

"You're not going to do anything stupid, are you?" he asks, narrowing his eyes at me.

I'm not going to do what he's thinking I'm going to do. I've got to let Maisie go, and it's going to be the hardest thing I'll ever going to have to do.

"Not what you're thinking," I tell him vaguely.

Brandon looks at me strangely for a few seconds before looking shocked. He's figured it out. He knows me too well.

"You're throwing Maisie away, aren't you?" he whispers so that nobody else can hear.

"Yes," I sigh.

"What the fuck are you doing that for? That girl is the best thing to ever happen to you," he whisper shouts.

I'm starting to lose my composure here. Out of everyone, I need him to understand where I'm coming from.

"She may not see it, but I'm just like *him*. It's only a matter of time before I hurt her. I won't allow that to happen. She has to leave before I have the chance."

"I'm not going anywhere," Maisie states resolutely.

How long has she been standing there?

"Yes, you are. You need to go with Brandon."

"No."

"Dammit, Maisie! Will you listen to me for once please? I can't have you here," I raise my voice, causing her to flinch.

I automatically feel bad. I've never raised my voice at her before. Maybe this is the way to get her to leave, though. Maybe she will end things with me. We can't be together after this. I can't give her what she needs, not after tonight.

"Please don't do this, Jesse," her voice trembles. "Please don't push me away, not after everything."

"It's for the best. Goodbye, Maisie." I look at her one last time before giving Brandon the sign to take her away.

"NO! DON'T DO THIS. PLEASE. BRANDON, GET OFF OF ME!" Maisie kicks and screams, trying to get out of his hold. I can't look anymore.

She carries on screaming until I can't hear her. I collapse where I am. Bringing my knees up to my chest, and with my head buried in my hands, I break down; for what happened to my mom, for not having a normal family life, and for throwing away the best thing to ever happen to me.

Fuck. I need to forget. I need a drink.

I rush down the stairs call an ambulance for my mom, put Drew in the garden, and then I text Brandon to ask him if he can dump Drew off at an abandoned place.

I wait with my mom until the ambulance collects her. The paramedics ask if I want to go with her, but I decline. I need to have a drink ASAP. I know I should be going with my mom and making sure that she's okay, but I just can't at the moment. I can't bear to see her in this state.

Once the ambulance has driven off, I hop on my bike and head for a bar that I know will let me in.

CHAPTER TWENTY-THREE
MAISIE

I can't believe him. I can't *fucking* believe him! He got his friend to drag me out of his house kicking and screaming. He wouldn't even give me a chance to be there for him. He's helped me with my problems, so why won't he let me help him with his?

I realize that he just broke it off with me, and my heart is breaking. I knew it would hurt so much more if he hurt me than it did with Matt, and I was right. I can't even explain what I'm feeling right now. I'm numb, back in the pits of despair. This time, though, I don't see myself coming out of it.

I didn't want to go back to my dorm. I didn't want to see Chloe, or anyone for that matter, so I asked Brandon to drop me off at the beach.

I found a deserted part and have been sitting here, just staring out at the waves. I don't know how much time has passed. I haven't even looked at my cell phone. If anyone is trying to get a hold of me, they won't be successful.

The last few hours keep repeating in my mind. Walking in and seeing Anna lying on the floor unconscious. The man, who I'm guessing is Jesse's dad, checking me out. It made me feel physically sick. Then, Jesse nearly killed his dad. That's what scares me the most. I didn't even recognize him when he was like that. I was shouting at him for ages with no answer. It was like he didn't even hear me.

I had to call Brandon in the end. I knew that he would be able to stop Jesse. I just didn't expect him to help Jesse get rid of me. I thought that he would at least talk sense to him. He didn't even try.

All those promises he made me? They were all lies. He gave up on me when the going got tough. He didn't even care how it would affect me or make me feel. He just tossed me away without a second look. I will never forgive him for that.

I sit staring at the waves until the sun goes down. I should leave. It's dark out now. I don't want to go back to my dorm, though. I wish I was home right now, so that I could lock myself up in my room and wallow in peace. I'm six hours from home, though, so no such luck.

As I start walking back toward the sidewalk, I notice a figure walking toward me. I can't see who it is, but I know it's a man by the way they are holding themselves. My heart starts racing. It's deserted out here. He's not even walking a dog.

Maybe he just likes taking a stroll late at night, I try telling myself. Or maybe he's a murderer. All sorts of scenarios play through my head, none of them good.

"Maisie?" the voice asks.

How the hell does he know my name? Maybe he planned this. Maybe he's been following me and has waited for the perfect time to strike.

Stopping, I ask timidly, "Who are you?"

He carries on walking until he's standing in front of me. I visibly relax. "Matt, what are you doing here?"

"I came here to apologize for how I was when I last saw you. I tried calling, but I couldn't get through. Have you blocked my number?"

He came all this way to apologize? Why would he do that?

"You can't have just come here to apologize. We're hours away from home, Matt." I'm confused.

He must realize that I'm not that bothered about how he spoke to me when we last saw each other. He knows that I'm getting on with my life. If he really cared, he would have come here months ago, not after some petty words have been said. Something doesn't add up.

"I'm here to see some friends, actually," he says casually, like he has friends everywhere.

I didn't even know he knew people here…

"Okaaaaaaay… So why are you on the beach by yourself at this time of the night?"

I'm one to talk.

"I felt like taking a walk. It's just a bonus that I bumped into you." He gives me his smile that used to make my heart melt, but it now just puts me on edge.

"Well, it was nice to see you, but I'm heading home. I'll probably see you around." I start walking away when he grabs my arm, spinning me around to face him.

"Let me give you a lift home? I didn't see any other cars over there, so I'm guessing you didn't drive. It's dark. Anything could happen to you at this time," he asks hopefully.

I don't really want to be anywhere near him, but he does have a point. It will take me ages to walk home, when it will only take him five minutes to drop me off.

Finally agreeing, I say, "Fine. Thank you."

"My car's this way."

I pull my arm out of his hold, and we walk toward his car in silence.

When we get to the sidewalk, I don't see any cars except for a white van. Where's his car?

"Matt, I think your car's been stolen..." I say, turning toward him with a confused expression on my face.

Something feels off here...

"No, it hasn't been stolen. I had to help a friend move down here, so we rented a van."

My throat is too dry for me to talk, so I just nod my head.

"Come on, then. Let's get you home."

I get into the passenger seat stiffly. Why am I getting in when I feel like something's wrong? I look toward Matt warily. He just smiles at me, again with the same smile that I used to love seeing every day. That smile used to reassure me that everything was okay. It settles my nerves some. Matt would never hurt me. Well, not physically anyway.

We drive off in silence.

I breathe a sigh of relief when the dorms come into view. I'm nearly home, where I can rest and try to slowly mend my broken heart.

That relief is short lived when he drives straight past them. "Where are we going? The dorms are back there," I tell him, pointing behind me.

"I have something I want to show you." He doesn't take his eyes off of the road when he says this. What could he possibly want to show me at this time of the night? Plus, he doesn't even know the area.

"Matt, what could you possibly want to show me at this time of the night?" I ask, voicing my thoughts.

"You will have to wait and see." He finally turns to look at me, giving me another sweet smile, just like he used to give me. It makes me feel sad. This is just like old times. Matt wasn't always controlling and a cheater. Once upon a time, he was so sweet, and I truly thought I loved him. But times have changed since then. I've met Jesse, who I love with my whole heart and, even though I feel sad about what's happened between Matt and I, I wouldn't change it for the world. His actions caused me to meet Jesse, and even though he's broken my heart to the point of no return, I will always be thankful that I met him.

A little while later, we park near an abandoned building. I look up at it, confused as hell. "What are we doing here?"

"There's something that I want to show you inside," he says, turning toward me.

"Erm, I'm not sure, Matt. It's pretty late, and I'm tired. Can we do this tomorrow?" There's no way that I'm coming back here tomorrow, though.

"I'm going back home tomorrow. Come on. You trust me, don't you?"

Do I trust him? I gave him my heart, and he broke it, but do I trust him not to cause me any harm now? "Yeah, I trust you," I sigh in defeat. I know he won't hurt me. I just feel uncomfortable being with him here after not speaking to him properly for months.

I cautiously get out of the van and meet Matt around the front. He grabs for my hand, and I let him hold it, not because I want him to, but because I'm pretty scared right now. This place is completely dark. Anybody could be hiding or living in it.

He squeezes my hand in reassurance, leading me through the dark corridors.

Finally, we end up in a damp room, which has lanterns scattered around. It's like he planned this in advance. But why? Then I spot the bed. He doesn't think that I will sleep here with him, does he? He will be sadly mistaken. That ship sailed a long time ago for us.

"Matt... Why did you bring me here?" I ask, letting go of his hand.

"Let's sit down first." He leads me over to the bed, where I sit down uncomfortably on the edge. "I love you, Maisie. I tried telling you…"

"No. It's too late for this, Matt. You need to leave it and move on," I interrupt him. I don't want to dig up the past. Like I said, that ship has sailed. He just needs to start realizing it.

"Please, Maisie. I need to get this off my chest. It's killing me not being able to tell you, and now I finally have the chance," he pleads, his eyes losing that glint that I saw in the van.

I'm not changing my mind on this, though. I don't want to hear what he has to say. I shake my head adamantly.

"I'm sorry," is all he says before he pounces on me, forcing my hands above my head. I'm no match for him. His strength is impeccable. He holds both of my arms with one hand, the other moving to his pocket. I watch to see what he pulls out.

Handcuffs.

I try to fight him as soon as I see them, but I can't fight him off. He has my wrists cuffed to the bed in no time.

"Matt, this isn't funny. Let me go!" I thrash around, trying to get my hands free, but it's no use. The handcuffs just cut into my skin.

I'm helpless.

I close my eyes, and the bed dips down next to me.

"I'm sorry, baby. I really am." Matt says.

"Then let me go," I cry.

"If I let you go, you'll go back to *him*. I can't allow that. If I keep you here, then we can be together. Have you missed me, baby?"

Has he lost his mind? He was being nice to me a minute ago, but now he's completely changed. He's like Jekyll and Hyde.

"You can't keep me here, Matt. You're crazy if you think you can. Someone will come looking for me. You know they will."

"Nobody will find you. Last I heard, your wonderful boyfriend dumped you, so it's not going to be him who comes after you. Chloe probably will, though she's got her own problems to deal with at the moment, doesn't she?"

He's right. Nobody is going to find me. Hope leaves my body, leaving me feeling numb.

"We can finally be together in peace," he says as he starts to get on top of me.

No, no, no, no, no. This can't be happening. Bile rises to the top of my throat.

I thrash my legs to no avail as he just pins them with his own.

"Stop, Matt. I don't want this!" I scream.

"You want this. Don't pretend you don't. You still love me, Maisie. I know you do. You don't get over a love like ours." His head dips, and he starts kissing my neck.

My body shakes. His lips on my skin makes me feel physically sick. I need to stop him. I can't let him do this to me.

"Get the fuck off of me, Matt. You disgust me. There's no chance in hell that I want to be with you again."

Bad move, Maisie.

I watch his face turn red, his eyes go hard. Then his fist is flying straight toward my face, and there's nothing I can do about it. Pain shoots through my eye; blinding, torturous pain. I scream.

"I'll make you want me again."

He starts ripping my top open, exposing my breasts. He greedily takes them in, his hand squeezing one hard. I don't feel the pain, though. My focus is on my eye, which is closing fast.

I can't look at him anymore, so I close my eyes.

I hear my jeans zipper, and then he's tugging at my jeans, trying to get them off.

"Matt? I need to talk to you," a female voice says.

Wait… Someone else is here? And that voice…

"I'm a bit busy right now, Tiffany."

Tiffany…

How do they know each other? Better question. Why is she here?

Turning to look at her as best I can, I see that she's looking in my direction with a huge smirk on her face. Of course she's in on this. She's been out to destroy me since day one. What better way to do it, than to get my ex to help; an ex who seems to have gone crazy. Just like her.

"You look good, Maisie. The eye really suits you," she says snidely.

"If I wasn't tied up, I would smack you. You really are disgusting. No wonder Jesse never wanted you. He could see right through you. Bat. Shit. Crazy," I tell her with a smile on my face.

It wipes the smirk off of hers.

She runs up to me, her fist in the air, but Matt stops her.

"Don't you dare! She's mine, remember? You get Jesse." That calms her down.

Wait… Jesse? He's here?

"What have you done to Jesse?" I ask frantically.

"Nothing, yet… He should be here shortly, though." She walks out without another word.

I'm too busy thinking to notice Matt getting off of me.

"I'll be back," I vaguely hear before he closes the door behind him, leaving me with my thoughts.

What is going on here? And why are they bringing Jesse here?

Oh, God no. Please don't let them hurt him. He's bound to be hurt more than I am, and I'm in a lot of pain.

Now that I'm finally alone, the pain is unbearable. I can't do anything. I'm cold, scared, and alone.

So I cry.

CHAPTER TWENTY-FOUR
MAISIE

I don't know how long I've been here. Trapped on this bed. Alone.
All I know is that nobody has come to save me yet.

Matt's brought food to me three times. I've not eaten a thing.

I don't speak when I'm spoken to.

I don't open my eyes when someone's in the room.

And when I'm alone, I cry or sleep.

JESSE

What day is it? How many days have passed? All I know is that it hasn't been enough.

I have a mega hangover this morning, but I need another beer. I need to forget, and if that means spending the rest of my days drinking myself into a stupor, then that's what I'm going to do. I don't even care that I'm going to be like *him*. I knew I would eventually. I just made it happen faster.

Opening the fridge, I'm sure I'm seeing wrong. Where the fuck has my beer gone? I had a whole case in here last night.

"I threw it away, and there's no point looking in the bin outside. It's not there," my mom says.

Closing the fridge, I stare down at her, anger seeping through my body. "What the fuck did you do that for?"

"Don't you talk to me like that, Jesse Cohen. Just because I'm not at full strength doesn't mean I won't kick your ass. I'm worried about you. You've spent the last two days drunk. I won't have you turning into your father. Do you hear me?" she says seriously, her hands on her hip.

"It's not up to you what I do, Mom. If I want to have a fucking drink, I'll have a fucking drink. Stop interfering. If you hadn't have had sex with that son of a bitch, I wouldn't have been born, and then I wouldn't have to deal with what I'm dealing with."

I know I shouldn't be attacking her. She's done nothing but try her best for me. I just need someone else to blame right now, and that happens to be my mom. I can't see past my anger.

"Oh, for goodness sake, Jesse. Sort yourself out! You want to end up like your dad? Fine. Go ahead," she says, opening her arms out wide. "But you won't be living under my roof, so pack your bags and get out. I refuse to watch another person I love destroy themselves." With that, she walks away.

Fine. If that's how it's going to be, I'm gone.

My cell phone rings just as I'm about to walk out the door. It's Chloe. Why is she calling me?

"What?" I answer, not in the mood for pleasantries.

"Well, hello to you too," she replies sarcastically.

"What do you want, Chloe? I'm really not in the mood."

"Geez, Mr. Happy. Fine. Is Maisie with you? I've been trying to get a hold of her, and her phone goes straight to voicemail."

"No. Why would she be with me? We broke up. I've not seen her since Brandon took her home on Wednesday." Has she not told Chloe that we've broken up? They usually tell each other everything.

"Wait… She left yours on Wednesday?" she asks, confused.

"That's what I said, isn't it?" Sarcasm drips from my voice.

"Fuck! Jesse, Maisie's not been home since Wednesday morning. I've not seen or heard from her since then. That was two days ago, Jesse…" She's panicking now.

"I'm sure she's fine. She'll come back when she's licked her wounds. Now, I've got things to do." I hang up the call and put my cell away.

What does she think I will do about it? Maisie's not my problem anymore. She's probably hiding for attention. Well, it won't work on me. I've got bigger problems to deal with.

I need to get drunk. Now.

MAISIE

The door opens. I keep my head facing the wall. I don't want to look at him. He's keeping me here, locked up like a caged animal. He's disgusting.

"You're beloved boyfriend will be here soon," he sneers.

That gets my attention. My head snaps in his direction, my eyes wide. "What are you going to do to him?" I croak.

It's all I can manage. I've not had a real drink in hours; only when he feeds me water through a straw, which isn't very often.

"Nothing for you to worry about. I'll be back soon." He closes the door before I can ask more questions.

I have a bad feeling about this. He's going to hurt Jesse. I just know he is.

He hasn't hit me since we arrived, but I know it's not over. It's far from over.

CHAPTER TWENTY-FIVE
JESSE

"Another, please," I ask the pretty bar tender.

She flutters her lashes and gets me my beer, just like she's been doing for the last two hours. She wants me. I can see it in her eyes. I might just take her up on her silent offer. She can help me forget about *her* for a little while. I'll take whatever I can get.

Leaning over the bar, purposely showing me her cleavage, she passes me my beer.

"I didn't get your name, darling," I drawl, putting on the charm I'm so famous for.

"It's Daisy," she coos.

"Well, Daisy, what do you say to leaving here with me when your shift is finished?"

Her eyes light up, a greedy look taking hold. Oh yeah, she fucking wants me.

"I finish in an hour. I'll come get you when I'm done, sexy." She winks, leaving to serve another customer.

"Tut, tut. You've only been single for what, two days? And you're already getting someone else into bed," Tiffany says quietly into my ear.

Great. Just what I fucking need is whiny Tiffany keeping me company.

"I'm not in the mood for your games, Tiff," I tell her bluntly.

"Oh, I'm not playing games, Jesse. I've never been playing games. I've always made it clear what I wanted. You just weren't ready for me. But I'll wait. Just don't sleep with her. You know I can show you a better time." Her hands slide down the front of my shirt, riding lower.

I have to agree with her there. She did always know what I liked. Looking over my shoulder at her for the first time since she arrived, I remove her hands from me.

"Okay. But you play by my rules. No touching unless I tell you to. You let me do whatever I want," I tell her seriously. She needs to understand my rules if she wants me. Otherwise, I'll go elsewhere.

"Understood."

I slap a bill down on the counter and grab her hand, stumbling out the door with Tiffany behind me.

"We'll take my car. You've had waaaay to much to drink, by the looks of things."

She's right. I can't drive in this state. I follow her to her car, get in the passenger side, and then we're off.

I rest my head against the window, closing my eyes. I guess I drank more than I thought I had. Everything is spinning. I better get used to it if this is how I'm going to spend the rest of my life. I just need a nap, is all.

****

"He fell asleep on the way over here. How are you going to get him inside?" a voice says, sounding far away.

"I'm going to have to knock him out. Do you think this will work?" another voice says.

"Yes, just be careful, please."

"This was your idea, remember? Don't change your mind now."

Opening my eyes, I come face to face with Tiffany and Matt, Maisie's ex. What the fuck? Where am I? Tiffany stares at me wide eyed. Matt just smirks at me before swinging something at my head.

Then everything goes black.

****

Ow, my fucking head. It hurts like a motherfucker. This is

230

definitely not just a hangover. What happened? And why won't my eyes open?

"*Jesse!*" Someone is shouting my name. It sounds so far away. What's going on?

Then it all comes flooding back.

The bar. Tiffany. Getting in her car. Falling asleep. Matt. Something hitting my head. Now I'm here. Where is here, though?

I pry my eyes open, and the light stings for a few seconds.

"JESSE!" that voice shouts again, louder this time.

"Shut your mouth, Maisie. I'm not going to warn you again."

Maisie? She's here.

My eyes snap open, searching the room. My eyes fall on Matt and Tiffany, both standing in the corner near a door. Where's Maisie?

That's when I see her, handcuffed to a bed with her clothes ripped open. One of her eyes is black and swollen.

What the fuck have they done to her? I'm going to kill them.

I try to get up, but I can't. I notice now that I'm strapped to a chair. *Fuckers!* When I get out, I'm going to rip both of their heads off for this.

I can feel my face heating up, the anger about to boil, but there's not a damn thing I can do about it when I'm strapped to a chair.

"Let me out of this," I warn, my tone biting. I'm in no mood to mess around.

"Nice to see you awake, Jesse, but I wouldn't get too demanding. I don't take well to being told what to do, and it's not like you can defend yourself now, is it?" Matt laughs in my face. He fucking laughs in my face. Is he trying to piss me off?

"When I get out, you're dead." I stare him straight in the eyes, letting him know that I'm serious. I've never been more serious in my life.

I watch his face contort with anger as he marches straight for me, his fist flying straight into my face. I hear Maisie scream, and it kills me. God only knows what they've done to her. I should have listened to Chloe.

Jesus Christ, that hurt. I can taste blood.

Matt roughly grabs my face, making me look at him. "You're as bad as she is," he says, pointing to Maisie. "Never listening. She seems to be starting to learn, though, and in time, you will too.

You're going to be here a long time, so you better start."

"Not fucking likely." I don't listen to anyone. I'm certainly not going to listen to a pussy like him.

My head snaps back as his fist collides with my face again. In. Exactly. The. Same. Spot. I act like it doesn't affect me, when really, it fucking hurts.

"Matt, leave him alone. I don't want you ruining his lips. I need those," Tiffany whines, giving me a wink.

Eurgh, I think I just threw up in my mouth. She better not come anywhere near me.

I look at her with disgust. "Oh, honey, don't look at me like that. Do you still want me to carry on with what we had planned not even an hour ago?"

Maisie's been quiet since I opened my eyes. When I look at her, I see tears streaming down her face. She's staring straight at me. *Fuck!* Now she knows that I was going to sleep with Tiffany.

That's not what's bothering me right now, though. We can deal with that later. What's bothering me is what they've done to her and the fact that she's tied to a bed, battered and bruised. It's breaking my heart, especially when I can't do anything about it. I just want to go over to her, apologize, and hope and pray we can work things out. Seeing her like this has made me realize how much I love her. I should never have kicked her out of my house. She wouldn't be in this position if it wasn't for me.

"I'm sorry," I tell her quietly. It's all I can say.

"Not as sorry as me," she whispers.

Those five words cut through me like a knife. I've royally screwed up, and this time, I have no one to blame but myself.

Matt walks over to Maisie, wraps her hair around his fingers, and says, "It doesn't matter. You have me now, baby, and I'll look after you. I've always loved you."

Oh, please! I watch Maisie shrink away from him, her face full of disgust.

"Get away from me," she croaks at him. That's my girl.

Next thing I know, Maisie's head is ripped back, causing her to scream out in pain. I try to jump up, but when I go nowhere, I remember I'm stuck. *Fuck!*

"Matt, please, I'm sorry," she begs, her dried tears no longer dry.

"You will be sorry. I'm promising to give you everything you could ever need, and you're throwing it back in my face. What makes him so special?" Matt asks, pointing at me, his eyes still on Maisie.

Because I didn't cheat on her, asshole? Or maybe because I didn't kidnap her? Yeah, that might be why.

Maisie looks at me, swallowing before turning back to Matt.

"Well?" he demands, his grip on her hair getting tighter, causing her head to go back further.

"N-n-nothing," she cries.

"You're damn right, it's nothing. He's made for Tiffany, just like you're made for me."

So this is what this is about? Tiffany's pissed that I blew her off, and Matt's pissed because Maisie started dating me.

I give Tiffany the coldest look I can muster up. The smile falls from her face, making her actually look scared for a second, before she covers it up. The smile returns to her face, only bigger.

She turns around facing Maisie. That's when I spot her cell phone hanging out her back pocket. I somehow need to reach it so I can ring for help. It's our only way out.

"What makes *her* so special?" Tiffany screeches, copying Matt and pointing at Maisie.

Maisie's head swivels around, as does Matt's. Anger flashes in his eyes.

A plan to get us out of here forms in my head. I'm sorry for what I'm about to do Maisie. I mentally tell myself that maybe, just maybe, she will be able to hear my thoughts. Or maybe she will hate me for a little while until she realizes why I'm doing what I'm about to do.

"Nothing at all. I've always wanted you, Tiff. I just didn't know how to tell you. You were never good enough for me." I put on the charm, giving her my famous panty-melting smile, as women like to call it.

She spins around, her hair nearly hitting me in the face, with a huge smile plastered on her face. I think she's happy with that answer. It physically pains me to say those words to her, though.

"Oh, baby, you have always been good enough for me. Do you know how long I've wanted to hear you say that to me? I've been waiting years."

"Well, I've said it now. Come here."

She slinks toward me provocatively, swinging her hips. I sneak a quick look at Maisie, and find her silently sobbing, but her body gives her away. It's shaking. Matt doesn't seem the least bit bothered. He must be happy to hear what I'm telling Tiffany. He probably thinks he can have Maisie for himself now. Stupid fucker.

Tiffany bends down. I pucker my lips, letting her know that I want a kiss. As soon as I get out of here, I'm washing my lips with bleach. Her lips touch mine, and all I can think about is how they aren't as soft or as plump as Maisie's.

I trail my lips toward her ear and whisper, "Untie me so I can touch you, baby."

She shudders, letting me know that I'm affecting her. Let's hope it's enough for her to let me go. She nods her head, not actually saying anything, and then moves to untie me.

Matt is oblivious to what's going on. Good. He might try and stop her. That guy never did like me. I never liked him either.

I feel the strings loosen, allowing some feeling to come back into my hands. Thank God. It feels wonderful. I can only imagine how Maisie is feeling with how long she's been here.

Finally free, I stand up and stretch. My t-shirt rides up, exposing my V muscles. I hear Tiffany sigh and, looking at Maisie, I see that her head is turned the other way. I've really hurt her. I just wish I could tell her that I don't mean anything I'm saying. I'm doing this so that we can escape.

I turn back to Tiffany, my smile back in place. I open my arms, which she willingly enters, and wrap them around her like I usually would Maisie. I'm trying to picture that it's Maisie I'm hugging, but the shape is all wrong. Tiffany doesn't fit in my arms like Maisie does. I just need to keep reminding myself that I'm doing this for her. It's my fault she's in this mess, and I need to fix it.

I run my hands down her back, settling them on her bottom. I give it a squeeze, letting her know that I'm interested. Then, I gently move my hand toward her pocket and try to gently pull her cell out. I give her other cheek a squeeze too try and disguise what I'm actually doing.

"That's it, baby. You squeeze my bottom. I know how much you like it," she purrs in my ear, getting the totally wrong idea.

I feel Tiffany run her hands down my back, moving them lower and lower. I need to do this quick, and then I can get her hands off of me.

Got it!

I step back, staring into her confused eyes. "Come on. Let's go find a quiet room." I wink, causing her to cackle. Yeah, she thinks she's going to get lucky. She's going to get a shock when she finds out what I plan on doing.

She grabs my hand, and I quickly put her cell in my pocket. Then I'm being dragged out of the room. I turn one last time, getting a look at my beautiful woman, who I plan on getting back as soon as we've been rescued. She looks like she's given up. I need to get that beautiful smile back on her face. I just need to do this one last thing first.

CHAPTER TWENTY-SIX
MAISIE

Watching Jesse walk out of the room, holding hands with Tiffany, guts me. I don't think I've ever felt soul crushing pain like I'm feeling now. Even when Jesse broke up with me, it didn't hurt as much as seeing him flirting with Tiffany. This is the girl that he claimed to despise more than life itself.

It doesn't help that I have Matt kissing my neck and whispering sweet nothings in my ear. It's not even like I can get him off of me. If I tell him to stop, he'll just hit me, and I don't want to be in anymore pain. So I just let him do it because that's all I can do.

"I told you he didn't deserve you. He's just gone to fuck another girl, leaving you here," Matt reminds me.

"Drop it, Matt," I tell him dejectedly. I'm not in the mood for his snide comments, especially when he's right.

"Just remember that I'm not the one who left you to sleep with another girl."

Did he really just say that?

My temper flies through the roof. "If I remember correctly, you did. That's why we aren't together anymore."

His face changes, anger returning and reminding me that I need to just keep my mouth shut. I know this isn't going to end well. He's right. I will never learn, it seems. "You just had to bring that up, didn't you? If you have nothing good to say, then keep your mouth shut. You're ruining my mood, and I don't want you to have to make me teach you a lesson again."

"Matt, you can't keep me here forever. Please, just let me go. We aren't going to work anymore," I plead, even though I know it won't help the matter. But I have to try, since Jesse's left me to defend myself.

"I'll never give up on you, Maisie. I'd rather die than never have you again, and if you decide that you don't want me, then I'll end us both. I can't stand to see you with anybody else. Do you know how hard it was to see you with *him*?"

My eyes widen. I'm shocked that he said he would kill us both. I can't have heard that right. "Did you just say that you would kill us both?" I ask, making sure that I heard him correctly.

He nods his head adamantly. Oh shit. "Yes, I did. If I can't have you, then nobody else can. The only way I can make sure that happens is if I take you with me."

"That won't be happening, son," a voice interrupts.

My head snaps in the direction of the new voice. I release a sob. It's the police. I'm going to be free. Thank you, God.

"Who are you?" Matt asks, standing in front of me and blocking my view. His body goes rigid, his hands balling into fists.

"Son, move away from her, please." Two men walk forward, slowly coming toward us. The one talking is tall and stocky and has a moustache. He looks scary. I wouldn't want to mess with him. The man with him is just as tall, but not as stocky. He looks even scarier, if that's possible.

"Stay away!" Matt raises his fists. Come on. Don't tell me he's going to be stupid enough to start a fight with them. He will lose.

I stay quiet. I know they will get me out of here eventually.

"That's not possible. I'm going to have to ask you to move out of the way please," the first one tells him calmly, as they continue slowly making their way toward us.

"TIFFANY?" Matt shouts, panicking. He's looking past them and out the door. He shouts so loud, I think my ear drums just burst.

"She won't be coming to help you. My partners have a hold of her, I'm afraid. Now, we can either do this the easy way, where you come with us willingly, or we use force. Choose wisely." They stop moving, waiting for his answer. The leaner cop looks over toward me, giving me a little smile. I give him the best smile that I can muster up in return.

"You can't do this. You have no right. You're ruining

everything! She's supposed to be mine!" Matt screams in hysterics, pointing at me. I've never seen him like this before.

They don't say anything; just move forward a little more. Matt turns and grabs me, squeezing the life out of me.

"I'm sorry. I love you so much, Maisie. I love you. I love you. I love you," he keeps repeating in my ear.

I don't feel anything. How can I, after what he's just done to me? He's ruined me in ways that he will never realize, and for that, I despise him.

"NOOO!" Matt screams as he's dragged off of me. I watch him leave the room, kicking and screaming. His eyes are pleading with me to do something. I don't do anything, though.

Two other officers take over, dragging Matt out of my view. I breathe a sigh of relief. It's over. I'm finally free.

"Are you okay, sweetie?" the stockier officer asks, crouching down next to the bed.

The tears come hard and fast now. I can finally see the light at the end of the tunnel.

"It's okay. We've got you now."

The other officer comes over to me with a key. I'm guessing all handcuffs use the same type. He doesn't say anything, but just looks at me with pity in his eyes. Usually, that would bother me, but right now, I'm just so relieved that I'm being saved.

Finally, a few moments later, my hands are free, and I'm shaking them to get some feeling back into my arms. I sit up, welcoming the feeling of my feet touching solid ground.

"Thank you," I tell the officers, giving them a grateful smile.

"It's our job. Come on. Let's get you checked out to make sure you're okay." I stand up, swaying from not walking for a few days.

Wait. How did they know that I was here? I never called anyone. "How did you find me?" I ask.

"We had a call from Jesse. He's outside waiting for you."

I stand still, shocked. He didn't leave me. He called for help. But how? I'll have to ask him when I see him.

The sunlight feels good as it beats down on my face. You miss simple things like sunlight when you're locked up, not knowing when you will next see it. I just wish I could see the sunlight properly, but my eyes are swollen, making it hard to see.

"MAISIE! HELP ME!" Matt screams. I turn in the direction of his voice and watch as he's shoved into a police car. The door shuts on his face, silencing his screams. Thank God. I can't deal with that right now.

I see Jesse standing there staring into the distance. He doesn't notice that I'm watching him, but I can see that his face is all swollen from where Matt hit him. I just want to run over there and make sure he's okay, but that isn't my place anymore, and I don't think my body would allow me to after the abuse it's been put through.

I should say thank you to him for rescuing me, except I don't know what to say. After everything we've been through, we're in an awkward place right now. He's not my Jesse anymore, not the person who I could talk to when something was wrong, and not the person who can comfort me when I need to be hugged. Those days are over. I just need to remember that.

"We'll go deal with him. My colleagues will take you both to the hospital, and we'll come and collect a statement from you later," one of the officers tells me as he hands me a card. I look down at the card. Detective Jones. I completely forgot that I didn't ask him his name.

"Thank you, sir," I tell him.

Then he's gone, walking over toward his partner.

****

On the ride to the hospital, the events of the last few days replay in my mind. Jesse and I don't talk. I guess both of us don't know where to start.

I'm seen straight away, and Jesse is being seen in another room. Thankfully, nothing is broken. I have a few bruises and am seriously dehydrated, so they put me on a drip to get some fluids back in me.

The door bursts open, and a head of blonde hair comes bundling toward me, wrapping me in a tight hug.

"Chloe, you're hurting me," I hiss through the pain shooting through my body.

"Oh shit, sorry," she says, letting go of me. "What did that asshole do to you?" she asks, her eyes watering up when she takes in my appearance.

Tears fall from mine too. "Everything apart from kill me. There were a few times when I wished he would. It was horrible."

"If I ever get my hands on him…" She leaves her sentence hanging. She would kill him, I know.

"I'm okay now," I try reassuring her.

"I didn't know what had happened to you. Then, when Jesse called me, I came straight here. I was expecting the worst. He didn't give me any details, just told me to get here straight away. I've been going out my mind!"

"Well, as you can see, I'm still alive, so you can stop worrying now."

"I won't stop worrying until that sick fucker is behind bars. Has anyone told your parents?"

I really don't need them worrying about this. They will be down here before I know it, babysitting me. I don't need that right now. I need to recover in peace.

"No, and I don't want them to know yet. You know what they are like. They will be down here and won't let me out of their sights. Or worse, they will take me back home. I just need time, Chloe. Promise me you won't tell them?" I plead.

She looks torn. I need her to be on my side for this one.

"Please?" I ask again.

She sighs, obviously not happy with my decision. "Fine, but you will have to tell them eventually."

"I will in a few days. I promise."

Knock, knock.

Detective Jones pokes his head around the side of the door.

"Come in," I tell him.

This is it. Time to spill my guts.

"Hello again. How are you feeling, Miss?" he asks, now standing in front of my bed.

"Please, call me Maisie."

"Okay, Maisie. I need to take your statement, if that's okay? Do you want your friend with you?" He looks toward Chloe.

"She can stay," I tell him. He just nods.

"Okay, first of all, how do you know Matt Davis?" he asks, pen and paper at the ready.

"He was my boyfriend in high school."

"And did you break up on good or bad terms?" I can't exactly tell him that I walked in on him having sex with another girl. Embarrassing.

"Bad terms."

"When was the last time you spoke to him?"

"When I went home three weeks after Thanksgiving, Jesse and I bumped into him in the store parking lot."

"How did he seem?" How am I supposed to answer that? We weren't friends anymore.

"I don't know. He was trying to rile Jesse. He took a disliking to him," I tell him, remembering that he tried to punch Jesse that day.

"So, can you tell me how you ended up in that building?"

I tell him how I was on the beach late at night, and that Matt randomly turned up. I go on and tell him everything else and all that happened over the last few days.

Chloe looks shocked once I'm done. I haven't had time to tell her what happened, so this is all new for her.

"And how do you know Tiffany Dawson?"

"She knew Jesse. She took a disliking to me when we became friends. She's always made it known that she didn't like me, and she even threatened to ruin me," I tell him. She definitely succeeded.

"Did she help Matt kidnap you?

"No, but they planned it together. Matt was to get me, and Tiffany was to get Jesse," I tell him what I know.

"Okay. I may need to ask more questions later, but for now, that will do. You have my card if you need anything, don't you?" he asks as he closes his notepad.

"Yes, I do. Thank you for all your help." I smile as best as I can at him, which he returns. Then he's gone, leaving the room in silence. Chloe probably realizes that I need a few minutes.

The door opens again, and this time Jesse enters. Chloe sees him, turns to me, and says, "I'll leave you two alone. I'll be back later. Call me if you need anything." Before I can protest, she's leaving the room.

Jesse stands awkwardly at the door. It's nerve wracking.

"Are you coming in or what?" I ask, breaking the silence. He doesn't reply, just comes and sits in the chair next to my bed.

"I'm sorry you had to be involved in all of that," I tell him, staring at the wall opposite me. I can't bear to look at him after what I caused him to go through. I know Tiffany was the one to take Jesse, but if they hadn't have met me, then she wouldn't have got in touch with Matt.

"It's not your fault. I'm glad I was there, to be honest. I don't want to think what could have happened to you if I wasn't," he says, his voice sad.

"I'm not your problem anymore."

I feel him looking at me, though I don't turn around.

"Maisie, you will always be my problem, for as long as I live. I shouldn't have thrown you out, and I will regret that for the rest of my life. You probably wouldn't have been in that_position if I had've let you stay. And then I also wouldn't have had to pretend to want Tiffany, but you have to understand that I did that so that I could get help. Unfortunately, I can't turn back time, though. All we can do is move forward, and I want to move forward with you. I understand if you can't forgive me and never want to see me again. I just want you to know that I love you so much, and I'm sorry for what I've put you through."

Even after everything, he still melts my heart. I should have known that he wouldn't have left me there by myself, especially after everything I've told him about Matt and Tiffany, but I'd given up. I know I'll never find anyone like him again. He is it for me, but is it enough to forgive him? What's to say that he won't hurt me again?

But if I've learnt anything from this experience, it's that life is too short to hold grudges, and you have to take life by the horns.

I face him, giving him my full attention. He needs to know I'm serious.

"What you did hurt me, Jesse. You pushed me away when I wanted to be there for you, like you have been there for me. That being said, I love you too, and after what's happened, I realize that life is too short to hold grudges. I forgive you this time, however there won't be a next time. I don't think my heart can take getting broken again."

Jesse's face transforms from a solemn expression to one of pure joy. I've missed that look on his face. Then he's lying next to me on the bed, wrapping his arm around me and trying to be careful of my bruises.

"I won't mess up again. I promise. I can't function without you. I was a mess, Maisie. I need you in my life. If I ever have a stupid idea about breaking up with you again, don't let me. Promise me?"

"I'll try, but you can be very stubborn when you want to be. I don't want to lose you, though. You're the best thing to ever happen to me. You helped me live my life again. I'll never forget that."

"Maisie, you were already in there. You just didn't know how to get out from behind the wall you had built. I just gave you a push in tearing that wall down."

"Well, thank you," I tell him.

I yawn. I must be tired from all the drama that's occurred over the past few days.

"Go to sleep. You're tired. I'll be here when you wake up," Jesse tells me.

"Promise?"

"I promise."

I fall asleep before I know it, with Jesse stroking my hair. I'm at peace for the first time in days.

EPILOGUE
MAISIE – ONE MONTH LATER

It's been a month since I left the hospital, where I was told to rest for a few weeks until all the bruising healed. The first few days were peaceful. I stayed at Jesse's house because it was bigger than my tiny dorm, and that way, I had someone there at all times in case I needed help. I didn't want to feel like a burden, so the things that I could do by myself, I did. The rest, I waited until Jesse was back so he could help me.

Then things got a bit hectic. Chloe made me tell my parents what had happened. They behaved just as I had expected them to, and were at Jesse's house a few hours later with a suitcase of their belongings. Anna told them that they could stay as long as they wanted, for which they were thankful. It was nice of her, but I hated that she allowed them to stay after the second day.

I wasn't allowed to do anything for myself. My mom would cry nearly every time she set eyes on me. And my dad? He was murderously angry. Even I was scared.

My parents have only just left after being down for nearly a month. Now, I'm dancing from the rooftops that I finally have my freedom back. It was exhausting, being under lock and key. However, when I felt like losing my temper with them, Jesse would remind me that they are just looking out for my safety. It was a big shock to them, and they didn't know how to deal with it. He was right.

With them staying at Jesse's, it gave them time to really get to

244

know him and Anna. My mom and Anna got along like a house of fire. I can see them being really good friends. They are so alike, really. My dad and Jesse are finally getting along without my dad doing his fatherly duties. I think he realizes that Jesse loves me and isn't going to turn out like Matt.

Well, I hope he doesn't.

After I made my statement, the police called me a few days later, letting me know that Matt had been arrested and was facing three charges; one count of kidnapping and two counts of assault. They told me that he will be sentenced to four years. Everybody said that wasn't long enough, but really, how long is long enough? At least he is still being punished. Some people get away with what Matt did. Thankfully, he was one of the people who didn't. I'm just grateful that I won't have to deal with seeing him for the next four years, which will allow me time to move on and heal. I'll deal with him getting out when the time comes. I hope he gets help while he's in prison. He's mentally unstable, and I see that now. Him seeing me with Jesse all those months ago was his breaking point, I think. It was enough to tip him over the edge.

Tiffany only got a fine and probation because she only brought Jesse to the building. She didn't play too big of a part in it, apparently. Since then, nobody has seen or heard from her. She hasn't been attending college. Rumor has it that she moved away, as she was too embarrassed to come back. At least now, I won't have to see her face and put up with her trying to destroy my relationship with Jesse. She deserves a lot more than she got.

Now that I'm finally no longer under lock and key, Jesse is taking me out. He won't tell me what he has planned, but told me to be ready by twelve o'clock. Which is now.

I'm nervous to be leaving the house. I know that I have to sooner or later, though.

"Are you ready?" Jesse asks, breaking me out of my thoughts.

He's standing at his bedroom door, wearing his usual white tee, dark wash jeans, and his black leather jacket. He looks yummy.

A smirk spreads across my face.

"What's the smirk for?" he asks, mirroring my face.

"Oh, nothing. I'm ready." I'm not going to tell him that he looks edible. His ego is big enough.

We head downstairs and out to his Ducati.

"Are you going to tell me where we're off to yet?"

Jesse turns back to face me. "To where it all started for us," he replies, giving me a wink.

****

Before I know it, we're pulling up outside the zoo. This is what he meant when he said 'where it all started for us'. This is where he brought me for our first date, gave me the beautiful elephant, and then took me for pizza. It was where I first realized that I was falling for him.

"I wanted to remind you why we are so good together. We had so much fun the first time we came here, and I want to see that smile on your face again. It seems like it worked," he tells me.

"I love the zoo. Thank you for being so sweet."

He truly is the sweetest guy on the planet, and I'm lucky to call him mine.

"Come on then. Let's go and see some elephants." Jesse smiles at me, grabs my hand, and then we are off to look at the animals.

This is the perfect way to spend my first day back in society. I have my amazing, beautiful man, who I love with all my heart. I have the animals, who always look so carefree. And I have my life back.

I don't know if I'm ever going to get over what happened to me. All I can do is see if therapy will help and try not to shut my friends and family out. I also don't know if Jesse and I are going to last, but I hope we do. I will never find someone like him again, so I'm going to spend every day with him like it's my last day. After everything that has happened between us, we are stronger than ever.

And thanks to Jesse, I am alive again.

THE END

ABOUT THE AUTHOR

Beth Maria is a mother and the author of Alive and Freedom in The Mended Heart Series.

She lives in England UK, with her two year old son. When she isn't doing her motherly duties, you can find her attached to her laptop writing new stories, reading books by her favourite authors or on the odd occasion, watching a film.

Her inspirations are Kirsty Moseley, Kelly Elliott, Tijan and Jillian Dodd.

Beth Maria loves listening to music that influence's her writing and searching the internet for pictures of men who could be her next muse.

Find me on Facebook and Twitter:
www.facebook.com/AuthorBethMaria
http://twitter.com/bethmaria1993

Or E-mail me at: bethmaria234@gmail.com she would love to hear back from you about what you thought of her books.

36610761R00144

Made in the USA
Charleston, SC
08 December 2014